THE
COMEDIAN

UNIVERSITY OF CALGARY
Press

CLEM MARTINI

THE
COMEDIAN

Brave & Brilliant Series
ISSN 2371-7238 (Print) ISSN 2371-7246 (Online)

University of Calgary Press
2500 University Drive NW
Calgary, Alberta
Canada T2N 1N4
press.ucalgary.ca

This book is available as an ebook. The publisher should be contacted for any use which falls outside the terms of that license.

LIBRARY AND ARCHIVES CANADA CATALOGUING IN PUBLICATION

Martini, Clem, 1956-, author
    The comedian / Clem Martini.

(Brave & brilliant ; 6)
Issued in print and electronic formats.
ISBN 978-1-55238-977-5 (softcover).—ISBN 978-1-55238-978-2 (PDF).—
ISBN 978-1-55238-979-9 (EPUB).—ISBN 978-1-55238-980-5 (Kindle)

    I. Title. II. Series: Brave & brilliant series ; 6

PS8576.A7938C66 2018   C813'.54   C2017-907068-1
                                       C2017-907069-X

The University of Calgary Press acknowledges the support of the Government of Alberta through the Alberta Media Fund for our publications. We acknowledge the financial support of the Government of Canada. We acknowledge the financial support of the Canada Council for the Arts for our publishing program.

 Canada Canada Council
for the Arts
Conseil des Arts
du Canada

Printed and bound in Canada by Marquis
♻ This book is printed on Enviro Book Antique paper

Cover Image: Andy Dean, *Fresco Ruins of Pompeii*, photograph, Colourbox #9887249
Editing by Aritha van Herk
Copyediting by Peter Enman
Cover design, page design, and typesetting by Melina Cusano

To all the ancient comedians who viewed their imperfect world through a comic lens, employed styluses and tablets, split reeds and home-made ink, wrote and left a rich legacy of laughter.

1

In my darker moments I take comfort in remembering the celebrated Jason of Thessaly. Hercules achieved renown for strength and courage; Theseus cleared the road of criminals and famously dispatched the Minotaur. Our distant kinsman, Romulus, displayed energy and wisdom in laying Rome's foundation. Jason appears to be the only great hero from ancient days to have never been troubled by a single good idea.

His failures—children massacred, marriage vows violated, assorted familial carnage and mayhem—are so varied and flamboyantly executed that they inspire a kind of awe. In one of his more noted adventures he proved capable of consummating intimate relations with a tribe of women rendered so especially malodorous by an extraordinary curse of the gods that their husbands had been compelled to abandon them. Hardly heroic! Even insofar as Jason was royalty he manages to underwhelm. We are told he earned his kingdom because of his inability to cross a river without losing a sandal. Surely, maintaining your footwear would be the least that could be asked of royalty!

Clearly, his greatest accomplishment lay in selecting and surrounding himself with others far more skilled and talented than himself. In preparation for his journey to retrieve the Golden Fleece, he convened a phenomenally gifted congress of problem-solving overachievers, gods, demi-gods, and heroes everyone. In fact, Jason may be the sole hero whose ship—the sleek *Argo* with its eloquently prophesying prow—was smarter than he was.

That someone so essentially inept could ascend so high offers great hope to those of us possessing only average skills. I am particularly drawn to these tales of Jason, though, because in a sense his journey can be said to parallel the process of a poet in the theatre, whose work can never truly be completed except through the collective efforts of others, and whose fame is reliant upon the creative invention, staying power, and skill of the band he gathers to complete a task he himself only ever begins.

Jason was a youthful and allegedly singularly handsome wayfarer, however, and I can't make that claim. At this point in my life I am no longer young by any means, nor do I cut the lean, athletic figure I once did. I meditate glumly upon this sorry state of affairs as I sit across the table from my colleague and reflect that while I may be no Jason, he is certainly no Argonaut.

I shift restlessly on the bench. The morning, which started fresh, has by the afternoon begun to cook. Even shade feels oppressively hot. I squint out from beneath the pale blue awning and view the great dusty pan of our city casually frying its citizens.

I mop my brow and return my attention to my associate across the table: a phenomenally hairy, wedge-headed individual. From top to toe he represents a veritable crisis of curly black hair. His sweat-slick neck is abundantly hairy, his pinched face likewise. His shoulders constitute a bristling, wiry thicket. Given that he is so prodigiously hirsute, I find it difficult to ignore the impression that I'm seated across from an animal—a kind of minor weasel perhaps. Something in his body odour lends itself to that notion.

"It's almost impossible to make money producing a play," he complains once more, his tongue darting pink across his thin and, yes, weaselly lips.

"*Miles Gloriosus* made money for Cosmo," I observe.

"Cosmo is dead," he replies bluntly. "I can't answer for what arrangements he made with you."

I remind him that we both made money on *Mercator*.

He sips his wine and shrugs. "That was *Mercator*."

I drink and allow the bitter taste of the posca to swirl about my mouth. "You've simply repeated what I just said," I point out after swallowing. "I don't know what that means."

"Times change, is what I mean. We performed *Mercator* eight years ago."

"And?" I ask.

"The public is fickle," he tells me. "Audiences have cultivated other tastes. They enjoy pantomimes. Charioteers. Wrestlers. They love dancers." An ant crawls up his leg, and I wonder what complications that must present from the ant's perspective. Would it be like struggling uphill through clinging bramble and thick forest? If it got lost, would it be forced to pitch camp and send for help?

"Pellio," I say, drawing my attention back to the matters at hand, "I don't need advice about the audience, wrestlers, or dancers. I need someone to purchase materials, construct the set, hire actors and musicians, and communicate with the Aedile. And perform. You still do all that, don't you?"

He frowns as if experiencing a severe bout of constipation. "It's a bad time," he finally declares.

"When," I ask, "has there been a good time for the theatre?"

"This is an especially bad time," he grumbles, and the way he waggles his finger at me puts me uncomfortably in mind of an old, much-detested tutor of my youth.

"How is it especially bad?" I ask.

"If you haven't noticed," he says, gesturing vaguely to the world beyond the caupona, "there's a war."

"When hasn't there been?" I inquire. "And this one is nearly ended."

"Anyone who wants to build has to compete with every shipbuilder for every timber. They're hammering together a navy down in the harbour to carry the battle to Africa. They want timber—I'll need timber. They want carpenters—I'll want carpenters. I have to hire labour, and right now labour is dear. I couldn't do it for less than a third of overage on the commission."

I shake my head. "A tenth."

He downs a great smacking gulp of his drink, then sits sucking his teeth silently and grimacing to himself. I allow him to grimace and suck in silence for what I feel is a more than generous length of time.

"Do you have something caught in your throat?" I finally ask.

"I'm trying to calculate," Pellio says, "how little a tenth will cover. It's so small that I haven't been able to do it."

I seize the edge of the seat in an attempt to suppress my frustration. "Calculate this," I suggest. "Assemble your team, build the set, keep an eighth. You walk away rich."

"Rich?" He laughs and it isn't a pleasant sight. It displays too much moist, pink throat, too many discoloured crooked teeth, and releases too potent a vapour. "Rich? It would be a miracle," he says, "if I walked away with my skin and skeleton at an eighth."

I remind myself that it is not necessary to like someone to work with them. "The Aedile can be very supportive," I tell him, "of an event that raises the spirits of the community."

"Oh, well. Spirits. Everyone enjoys seeing spirits raised." He swirls his wine around in his cup as though trying to conjure some. "Not sure that you raised many spirits last go-round, though."

"What do you mean by that?" I ask.

"I mean *The Runaways* was a disappointment."

I suppose this remark was inevitable. It's never your best play people remember. What everyone recollects is your last.

"Well," I reply, ignoring his slight, "if you can't do it, Marcellus or Lucius Vallerius will."

He snorts. "Lucius caught fever and retired to his family home. My opinion, he's not likely to recover. Marcellus is way the gods and gone up in the backwoods of Campania presenting *Daddy the Farmer,* or *The Lovesick Cowherd* or some other of those charming Atellanae."

"Marcellus," I contradict him, "is in town now."

"Your sources have failed you," His Hairiness maintains. "He left two days ago and is out performing for the yokels."

"If he's in the forests of Dacia he will return as quickly as he can to do the kind of job that he's capable of," I insist, "for a tenth."

"If you can get him to leave Campania for a tenth, more power to you. If you come to your senses and change your mind, I'll do it for half. "

"Half?" I've attempted to maintain an appearance of restraint, but my voice catches at this provocation. "*Half?*"

"Half," he says coolly, "would be reasonable under present circumstances."

"Moments ago, according to *you*," I say, pointing at him—and if I could thrust my outstretched finger and pierce his greedy, faithless, self-absorbed, money-grubbing heart, I would, "it would have been reasonable to do it for a third."

"That was before *you*," he barks, leaning forward and propping himself on his hairy knuckles, as though preparing to vault the table, "questioned my integrity and insulted my intelligence."

"I never questioned your integrity," I deny, "and there's nothing I could say low enough to insult your intelligence."

He stands and throws some coins onto the table carelessly, one rolling and falling to the floor. "Things have changed since you last presented in Rome. Here are a couple of semis for the wine. That's about what I imagine you can expect to receive from your next play—if you get it done. And for the record, *Asinaria* was a disaster as well."

"Thank you for your change, if I want a critique from a monkey, I'll ask," I say, and call after him, "Have a good day! In Hades."

He stalks away without looking back.

The server returns wiping her hands on a towel and looks about. "More to drink?" she asks me.

"No," I reply. "I'm enjoying this right now."

"Is the posca too bitter?"

"No, it's perfect," I tell her. "Sour wine suits the occasion."

She leaves. One of those shifty, skinny youngsters with scabby knees, loitering at the edges of the market, scans the room and saunters through. He crouches momentarily near my table, and I grasp him by the arm.

"Where are you going with that?" I demand. "That's money left for the bill."

"Ow!" he yelps, and wriggles to escape, but I tighten my grip. "It was on the ground," he says, "I didn't think it belonged to anyone."

"Let me see it," I insist.

He extends the hand holding the fallen coin.

"And you palmed one from the table just now," I point out. "Give that back too."

The boy doesn't display any expression. He simply opens the other hand and lets the coin drop to the floor. I scoop it up and hold it in front of him.

"You can keep this one," I inform him.

"Thank you," he says, snatching it and turning to leave. I continue holding tight to his arm.

"But," I add, "you'll have to work for it."

He tries to escape. I slip my hand to his wrist and wrench it into a locked position.

"Ow!" he grunts, his grimy face twisting in pain.

"Settle down," I reassure him. "I'm not asking for anything difficult."

His face continues to express doubt. "What do you want me to do?"

"Tell me a story," I explain. I can see him turning that over in his mind, searching for the catch.

"Just tell you a story and I can keep the coin?"

"That's right."

"And you'll let me go?"

"Yes."

"What kind of story?" he asks suspiciously.

"A good one."

He mulls that over. "I know one about Mercury," he suggests.

"Tell it to me."

The boy shifts from one foot to another as he thinks, then begins in a rush. "He was just born, but a god can do things smarter than your average baby. He wanted to play a trick on his bossy older brother, Apollo, who his father loved best. Apollo owned a big herd of magic cattle. One day, Mercury stole them to teach big brother a lesson. He made the cattle walk backward so they couldn't be followed, then hid them in a cave. Someone squealed on Mercury, and bossy older brother found out. Whack, whack, whack—he whipped Mercury up and down with the switch he'd used on the cattle. He hit him alongside the head too, he was so mad. And wah, wah, wah, Mercury gave the cattle back. Then Apollo grabbed him by the throat, pressed him to the ground and choked him and said, 'Next time you do that I'll tear your ear off and feed it to you.' And the father said, 'You pull that kind of stunt again and you'll be *out* on the street, do you understand, *out*, and I won't care if I ever see you again.'"

I consider the tale. "Every story of the gods illustrates something to us. What does that one illustrate?"

The boy looks at me as if I have suddenly started speaking another language. "What do you mean?"

"What's the moral of that story?" I ask.

"There are two," he replies. "Every father has a favourite, and don't steal and get caught."

"Fair enough. Both good morals," I conclude. "What's your name?"

"Tertius."

"All right, Tertius," I say and release his arm. "Run along." The boy turns and quickly disappears into the street.

Orestes joins me shortly before duodecima. He's tired, and that lends his already slender form a slightly gaunt appearance. With his high cheekbones and neck like a swan, I've often thought of Orestes as a kind of very good-looking skeleton. I motion to the server to bring us wine and water. My lanky Greek friend folds his frame onto the bench and rubs his face.

"Any luck?" he asks.

"No," I reply, and motion to the server to set a cup in front of Orestes. "But he wasn't negotiating seriously."

"What did he say?"

"A lot of nonsense too boring and obvious to repeat. It's expensive, he told me. There's a war." I shrug. "I imagine he already has something in the works with someone else."

"Pellio was never the most trustworthy Dominus Gregis in Rome."

"True," I agree, "but he continues his glorious tradition of being the most universally covered by hair."

The server pours us our drinks. Orestes measures some water in as well and lifts his cup. "To His Resplendent Hairiness," he toasts.

"His Hairiness," I echo, as we touch cups and drink. "Why hasn't he recruited you to accompany his grex?" I ask him.

"He has Avitus arranging music and playing the tibia for him," he explains.

"Avitus?" I scoff, "Avitus is a frog piping in a swamp compared to you."

Orestes's lips tighten in disapproval. He cleaves to an annoying philosophy that doesn't permit him to speak ill of others. "Avitus is a decent musician," he corrects me primly. "And I haven't worked with Pellio for nearly six years. What will you do until you find a Dominus?" he asks, changing the subject.

"I don't know," I tell him, and I don't. "You?"

"I play the tibia at dinner parties."

"That pays sufficiently?" I ask.

He shrugs. "There's always food to take away after."

As if on cue, a plate of olives, crumbly white cheese, and a tawny end of bread is set down at our table. I consider the plate, and then glance at Orestes to confirm that he hasn't ordered this, and is as confused as I am. I quickly hold my hand up to catch the server's attention before she turns away. "Excuse me? What's your name?" I ask.

"Pomona," she replies. She's a tall, pretty, ample-figured girl. Maybe twenty, and I take from her Samnian lilt that she comes from away east.

"Pomona," I say, "I didn't order these."

"They are sent," Pomona informs me, "with the owner's compliments."

"Free?" I confirm.

"Yes."

Orestes and I exchange a look. I pop one of the olives into my mouth. Tart, with a firm, dark, zesty flesh. "These are good."

He samples the cheese. "This isn't bad either."

"And it's free?" I inquire once more for reassurance.

"Yes."

"Your good health, and send our thanks to the gracious proprietor," I tell her.

Pomona nods and carries on. Clearly the Cerium has changed for the better under new ownership. I glance around to determine what other adjustments have been made. The light blue awning that stretches over the street is the same, as is the whitewashed interior. The rough wood benches and tables have the same lewd carvings etched into them years ago. There are a respectable number of patrons for the time of day, fifteen or so, and the floor looks to be kept in a cleaner state than when I frequented here last. The gods represented in the Cerium are familiar: Janus, vigilant at the doorway, and Vesta in her quiet alcove off the north wall. Priapus, with his massively erect penis—polished to a glossy sheen from the repeated rubbing of gamblers hoping to receive good luck—remains in his place of honour on the wall next to the archway exiting to the stairway. But I note that a new statue of Minerva, stern goddess of wisdom, has been added, and she stands watchfully at the base of the stairs, scrutinizing those who ascend and descend.

"If not Pellio," Orestes asks, returning to matters of the theatre, "then who?"

"Good question. I thought maybe Marcellus."

Orestes shakes his head. "He left the city."

"That's what Pellio said. What about Lucius?"

"Sick as a dog." He drops his chin to his chest in reverie and taps the table with his index finger. "Who," he murmurs to himself, "else?"

"There must be someone …" I begin, but am interrupted by the arrival of an unfamiliar woman at our table.

"Your health, gentlemen," she greets us. "I understand you found the cheese, olives, and bread to your liking." From the way she says this I take her to be one of the new owners of the Cerium—a number of these cauponae are husband/wife operations.

"Your health," I reply. "And thank you—that was entirely unexpected, and very generous of you."

"I'm happy if I make my customers feel like they are at home."

I try to decide whether she is attractive or not. She's petite, trim, older—approaching the far side of forty perhaps—but smiles readily and carries herself with a certain easy confidence. Her dark hair is braided into a tight knot over her right ear, a simple style, a little severe, but elegantly arranged. She's adopted a no-nonsense air that I imagine comes with managing a caupona. On others it might seem brusque, on her it feels open and honest. She turns her full attention to me.

"Pomona tells me that you inquired about room rates earlier," she says. "Would you like a place for the night?"

"I haven't decided yet—I have relatives I feel obliged to stay with. But you know how that can be, children poke fingers in your eye to wake you, relatives bicker—and at one time I slept in the Cerium back when it was under the previous management. What rates would you offer a returning customer?"

"I'm sure I can find something that would suit you. Perhaps we can discuss this after you have finished your drink." This would normally be when she would leave, but she doesn't. "I overheard your meeting with Pellio," she remarks.

"Yes. My apologies." I flush with shame and once more curse Pellio, this time for the bad impression he's caused. "I didn't mean to create a disturbance."

"No need to apologize," she assures me. "Business negotiations can sometimes run hot. I take it that your discussions didn't go well?"

"Well enough with me. For him," I say shrugging my shoulders, "perhaps not."

We grin at one another. She has a nice smile, I decide, a little lopsided, but warm. On reconsideration, she could be in her late thirties.

"Well," she says, "I'd be pleased to offer a famous writer a special rate."

I take a moment to suppress the all-out-of-proportion pleasurable sensation that accompanies receiving a compliment. "Oh," I say, "you've seen my work?"

"Not recently," she replies, "but I attended one a few years back and enjoyed it very much." She lingers yet and I feel she must want to inquire about something. "If you don't mind my asking, what problem was it that Pellio had?"

Orestes frowns. "Excuse me," he says. He's not a patient man and can adopt an abrupt manner with women. "What business is that of yours? It's one thing to be hospitable, it's another to pry."

"It's all right, I don't mind," I placate Orestes, and turn back to the proprietor. It's an odd request, but I assume she has her reasons. "I've heard it on good authority that there's an older man who has taken ill—I can't mention his name. His family expects he will pass on very soon. As a younger fellow he enjoyed the theatre and it's my understanding that his family will ask that a play be staged as part of the funeral ceremonies."

"Ah," she says, "good news for you."

"Good news for me," I agree. "But the Dominus I previously worked with fell sick last summer and died. Pellio and I worked together at one point several years back, so I was inquiring if he'd be interested in partnering up again. As you might guess from his response, he wasn't."

"It sounds," the owner says, "like you're better off looking elsewhere."

"She has no idea," Orestes tells me and takes a deep drink.

"It's not that simple," I carry on, attempting to ignore Orestes's curt manner. "The Dominus hires and runs the company, he performs in the play, he negotiates with the Aedile, sets an inflated price for the overall commission, and in addition to his set fee as an actor, keeps a percentage of the overage at the end—that is, what doesn't actually get spent. He has to be canny, he has to be thrifty, he has to be able to perform and sufficiently famous to draw a crowd. A Dominus is necessary to any performing grex, but these kinds of people aren't just found."

"What does he do?" she tilts her chin in Orestes's direction.

"He's a musician, and Choragus."

She nods. "And the Choragus does what?"

It's evident that Orestes doesn't understand why I'm pursuing this conversation, and I'm not entirely sure why I am myself. Perhaps, if she's a fan of the theatre, she can be convinced to subsidize my lodgings. In any case, wanting to indicate how bored he has become of her questions, Orestes pops another olive in his mouth and shifts his attention entirely to the street and passersby.

"He collects the performance materials," I explain, "and directs the actors. The Choragus is like the general of an army, only fiercer, and more musical."

"If he," she continues, indicating Orestes, "can organize your actors, and you have the men you require . . . ?"

Orestes swivels on the bench and looks at me. "She doesn't understand." He turns his deadpan gaze on her. "You know nothing about theatre, and what does it matter to you? You should simply concentrate on serving food and drinks, where I assume you and your husband have greater expertise."

The proprietor narrows her eyes and considers Orestes a moment as though prepared to offer a sharp response. Instead, she returns her attention to me.

"Explain it to me," she continues evenly. "What else would be needed?"

I have told Orestes in the past that he must be patient with people who have no involvement in the theatre. They attend a production, and think they understand how a play is produced, which is like seeing the antlers mounted on a wall and believing you comprehend the stag. "First of all," I explain, "we'd have to find actors for the grex—the company that will form the core of our performing group. This will take some work. We would also need to build a theatre on which to rehearse and perform; and then we'd need costumes, sets, props, masks."

"I have masks," Orestes grumbles, still studying the streetside activity. "A few."

"And you could get others from someone else, couldn't you?" she says. "On loan?"

I look at Orestes and raise my eyebrows in question.

"It might be possible. Most of them," he permits. "There would be some we'd have to purchase."

"What else would you need?" she asks.

I hold up fingers, counting them off. "Set, props, and costumes."

Orestes breaks off a piece of bread, and inserts it in his mouth. "I own some costumes too."

"Couldn't you borrow the rest?" she suggests.

"Perhaps," he allows. "I could ask around."

"So," she continues, "it seems if you could find someone to construct the theatre—"

"That's not a problem," I correct her. "I can do that. With a couple of helpers. And I could build the props too."

"You're not just talking?" she asks me. "You're capable?"

"I was immunes in the Legions led by Appius Pulcher, engineering division," I tell her, "and there isn't much I can't build."

"Then, if this one," she says, nodding at Orestes, "can organize the play and the actors, and you have a script in hand. And you can construct the theatre—"

"The biggest impediment would still exist," I interrupt. "That indispensable ingredient everybody needs and can't make. Money. I would require a Dominus with enough financial heft to initially contract actors, cover wages, purchase materials, and form a viable grex until the Aedile dispensed—"

She refills our drinking cups. "I have a little money."

That catches me short. I had thought at best I might get free lodging. I study her as I take a drink. She doesn't appear to be joking.

"What are you suggesting?" I ask.

"I'm interested," she answers.

"It could be a considerable initial investment," I caution her, "as much as several hundred denarii. Maybe a thousand."

If this surprises her, she doesn't show it. "In the past I have directed profits from the Cerium into a variety of activities," she says.

"How much would you expect in return?" I inquire.

"I've actually done a little poking about in terms of the fees normally charged for performances," she tells me. "If I have a hand in setting the overall budget, I would expect a seventh of overage when the play closed."

I study her. Her gaze doesn't waver.

"You're serious?" I ask.

She nods. "Yes."

I turn to Orestes, who is as astonished as I am by this unexpected shift in the conversation. "See if you can recruit actors," I tell him. "I'll take care of the assistant carpenters. We'll compare notes in a day or two."

"Where will I find you?" he asks.

I glance over at the proprietor. She nods again.

"Here," I tell him, "but send notice before you come, to ensure I'm not off recruiting."

Brushing crumbs from his lap, Orestes stands and leaves.

"Your associate is surly," she observes as Orestes steps into the street.

"And cheap," I add, noting that he has left no money for his drinks. "The two most important traits of a successful Choragus."

"I appreciate thrift in a man," she reflects, "but I can see why he won't do for your Dominus, who I assume must demonstrate greater social graces."

I pull my bench closer to the table. "I don't know your name."

"Casina," she replies.

"Casina," I start, "if you and your husband—"

"There is no husband," she interrupts me. "I am the sole owner of the Cerium."

"I see." That's unusual. The war has created many widows who, barring any male children, end up inheriting their husbands' businesses. Normally, though, she would be expected to sell her holding and retire to live with relatives.

"You understand that there's no absolute certainty that there *will be* a funeral," I explain. "Only the gods can predict with certainty when someone will die."

"I assume," she says, leaning forward, "that you have some reliable inside knowledge."

"I've received information from people I trust that the old man cannot possibly last longer than two months." I pour myself more wine as I try to figure this woman out. "So. You're fond of plays."

"I attended your *Miles Gloriosus* three years ago," she recalls. "Enjoyed it very much."

"But there are a number of uncertainties associated with this affair, and you don't look to me like a person devoted to works of charity."

"I'm not. I feel I should be able to use my connections to trim costs, widen the margin of profitability, and make us money, and it will open up other opportunities for me. And . . ." she begins, then hesitates.

"And?" I ask, when she doesn't finish her thought.

I can see her appraising me. "You say you've done woodworking when you were with the legions."

"Yes."

"If I provide the investment, I'd ask that you do me a favour in return."

"You're going to get your investment back," I remind her.

"Eventually," she replies. "This job you'd perform for me could act as my security, and of course, in the end I would deduct your labour from my investment."

"And if Orestes is not able to gather a grex, or if the funeral ceremony fails to appear, or if for some other reason the production doesn't materialize?"

"I will pay you for your duties, and in the meantime you'll have a roof over your head."

"What job?" I ask.

The pit she leads me to in the alley has already been excavated and carefully lined with cut stone. At the bottom, a drain has been positioned emptying down the incline and under the adjoining street. I stretch flat on my belly and stick my head into the hole.

"Who was the mason?" I ask over my shoulder.

"The water commissioner is an occasional patron of the Cerium, and kindly volunteered men and material."

"Generous of him," I say, and reflect that she must be very well connected to some influential citizens. I sweep my right hand along the rock face. Smooth, dry, carefully placed, no holes that I can detect. "It's good work. There's an incline that routes it right into the—"

"The Cloaca Maxima, that's right."

I stand. "Smart. Won't have to pay to have it emptied. And you're getting water for drainage from . . . ?"

She nods in the direction of the crossroad. "There's a diversion the commissioner tapped off the fountain in the square."

I perform a little mental calculation. "How many seats would you want?"

"Six and three."

I consider the wall of the taberna rising next to us. "Coming off where?"

"The second floor landing." She points. "You would knock out the rear wall there."

I envision it coming down and the latrine replacing it. The construction wouldn't be particularly difficult. "I could build it," I tell her.

"I'd provide meals and drinks as well. And there's a vacancy, so I'll have a cubiculum set aside for as long as you need to get the play completed."

I picture the structure she's asked me to build. "I'll need tools as well," I say. "Saws, chisels, a bow drill—"

She hands me a wax tablet and a stylus. "Make a list."

I take it away with me, and move into the Cerium that night. The cubiculum she's set aside is on the second floor, up the flight of wooden stairs and to the left, third door down. It's small, but that's fine. I travel light. It's sufficiently comfortable and I'm sufficiently exhausted that when I sit upon the bed to contemplate my next move, I fall dead asleep in my clothes. The next morning I wake, clean myself up, and after Ientaculum, Casina brings me to the lane in the back. She has tools laid out.

"The hammer is good," I tell her, "and the planes and saws will do. The pumice stone can serve. I'll need a smaller drill. Here are a few other things I'd forgotten." I return the tablet to her.

"I'll have these tomorrow, waiting for you in the cellar."

"Good. And I've made a bit of a drawing so you'll know what I'm doing." I indicate the sketch at the bottom of the tablet. "This is how it will look."

She spends more time studying it than I had anticipated. She's cautious—I like that in an employer. Better she should know what she wants than that we argue about it after it's built. "I want the six and three separated by a wall," she tells me, and traces a line across the drawing. "—and with separate entrances."

I look at the line she's inscribed. "That will take more time."

"And put doors on the entrances," she adds.

"Really?" I ask, surprised. "Doors?"

"Yes."

"That means extra lumber, and time," I point out.

"The girls are chased everywhere. They should have at least one place where they're left to themselves."

She provides me with the names of people to see in order to collect the lumber and tools I'll need. It takes most of the day, but by late in the afternoon when I return to the Cerium I have all the necessary materials. I find a seat in the common room, and congratulate myself on a day well spent.

As the sun drops in the horizon the rhythm of the caupona changes. The tables fill, customers order food and drink, the conversation grows livelier. The mix of people is about what you might expect for a place of this kind. Soldiers and ex-soldiers boasting and gaming, artisans, merchants, and tradesmen drinking and doing business. A few farmers or men working the boats, and the odd citizen or senator out slumming and seeking entertainment.

The awning is extended a little further, and tables are shifted streetside where customers are most likely to catch a bit of a breeze. Food is served briskly from the six immense amphorae set in the L-shaped stone counter along the front of the caupona and the north sidewall. I order soup and hot spiced wine. Pomona and four other servers, young, attractive women all, move swiftly from table to table taking orders, hoisting laden trays, refilling empty cups. One of the servers, a slight young thing with surprisingly long, delicate limbs, gets a good deal of attention from a cluster of half-cut soldiers seated nearest the counter. Another extremely limber server with a cascading mane of blue-black hair is referred to as The Scythian by customers, so I assume she dances. It's doubtful she's actually Scythian, but she carries herself a little like she might know something about dance, and I wonder if she'll perform tonight.

"I remember you," a man one table over says, interrupting my musings. I turn to see an older citizen who has ordered and consumed several drinks since I've arrived. He is seated at the edge of a group of what I take to be his younger relatives. They don't appear to be paying him much attention. His eyes are rheumy and a little unfocused, but he is neatly put together, and only teeters slightly as he shifts his attention to me.

I try to put a name to his grizzled face, but am unable. "I can't say the same," I tell him.

He continues staring intently at me, as though trying to place where we have met, then announces, "You wrote that Greek play. In Latin."

"Well," I agree, hesitantly. "Maybe. I've written several."

He doesn't reply, just carries on studying me and nods, as if something important has been revealed. After a slightly uncomfortable moment, I conclude that our brief, odd conversation has terminated, and return to my meal, when abruptly, he continues his thought.

"Everything is changing," he declares.

Out of respect for his age, and because I don't know what he's getting at, I respond with some rather vague murmur of agreement. Instead of extinguishing the conversation, as I'd hoped, this encourages him.

"The Latin League is changing, everyone can see that it's all a façade. The League has become Rome and Rome alone. Rome is growing, everyone comes to Rome or wants to come to Rome or is selling their belongings to come to Rome. The countryside vomits up its trash—and dumps it here." He gestures with a wavering hand at those seated around him. "Where will it end?"

"Good question," I answer with what I hope is a sufficient lack of enthusiasm, but I realize that while he is addressing me, it is not only me he is talking to—or even primarily me. He is offering up a lesson, of sorts, and it is through instructing me that he hopes to educate others. His voice rises and more people begin to take notice.

"Greek plays," the old man quavers, "and the corrupting disease of Greek ideas. Now it's required to sit through *plays* when one attends the ludi."

"Well, it's not actually *required*, and believe me, many people don't," I joke, hoping to dampen his ardour, but he is in full stride now.

"I remember when there were fewer ludi, and they were more devoutly observed. There are more attendees at the ludi now, oh yes. But why do they attend? Is it to *praise* the gods? Is it to *make sacrifice*? Is it to demonstrate *devotion*? No, no, goodness no, now it is to witness the games, now it's to participate in feasts and watch charioteers, now it's gambling and foreign rituals and throwing yourself upon some whore and riding her like a pony."

Someone at another table cheers. I believe some other wit neighs. This provokes the entire room to laughter. The old man is not deterred. He pushes himself up to a standing position, wavering on his two skinny legs as he glares about. He has at last succeeded in attracting everyone's attention. One of his relatives nervously plucks at his toga, but he brushes the interfering hand away.

"Before, we attended to sacrifice. To supplicate. To humble ourselves. *Humble* ourselves?" Here he offers a dismissive little laugh as he scans the room. "Is there any genuine humility in Rome anymore? Is it possible to find even *one* humble individual? Now, even the beggars are proud. Proud to be begging in Rome."

"Sit down!" one of the larger soldiers calls. "Take Father Socrates home," someone growls at another table, "we don't need his lectures." The relatives, realizing the precariousness of their situation, begin to take things in hand. One fellow quickly settles the bill as another quietly suggests that it's time to leave, and together they attempt to urge the old man out. He ventures a few faltering steps in the direction of the exit, but then shrugs the hands from him and balks at the edge of the street.

"We barely escaped destruction!" he declares, his jowls quivering, "Are any of you sober enough to remember? Hannibal held us by the testicles. Do you recall the humiliation of the Trebia? The despair felt after the defeat at Cannae? Greasy, murderous barbarians loped up and down the length of Latium, cutting down whomever they pleased, pissing on our sacred sites. That was a divine warning to us."

"Get him out of here!" a chorus of angry voices respond. "Take Grumpy home before we toss him in the river."

"I say," the old man shouts over their objections, "it was the gods' doing. We know that the gods exact revenge through men—wasn't it the gods who destroyed Troy, through men?" The soldiers are turning around and showing signs of being ready to guide the old man to the river, but still he resists his relatives' urgings and struggles to speak.

"It was a sign! It was a caution not to succumb to decadence, or wallow in corrupt, profane, foreign ways. One-eyed Hannibal is fleeing now, they tell us. Climbing aboard a ship and returning to Africa." His relatives seize him firmly by his shoulders and thrust him up the street, but he has sufficient vigour to wave a single, crooked admonishing finger in farewell. "But do you think that will end our troubles? I tell you no—because the trouble is here." He thumps his narrow chest with a bony hand. "It is in us."

He is jerked, rather roughly, out of eyesight. And only just in time, since several of the rougher soldiers are just preparing to make good on their threats. Once gone, however, he is instantly forgotten. New customers arrive, crowd the tables, and the old man's vacant spot is filled. Like bees clustering to the honeycomb, they eat, wiggle, and hum, some throwing dice, some singing, some slapping the tabletop to make a point.

I finish my dinner and drain my cup of hot spiced wine, now only tepid. Once done, I mount the stairs at the back, and crack the door to my tiny, stuffy bedchamber. Slightly more aware than I was the previous night, I reflect on the space, which is really no bigger than a rather cramped rowboat. Along one side, a bed with a lumpy straw mattress atop it, and next to the bed a three-legged wooden table. A coarse wool blanket is folded neatly on the table. I pick up the blanket, place the lamp by the bed, drape the blanket across the mattress, undress. I extinguish the lamp, stretch out, and stare up into the impenetrable darkness. A lonely dog barks and is joined by the wild, shrill chorus of neighbourhood mongrels. What can it mean to them, I wonder? A warning? Commiseration? Are they singing in celebration? The noises from the bar below filter up. More raucous conversation, more drunken laughter, more plates clattering. A few doors down, a couple share a joke, what appears to be a kiss from the sounds of it, and then fall into bed. It isn't long before I can detect rhythmic thumping, and the subdued but desperate whispers of lovemaking. Having been womanless myself for an extended period, I am compelled to reflect uncomfortably on the absence. I roll over, but the sounds, once heard, are impossible to ignore. It isn't long before they finish and there is some subdued concluding conversation, followed by relative peace. A few moments later, though, I hear a new pairing of feet stumbling up the stairs followed by more groping, urgent urgings, bumping against the wall just outside my bedroom. Obviously, the Cerium is doing a thriving business. The passionate couple finally navigates their way to a bed a few doors down, and the amorous cycle begins once more. This time I manage to fall asleep before they reach their cataclysmic finish line.

2

I wake to the thunder of wagons rumbling up the street, the
whips of drovers chastising mules, the rough shouts of men
unloading goods. I stretch and kick off my cover. There are
some who berate Rome for its nighttime disturbances, but I'm
not one of them. Having spent years on guard duty, listening
fretfully to nighttime silence and testing it for indications
of trouble, I regard the friendly commerce of early morning
as a comfort. And regardless of one's state of distress or the
anxieties that trouble one's sleep during the night, the sun rises
at dawn to anoint everything. I rise and fetch water from the
fountain at the end of the street.

Garlands of woven olive branches hang from the fountain
spigot, and I am reminded that today is the Fontinalia,
celebrating the god of springs and fountains. I quickly ask a
blessing, then wash myself from a metal basin. I adjust my
tunic and get to work. I descend into the cellar of the Cerium.
The additional tools are there, as Casina had promised. I begin
by measuring and marking. I spend more time at it than I
would have liked, but this is where things either go wrong or
right—in preparation. Any flaws in structure can ultimately be
said to be flaws in planning.

I haul out beams, plane them even, rub pumice up and
down the length to remove splinters. The sawing I find oddly
relaxing. The burr of the toothed blade cutting the grain, the

smell of fresh pine wafting up from the sawdust. I love the slick feel of wood that's been smoothed and oiled.

I lay the beams out on the floor, count, and number them. A metal poker leans near the brazier in the culina. I heat it and brand an identifying mark into each plank. This is a habit I developed back in my army days. A simple brand won't prevent anyone from walking off with your goods, but it will warn a thief that each piece is part of an identified set, and will be missed. I can't say if any of Casina's staff are prone to pilfering, but better safe than sorry.

One of the servers—the one who received the lion's share of attention from the soldiers the other evening—brings me a tray with wine and water and small plate of bread, oil, and olives. A few black figs are arranged alongside.

"For you," she announces, and sets it down.

I drink thirstily, tear a piece from the loaf and stuff it in my mouth. "It's good," I tell her. "Thanks."

"We used to get the best bread right next door, but that baker recently closed. This fellow we use now is second best." She sits on a stack of lumber, eyeing the work I've done and dangling her sculponeae at the end of her long legs.

"Those wooden-soled shoes can't be very practical in a place like this," I observe. "Running up and down stairs in those hard things. Why not get yourself sandals?"

"Oh, I'm used to these old friends," she says, "and wood soles last longer—don't have to buy something new all the time. You should see how Prima goes through her sandals. Plus," she adds, "when patrons get fresh, I use these to provide a reminder."

She snaps a dangling clog up against the base of one foot with a slap.

"That'd hurt," I agree.

She continues to linger as I eat, watching. "You write plays?" she asks.

"Yes," I reply, and mop my face with a rag. The day is heating up.

She eyes the sawdust, timber, and tools lying around. "When do you do it?"

I move the container of nails closer and select a handful. "How do you know I'm not doing it now?" I ask.

She peers at me skeptically. "I don't see you writing anything."

"It's all happening," I reply and tap my brow with a finger, "here."

She snorts disparagingly. I hold up a hand to restrain her comment. "There's a character named—what's your name?"

"Felicia," she says.

"The character's name in the play I'm writing," I tell her, "is Felicia."

"Hussy!" Casina calls from inside the culina, "did I send you out to talk? There are customers waiting."

Felicia stands, slips her right foot further into her wooden-soled shoe. "I've got to go," she says.

Later, Orestes joins me for coena. The meal—chickpeas and nettles, with fresh curds crumbled over top—is satisfying, and again, better quality than what I remember being served by the previous management. As somber and restrained as Orestes naturally is, I can sense he's excited. He orders wine and water, and as he's calculating and mixing it to his precise specifications he tells me. "We have our grex," he announces, and permits a tight, crooked grin. Coming from him, that almost qualifies as laughing out loud.

"Who?" I ask.

"The better part of our grex, anyway," he corrects himself. "Antipho has agreed to join us."

"Really?" I'm completely caught off guard. "Antipho? I thought he was performing down south."

"He was," he replies. "Then the troubles erupted, squadrons of armed men took to the countryside and it became too dangerous. His grex disbanded. He left, returned here looking for work."

"There are a lot of southerners moving up," I note.

"The whole world is stirring," Orestes says as he selects a boiled egg. "Poke a stick into an ant's nest and ants will run in all directions. Level their hill and they must find another mound to settle in. For now, and I believe for the foreseeable future, as cities are unsettled and people unhoused, Rome will be their pile of dirt." He takes a drink. "Now, Antipho's old," he reminds me.

"He'd have to be." I try to recall his age. "What is he, sixty-eight, sixty-nine?"

Orestes glances off as he does the mental calculations. "He could be."

The last time I saw Antipho, he was frail, but still a brilliant comic actor. No actor has been able to extract more undeserved humour from a single joke than that man.

"Too old to be our Dominus," Orestes says, thinking aloud, "but good enough to perform the lead, depending on the part. We couldn't ask him to do anything athletic, but his voice is still strong."

"Certainly," I agree. "And he can draw a crowd," The more I think about it, the more confident I become. Antipho has always had an excellent sense of timing, and will be able to play a range of parts. "That's very, very good news."

"I recruited him and two others, Quintus and Fabius, and listen, you'll be pleased with this—Fabius can sing the female parts."

"His voice?" I ask.

Orestes casts his eyes toward the ceiling and purses his lips in thought. "He has an adequate voice," he allows. "Very passable."

Coming from Orestes I know this to be high praise. "So, we have three?" I confirm.

"Four," he corrects me. "I've had a conversation with a younger fellow as well, whom I've only told we'd consider. Fronto. Hasn't much training, but he has potential. And, with an actor of Antipho's reputation, we can count on others to express interest."

I consider the group and feel my heart lift. "Excellent— even if the others haven't as much experience, even if we have to limp along with just the ones we have now, we'll be fine."

We toast one another, drink, toast again, and then make plans. I scribble a few alternate names to fill out the grex, depending upon the play we select. We argue about it, drink more, get excited, work in earnest again. Orestes strokes the previous names out and jots in some others. We haven't yet received confirmation that the funeral ceremonies will take place, of course, and until that happens, we have nothing. It's all just vapour. Still, just being able to think and plan for the future feels wonderful.

As the sun drops, the night deepens, and bats emerge to career drunkenly across a darkening sky. The usual customers merge on the caupona. Conversations rise, and it becomes more difficult to shout over their racket. Abruptly, Orestes dusts himself, drains his cup, and stands. This is his manner, I recall, abrupt in his opinions and swift to make decisions. He gathers up the wax tablet containing our notes, nods his goodbye. As he exits, I finish my final mouthfuls, and make my way up the rear stairs. Revellers previously hovering by the entrance squeeze past me to occupy our empty seats.

Next morning, after I've wakened, I continue work on the latrine. I bang several planks together, and lay them in units according to size and function along the floor. Felicia emerges from the culina fanning herself. It's still early but already hot. She perches on the stairs and watches me.

"What are those?" she asks.

"Doors," I tell her.

She laughs as though I'm joking. "Doors for a latrine?"

I shrug. "Apparently your boss doesn't want the wind to blow in on you."

Felicia leans forward, runs a hand over one of the planks, and shrugs. "Funny, her tastes."

I glance down at her hand, and note how delicate it is. A lock of her hair falls loose, and she winds it around one finger and tucks it behind an ear.

"Last place I worked—before Casina—we girls peed in a bowl, threw it out the window. If the pot was in use or full," she splays the fingers of both hands out in a gesture of, 'what else could we do,' "we squatted in the alley."

I grimace. "That's a dog's life. Even back in the country we had a hole we used, and a shelter to maintain some privacy and to keep the wind off our parts."

"It didn't matter," she says. "It's not a very private occupation."

I nod and hammer a few of the planks to the frame. She continues watching.

"Are you still writing?" she asks as I lay the hammer aside for a moment.

"Yes."

She grins. "In your head?"

I nod again. I'm often asked this kind of question. If you've never learned to read or write, I think the process must seem mysterious. One moment there's nothing, then words, characters, tears, and laughter.

"What part are you working on?" she asks.

"The most difficult part," I answer. I drink deeply from the water jug I keep near me when I work. I'm sweating. When I was young and in the legion, you worked quick, hard, and when you finished, recovered instantly. Now a whimsy like this latrine feels like a serious effort. My back aches, and I find I can't remain bent over the way I used to. "The planning part," I tell her.

"What plan?"

I sit heavily on the floor, stretch my shoulders and lower back. If it takes a day longer to build the latrine, I conclude, it's not going to kill anyone. "I'm laying the trap."

She searches my face, not sure if I'm teasing. "Didn't know you had to trap anything to write."

"Catching a story is like trying to catch anything," I tell her and offer her the jug. She takes a drink. "Have you ever caught a weasel?" I ask.

She shakes her head.

"You never lived on a farm?" She shakes her head again. "Well. You lay your bait and set the trap. You walk away from it. You watch for signs and tracks. The story remains hidden and avoids your traps. You set others. Those don't work either.

You despair. And then one day you see it, just a glimpse of a tail as it darts from one building to another. Then you know."

"What do you know?" she asks.

"That you've attracted its attention," I say. "That eventually you'll catch it."

She considers this, still not sure if I'm being serious or not. "That's a strange way to write a story," she says.

"Writing's a strange business," I look at her again, sitting on the steps, her chin on her knees. "I would have taken you for a country girl."

"I was when I was little," she confesses.

"What region?" I ask.

She makes a vague directional gesture with her chin. "Up north."

"Same as the cook then," I conclude. I've noticed that the cook, a massively muscled man with an enormous red beard, has the look of a Gaul.

"Oh no," she laughs, "not that far—the cook's from so far north he's half bear. Have you seen how thick his hair is? Ligurian Gaul, that's my homeland. Then fighting came, my village was put to the torch, and soldiers carried me off. I was purchased by a procurer when I was nine."

"That's how you came to Rome?" I ask.

"Not right away. Old Ballio, our procurer, owned a rickety, lopsided wagon and bumped along after the legions in it. He was eager to do business and we rattled everywhere in that old back buster. That was a harder life than this, I'll tell you. To encourage us, he'd proclaim every day that we girls followed the greatest god there was, because Eros sprang from Chaos right alongside Gaia—and what's more powerful than the Earth Goddess, right? He wasn't a bad fellow, but his breath?

Awful. It'd stun you." She leans forward, tugs a sliver from a piece of scrap lumber and uses it to pick food from between her teeth. "He named me. Felicia, because I brought him good fortune. He saved enough money from what we made that he sold the wagon, and rented a place in Rome—a shabby little operation maybe a third the size of this, just a hallway with square chambers off of it."

"Can't have been much bigger than your wagon," I say as I try to picture it.

"It wasn't. But Castor's nuts, it was *so* much better than living out of that wagon. You know, when you're travelling like that, six girls crammed together, there's no room to store nothing. Living on top of each other, no place to bathe, no place to change, nothing to change into even if you had a place, mud when it rains, dust when it doesn't, the pong of mule dung clinging to everything. The Rome operation was a crumbling bit of nothing held together with cobwebs and stolen street stones, but it was a palace compared to life on the wagon. And, it was in Rome."

"How'd you end up here, then?" I ask.

"A year and half into the new place, a shipload of soldiers fresh from troubles in Sicily dropped anchor. We were busy as cats with kittens for two weeks, then plague swept through and Ballio and three other girls were dead in a hiccup. Just like that. It hit them; they took to their beds with a headache, and were gone. I caught the fever, thought I'd die but didn't. I was recovering when the landlord threw our things out on the street. So, still weak from the sickness, no place to earn money, I went searching for shelter." She wraps her arms around her knees, as though even thinking about those times makes her uncomfortable. "Casina," she continues, "was running a successful little operation not far from where we worked—it was a different place then—in Subura—and I went to her, the clothes covering my bum, and that was all. I offered to sell myself to her. She cleaned me up, took me in, and now I'm working off my price. She doesn't promote me the way old Ballio did, and I have to look after tables too, but she doesn't take the same cut as he did either. She calls what she takes from me 'rent'—it's high for rent, and I could never make it just on what I earn from tables, but she doesn't care how many men I turn, so long as I pay her what's owed monthly. It's better here, the best I've ever had." She smiles at me. "And now we have a latrine—with doors—so I must be good luck."

She excuses herself. I work steadily, throughout the day. Prior to sunset I lay my tools aside, stack the timber, and after washing myself, retire to dine. I request lentil soup, and some water and wine from one of the servers—a dark-haired, dark-eyed, wide-shouldered young woman. She brings me the soup, and a vase and a cup. I lift the candle, spill hot wax upon the table and spread it with a finger. I extend my hand, grasp and snap a twig from a nearby mimosa, and begin to scratch a few hasty thoughts in the cooling surface.

"That's quite a mess you're making," a gravelly voice says. I look up.

An older man, medium height, steps into the protective shade of the awning. Short grey hair, neatly trimmed beard. Serious lines around the eyes. Dusty toga clutched about him.

"It's nobody's business but mine. And it's how I make my livelihood," I reply, as I scrape the excess drying wax from my finger.

He raises his eyebrows. "Must be nice to be professional maker of messes."

"It has its pleasures," I agree. "Then again, I didn't say it pays well." He stamps and brushes dust from his legs. "Looks like you've had a hard journey."

"I'm parched," he says, "My lips are cracked. I am tired and weathered and quite frankly it has almost done me in."

"You speak like a tragedian," I tell him, "which would explain your frailty. Here, take some wine." I offer him the remainder of the flask at my table. He drinks thirstily, directly from it.

"How is it?" I ask as he finishes.

He holds it away from his mouth. "I begin to feel some slight restorative powers."

Having been stirred to activity by the sound of voices, the server emerges from an inner room, blinking at the light. She glances first at the flask being upturned and emptied, and then the tabletop and my spilt wax.

"What's your name?" I ask her.

"Domitia," she replies.

"Good. Domitia, don't remove that wax," I tell her. "I'll peel it off and take it with me."

"You should bend your will to some more serious endeavour," the man says, returning my flask to the tabletop.

"Writing, my friend," I say as I dip a corner of bread in my soup, "writing is a serious endeavour."

"Writing comedy," he corrects me, "which is what I take you to be doing—is a masturbator's craft."

I tuck the bread in my mouth and chew. "You are mistaken," I tell him. "Comedy is a godly craft, and a tonic for what ails you. Perhaps for whatever ails *you* specifically. More than that, comedy is a lash. Comedy howls and compels us to confront our fears. Comedy illuminates, it illustrates. Comedy is bread, and cheese, and wine for the soul.

"Tragedy, on the other hand—which I would guess *you* prefer," I say, pointing at him with a crust of my bread, "harangues and harasses. It is heavy. It oppresses the soul. It says to the soul—'soul, sit down and quench your thirst'— and then slakes it with seawater. It plunges you into mayhem and bloodshed and the most outrageous excesses and vices of mankind. It's noisy. It's bossy. It lectures and moralizes in a way that you would find unacceptable coming from even your most beloved aunt. It makes you sit on hard uncomfortable seats studying unpleasant, long-winded, self-absorbed characters, people you would not generally wish to share a moment's piss with."

The man suppresses a belch. "I feel you are too hard on tragedy," he says. "Tragedy teaches rigour. As you have indicated, tragedy is neither gentle nor quiet, nor is it meant to be, but it will make a man of you. You sit here eating thin broth and cold bread. This is not a tragedy, but it is a little sad. If you viewed more tragedy you would eat a more robust meal of bloody meat, and consequently would do everything manly better. Fight, fart, fornicate."

Puzzled, Domitia blinks as she looks from the newcomer to me.

"Can I get you anything?" she inquires. "Either of you?"

"Don't give him any wine," I caution her. "He's trouble if he gets a bellyful."

"I'll have what he's drinking," he says. "Only more. And without water." Domitia nods and gratefully exits.

I stand, embrace him, clap him on the back. "Naevius. Good to see you. How are you?"

He runs a hand through his beard. "I'll be better once I've had another drink."

"I heard you'd been released," I say, "but I hadn't seen you so wasn't sure what to believe."

"I had to put my things in order," he informs me. "I'd heard you were staying at the Cerium. I remembered staying here myself back in the day. It looks like it's improved." He draws up a bench and sits, spends a moment considering me. "You appear hale, so the writing must be going well."

"I'm building a latrine," I tell him.

"Good, then you'll have a place to consult your most natural muse. I'm staying with relatives."

"It must agree with you. You look healthy," I point out, and he does. He may have been in confinement for the past years, but he has kept his appearance. He's not young, but he's always been a good-looking man—tall, lean, muscular—and that hasn't changed. But he's aged more than two years in the two years' time since I've last seen him, and his beard has gone completely grey. There's a bit of a shaggy, old, Tiresias look to him—a prophet returned home to deliver some bitter divination.

"If I can survive the food my nephew's family serves," he grouses, "I must have the constitution of an Olympian."

"Bad?" I ask.

"Beyond bad." A tight grimace crosses his face. "It beggars the imagination."

"Considering the poverty of your diet," I observe, "you look remarkably fit."

"I'm resilient," he replies, and drums his fingers on the tabletop. "Truthfully, I've struggled since I returned to Rome.

I've tried to secure a patron—so far no bites. They're all frightened that I'll write something that will give offence."

"And given your history," I observe, "you can see their point."

"A little offence is a tonic," he answers. "And there was a time when that was understood. But times have changed, or maybe I've changed. I don't know what people want anymore."

"People always want the same thing," I tell him. "They want a story. They want a laugh or two. Give them that."

He groans and rubs his face with one hand. "I don't want to give them that."

"Then go into shipping. It didn't work for me, but there's nothing to say that it wouldn't work for you."

"You need money to enter into shipping, and it's a hideous business. Shipping," he repeats, pronouncing the word as though it leaves a bad taste. "It's damp and smells of fish."

"Sea air is healthy, I'm told."

"Sea air gives you bow legs and scabies. Do you have money?" he asks, changing topics.

"Do I look like I have money?" I reply.

"Well, you've always looked a little like a beggar," he allows, "but I never thought that had anything to do with whether you had money or not. I thought it was a style you cultivated."

I perform a quick tally of my meagre resources. "I can lend you thirty semis," I tell him, and reach into my money pouch to count out the coins.

3

Next day, after rising and eating, I erect the frame of the latrine, hammer it into place. I kneel at the base of the stairs to piece together the interior benches. From the corner of one eye, I catch a subtle movement in the shadows near the culina's doorway. At first I can't make out what it is precisely—it seems so disproportioned—then realize that it's the skittish female cat that haunts the caupona, wrestling an immense portion of smoked ham. She's grasped it firmly between her jaws and is resolutely marching it backward, one paw at a time. Suddenly her ears lift, she releases the ham and spins about in that fluid, seemingly boneless way cats can.

"Get oouut of here, you!" A hoarse, thickly accented voice hollers. A dripping dishrag hurtles out the door, landing wetly against the corner post of the stairway.

"Vulcanus!" Felicia shrieks from the top of the steps. I know she has a soft spot for the cat—I've seen her leave it snacks out on the landing. "Watch where you throw things. I might have been sitting there."

The cook, a massive red-haired, red-cheeked, red-bearded titan, squeezes through the doorway, glowering. He's big in every sense of the word, filling his cooking alcove like a snail fills its shell. The cat—his intended target—has already nimbly escaped and leapt into the street.

Grumbling, the cook bends to scoop the rag up from the base of the stairs, and hauls the ham from the floor. With the wet cloth grasped in one immense hairy fist, he gestures at Felicia.

"She bad spirit," he complains. "Prowl kitchen. Climb shelves. Steal pork, scatter fish, come back, come back, too much come back."

"She's just trying to survive," Felicia answers, in a way I would consider ill advised if someone as large as Vulcanus was waving his arms at me, "same as anybody. Everybody gets hungry."

"Her get hungry someplace else," he grouses. "Next time I chop off head, cook with side of garum." And having shared that culinary enticement with us, he wedges himself back through the doorway and returns to his steamy, smoky domain, muttering, "Never worry 'bout her again."

"Cooks," Felicia says, rolling her eyes. "They're so emotional." She stands looking down at me from the stairs. I nod my agreement, but continue hammering. I have no interest in offering an opinion on any matter that would position me on the wrong side of the person who makes my meals. And besides, I'm hoping he'll share the much-coveted recipe for garum with me someday. When I glance up, Felicia is still leaning against the banister, staring.

"Have you been sent to make sure I'm working?" I ask.

"I'm trying to figure out what to do next. One of my regulars was supposed to meet me and hasn't shown. He didn't warn me, hasn't explained his absence, didn't send a message. That's the third time. Now I'm behind on rent," She descends halfway down the staircase, sits heavily and sighs. "I don't know how you write funny things. Life isn't funny."

I remove a nail from the corner of my mouth and hammer it into a plank. "Sure it is."

She folds her arms on her knees, and props her chin in her hands. "Not the life I've known."

"You're young," I say, and reach for more nails. "Tomorrow, you'll find a different client. Then all of this will be a comedy."

She shakes her head. "I don't think I'll ever laugh after the unreliable couple of clients I've had."

I shrug. "You might. Comedy doesn't wait its turn—it pushes right up alongside tragedy, and they both vie for your attention. Your sassy cat a moment ago, chased away from her food by the cook. Is that a tragedy—desperate, hungry cat loses her meal, only barely escapes with her life? Or a comedy: wily, resourceful pussy outwits cook, escapes, and will return for a rematch another day?"

Felicia scrunches up her face in an extreme expression of skepticism, "You only see it that way because you're a poet. You can't live your life like that."

"Yes, you can," I reply. "You do."

"You can't just suddenly *decide* to feel happy."

"Why not?" I ask.

"Because that's not the way things are in real life," she insists. "In real life, you get hit, you hurt."

"Yes, you hurt." I sink a row of nails into a timber. "And what else?"

"Nothing else. That's it."

"There's always something else," I repeat.

"No," she insists. "That's what I'm saying, there's not."

"I remember a fellow I fought alongside," I tell her, "Got fastened to a pole and flogged for backtalking a tribune. He initially maintained that at the time he felt nothing. But I know for a fact that he spent that entire whipping planning how to take his revenge. I know, because later, in a frenzy of drunkenness he confided his plan to me. So, he felt pain—one response—yes—but there was another emotion he experienced at exactly the same time, something more closely connected to these other unfortunate notions he had of vengeance."

She twists a lock of her hair between her fingers as she considers this. "And did he?" she asks. "Get his revenge?"

"Oh, yes." I remember Titus. A big-boned, happy-seeming fellow, with a loose-limbed, ambling stride, and truly unquenchable thirst when he drank. "During a skirmish several months later he picked his moment and when he thought no one was watching, planted his gladius deep in the tribune's throat."

Felicia winces. "Eww."

"Blamed it on the Liburnians, but of course, someone was watching—someone is always watching. So he was executed." I don't bother going into the bloody way he'd been executed, as an example to others who might consider avenging themselves on their superiors. How he had been stretched between trees, his fellow legionnaires outfitted with staffs and then instructed to club him to death. No point in sharing those kinds of gory details early in the morning. "There is nothing you will ever end up paying more for than revenge," I tell her.

"There. Just like I told you," she exclaims, "people feel what they feel—he felt hurt and it caused his death."

"You're missing the point—he felt hurt, yes but he also felt angry and vengeful, and he chose to act on the latter." I put down my tools. "Look, you've been to the theatre, yes?"

"Yes."

"Then you've seen masks. In any given show, an actor switches masks two, maybe three times. Do you think a mask—which has just one fixed expression—permits you the luxury of gradually working your way around to feeling the emotion it expresses? No—once you remove one mask to put on another, you shed one emotion and get on to the next, *instantly*. You have to feel something—so you do." I brush the dust from my hands against my tunic. "There's no point in discussing it. I'll show you." I stand and stretch. I could use a break anyway. "I'll make an angry face, you imitate it back."

Felicia shakes her head. "I'm not making faces."

"Just try," I urge her.

"No," she objects, "you only want to make me look silly."

"I'll do it too, so we'll both look silly together. Imitate me," I wrinkle my face into my fiercest expression. At first she just gazes at me, shocked, then doubles over laughing.

"Now you're frightening me," she says.

"Go on," I encourage her. "You do it."

She concentrates, and her face folds into an expression that might be described as mild annoyance. It will have to do.

"Make an angry sound," I instruct her.

She shakes her head in disbelief at what I'm asking, closes her eyes and releases a timid, ineffectual mewl that wouldn't scare your average kitten.

"That's the most feeble, half-hearted, *pitiful* sound I've ever heard. Growl!" I tell her and release a low growl myself.

She rolls her eyes, astonished at her own credulity and compliance, then growls.

"Good!" I compliment her. "Now say something angry."

"What?" she asks.

"Anything!"

She thinks a moment, then pipes, "I'm angry."

"What's that?" I scoff, "Have you never been mad?"

"I don't know what to do!" she protests. "I feel ridiculous!"

"Make something up!" I tell her, "Get angry! Threaten me."

"I'll crush you," she says in a voice you might employ to lull an especially sensitive infant to sleep.

"I don't believe you!" I tell her, and I give her a push.

"I'll crush you," she repeats, startled by the shove. She's louder this time.

"Angry!" I bark, determined to provoke a real response.

Her frustration and anxiety combine to generate a sudden surge of intensity and emotion. Her face flushes.

"I'll crush you!" she snaps at last.

"Good!" I say, and growl back at her to keep her focused, "Again!"

"I'll crush you. I'll *crush* you! I'll stomp on you till you're nothing but bone chips and bloody pulp and throw your bones to my goats. My goats will butt you and then, and then, trample you too!—and then I'll throw what remains into the pigpen and feed you to the boars."

"Better! Now make a frightened face—like this." I stretch my mouth and eyes open wide in shock. "And make a sound like you're terrified," I tell her, and release a startled yelp. "Back away from everything! See that fly buzzing on your right?" She turns her head. "Gasp and back away from it, it's hideous!" She's enjoying herself now. She steps back from the fly and gasps. "There's another behind you!" Squealing, she whips about.

"Excellent," I commend her. "Now, make a happy face, and look at the fly again, only this time make a happy sound." I smile widely and release a sigh of astonished pleasure. "Doesn't it have delicate wings? And look at the sunbeam beside it, pretty thing, isn't it?" A dazzling finger of sunlight lances the room, brilliant specks of dust swirling about in it like so many glittering jewels. "Sweep your hand through it and make it swirl."

She does, then throws back her head, laughs, and claps her hands.

I find myself laughing as well. "We feel what we feel, yes—but we can switch those feelings just by choosing what we'll focus on. That's the incredible thing comedy tells us. Cry or laugh—your choice."

Pomona appears at the top of the stairway, frowning at the noise we're making, one hand on a hip. "What's going on?" she inquires.

"Nothing," Felicia answers, and quickly stoops to kiss me. Just lightly on the lips, and then slips off to the coenatio.

I taste salt where she kissed me. That was interesting.

It takes five full days to complete the latrine, but in the end, I'm pleased with the results. I open the doors and shut them again. They close quietly and hang straight. I step inside. It is dark and secret, like a temple. The air is thick with the smell of fresh-cut pine. Honey-coloured light slants through holes chiselled in the door. I hoist up my tunic and sit on one seat, then stand and move to another. The wood is warm to the touch, smooth and even.

I stand once more, lift the front of my robe and relieve myself. The stream arcs through the air, then clatters as it strikes the stone below, sounding a kind of inaugural offering.

I shake myself, lower my robe, and step out only to find Casina considering the work. I gesture to the latrine. "Done," I announce.

"Very good," she replies, as she opens a door and glances in to judge the craftsmanship. "Very, very good." Then she peers back at me. "There's someone wanting to speak to you downstairs," she says.

"About what?" I ask.

She shrugs. I descend the stairs and find a short slave slouching against the wall by the entrance to the caupona. "Are you looking for me?" I ask.

"I have a message for Plautus, the writer," he announces, eyeing me and my dust-covered tunic suspiciously. "Is that you?"

I feel a rush of impatience at his attitude. "Would I have asked if it wasn't me?" I snap. "Hurry and tell me your message."

"You are requested," he says, "to meet with Gnaeus Lentulus Caudinus."

I feel blood rush to my head. Someone from the family Lentulus wishes to meet. That can only mean one thing.

4

We agree to meet in the Comitium near the Rostra at midday.
I quickly clean up, then hasten through the forum, hurrying
past the sharp horns of captured ships that project off the
speakers' platform. I spy Gnaeus Lentulus Caudinus standing
by a series of long wooden benches. A tallish young man, I
assume to be another of his slaves, sees me at about the same
time as I see them, and tilts close to whisper to his master.
Gnaeus Lentulus turns, scans the surroundings, and we make
eye contact.

He is sharp-eyed, lean, and in every way a very serious-
seeming elderly man—he looks something like his brother
Cornelius Lentulus Caudinus, a rising star, who has been
recently elected to attend the Macedonian negotiations. Of
average height, Gnaeus Lentulus has chosen to maintain a
neatly trimmed beard, after the Greek fashion. He continues
studying me as I draw nearer, which I find unnerving. "Titus
Maccius Plautus?" he asks once I am close enough. I nod. He
gestures for me to sit beside him on one of the benches.

I've never had occasion to meet any of the Lentulus family,
but they have a reputation for being both blunt and cheap.
He's certainly blunt—he dispenses with all the standard
pleasantries and cuts straight to business. "My father has not
been well," he observes as he adjusts his toga. "It's clear he
won't survive another month."

"The gods give him an easy passage," I reply, but inside, hypocrite that I am, I secretly exult. At long last, I think to myself, this is the event we have been waiting for! Instantly I experience a corresponding pang of guilt. What a world. For someone's loss there is always someone who profits.

"Thank you," he says to me, unaware of my blasphemous inner dialogue. "Still, it is necessary to make suitable preparations."

"Certainly," I assure him. "In whatever way I may be of assistance, please let me know." I wait, confident that we will now attend to arrangements for a performance, but instead an uncomfortable silence descends. We peer at one another shyly, like hesitant lovers.

"Yes. It is so essential to think ahead," I chatter without any real idea of what to say next, simply trying to fill the void, wondering why he would delay outlining our agreement, an agreement I assume he has invited me specifically to address. Suddenly I feel an inner spasm of doubt as it occurs to me that I may have entirely misjudged the situation. Maybe there is something else he wants from me, something entirely unrelated to plays or the theatre—although that scarcely seems possible. Why would someone from a family of his stature wish to speak to someone like me, except to arrange for a play?

"As part of his f-funeral ceremonies," he continues, finally, "he has re-re-requested that a play be dedicated to Ap-pollo and p-p-per-formed."

At first I am taken aback at the enormous effort this simple statement represents, then I breathe a sigh of relief. *This is the reason that he has been reluctant to broach the subject.* I recall a fellow I worked alongside in the engineering corps who had a terrible stutter. When he was calm, the disorder was almost unnoticeable; when he became anxious, even the simplest phrases erupted as a tortured exchange. "Your father was famous," I assure him, "for his pious nature and love of the arts. I'm certain this will be a great comfort to him."

He nods his head in agreement, and I can see that the nod itself is also his way of deflecting attention from his speaking disability. "I enjoyed an earlier p-play of yours a great deal."

"Thank you," I say.

"It m-made me laugh very hard," he remembers. "W-what was its name? About the boastful soldier?"

"*Miles Gloriosus*," I reply.

"That was it," he says, smiling at the recollection, the first genuine smile I have seen him make. "You should employ my fa-father-in-law as a ch-character in one of your performances." He dips his head, as though affirming the absolute appropriateness of the suggestion.

People often say this sort of thing to me. 'You would find my uncle so amusing,' or, 'You would find my grandfather interesting.' I rarely do. Over the years I have struggled to calculate a response that doesn't explicitly label the idea boring and worthless, which it often is, and still allows for the remote possibility that the idea may be a genuinely good one, which it almost never is.

"The things he says!" he continues and shakes his head in mock astonishment. "They're ast-ast-astounding."

"Really?" I ask.

"He grumbles about the softness of city people sleeping on their mattresses, prides himself in his hard living upon campaigns, boasts of his times fighting Carthaginians in Sicily. You would think he won the war single-single-single-handedly.

His role increases dramatically with each telling. He becomes a Her-Her-Hercules. He draws maps of the battles, and charts, so many maps and charts—but, do you know—it is impossible to decipher a single one!" He taps the benchtop, as though one of these anarchic maps was stretched between us. "If you developed a character scratching incomprehensible maps on every imaginable surface; table tops, walls, railings, you would be close to the truth—your audience might appreciate that."

"That's very generous of you to offer that suggestion to me," I say, supplying the stock answer I have arrived at over time.

"Well p-p-perhaps it will provide you with a new comic character, call him the Old M-Map Maker." Returning to business, he asks me, "What play would you perform?"

"What play would you prefer?" I ask.

He considers this a moment as he gazes into the distance. "Is a new play possible?" he suggests.

Clients always wish to make their mark on posterity by commissioning new writing—but they rarely consider all the additional work. "If there were more time," I tell him. "It requires thought and effort to translate and find the correct way to turn the play to a Roman sensibility. How much time would you say there is?"

He frowns as he considers his father's illness. "Not much. My father has been getting weaker each day."

"Perhaps an earlier, already written play, then," I propose. "Did he have a favourite?"

The idea of performing a 'favourite' seems to encourage him. He tilts his head back to think. "Would *The Pot of Gold* be possible?" he inquires, his chin still lifted. "He was fond of that."

I nod. "That would be possible."

He drops his right hand against his right thigh, generating a soft but resonant thud. "Let's d-d-do that then. I'll provide you with the money you'll need for the staging. Do you have a general s-s-sense of a b-b-budget?"

"I do," I tell him, and withdraw some documents from my shoulder bag, "and I have written notes on that matter that I can leave you."

"Just pass those to my servant on your way out. He'll take care of it. I'm sure the p-p-production will be sp-splendid." He hesitates as if the thought had just occurred to him. "There is the real possibility that my father will fail earlier, so I suggest you begin work at once."

He peeks at my notes before passing them along to his slave, and stops. "I have some used lumber that you may wish to salvage for construction," he says, and reads a little further. "And it won't be necessary to build separate chairs for the audience—a few planks for benches along the front, for family and honoured guests will be suffi-suffi-sufficient. The rest can bring their own seats or stand."

I nod my agreement. The rumours, then, are true. He is cheap. So, I should not anticipate great wealth resulting from this play. By the time he has had his slave analyze and edit the budget, it will be a thin document presenting only the smallest possibility of any surplus. Nevertheless, nevertheless inside I am exulting. I have negotiated a guaranteed production. At last, we may begin rehearsing.

I take my leave of Gnaeus Lentulus Caudinus and his servant. At this point it becomes necessary for me to compose myself and visit Lucius Caecilius, something I have been avoiding.

The industrious Lucius Caecilius can generally be found at the other end of the forum by the temple of Castor, doing business, and sure enough, he is there today as busy as ever. He occupies most of a short stone bench near the base of one of the white marble pillars. He is a wide man and he radiates width. He has a wide face, a wide chest, and infamously broad and expansive buttocks. I sit at the other end of the bench and feel the impressive sense of space he commands. He stares impassively at me, but he too wastes little time on niceties.

"Plautus," he says, "I had heard that you had returned to the city. Have you come to clear your debt?"

"I'm afraid not," I answer.

If he feels disappointment at my answer, it doesn't register on his broad face. "Have you a payment with you?" he inquires.

"Not with me," I reply, and he continues staring at me without expression. "But," I hasten to add, "soon I will. That is why I have come. I have received confirmation that one of my plays will be performed very shortly."

He raises his thin eyebrows in an expression of doubt. "In which of the ludi is this play to be presented?"

"It will be part of the funeral ceremonies the Lentulus family is arranging and you will receive a payment shortly after."

He opens a tablet and raises his stylus. "How much and how shortly?"

I have been trying to develop an answer to this anticipated question as I walk the Sacred Way approaching the temple. The complete payment won't be received until the production has been offered, and that cannot happen until the elder Lentulus passes away. "I will be able to pay quite a bit," I answer, rather vaguely, "and soon."

He sighs, lowers his stylus to the bench, and presses the fleshy tips of his fingers together. "We are both too old for stories and games. Precisely how much and precisely when?"

"200 sisteres," I tell him, "by the end of the month"

His fingertips flex and relax. "Considering the previous lapses, that's insufficient."

I perform a quick mental calculation. "400, then," I suggest.

"And that would be followed by additional, regularly scheduled payments?"

"That's correct." I agree.

He meditates on that, and it is as though he is meditating on the errors and failures of all of humanity. "Your payments have been erratic," he admonishes me finally. "You have promised, in the past, to pay, and then haven't. Over the last year and half you have been impossible to find."

"I realize that," I say, "and I'm sorry."

He leans back, folds his hands over his expansive belly and considers me. It is the consideration a large fish gives a much smaller fish as it weighs whether to swallow it or permit it to swim on.

"It is thrifty to prepare today for the wants of tomorrow," he quotes at last. "Aesop. Learn from his sage instruction. If you don't get me my money, on time, I will have to apply other more severe legal remedies. Do you understand?"

"I understand," I answer. "But that won't be necessary."

"See that it isn't." He places a note in his ledger. "Or I will take the necessary action." As he closes the file he asks me, "What play?"

"Pardon me?"

"What play?" he repeats.

"*The Pot of Gold.*"

He places the document in an urn. "Fortunate title. Let's hope it proves to be your pot of gold. Be here, end of the month, with the payment."

5

Casina hires drovers and oxen to haul timbers to a field in
Campus Martius north of the Circus Flaminius. The area
set aside for the ceremonies is a flat grassy space edged with
olive trees and flecked with poppies. Casina has also procured
the services of two carpenters I've recommended: one, an
older, long-nosed fellow of medium height named Grippus;
one younger, bald, and shaped like a squat Egyptian oil lamp,
Papius—both Samnites. They are taciturn and not much use
at first, but as I begin speaking to them in their native Oscan,
they cheer up. Our priority will be the pulpitum, of course.
Once that has been knocked together, the grex can move out
and begin rehearsals. After that, we will continue to build
around them.

I explain the way the theatre should be positioned. Sun
behind the audience, so that the slanting light will illuminate
the performers. Using a piece of charcoal, I quickly sketch a
plan on a slab of wood and peg it to a tree where we will be able
to consult it. I discover that Grippus speaks Latin reasonably
well, and is able to translate most of what I say to Papius,
so I'm not compelled to organize all my thoughts in Oscan.
Together, we take measurements, make the ground level, dig
postholes, hammer a frame together. It takes three solid days
of hard digging, boulder removal, hammering, and sawing,
but by the end of that time we have created a stable platform

the company can run, jump, and perform upon. Surprisingly, that little street thief, Tertius, follows us, perhaps with the expectation of getting fed. He hovers at the edges of things like a crow, hopping from perch to perch, watching silently as the pulpitum is assembled. Eventually out of pity I toss him a crust of bread and a dried apple or two, and have him fetch things for me in exchange. At the end of three days I have him take a message to Orestes telling him the grex can set out. My carpenters and I will still require daylight for building, but the actors can rehearse by torchlight tonight.

After we have cleaned up the site, laid things aside, and gathered and put away our tools, Grippus and Papius trudge off to their homes. I remind them to return promptly at daybreak.

I savour my evening meal of bread, olive oil, and slices of onion and wait for the actors to arrive. A breeze slides up the valley and the leaves rustle their thin, dry, wait-and-see music. I chase my meal with a ladle of warm water, then sit and let the air play over me. The cast arrives shortly before sunset, drawing behind them a creaking wagon containing the costumes, masks, props, and another small barrel of nails for my use in the morning. There are the usual greetings, and introductions. Orestes invokes a blessing from Dionysus, asks that the play be a success and that it meet the approval of all the gods and the audience as well. Then he pours and offers the libation. He makes a brief introductory remark, I say a few words in my turn about the script. We begin to read.

I love rehearsals—more than performances, if that's possible. In a performance, each decision has already been set. In a rehearsal every moment is its own discovery, every spoken word a freshly plowed furrow in the larger field of story. An actor will apply particular weight to a phrase and reveal a certain tenderness in a relationship, or an aspect of a character that had previously remained hidden. If you enjoyed the play originally, it can feel very much like having old, beloved friends back for an extended visit.

After the first reading we talk. I tell the cast that they must feel the current of the story and allow it to move them. If they resist, it will dash them against the rocks along the banks. If they pole along with the current they, and the rest of the cast, will be carried successfully to harbour. There are a few questions asked, mostly intelligent. I believe some of the new talent will prove strong. The young man playing Lyconides is already very good. Following our conversation, Orestes guides them through the music.

In addition to packing the necessary theatre materials, Orestes has had the great good sense to bring along an amphora of wine. I break the seal, fill a cup, and drink. It is delicately sweet going down, dark as blood, fragrant as blossoms. As the wine cleanses the dust from my throat, I listen to the actors sing, the music of the tibia softly swelling behind their voices. What a magical thing our craft is! The public is deluded in the belief that anyone can act, but acting is by no means an easily understood or simple craft to execute. If it appears easy it is because actors strive mightily to make it so. The truth is that the average citizen is barely competent to deliver the simplest pun.

The fault for this can be laid at the doorstep of our so-called tutors of rhetoric. Instead of instructing students to be clear or at the very least entertaining, they train their initiates to spew streams of sterile logic. Speeches delivered at the forum now extend so long you would think the speakers were paid by the word. I attended a trial the other day so convoluted that I believe I aged decades before it was over—a moment longer and I am sure my hearing and ability to maintain an erection would have been impeded.

In any case, someone who is trained in rhetoric cultivates the ability to speak. Spend enough time and you can train a goat to speak. That's not the goal of acting. A good actor must possess the ability to open a door that exists only in the imagination, and then coax a reluctant audience to walk through it. Rhetoric can't accomplish that. I have seen many a mediocre play made passable through the exertions of a good actor, and have observed good plays made sublime through the efforts of a great one.

Following the evening's musical rehearsal, a few actors linger to have their masks fitted. Antipho approaches me. "I wonder," he says, "if there is a bit that Euclio might perform as he tries to hide the gold. Perhaps some comic mime as he searches?"

"Try it tomorrow," Orestes suggests. "We'll see how it plays."

He ambles off, and I can see him gesturing to himself, working it up even as he is swallowed by darkness. When the cast reconvenes tomorrow, I'm sure he will have tricks to demonstrate. Frail as he is, he might even try a tumble or fall if he thinks it will elicit the right response.

"He *loves* getting his laughs," Orestes observes.

I lift a ladle of wine and refill our cups. "Yes," I agree, "he's very eager to please." Just beyond the torches, fireflies trace a flickering pattern of light, night unfurls its shimmering fabric, and bats loop among the branches. What a delightful evening. "You want a bit of that in an actor," I note, "that hunger to be loved by the audience. There are actors who are strictly business—and can be wonderfully capable—but possess no magic. Then you have ones like him, who would swallow fire if they thought it would amuse."

Orestes mixes his water and wine carefully before sipping it, religiously careful in the proportions. "Have you seen anyone swallow fire?" he asks.

"I have," I tell him. "During the Illyrian campaign. A tall, wild-haired Thracian. He would light a branch, hold it to his mouth, breathe in and exhale a great billowing flame."

Orestes squints into the darkness as he drinks, his austere, angular face silhouetted against the torches, now flickering low. "How do you think they do it?" he asks.

"I believe they must prepare a salve of some kind that they anoint their mouth and the back of their throat with."

"But how do they eject the flame?"

"I don't know," I say, tossing the sediment from the bottom of my cup into the bushes. "Indigestion? Thracians, a mysterious breed."

"Do you think Antipho's mime business will generate anything useful?"

"It's possible," I allow. "One thing's certain, though. You'll have to caution him about the time he's spending on his monologues. Right now he's making banquets of passages that can only be snacks, and it's adding unnecessary heft to his performance. I will skin him alive if he turns *The Pot of Gold* into a fat, fussy production."

"It's early in the process yet," Orestes objects, "and I don't mind what he's doing for now."

"It's indulgence," I correct him. "It's that extra drink or sweet you order when you know you really shouldn't. It feels good in the moment—but it's not so pleasant later when you vomit in your hat."

"Do you normally do that in your hat?" Orestes asks me.

"Normally I don't wear a hat, as you know. I feel proud to show my face, but if actors impede my production with their cheap and indulgent humour, I'm embarrassed, and I wear a big hat, to hide my shame and vomit in, if the need arises."

"You're too sensitive," Orestes says dismissively as he adds some additional water to his cup. "And remind me not to borrow your hat."

"That passage, for instance," I continue, "when he calls for help, should be like two people hitting each other with sticks. You can't hit someone slowly with a stick."

"I'll warn him to be careful," Orestes assures me. "But again, I don't mind the direction he's taking."

"I'm telling you it will come back to bite us."

"And I'll caution him," he repeats.

"Good."

He drains his cup. "When have you ever been opposed to cheap and indulgent humour?"

"I delight in cheap, indulgent humour—so long as it is delivered quickly."

Once we've finished our drink and put things in order, I stroll back to the caupona to continue some writing I'd begun earlier. As I leave the fields of the Campus Martius, I pass by a villa on my left, and am momentarily arrested by the unpleasant sound of leather striking flesh. I glance through an archway and see a slave, shackled in irons, receiving correction. From his place, kneeling on the floor, he begs forgiveness. "Please," he keeps saying, "please."

The sound of the leather thong whistling through the air follows after me long after I have left the villa behind. There's an enormous appetite for violence in Romans that sometimes seems insatiable. Other activities will tire our citizens, but how infinitely inventive we can be in ways to inflict pain!

I carry on south, avoiding the darkest alleyways where disreputables convene, and end up shoving my way through the street of the Oil Merchants. It turns and narrows and for a short time I am crowded on all sides by other passersby. I sense rather than see the torchlight of someone approaching from behind, and am abruptly elbowed to one side. I stumble and find myself pressed flat against the rough stone wall of a storefront. Behind me, a team of six sweaty, burly men carrying a veiled litter on their shoulders forces its way past. The slaves show little regard for the crowd, which is compelled to either part or be trampled.

"Who was it that they carried?" I ask a merchant who, like me, has been unceremoniously shoved up against the building.

"A member of the Regulus family," he grunts, his face pressed against the brickwork. "I recognized their porters." The litter past, we push off from the wall. I turn and see an elderly man has ended up hurled to the ground.

"What reckless haste and disregard," the merchant grumbles, as together we help the grandfather to his feet. "What arrogance these old families display—whisked about on their litters like demi-gods! Could they not just shout ahead and wait for a person to step aside?"

The old man stands unsteadily, retrieves a sandal that had sprung free when he took his tumble, and places it back on his foot. "My rear end will bear the imprint of this flag stone for days," he groans, rubbing his thin buttocks.

"Look at that," I observe, as I watch the torches and the team of men disappear around a bend, "not a single glance back."

"Glance back?" The merchant laughs bitterly. "Not much chance of that. When has the ox ever worried that it bruised the mouse?"

I arrive late at the Cerium, grumpy and hungry after my hike. I find a spot on a bench near the street and make myself comfortable. Domitia brings me my order, and as she sets down my stew I note that she possesses a superb body—but only an average neck.

This may seem a small point, but the neck is the pillar of the soul. Examine the way a neck inclines and so inclines the inner person. If the neck is sunk into the body, the soul is a shrunken one. An elegant neck reveals an elegant spirit. A neck belligerently thrust forward is the sign of a belligerent character, a retreating neck indicates timidity. Look to the neck. Always look to the neck.

I withdraw my writing tablet and stylus, and review my thoughts regarding the next play I'll work on. I'm drawn to developing a theme of mistaken identity. There would be no difficulty finding a work of this sort to adapt—mistaken identity is the compelling theme of so many plays, and why not? Mistaken identity is a lifelong theme, maybe our only lifelong theme. What do we do as we age and mature but try different identities on, find we were mistaken, shed them, and slip into others? We hold friends close and are disappointed to learn of their envy, defend ourselves from perceived enemies and discover they secretly support us, believe we loathe someone and then suddenly fall in love. Life is a long series of unexpected, misjudged, misidentified, mistaken identities. I have been taking notes in this vein for some time when I hear a murmuring, glance up, and see Naevius pacing restlessly on the street in front of the caupona. He sighs heavily once more and peers into the darkness. "How long," he mutters to himself, "must a man wait?"

I glance in the direction he is staring, but can see nothing. "Wait for what?" I ask at last.

"For you," he says, "to buy me a drink, of course."

Laughing, I push a bench out with one foot. "Sit, then. You can't expect me to lob you a drink."

I motion for Prima to fetch me another cup. "There," I say, filling it.

"That's more like it," he sighs, taking a long pull and wiping his moustache. "Better pour a little more. I've been waiting a long time." I do so, as he glances at my writing tablet. "Ah, you're working?" he asks.

"Yes."

"Bravo. Good for you. That'll keep you occupied and out of trouble." He settles comfortably in his seat, clearly more at ease now that his thirst has been abated. "On a comedy," he inquires, "or something of consequence?"

"I tried writing tragedy," I answer, "but the intense boredom I felt was like a stabbing, physical pain."

"I can understand that," he says, nodding sagely. "It takes a certain degree of sophistication and maturity to write tragedy. People raised in the country rarely possess either. But it's going well, as best you're able?"

"Yes," I answer simply, not wishing to prolong this line of argument. I've heard this kind of thing before, from him and others. Romans have always enjoyed having their fun at the expense of outsiders, although this has gotten thin in recent years. More and more, between slaves, freedmen, foreign merchants setting up shop, and displaced smallholders looking for work, 'outsiders' make up the majority of residents.

"Excellent," he exclaims. "Perfect. I look forward to attending the eventual performance. And whose work are you adapting?"

"I'm contemplating another of Menander's," I tell him.

"Agh," he groans loudly, and his entire frame collapses in on itself in an attitude of utter defeat.

I shake my head at these pitiful theatrics. "And what could possibly be wrong with Menander?" I ask.

"Nothing, I suppose, except couldn't you choose a grown-up's work?"

I set aside my writing tablets. Clearly there will be no more work while this mood is on him. "Menander is an acknowledged master poet and playwright, one of the finest of his age. Everyone agrees his use of language is impeccable."

"Oh, his language is fine, but he's . . ." Naevius squints as though searching for the correct word on a distant hillside, "soft."

"It's comedy," I object. "You don't need a bloodied dagger and a severed head."

"Yes, fine," he says, managing to dismiss my objection at the same time as appearing to agree with it, "but what does he actually have to offer?"

"Everything!"

"Nothing," he contradicts me, "except a lot of nonsense about incompetent sexed-up masters chasing their nubile slaves—"

"And an abundance of profound insights," I interrupt, "into loyalty, love, duty, and devotion. *You* have adapted Menander many times in the past."

"Yes, yes, I had a slight interest in him some years back, and I agree that he's not totally worthless," Naevius allows, "it's just that he's just so, so . . ."

"Brilliant?" I suggest.

"Banal," he corrects me. "There are more important things to write and more legitimate writers like Phrynichus, or Pherecrates to consider. Or why not stiffen your spine and adapt Aristophanes?"

"Ho!" I snort. "I'll leave that adaptation to you."

"Aristophanes," he says, adopting his familiar lecturing posture, his finger wagging under my nose, "is a thousand times the writer Menander was." He snatches a chicken leg from my stew—apparently he is thirsty *and* hungry—and points it at me. "There is more man in the smallest end of Aristophanes's dick than there is all of Menander's words and works."

"Don't talk to me about Aristophanes," I object. "When have you ever seen Aristophanes produced in Rome? Aristophanes, were he writing today, here, would have been crucified before the end of scene one. You, of all people, should know that."

"I do know that," he says, suddenly serious. "I do know. That's the way it is in Rome now. A corrupted Rome. A Rome with its hand up everyone's toga and in everyone's purse. But it's not true of the Rome we could or should be." He finishes the chicken leg and flings the bone into the street. He broods a while, his sense of humour suddenly dispelled. He pours himself another cup of my wine and drinks it. "I know what you did for me," he says suddenly. "I know that you mentioned me in your plays. Kept me in the public eye. Worked to keep me visible. You didn't have to do that, and I appreciate it."

"I was just trying to keep things lively," I tell him. "I needed someone to complain about my writing and borrow money from me."

"No, no. Joke all you want. I know you took risks to support me. No one knows better than I. I know." He swirls the wine about in his mouth. "Merciful gods but this wine is awful. I'm not sure it's legal for the Cerium to sell it. Could you not spend a little more to get something a little better?" He takes another mouthful, and after a slight hesitation—for show—swallows it. "I wasn't sure that the Metelli would let me return, you know."

I am taken off guard by his candour. It's the first time I've heard him talk about his confinement, and I haven't felt invited to inquire. "I wasn't sure either," I admit. "A year ago I wasn't absolutely certain that you were still alive."

"You know how they took me?" he asks. "Those brave, upright Metelli. Those fine citizens."

"No," I admit. "I knew they had confined you to your house for some months. Set guards outside. Then you disappeared."

"They came like bandits one night. They sent criminals who broke into my house, dragged me from bed by my feet. Beat me. Blindfolded me. Stuffed me into a leather sack. Threw me first into a wagon, then into the bottom of an old boat to soak among floating fish heads and bilge water. Finally, they unloaded me on some remote, rocky island—I still have no idea where it was. Barren. Treeless. No way off. No well water. I collected rainwater in a hollow in a rock, lapped it up like a wolf pup. Spent two years peeing behind a bush, swept by wind, burnt by sun. I slept in a hut of piled stones, and had goats for guests. To prepare me for my residence, on the tenth day after I had been unloaded, the boat returned, and I was presented with a sack of wooden slats."

"To build shelter?" I ask.

He shakes his head. "They were my writing materials. I was informed how I might earn my freedom. The next play I wrote, they told me, would be the indicator of my penance. When I finished the first play, *Ariolus*, they gathered all the slats, consulted a short while, then built a little bonfire and burnt them. *Ariolus*, they informed me, was insufficiently convincing. I don't think they even read it, they may not have been able to read, they were just hirelings sent to break me. I was set to work on a second, more contrite play."

I imagine him on that solitary island, and view in my mind's eye that bonfire of wood and words. "That must have been hard," I reflect, "seeing your writing destroyed."

He nods to himself, remembering. "It took me fifty-six days, nonstop, writing to complete it. Rough draft on broken stone shards with a piece of charcoal, then copying the final version to the slats. When I watched those villains incinerate them, watched my words consumed by flames, I almost gave up. They're just toying with me, I thought. They mean to keep me here forever, starve me or kill me. Why hang on if they're just going to make me play at living? But eventually I realized I had no other choice. To get off the island I had to produce whatever was required, and trust that if I grovelled sufficiently they would be satisfied. The piece that I next vomited up, *Leo*, apparently contained the necessary proportion of abasement and servility. I was summoned back to the mainland. When I disembarked, I was thrown to the ground, held face down in the mud by a slave, whipped with a leather strap, made to shout my thanks with each stroke of correction, compelled to promise never to offend again. You can't imagine the humiliation I felt." He grips his cup so tightly that I believe he may break it. Then he sets it back on the table with a light, dry click. "But I'm free now, and a Roman citizen, and by Castor, I earned my freedom with my writing and I will write what I please now."

I cock my head. "Have you become so powerful that you are able to challenge the lion in his den?"

"Not yet," he agrees, "no, not yet. Never mind, one thing at a time." He dips bread into my stew, tucks a piece into his mouth, then leans in close, and lowers his voice. "But you keep your ears open. I have had words with a few other well-placed individuals and there is potential for a new opportunity."

This is the Naevius I remembered, who could never resist presenting himself as powerfully connected and able to forecast important events. I pick up an olive, chew the flesh, spit the pit into my hand, and try to sort out how much of this talk is pure boast and how much authentic news. "What kind of new opportunity?" I ask.

"I can't share anything more right now, things are uncertain. But I still possess some influential friends, and it wouldn't hurt to begin thinking about which Greek play you wish to turn to next—maybe something other than bland, boring Menander." He pats me on the shoulder. "But all this talk is thirsty work. Can you lend me ten sesterces?"

"I only have eight."

"That'll do." I shake some coins from my purse and push them across the table. He sweeps them up, waves Prima over, and then treats me to better quality wine bought with my own money.

6

The theatre is finally completed. I walk around it, giving it a final inspection. It is modest but well proportioned, sturdy, and suited to the requirements of *The Pot of Gold*. It took longer to erect than I had calculated, but the results show in the details. I am particularly proud of the work my Samnites have done constructing the pillars of the scaenae frons. Both functional and decorative, they're solidly anchored so that the actors can swing from them without their waggling. I've seen this kind of shabbiness happen in other productions and cannot help but feel embarrassment for both carpenters and performers.

Rehearsals proceed well this evening. Orestes asks the cast to wear their masks and pieces of costuming. Performing with masks is hot work, but is also a spur to inspiration. Antipho immediately draws fresh life to his part. He becomes louder, clearer, more energetic—transformed into another character entirely. This stimulates the others to greater efforts, and for a time you can see the play lift and take flight. In the latter half of the play, though, the actors run into music difficulties—it's always challenging when performers are still uncertain of the musical arrangement, and I'm aware that I've embedded demanding rhythms and metre changes. Orestes halts the rehearsal, pulls the cast together, and straps on his aulos. They sing a section through slowly, as Orestes guides them with the double pipes. He makes a number of small, precise corrections and they start once again, sounding more confident. A thunderstorm blows in before they can finish the run, and a hard rain soaks us all. We huddle at the rear of the pulpitum for protection, throw the masks and costumes in storage containers, and wait for the weather to pass. Tertius, who has become a regular at our rehearsals, races, head down, through the downpour to the equipment wagon and, drenched, fetches wine back. We pass a vase about hand-to-hand as Antipho and Orestes entertain us with outrageous stories of their tours with the Acting Guilds.

I've known Orestes long enough to have heard some of his adventures performing music with the Athenian Guild of Artists, but it seems he still has fresh stories to share. As the rain pelts down, we prop ourselves against the colonnade, protected by the sheltering architrave above us. I lean my cheek against one especially smooth pillar, and relish the rich scent of wet timber and damp earth. A deep belch of thunder ricochets through the valley, shivering the floorboards. Orestes pours and prepares his wine and water mixture into a bowl he has fetched, fastidious about the proportions as always.

"The grex I originally toured with were extremely devout," he informs us as he passes the vase to me. "Attentive to the gods, ready to perform all the necessary preparations and rituals. But one time, in Syracuse, we were in a rush. Our ship had been delayed by bad weather. I'll tell you now, I would rather travel overland by donkey a thousand miles than by ship, one. You can whip a donkey if the trail proves difficult, and it will trot faster, but if you run up against bad weather in a ship, you are truly at the mercy of the gods. Not to mention the stomach-churning, soul-destroying wretchedness of seasickness. In any case, we were late for our engagement.

When we finally unloaded, we didn't set up correctly, we took short cuts, didn't offer the proper prayer or sacrifice. Next day, we performed *Agamemnon*. That's a delicate story, you know, very sacred, and has to be presented just so. You don't want to mishandle it. When we arrived at the prophesying—where Cassandra enters—a wind sweeps in from the ocean side, low and threatening. We ignore it, hoping that if we persist and move quickly, we can finish before the storm gets too bad. Cassandra begins the 'Oh misery, Oh misery' speech. All at once, the skies blacken dark as octopus ink. Well, what can we do? We're nearing the end of the play. We make eye contact across the stage and decide to carry on. An older fellow by the name of Theocritus—any of you remember him? No? He's dead now—brilliant artist, playing Cassandra, uses that darkening sky as atmosphere to underscore the seriousness of the situation, and then—just as he says, 'Ah, what fire it is!'—lighting strikes. Deafening."

"No!" Antipho exclaims, interrupting his drink. "Right on the line?"

"You couldn't have set the cue tighter if the weather had been working from our script."

"How close?" I ask.

"Close enough that his hair and robe flared as though fanned by spirits. Then, when Cassandra enters the doomed household, her fate sealed, anticipating blades, bloodshed, and regicide—lightning strikes twice more. Even closer, if that's possible. One actually striking so close," Orestes says, tracing a circle with his fingertip on the wooden planks we're seated upon, "that Theocritus is illuminated in a perfect yellowy halo against the scaenae frons. The twin thunderclaps, louder than before, followed instantly."

I imagine trying to act in a storm of that kind. "So you halted the performance at that point?"

"We did not," Orestes replies, shaking his head. "Remember—there was still the final fee to collect from the town. We couldn't afford to forfeit. Also, we were afraid. The way we saw it, the gods had paid a special visit—were present in the theatre with us—and if the gods come for a viewing, you don't shortchange them."

"But the audience," Grippus asks, "they can't have remained seated?"

"They did. I think they realized that they were participating in something beyond the human realm. We finished that show, and though by the end the wind was wild, bending trees, stripping branches—the audience filed out as silently as supplicants before an oracle. We all knew, actors and audience alike, that we had been part of something special. Next day, our Choragus doubled the libations, and made a special sacrifice of a young goat to Dionysus."

"Resourcefulness," Antipho, agrees nodding his approval. "That's exactly it. Each presentation is a solemn vow you take, and you perform whether it's raining, blowing, currents coming against you. Whatever. You perform." He pours himself another drink and settles himself comfortably against a basket that we've been using to store masks in. "Libations?" he asks, holding out the vase. "More libations anyone?" Hands fly up, and I can tell at this point that there won't be much more rehearsing this evening, whether the storm passes or not. "And the way I see it, you have to learn to take the fat with the lean, the bitter with the sweet. We've certainly seen that recently with all the troubles and upset around Tarentum. Soldiers, bloodshed, the torch laid to homes, exquisite theatres completely destroyed, everything everywhere in chaos. Many good artists have just given up. Yet here we are, rehearsing another production, our next production, thanks to our brother in the theatre, Plautus."

"To Titus!" Fronto and Quintus murmur, and I see Grippus raise and tip another vase. It seems Tertius has been asked to retrieve more wine from the wagon.

"I recall," Antipho carries on, "one particularly long tour when we tasted both the bitter and sweet. I was with the Isthmian and Nemean Artists of Dionysus at the time. The first leg of our tour took us to Crete, and then Egypt, where we performed in Alexandria." Envious sighs erupt from the lips of virtually everyone. Alexandria has a reputation for being a genuinely sophisticated city, and none of us—with the exception of Antipho—have been there. "And let me tell you, theatre there is appreciated," he says, licking his fingertips to catch a few drips of spilt wine. "Appreciated in a way you would not recognize here. They *adore* actors. There, the citizens *wait* upon you. Can we get you food? Can we make you more comfortable? Will you stay longer? Will you bless these rites? We performed the entire Achilles cycle by Aeschylus, and were *worshipped* by the audience. Worshipped. But of course," he says, raising his eyebrows, "it wasn't like that everywhere we went."

"Same tour, we've finished at Alexandria and are performing in Cythera on the return leg. It had long ago been scheduled, but as it turned out the islands had recently experienced a drought, crops had failed, and things were tight among the islanders. Still, the last message we'd received before we left Corinth was that they insisted that we carry on. But when we arrive at Cythera, dock and unload, our hosts send a delegation to say they can't afford to pay us, many apologies, very regretful—you know how townsfolk can be. They can provide us with a smidgen of food, they inform us, a little clean water, maybe a jug or two of their—poorer—wine. Of course, they hadn't sent any notice ahead or any warning while we were still in Alexandria, and might have been able to change our plans—and they knew that once we docked it would be impossible to just turn around and go. We would be hungry and thirsty, and they could afford to withhold provisions if we didn't perform. So, there we were. Stiffed for our fee. Stuck on the island, starved, thirsty. What could we do? Well, we agreed to perform, of course—but we switched plays. We decided we'd present *The Persians* that afternoon. As you know, that's a compact play—powerful—but small, you trim the chorus, and it doesn't require many actual bodies. And we tell the musicians to play especially loud. The audience loved it—it was a good performance—and those miserly Cytherians delighted in the money they'd saved. They enjoyed themselves so thoroughly, they insisted that we present the finale again. Which our grex thoughtfully reprised. But while the actors were performing *The Persians* and repeating the finale—we sent the actors not performing, as well as the stagehands up and into the town, quiet as mice, and they put their hands on every precious item they could possibly carry. We took everything, and I mean *everything* that wasn't strapped down: goblets, silver shields, trinkets, charms, cheeses, chickens, lambs, and olive oil and returned and stowed it all away under wraps on the ship. As soon as the audience left the theatre—completely satisfied with their free performance—we struck camp, stowed the luggage, props, costumes, masks, everything—shipped anchor and set out in the dead of night.

Of course I wasn't there to see, but I understand that the townsfolk woke up next morning in a state of total confusion. How could their valuables have been taken? Hadn't they watched us closely? Hadn't we been performing? And after the performance, weren't they careful to make sure that we didn't approach the town? And how had we possibly packed up so swiftly and silently? It was all done so quickly there were some of the more pious citizens who said we must have had the gods' help. And in a way, I think we did, because I personally took a vase of their best wine from a wine shop, and when we slipped from the harbour, I cracked the wax seal and my fellow guild members and I toasted Cythera's health. And let me tell you it was some of the most blessedly delicious wine I have ever tasted—I'm sure Dionysus had a hand in it."

Everybody laughs, toasts Antipho and the ingenuity of actors, with the exception, I note, of Orestes—who, being especially devout, doesn't care for what he sees as the impiety of holding Dionysus responsible for an act of theft.

As I wind my way back to the caupona, down a path running alongside the river, I wonder if it's possible to perceive the future in the telling details of small events. I wonder if my feeling of well-being tonight forecasts happier times, or if I am simply treading through one of the many narrow valleys that exist between the towering mountains of discontent and dusty crags of hard times and privation. I review my debts. I think about how little security life offers. It is in the midst of this reflection that I feel rather than hear a tiny popping sound, and glimpse a brilliant flash of light behind my eyes. My knees buckle and I find myself on the ground scrambling in wet dirt.

CLEM MARTINI

I try to rise, but a vicious kick to my ribs sends me sprawling into the mud and the reeds. It's only then that I realize I am being attacked.

A fist-sized rock skins the knuckles of my right hand. I grab it, twist, and strike out. It connects with something fleshy, and I hear a grunt of pain in response.

I still can't see anything, so elect to crawl further into the underbrush where it may be more difficult to reach me. I hear branches snapping behind me, feel the ground shudder next to me and a kick strikes me in the kidneys. My teeth clatter together and a warm pulse of blood fills my mouth.

I give up attempting to rise and simply try to avoid the worst of it. I wrap my arms tightly around a tree trunk to hinder being dragged back into the clearing. I briefly wonder what might have motivated this attack, and am still turning it over when I lose consciousness.

I wake, the right side of my face resting in a cold puddle. I brace myself against a tree trunk, and gasp at the dizziness that sweeps over me. I grasp the branch above me and slowly haul myself into a standing position. First taking a moment to orient myself, I push off, and weave unsteadily along that dark track. I'm uncertain how long it takes, but am compelled to sit and rest several times. Eventually I arrive at the Cerium, and immediately upon entering, trip and upset a bench. The clatter draws Vulcanus and Casina from their beds. They approach, Casina with a lit lamp in hand, Vulcanus with a cleaver. I am able to make out the dim shadows of several of the servers glancing down from the top of the stairs.

"What happened to you?" Casina asks when she realizes it's me. Vulcanus drops the cleaver to a table, hooks his hands under my arms, and guides me to a bench.

"Are you all right?" she asks.

I tilt my head to view her, and realize my right eye must be swollen shut.

Casina grimaces as she catches sight of this side of my face. "How did this happen?"

I struggle to speak, swallow blood, and trace my tongue around the frayed edges of my mouth. "I was waylaid," I say finally. Casina has Felicia fetch me a wet towel, and sends Prima for a cup of the medicinal herb wine she keeps warming in the culina. I take the wet towel from Felicia when she returns and swab my face. The cuts sting, but the cool press of the cloth feels soothing. Nevertheless, it's difficult having others observe you after you've taken a beating.

"Send them away," I mutter.

"You can return to bed," she tells the girls and Vulcanus. "It's all right."

She takes the towel from me, rinses it in a pan of water, wrings and returns it to my hands. "There's a Greek doctor I know. Should I have him summoned?" she asks.

"No, no."

"Do you have any pain inside?" she asks.

"No. Nothing's damaged," I say, and perform a quick inspection of my teeth. Nothing missing. Nothing broken. "This was just a reminder."

"You're not making sense," Casina says. "A reminder? Of what?"

"The man. As he was hitting me he said something." I try to recollect the phrase he had employed. "It's only becoming clear to me now."

"What?" she asks again as Prima arrives with a cup in hand.

I think back. "As he gave me a kick he said, 'To the late are left the bones.' And he repeated it, so I assume that is the message I am to take away."

"Here, drink. It's warm wine and has healing herbs in it." She places the cup in my hands. "I'm not educated enough— what does that mean, what this criminal said to you?"

"It means I was late," I tell her, and drink. It stings where it touches the open cuts in my mouth, but the wine takes the edge off the pain.

"Late?" Casina asks. "In what way late?"

"Late with a payment," I explain, "to a money lender."

"Ah," she sighs, and her mouth tightens into a thin crease. "I thought this might have more to do with jealousy, or an angry lover, but it's a money matter."

"Yes."

"How much?" she asks.

I press the rag to the large, painful lump that has risen on the back of my head. "A considerable amount."

"Who have you borrowed from?"

"Lucius Caecilius."

"And you hadn't paid him?"

"I'd begun paying him," I tell her, "but I paid late. Two days late, after we had received our initial payment from the praetor. And after my previous inattention to my debt, he must have felt this warranted a reminder."

"Why didn't you tell me?" Casina asks. "I would have advanced the money to you."

"I hadn't thought it was critical that it be there on the day, but," I take another drink, "it seems it was. To him."

"And you believe he had you beaten for that?"

"It was his way of warning me that this time there's to be no deviation from regular payments."

"You're certain," Casina asks, "it was him?"

"He wasn't present when the beating occurred. His name wasn't mentioned. But still," I say, recollecting with sudden clarity the expression that had crossed Lucius's face when he had told me to be on time with my payments, "I know it was him."

She rises and walks to the doorway, stands there a moment. "Well," she tells me. "You are a free man, not his dog to be whipped if it returns from the field without a partridge." She studies the night and the empty street. "I have *been* a slave," she says at last, "and once you are free, you cannot permit anyone to reduce you. How did you come to be in debt to this man?"

"Two and a half years ago," I tell her, "after the success of *Milos Gloriosos*, the plays that followed failed. I became discouraged at the hazards of my craft, gathered the money I had saved, and decided to pursue shipping."

"You bought a ship?" she asks, her eyes widening slightly.

"No," I say, shaking my head impatiently, and instantly regretting it. I grip the table a moment as I wait for the nausea to pass. "I'm not totally deranged. I invested in cargo."

"What happened?"

"I had divided my cargo evenly between two separate ships, and stood to get a return of ten times my investment. They weighed anchor on different days." I recollect watching the ships slipping out of the harbour and feeling a flush of excitement, a thrill that was remarkably similar to the sensation felt at the opening of a play. "Weather rose that night and the first ship sank three days out."

"The other?" Casina asks.

"Sailed straight as an arrow then struck a sand bar on the fifth day. Pirates swept over it like ants over honey and picked it clean."

"So you lost everything?"

I take a large gulp of the medicinal wine and feel it glide, warm and soothing, down my throat. "More than everything."

"Meaning?"

"I lost money I didn't have," I confess. "I'd borrowed against money I'd saved, and money I hoped to make. I'm deeply in debt. This play needs to succeed."

"Well." Casina returns to sit across from me with her hands in her lap, contemplating the story. "You have been very imprudent."

"Yes," I admit.

"This Lucius could sell you into service."

I nod. "That is what he has threatened. But he won't. He doesn't want me as a worker. I'm too old. Who would buy me? How much would he stand to gain from it? He might have me whipped a bit to teach me a lesson, and spur me to greater assiduity."

"Have you thought about seeking the assistance of a patron?" Casina suggests. "You might coax a wealthy Senator to forgive the debt on your behalf."

"No," I disagree. "I need first to secure other opportunities at upcoming ludi. If I'm viewed as a liability or a nuisance, I'll be passed over in the selection. For now, I must dig my own way out."

She considers me a moment, drumming her fingers against a tabletop.

"While we are working together," she says, finally, "I will arrange to have your payments sent on time."

"You'd take that on?" I ask, surprised at the offer.

"Consider it one of my duties as a financial partner. It doesn't make any difference to me. I will simply deduct it from the funds owed you in the final accounting. After the play finishes," she says, "you will have to make other arrangements."

She takes the empty cup from my hands, helps me to stand, and lights my way to my cubiculum. I thank her for her assistance, and we both retire. I throw the blankets back and stretch out on my left side, but despite the herb and wine concoction my battered spine and legs ache badly, the back of my head throbs, and I sleep restlessly. At some point in the evening I open my eyes and sense rather than see a vast darkness stretching into the distance. Water drips from a ceiling high above me, and immediately to my left a broad, slow-moving river silently glides past. Pale, plate-sized objects regularly rise to the surface of the water, emitting feathery bursts of luminescent steam, before submerging once more. It is from the faint light they cast that I am finally able to make out my surroundings. In front of me an immense, three-headed dog crouches. Massive. Powerful. Muscular. Knotted muscles rippling beneath his black, glossy pelt. Three fierce pairs of yellow eyes gleam and follow my movements. Teeth like polished ivory jut from lips stretched around their three enormous mouths.

The ferryman, a fleshy, disreputable-looking individual— Charon of the underworld, I assume—slouches against a railing that snakes up from the dock. He stares at me insolently and picks his teeth.

"They look upset," I whisper to him, nodding at the dogs.

Charon glances back to Cerberus. "They are immortals. Not everything holy is happy."

The three canine heads appraise me dourly, each testing the air for my scent. "Worthless," rumbles the most senior-looking head, dismissing me.

"He looks," murmurs the hungriest-looking head, "delicious." And his red tongue performs a quick, sodden swipe of his lips.

"Write," commands the last head, speaking directly to me.

"I have been writing," I object. "See." And I hold my script in front of me as proof.

The three-headed dog shuffles forward, the heavy chain-link leash clinking dully behind. I can feel the moist heat of the sour breath against my face. The third head leans in to sniff the script, the first ignores it, the second clamps the scroll between his teeth and, with a quick jerk of his muscular neck, yanks it from my hands. I look to Charon for some kind of mediating action and support.

"Stop him!" I demand.

"He's not my dog," he replies.

"But he's chewing up what I just wrote," I protest. "Look!" And he is. Pieces of the shredded document flutter about me like a cloud of milky-coloured butterflies.

Charon considers the dog and the devoured script a moment. "But he doesn't appear to like it very much."

The first head lowers, narrows his eyes, and growls at me.

"And I would say that one," says Charon, indicating the angry-looking head with a nod, "doesn't like *you* very much."

A gust of wind blows off the river at this point, gathering up the scraps of paper and scattering them. I detect something like faint mournful whispers, turn and realize that the pale shapes in the water are, in fact, faces of floating corpses; the eruptions of steam their souls emerging briefly from their open mouths, to stretch and share the sad secrets of their past lives.

I take one hesitant step back. "I am chased by competitors and debts and time," I declare, "but I will outrun them all."

Charon considers me pityingly. "You cannot outrun time," he tells me.

"You can outrun it for as long as you can outrun it," I tell him as I move rapidly and smoothly into the distance, sprinting backward, I assume.

Cerberus strains at his chain, and howls after me. "Worthless!" the three enormous heads bay, their mouths gaping wide. "Worthless, worthless!"

I recall that my father used to thoroughly beat his olive trees at harvest, to draw down the fruit. I wake from my dream feeling very much the way those poor olive trees must have. I rise from my bed aching in places I did not even know I had, and decide to forego attending rehearsal. I gingerly descend the stairs, and after eating a bun and washing it down with warm water, I contemplate returning to bed. Instead, Casina urges me to accompany her to the docks on errands. She maintains that this will stretch my legs and prevent my body from stiffening. We are to pick up an additional barrel of nails, two bolts of cloth for costumes, and material to stretch as awning for the audience. I express reluctance, but she insists that my help is required. Given that she has a donkey to carry the material, I am uncertain why she will need me. I soon realize that it is precisely because she has a donkey that she will need me.

The donkey's name is Dulcina. Casina asks that I lead the wayward animal through the streets, but it would be considerably less work to carry her. Headstrong, and an incorrigible glutton, she thrusts her tawny muzzle out to graze on shrubs we pass, or on produce carried by merchants. As the sun rises and the day begins to warm, the crowds press closer, and Dulcina finds this intimacy disagreeable. She grumbles and slows her pace.

We cut through the Forum Boarium to save time. The meat market is rank with the smell of pigs, sheep, and cattle, noisy with squealing, bleating, and people haggling. It's hot work navigating through the crowd and across ground slick with manure and blood. Every individual in that noisy throng is intent upon business, bringing an animal to market, or fetching away freshly butchered meat. Dulcina, made wary by the smell of death and the frightened cries of sheep and goats, displays even greater reluctance. I, for my part, feeling the blows from the night before, turn impatient. I jerk on her lead rope. Dulcina digs her hooves in. I yank harder, the stubborn creature lowers her ears. I snap her rump with the knotted end of the rope and she responds by planting two hooves just above my bruised right thigh. Searing pain shoots directly from my thigh to my head.

Casina relieves me of the rope. While I double over, roundly cursing the wretched Dulcina, Casina feeds handfuls of grain to her precious donkey. Moments later, the treacherous creature trots after her, amiable as a kitten following her mother. I limp after them, massaging my upper leg.

Before we reach the docks I detect a throaty lowing. We round a corner and encounter oxen straining to haul cargo attached to the draglines up the tracks alongside the river. I listen to the raucous back-and-forth call and response of workers unloading the barges, and feel my heart lift. Despite my failure as a sea merchant, I retain an almost irresistible attraction to boats transporting goods. The crafts appear so uniformly happy to me, swaying merrily side to side on the water. I glance over at Casina but see that she's frowning.

"The sounds of the docks don't appeal?" I ask.

"It's not the sounds," she says as she threads Dulcina past a slippery load of mackerel strewn across the pavement, "but the smells of the docks that are not to my taste."

"It's only marginally worse than the meat market," I object, "and it is the smell of commerce and the future. And look. Look at that plucky little boat, and the way it rides the water."

She dubiously eyes the craft I've indicated.

"Imagine just a moment, its far-off points of origin," I say. "Imagine the places all these boats will travel. The adventures these sailors will experience."

"Boats are wet and dirty," she declares, "and carry rats big as goats. These workers will hump their goods onto other carriers, ride the current downriver to load the cargo on to larger ships, then sweat again as they off-load land-bound freight."

I nod. "But what a glorious, intrepid enterprise."

She glances at me and shakes her head sadly. "You have dangerous tastes. You should never visit the waterfront without someone holding your hand."

"That's probably true," I admit.

The arrangements at the docks are chaotic, but Casina finds the goods she's looking for amid a tangle of ropes and crates and amphorae. Through the judicious application of flattery, bullying, and surprisingly coarse language, she ends up paying half what I would have imagined possible.

We strap the goods to Dulcina's back. As I cinch the ropes tight, I observe, scrawled on a brick near the ground, a crude and improbable figure drawing accompanied by the terse statement, 'I fucked Rufina against this wall.' I ponder what impulse spurred this clumsy confession. Pride? Romantic attachment? A sense of occasion? In any case, I hope neither of the participants looked anything like this unsophisticated rendering. I point it out to Casina, who simply sniffs, and notes that it is never the Rufinas of the world who commemorate these intimate moments.

The crush of the market is more than we can endure a second time, so we take the longer but quieter route south along the Tiber and then east. Swallows skim and dive, and Dulcina seems put in better spirits. Casina withdraws a cloth sack containing chestnuts. We crack the shells as we walk and fish out the tender flesh. She asks what led me to write.

"Chance," I confess. "Accident."

She snorts. "Only the lazy set their fate at the altar of Fortuna."

"Does anyone's life conform to plans?" I challenge her. "Did yours? I could as easily ask what brought you to become proprietor of your own caupona."

"You switch topics too quickly," she replies. "First things first, answer my question—what led you to write?"

I shrug. "I was a boring and untalented child."

She lobs a chestnut shell at me. "False humility," she replies, "is hateful to the gods. People say things of this sort, and they're never true."

"In my case," I say, brushing away the shards, "all too true. My father died young. My uncle adopted and raised me. He concluded, rightly, that I demonstrated no skill as a smallholder and farmer—my father's profession—or as a woodworker—his. He decided I should, instead, become educated. I believe he had notions that we might attract a certain kind of client if I were able to read and write. He made the arrangements. Off I went each day."

"And you enjoyed your studies?" she asks as she passes a nut to Dulcina.

"Hated them," I tell her. "Loathed them. My tutor's humble pedagogy extended to wandering the rows of seated students, flailing randomly. It was impossible to predict where or why his birch rod would fall."

"Yet there you stand," she observes, "a poet. The man, or his birch rod, must have done something right."

"Luck," I reply, and another shell bounces off my shoulder. "He introduced Homer's *Odyssey* to us," I confess, laughing. "From that moment, everything changed. I learned to read Greek well, not because I was taught better but because I enjoyed it more than the other students. He'd borrowed some Euripides, I consumed it. Next came Phrynichus, and Sophocles. As a lark, I translated Menander's *The False Accuser* into Latin. I became the most gifted scholar of a supremely mediocre tutor and fell in love with words. My uncle had envisioned that my education would transform coarse wool into fine cloth and instead bitterly realized—too late!—that I had been corrupted by learning and rendered even more useless than before. I wasn't surprised that when conscriptions were summoned, I was selected for the legion, Hastati division."

Casina shakes her head. "For a poet you advance your story badly. I can imagine that soldiering taught you to fight. I don't see how it taught you to write."

"Patience," I say. "When our centurion observed that I was woodworker enough that my fellow soldiers relied on me to organize our section of the camp barricades, he seized his opportunity. He swiftly transferred his least adept soldier to

the engineering division, where, fortunately, I thrived. My
uncle had hated it when I took shortcuts as a woodworker,
but in engineering this was rewarded. I found quick ways
to repair broken machines. Learned how to shore up a wall
economically. I believe I could still knock together a very
serviceable ballista in short order if I put my mind to it. And,
in an odd way, that construction aided me in adapting Greek
plays to Roman sensibilities. Part of what I do now is assemble
a machine that will vigorously propel a story forward." I reach
for the chestnuts, but she withholds them.

"I asked how you began writing," Casina scolds me, "and
I am no closer to knowing. Before you are permitted a single
chestnut more—when do you encounter the theatre?"

"Stay calm. Between campaigns I was permitted to see a
play—"

"Aha!" she exclaims, and extends the bag to me.

"Exactly. Aha. *The Gamblers* by Diphilus. I'd loved reading
plays, but actually *viewing* one—seeing one performed—was
a revelation. The thrill of observing a story made live was like
nothing I had ever experienced. After that, whenever possible,
I would attend the theatre. When I was released from military
service, I realized that I had nothing at home to return to.
A grex visiting Syracuse needed a carpenter. I knew enough
to hammer together a set. In return for food and a place to
sleep, I repaired things, built props, and performed the odd
small role—usually as a servant delivering a message. One
evening, an argument erupted and half the grex walked. I'd
read other scripts and seen plays, and said I could recall at least
two that the remaining actors might perform. The Dominus
was too despondent to argue. I stitched together something
in two and a half days—some hideous, bastard portion of

Menander's *The Ship's Captain*, a play that I attended a couple of times in Apollonia. My rendering was very imperfect—half remembered, half invented. The rascals who'd remained with the grex were more gymnasts than actors, and where my script wasn't funny enough they substituted tumbling, juggling, or stage fighting."

"And did you perform it?" she asks.

I pry a sharp bit of wayward chestnut shell from between my teeth and flick it into the river. "We did."

"And?"

"It was a thoroughly disgraceful, disreputable venture," I confess, "which, to my great surprise, apparently held wide appeal for the public."

"Really?" she laughs.

"Maybe they enjoyed it as much as they did because their expectations were low, or perhaps they hadn't been exposed to much theatre, but in any case, the play proved very popular. The Dominus asked me to write another. I obtained a comedy by Diphilus, *The Busybody*, and translated and threw that together. That proved a happy experience as well—and away I went. And *that's* how I stumbled into theatre—my 'plan,'" I conclude. "Life amounts to what we salvage from our horrible accidents."

We arrive at the caupona, and I tie Dulcina to her post. "Now, you will have to tell me how you came to own the Cerium."

"Another time," she says. "You're being signalled." I look in the direction she is indicating, see Felicia wave, and return it.

"You should listen to what you write," Casina advises me as she unstraps the goods fastened to Dulcina.

"What is that supposed to mean?" I ask, unloading the nails.

"In your plays," she replies as she lowers the bolt of fabric to the ground, "you write about the fools that old men become when they throw themselves at young girls."

I still don't see her point. "Yes?" I ask.

"Obviously," she tells me as she rises, "you are at risk of becoming a fool."

I raise my eyebrows. "I've hardly done anything scandalous," I protest.

She shoots me a look. "Your interest in Felicia is obvious."

"And," I point out, "I'm hardly old."

"Yes," she says, "but you're no longer young."

"I feel young."

"We all feel young. The wine in the amphorae feels it is young, but there comes a time when even the most incorrigible drunk knows it's not. I can handle Dulcina from here," Casina tells me, and dismisses me with a wave of her hand.

I spend the remainder of the day recovering from my beating, then attend rehearsal the next morning, and immediately wish I hadn't.

There is an especially intense kind of agony that accompanies observing a rehearsal that has gone wrong, like coarse salt jammed under the eyelids. Dialogue that previously appeared funny is exposed as painfully obvious. Characters that once felt rich and original appear flat, lifeless, and pedestrian. The singing falters. The performances slow to a crawl. I recollect seeing a dog that accompanied a particularly ragged beggar through the market, once. The dog was ancient, scabby, and had only two remaining legs, his front ones. The beggar had strapped a kind of ingeniously conceived, primitive wagon to the dog's hind end; but the wheels, carved from wood, were chipped and battered flat in places, so that they only occasionally actually turned. The dog dragged himself along, whining whenever its sorry rump landed hard on a rock. That's the way my play moves during this dismal rehearsal. Slowly clattering along, bumping its bruised ass, and moaning sadly to itself.

The most excruciating aspect of it all is that there's nothing you can do to remedy a bad rehearsal. Despite their boisterous, resilient appearance, actors are surprisingly delicate creatures. At a certain point in the process they cannot bear to receive even the mildest criticism from anyone but the Choragus. They need to cling to the belief that they will be applauded, and not reviled and despised by the audience. If this belief is punctured, their spirits can collapse in an instant. Consequently, after the rehearsal ends, I dredge up some vague and completely inaccurate platitude about how wonderfully they have made sense of the story. They smile wanly at my encouragement. I wander off on my own to consider the impending calamity, and select the tree most suited to hanging myself.

Later, Orestes finds where I am hiding and sits next to me.

"You played your instrument well," I compliment him. "Thank the Gods. You were the only thing on key."

"They're all sick, you know," he says by way of explanation. "Fevers. Terrible coughs. You should be grateful. We were lucky to coax any kind of performance out of them today."

"*They're* sick?" I return. "Well, I'm not feeling so good myself right now."

"It's going to be fine," he assures me.

"Will it?" I ask, "Will they be healthy in four more days?

"They should be. Why four more days?"

"Because the elder Lentulus has expired," I inform him. "It was announced just before I left for rehearsal. His body will be held in attendance for three days at the estate. The ceremonies and *The Pot of Gold* will commence the day following."

7

Orestes was correct—the actors more or less recover and their voices become passable. When I return to rehearsals two days later, Antiphos—Aesculapius the Healer be praised—is much improved. Given that he has the lead role, this is a major blessing. If he falters, the play cannot succeed. The rehearsal fails to inspire, but at least is no longer a travesty.

After, to raise everyone's spirits, I open a vase of good wine. I toast the grex, and then Orestes toasts me, and together we toast our patrons, the Lentulus family. Nothing else can be done, but pray that the gods look kindly on us. To this end, I bring an offering to the statue of Janus at the Cerium.

"Janus," I say as I lay my offering at the base of his statue, "blessed god of beginnings, guardian of gates, watchful supporter at the start of all journeys, help me. I give you this cake of barley and honey, I give you this sacrifice and ask that you encourage this adventure to thrive. All plays are uncertain, who knows how they will go, if the actors are well or sick or can perform their parts or if the audience will receive the play favourably? You know the beginnings of things and can read their endings as well, and I ask that you shepherd this performance."

Naevius sees me placing my offering and when I've finished calls out. "I've known you to bring offerings to Apollo and

Minerva in the past," he observes, "but have never before seen you honour Janus! You must be desperate."

"There are many gods," I call back, "and it's never wise to exclude any."

"Keep your head up," he tells me as he leaves the caupona, "important events are in the wind." He refuses to say anything more and seems in a great rush to get somewhere. It's impossible to tell from his vague hints if he has actually learned something of significance, or if his intimations are merely a delusion.

The morning of the ceremony arrives draped in fog. I step out into a clammy, enveloping mist to attend the funeral procession. I hear it before I see it: the bold music of the cornu and tympanum, the heavy tread of many feet, the murmur of voices, then out of the obscuring vapours emerge men in masks—honoured members of the Lentulus house wearing representations of their ancestors—followed by the rest of the throng. The procession winds along the Sacred Way to the Rostra in the forum, gathering more participants with each vicus we pass. By the time the senior member of the family ascends the Rostra to speak, the forum is packed. Publius Caudinus delivers fine words of remembrance in the laudatio. The swollen procession then proceeds to the temple of Ceres, where ten immense white sows are sacrificed, their entrails offered to the god, and the remaining meat cooked and shared with the crowd. Once Ceres has been properly honoured, the procession migrates beyond the pomerium of the city for the cremation. Later, horse and chariot races will be held at the Circus Flaminius, as tribute to the senior Lentulus. I forego these races and return to the theatre to ensure that all is in order for a final rehearsal. Orestes has arranged for a small invited audience to attend.

As the actors prepare, I stand watching with a certain feeling of helplessness. "Are you nervous?" Casina asks, detecting some aspect of my inner thoughts.

"Of course I'm nervous," I answer testily. "Anything can go wrong. We've already seen that the cast can get sick—and they can get sicker than this. I recall once an actor vomited noisily each time he exited the pulpitum. It was repulsive, and drove spectators away by the droves. The actors can deliver their lines too quietly. They can sing badly. The audience can become restless, find they're too hot, too cold, or the cursed wind can blow so hard that it impossible to hear. It can rain." I survey the crowd, at this point still socializing. "Look at them. They can be distracted by the slightest thing: dancers, or wrestlers, bees, the smell of fresh bread." I take a deep breath to still my feelings of anxiety. "Really, when you think about it, writing for theatre is an activity only an idiot would take up."

"The actors know their duties," she assures me and pats my arm. "The play will be perfect."

"Let us devoutly hope so," I respond glumly.

Talking about it just makes me more restive, though, so I adopt my usual position behind the audience, fold my arms, and attempt to compose myself. Sitting isn't an option, but standing in one place is only marginally better, so I pace.

The crowd takes its time settling. Vendors attempt to sell things—Orestes has them chased off, as it's still a rehearsal. A couple of mothers have brought babies. They require quieting, so the cast waits. Then I see signs of the actors making themselves ready.

Whenever I view one of my works, I separate into two parts. One part observes the play, another focuses upon the audience. These two parts communicate throughout the performance. Sometimes this internal chatter grows so loud that it becomes difficult for me to hear the play.

"So," the Part of Me that's Viewing the Play says, "the cast looks strong and confident. Things should go well."

The Part that's Viewing the Audience replies, "Yes, and the audience, while small, appears attentive. I'm sure they will be entertained."

Both portions are getting along well. They are in agreement, more or less, patting one another on the back for a job well done, and prepared for success.

Then Orestes mounts the pulpitum to thank the viewers for attending this final rehearsal. The cast takes their places, and at last the Lar Familiaris of the play appears to deliver his prologue. The audience responds with polite applause.

Everything goes as planned, the story is advancing, the audience seems responsive, until the actors come to the scene where miserly Euclio, worried that Megadorus has learned from his servant about his hidden pot of gold, fumes: "By Jupiter!" he says, "the old woman has told him about my gold! I'll teach her a lesson!"

To which Megadorus, played by Quintus, replies, "Are you talking to yourself?" The audience laughs appreciatively.

Euclio, played by Antipho, begins to answer. Then I hear a hitch in his voice and a pause follows, and instantly my stomach drops. I have written no pause there. The play has never been rehearsed with a pause there. "Stay calm," the Performance-Watching part of me cautions. "Perhaps he's just clearing his throat."

Orestes repeats the musical line, cleverly making it seem that this aberration is part of the stage business, but Antipho in his role of Euclio says nothing. The Audience-Viewing portion of me adopts a shriller tone. "What is he doing? There's no pause there! He's forgotten his lines, the bastard."

Performance-Viewing Me maintains a cool calm. "You're jumping to conclusions," he argues. "He's a veteran, and even if he has blanked, the audience hasn't noticed anything yet."

Antipho clears his throat. Performance-Viewing Me observes this and says, "Oh good, he's started again. Thank the merciful Gods. Maybe he can find his way back."

"It's just, ah," Euclio/Antipho stammers. "That is, I'm just, ah . . ."

He keeps repeating the same thing! It's obvious he's stalling. "Listen to him nattering away," the Performance-Viewer in me complains. "He has no idea what the next line is. Jupiter with a raised fist, *say* something, something other than "ah, ah, ah!""

Audience-Viewing Me mops his brow—*my* brow—and calms the other part of me, "Wait, wait, wait—the audience hasn't understood what's going on yet. They, poor innocents, still believe this is part of the play."

Both parts of me croon in unison, "My play, my poor play."

"After this is finished," Audience-Viewing Me rages, "I will have Antipho skinned alive, and take that skin and stuff it like an olive, and mount the stuffed representation somewhere at the forum as a caution to writers everywhere."

"Wait," replies the Performance-Watching Me. "Listen."

Megadorus/Quintus intervenes at that moment, saying, "Just speak up, I can't hear you."

"Oh, good for him," Performance-Watching Me cheers. "Good old Quintus, that's the way to do it! He's playing along, trying to buy him time."

Antipho/Euclio scans the audience as though he might detect his lines among the seats and repeats "It's just. Just."

"More stammering!" Performance-Watching Me almost weeps with frustration. "By all the lost souls that crowd Hades, he can't just keep repeating the same thing over and over again! Say *something*."

"Look!" Audience-Watching Me shrieks, "The audience is beginning to shift in their seats! Once they comprehend that the lead actor hasn't the foggiest idea what he's saying they will lose patience and leave. We're finished. Finished!"

"You've got a cough," Quintus improvises. "Let me help you out." And he pounds Antipho on the back. The audience responds with guffaws—Romans love it when someone gets hit. Doesn't matter why. They can't get enough of that kind of cheap, unmotivated violence. Quintus then stares intently at Antipho and asks pointedly, "Are you all right now?"

Grimacing, Antipho says, "I will be, if you stop breaking my back. It's just how wretched it is to be poor. And to have a daughter with no dowry, and no chance of getting a husband."

And in an instant, he finds his way back! Orestes, who has cleverly covered the lapse, with some trills indicating rising tension, immediately returns to the former musical line. "Thank you, thank you, thank you," both inner voices repeat fervently.

"Who are you thanking?" Casina whispers. Apparently I have muttered this aloud.

"Every god and spirit that is looking on," I answer.

When Euclio/Antipho sings the next line, "When he says he'll give, he means he'll get! His mouth stretched wide to swallow all I've gathered yet." Everything seems back in order and when he finally rages, "You can't trust the rich when they're kind to the poor!" he sings with such fervour that the audience spontaneously cheers.

Sometime later, it may be only moments later or it may be days, the cast reappears on stage and says, "Spectators—miserly Euclio has been transformed! If you've enjoyed yourself, prove it by clapping as loudly as you can." The actors bow, and the invited audience cheers and hollers as though there were thousands of them and it was the finest entertainment they ever witnessed.

After the spectators depart, I hurry behind the stage to meet with Orestes and the actors. I see Orestes swiftly approaching Antipho.

"What. Is. This?" Orestes demands, marching up to Antipho, a scroll clutched in his fist.

The older actor blanches at the anger simmering under the question. "What?" he asks.

"What is this?" Orestes repeats.

"It's a script," Antipho answers timidly, and leans in and squints at it. "It's our script, I think."

"Is it?" Orestes barks and shoots a look at the scroll. "I thought it must be your worst dog, because of the relentless, uncompromising, abuse you gave it."

Antipho vacillates a moment between defending himself and apologizing and opts for the latter. "I admit," he says, "I got a little lost—"

"A *little*??"

"—for a moment," he allows, "for a few moments, but we recovered—"

"Recovered?" Orestes continues, his lips hitting each consonant. "Is that what you call it? Recovered? You," he says poking the old actor in the chest, "are an ancient, derelict billy goat, burping, farting, baaing, and in general *eating up* the scenery. If you were more intent upon your actions, your actions as we have rehearsed them, rather than upon *preening* for the audience, you wouldn't forget your lines. *And* by all that's holy, if you can't remember the lines, then *at least* improvise something clever. By Jupiter Maximus and all his punishing power, that stammering and umming and awing was pitiful."

Antipho is beginning to sweat. He places a placating hand upon Orestes's right arm. "It turned out all right. In the end—"

"Did it?" Orestes casts the old man's hand from his arm. "If it did, it was no thanks to you. I should have you donate your fee to Apollo as a sacrifice, because you were the luckiest man alive out there today. You were *saved*."

"It's true," Antipho admits, "Quintus helped out."

"Helped?" Orestes repeats with a scornful laugh. "He absolutely saved you. He saved all of us."

Antipho hangs his head, his fleshy lips drooping. "I'm sorry. It won't happen again."

Orestes brushes a hand through his hair. "See that it doesn't. If that happens this afternoon, of course it'll be a disaster. I'll deduct your wages, distribute half to the rest of the cast and scatter the other half to the beggars in the audience. Go on."

Chastened and mumbling apologies, Antipho scurries to change. I was going to have my own say on the matter, but after viewing this scourging I haven't the heart. Orestes catches me looking.

"You were hard on him," I say.

"I have to be," Orestes replies in a low voice. "He is a wonderful actor, and you saw that ultimately he won the audience over; but truthfully, his memory isn't very good anymore."

I hadn't noticed that prior to this. "How bad?" I ask.

"Not awful. Just the odd line, the odd scattered glance off stage. Most of the time he can cover up, and find his way back. But he's the *vainest* old fart. Once he hears his audience laughing, he just can't help doing a little twirl, and then . . ." He draws a breath. "Agh. It could have been much worse—he could have done it this afternoon in front of the Lentulus family." Orestes glances off in the direction Antipho has exited. "He still might."

I nod my agreement. What else is there to say? "Have him run his lines before this afternoon's performance," I tell him, and leave.

Rehearsals concluded, masks, costumes, and set pieces are returned to their places. The performance is scheduled to occur two hours before sunset, and spectators begin drifting back well before that. The sun is falling behind the audience at this point in the day, and the stage is bathed in a rich, amber glow. This showing draws a boisterous crew. They holler greetings to one another as they convene and find their seats. Merchants hawk trinkets and good luck charms. The Lentulus family arrives at the head of a ceremonial procession and takes their seats of honour in the front rows. Other respected members of the Senate follow. As the audience settles, the cast attends to the rituals that are required of their craft, growing progressively more focused. I visit backstage briefly to wish everyone well and glance over at Antipho. He is seated off on his own, hands clasped upon his lap, his eyes turned inward. From there I take my station once more, pacing at the rear of the audience. Then it's time.

The actors stride onto the pulpitum and request the audience's blessing. Right away the crowd responds with shouts of approval. I recall once more why performances both thrill and terrify me. It is like watching charioteers lunge out after the flags have dropped. The actors surge forward, into and through the story, buoyed by music, by their energy and intensity, and by the audience, who applaud and cheer and laugh and urge them on. Once embarked, there is no turning back. Confusion and complications arise, struggles and tears are encountered, intimacy and calamity intermix. Whatever Antipho's thoughts were prior to the performance, he is now a man possessed. He sings his part full-throated like an actor twenty years younger, vigorously attacks each scene, squeezes laughter from the smallest turns of phrase. The others in the cast follow his lead, and the performance becomes a kind of combustible, exploding in bursts of heat and sparks. The conclusion approaches, the tempo mounts, the tension builds, climax and resolution and then, abruptly, the cast are removing their masks to beg the audience's applause. It is gladly given. Coins thrown. Flowers thrown. The actors salute the audience, and exit. Gnaeus Lentulus Caudinus approaches, gruffly slaps me on the shoulder, and says, "My father would have heart-heart-heartily approved!"

Hugs and congratulations are exchanged backstage. Fronto, Fabius, Quintus, and Antipho pound one another's backs so fervently you would believe they were smothering flames. All who shared in the responsibilities share in the glory—actors, stagehands, and carpenters. Grippus and Pappius grin their wide, gaptoothed smiles. Admiration is expressed, pronouncements made of reverence and loyalty, vows pledged to work together again. Hands clasped. Orestes laughing. Orestes! Laughing! The crowd lingers out front, clamouring for Euclio/Antiphos. He runs out once more, salutes and bows. More cheers. Then the old fool suddenly slips into a relatively adept backward roll and emerges on his feet, arms outstretched. The audience breaks into wild applause—you'd have thought he was a genuine acrobat. A servant approaches me—at first I can't hear him over the noise—he raises his voice to inform me I am invited the following week to share an afternoon meal with the Curule Aedile, Titus Quinctius Flamininus. I thank him as he slips back into the crowd. The Curule Aedile controls matters pertaining to the ludi, which can only indicate that he means for me to submit a play! I am unable, in the moment, to conceive how to respond properly and so simply release a laugh so loud and abrupt it frightens a stranger next to me. The wax seals on several amphorae are broken, wine is poured into mixing bowls and served liberally. Skewers of roast lamb suddenly emerge. A dusty wheel of cheese is cut up. Platters of figs and olives and are distributed. Crusty buns. Plums. Grapes. A flushed Casina finds her way through the crush. She clasps my hand, tells me how much more exciting the theatre is than operating a caupona, then surprises me when she grabs me by the ears and kisses me on both cheeks. Old friends wind through the crowd to offer their compliments. Nothing compares with the variety of strong feelings that accompany a successful performance: elation muddled with relief, exultation with exhaustion, sheer joy with still more relief. Strangers caught up by the performance shout your name as though you were long-time companions, clap you on the back, press close. The actors appear at last among the audience, having changed out of their costumes—their hair strewn, their clothing adjusted, their faces flushed, laughing now instead of solemn. More clasping of hands, and exchanging of small gifts. Antipho thrusts his mask above his head and shouts to onlookers that he will dedicate it to the gods, vows to hang it in the temple of Minerva. The actors reprise a song from the show, and the crowd picks up the melody, clapping and singing. The women who had lingered near the edges of the audience begin dancing. A drum that was tucked away somewhere emerges, and the music changes tempo and tenor, becoming wilder. Three of the dancers weave through the crowd—one, our own Scythian, Candria; sinewy, fluid, seemingly boneless, possessed by the rhythm. The sun sets completely, stars appear, still the crowd won't disperse. Lamps are lit. Others who had departed earlier return and more wine is poured, poured, poured—this time straight. Nothing mixed. Nothing weakened. The music grows louder, members of the crowd disappear with this or that partner. The crowd is an ocean, swelling and ebbing and rolling together. Eventually it breaks into smaller groups for more drinking. Laughing all the way, and toasting. Blessings invoked for every eventuality. For future shows. For individual careers. For success. For luck. Riches. Love. More singing. Singing fading in the distance, into the darkness, into the night. Smaller and smaller and smaller groups linger until finally the group is just two and I fall into bed and at last the lamp is blown out.

The next morning I waken in the dark, stretch, and feel a warm leg thrown over mine. I open my eyes, and in the dim light realize that I am not in my chamber. I see Felicia's face pressed up against my shoulder. Gently, I shift her leg to one side. I silently extricate myself, stand, and dress.

I take a basin to the fountain, fill it, and wash myself. I lean against the moist stone lip of the collecting pool, listen to the water splash. There's a quiet, contemplative feeling that possesses you after a night of heavy drinking. Everything slows. Light takes a little longer to reach the eye, thoughts crawl through your mind on all fours like old men searching for a couch to rest upon. If you don't have to perform athletics or complex mathematics, it's not an altogether unpleasant sensation. I find myself reviewing the night's events once more. I had presented my play, successfully it seems, secured a meeting with the Aedile, and ended in bed with a young and attractive woman. Life looks considerably better than it had only few months back, when I returned to Rome with nothing but a tattered tunic and a handful of bad debts.

I toss the used water into the gutter, rinse the basin, return it to the alcove I found it in. I sit down at a streetside table at the caupona, stretch my legs, and wait for the day to unfold.

Pomona catches my eye. I mime eating and she fetches me hot puls in a bowl. I stir it, eat slowly, and gradually begin to draw my faculties together and form some general plans. The first thing I must do is determine how many of the cast will remain with the grex now that *The Pot of Gold* has closed. Some will certainly have plans elsewhere to attend to. This is a small hurdle, there should be others we'll be able to attract.

The bigger matter will be to put out feelers to recruit a young and promising Dominus-in-the-making. Someone with acting talent, someone whose star is ascending and can look forward to a still more successful career, someone who won't feel threatened at the prospect of working alongside and in the shadow of another artist as genuinely popular as Antipho.

"Congratulations," a voice says, interrupting my thoughts. I glance up and see Casina, gathering her tunic about her and sitting opposite me at the table. "I thought the play went very well."

"Yes, it did," I agree.

"You must feel pleased," she says, then cocks her head to one side and squints at me. "If you can feel anything. After all your drinking and foolish misbehaviour."

"I feel very pleased, thank you, and only a little blunted as result of the drinking and misbehaviour. And thank you as well," I add, "for your most generous financial help and coordination. You should be receiving your investment back and more."

"Good. So," she asks as she folds her hands on the tabletop, "what will you do now?"

I glance out at the beam of sunlight cutting through the street, and shrug. "We have gathered together a young, inexperienced grex. With this next production, we will want to attract greater attention. Antipho is wonderful, and I believe he will stay with us a while longer, but it will be necessary to recruit someone he can mentor for the future."

"Good," Casina says, nodding. "And after I receive the official return from this performance, I believe I will have additional savings that I could invest."

"Really?" I reply. "You'd loan the company additional money?"

"That's not exactly what I had in mind," she advises me.

"No?" I ask. "Then what?"

"I thought," she says, leaning forward slightly, "we might become partners."

I chuckle, and shovel more puls into my mouth, but when I look up I see that she's not laughing.

"You seem surprised," she says.

I run a hand through my hair, and try to formulate a reasoned response, but am unable to compel my mind to perform at its normal speed. "Of course, it's out of the question," I correct her, more bluntly than I mean to. "A woman as partner? The Aedile would think I was mad."

"I imagine," she begins, "he would be perfectly content with any arrangement, so long as he was convinced that the operations were being competently managed—"

"He would consider it *blasphemy*. Members of the Senate would share his feelings. He would announce—rightly—that we had profaned the sacred rites of the event."

"What matters most," Casina tells me, "is what you think."

"It's very nice that you should say that, but of course," I say, as I finish the last of the puls, "you're completely wrong. You have *no experience* in the theatre."

She reaches into her apron, pulls out a ledger, and drops it on the tabletop. "We made a profit on *The Pot of Gold* when it was never certain that it would open. There's your experience."

"That's for one play. One. And it was performed at a funeral. The Ludi of Apollo will be different, this will require—" The words escape me. She seems so uncomprehending that I don't know where to begin. "This ludi will be a bigger event, do you understand? Of a completely different scale. There will be other greges competing. Prizes will be awarded. Senators and magistrates will be there to pass judgment. This next production will be based upon a new play and will truly establish the character and stature and qualities of our grex as compared to others, and we can't afford to falter. Can you see how critical this will be?"

"Which is exactly why I should be involved," she replies patiently. "I have experience running a successful business."

"You don't know theatre. Who will *hire* people, who will meet with the Aedile and negotiate on behalf of the play? *You?*"

"No," she answers, and nods at Orestes. I hadn't noticed him entering. He is standing in the archway, silently observing. "Him. The reality is that I will handle all the financial affairs, business transactions, and delicate negotiations, but I understand that I cannot present the public face of the grex. He will perform the role of the Dominus Gregis, as well as maintaining his position as Choragus," she continues. "Ask him. We've discussed it thoroughly already."

I'm stunned. I have always been able to count on Orestes to be my voice of sober second thought. "You've agreed to this?" I ask.

His face remains impassive. "This production went well, no one can deny it," he replies. "And we couldn't have done it without her."

I throw my hands up. "You've bewitched him."

Casina shakes her head. "He understands that together we possess the skills—"

"We had a *temporary* solution," I interrupt, "an improvised solution. You run a caupona." I take to my feet—recklessly. The world shudders, and I have to brace myself against the tabletop. "Have you ever seen any other grex operated by a woman? Have you ever heard of any other grex, that—beyond musicians or dancers—even *involves* a woman?"

"For the moment, see me only as your business associate," she urges me. "*The Pot of Gold* didn't suffer from my involvement."

"We got lucky," I tell her.

"Fortune is the blessing gods endow on those who prepare," Casina insists. "We ran a tight operation. Surely you can see that. Did I or didn't I get you lumber at lower than average cost?"

"You did," I allow.

"Were the labourers I hired prompt for work, and diligent?"

"Yes," I agree once more.

"Did you have sufficient funding when you required it?" she presses. "Were things in order, exactly as you requested? Was I honest in my dealings with you?

"Yes, but—"

It's her turn to throw her hands up. "But *what?*!" she demands.

"There's no point in speaking to you," I say, "if you can't see how impossible it is, it's, it's . . ." I step into the street, but it is still too early to actually go anywhere, and my body isn't prepared to move in any case. I feel sleepy, dazed, and bewildered. I stand rooted in one spot at the edge of the street and watch a woodpecker hammer away at a fig tree. It shifts a little higher on the tree trunk, then leans its broad head in to try once more. This, I think to myself, is how we advance, knocking our heads against the barriers we encounter, moving a few steps over in search of a new solution, only to batter our heads against a new obstacle.

I feel a hand on my shoulder. I turn, and Casina thrusts a hot herb drink into my hand. "Drink this," she says, "and have another bun." I take the bun from her and bite into it. It is soft, warm, freshly baked. "I understand your anxiety, the concerns you have about how things will turn out—but you've seen that I can be discreet. I will remain in the background, paying bills and mopping up spills. I have long experience working around and between the rules to ensure that things get done. If you'll just listen and relax, you'll see how Orestes and I have organized matters to make your life simpler, not more complicated."

I start to voice another objection . . . but the bun is very good. I possess a terrible weakness for fresh bread.

"We've gone over this together," she tells me, "what we can salvage from the previous production, what you will need to purchase new." She hands me a tablet with a long list drafted upon it. "You should review it before you meet with the Aedile. And this," she passes me another tablet," is a list of artistic considerations you must request when you meet with Titus Qunctius Flamininus. If you review the two lists you'll see that between them they're very complete. You and Orestes are steeped in theatre practice and possess all the requisite relationships and connections with theatre artists, musicians, and their guilds. I have the business knowledge, my own connections with tradesmen and merchants, and I own a commercial organization that will provide financial support." She passes me what look to be notes I am to study in preparation for my meeting with Titus Flamininus. "By the way, where were you planning to store the material from the theatre?"

"I hadn't thought that far in advance," I reply.

"Some of it can be tucked beneath the Cerium with the timber you haven't used for the latrine. The rest can go into storage at the docks—I have a special understanding with one of the clerks there. Budget for new masks, new props, new costumes. You'll want to build up inventory. And you'll want to ask for funds for carriage. People forget the costs associated with transportation."

I start reading ahead in her notes. There are small but significant subtractions everywhere. I admit that one of the great joys in life lies in working with a true miser, because they have an eye for every possible detail. "What's this?" I ask, pointing to the end of the notes.

"Ah, that," she says, glancing over my shoulder. "That is a little delicate. You should wait and judge how things have gone once your conversation with the Aedile has come to a close. I wrote that as I was meditating upon your finances—you will still be considerably in debt to Lucius when *The Pot of Gold* has closed."

"Yes, I know," I say as I finish the bun. "And?"

"I was turning that about in my mind. If you wanted—and you don't have to, this is just an option—but, there is a quick way to increase profits, and eliminate the majority of your bad debts in a single throw."

I hadn't thought beyond simply keeping up with my payments. The notion that I might be able to terminate them takes me by surprise. "How?"

"Request a bonus," she says, "if the crowds exceed expectations."

"A bonus?" I repeat.

"Yes."

I scan the numbers once more, to determine if there is some information there that will help me understand. "He won't agree to a bonus," I say as I come to the bottom of the column. "Why would he agree to a bonus? Out of the goodness of his heart?"

"The Curule Aedile is interested in reaching the plebeians, and the theatre can do that. That's why equites compete for his position, for the chance, through the events of the ludi and the theatre, to promote themselves to the merchants, artisans, and storekeepers they would never otherwise meet. The more plebeians attending and entertained at a performance, from his point of view, the better."

"I understand that," I tell her impatiently, "but why would he provide a bonus? He expects the play to do well. He'll pay to ensure that it does well, but he has no incentive to pay any more than the initially agreed-upon fee."

"He will—if you frame it as a bet. And this is how you bait the hook." She leans forward to explain. "You provide him with an option. Tell him he can pay us nothing if we attract a smaller crowd than what we guarantee, but that he will double it if we exceed expectations."

Orestes and I exchange a look. My sense is that this is the first he's heard of this plan.

"What makes you think he would do that?" I ask. "Titus Quinctius Flamininus belongs to one of Rome's oldest, noblest, wealthiest families. He's not going to want to place a bet with me."

She laughs as though she's heard an especially innocent toddler utter his first guileless words. "Titus Quinctius Flamininus is a notorious *gambler*, which means he will wager with anyone. You're correct in assuming that because he's one of the noble families the stakes will have to be high."

"Which means I can't afford to wager," I point out.

"Not at all," she contradicts me. "That you can't afford to lose will make the venture that much sweeter."

I hold the thought a moment. "But what if we don't attract the audience we require?"

"Then we will lose money. That's why it's a gamble." She pats my shoulder encouragingly. "But don't worry, we won't."

"You're right about that," I assure her, "because I'm not about to risk my professional reputation, or the future of the grex—everything really—on some throw of the dice."

"Fair enough," she says, and reaching over my shoulder, erases the notation with the blunt end of the stylus. And that's how, without ever formally agreeing to anything, in fact, the management of our grex falls into place.

8

I strive to put my thoughts in order, which is a little like attempting to stack gnats. As I prepare to meet the Curule Aedilis, what story should I select? How can I inspire trust in Titus Quinctius Flamininus with a group of artists that has only performed once? How can we set our grex apart from all the other more seasoned greges submitting plays?

I put all these matters aside and return to the matter of writing the play. A comedy of mistaken identity—good. Perhaps not just a mistaken identity, but a doubly mistaken identity, that then, in turn, masks a third, new and genuine identity. There is some novelty in this approach. I feel I am making progress.

As I scratch notes onto a tablet, Orestes arrives to store materials from *The Pot of Gold* in Casina's cellar. He instructs Grippus, Papius, and Tertius to stack things below, then sits across from me.

"You're working up the story?" he asks, wiping his face of sweat and peering over at my notes.

"Yes."

Pomona brings him his usual water and wine. He drags my plate of nuts closer to his side and fishes through them. "What's its name?"

"The majority I'll pull from Menander's *The Shield*," I reply.

"I'm not familiar with it. Tell it to me," Orestes says as he cracks a chestnut and discards the shell, "the way you would tell a child."

"Daos," I begin, "is the clever slave."

He pops the nut in his mouth. "Good."

"He will have a beautiful opening song—I can hear it already. He enters the city, announcing that his master, Kleostratos, a soldier, is dead. Killed in battle."

"So," he says, closing his eyes and cocking his head to one side to focus, "it begins with a song and a complication. Also good."

"The song, as it turns out, is layered with irony—the family should have been celebrating a great triumph, and putting into storage the wealth that had been gathered in the battles, had Kleostratos not been killed. But as it turns out, Daos is wrong. Kleostratos isn't dead," I tell him. "He's been taken prisoner."

"Even better," Orestes murmurs.

"The survival of Kleostratos will only be revealed later. In the meantime, there is a mix-up of marriage. An old miser by the name of Smikrines is the villain. He has his eyes set on the gold Kleostratos won, and plans to marry Kleostratos's sister to get it."

Orestes nods as he thinks it through. "There's an impediment?" he asks, raising his eyebrows.

"She's already betrothed to someone else," I explain, "whom she, of course, loves."

His mouth stretches in a satisfied grin. "Of course."

"The next part is cloaked in mist. In Menander's version the love story doesn't really amount to much, but we'll borrow from one of the others and make something genuine of the romance."

"So, in our version," Orestes clarifies, "you'll have a clever slave, a mistaken death, mistaken identities, and lovers as well?"

"Yes."

"The shape is good already," he says, dusting the nut debris off his hands. "Our actors can survive on what they have received from *The Pot of Gold* till spring. We'll begin work toward the Ludi of Apollo then, and provide initial payments. We should convene the actors to read the play and cast it in the winter sometime, perhaps just prior to Saturnalia. If we do that, it will commit them and keep them from being poached by another grex. How quickly can you have it written?"

I perform a few mental calculations. "It will take some thought to graft the new plant onto the old roots. And determining the correct rhythms takes time. It all takes time."

"How much and how soon?" he repeats bluntly.

"I can guarantee I will have some, a good portion, completed by Saturnalia."

He responds with a quick, emphatic clap. "Perfect," he says, and then looks down at the floor. "When are you going to visit the Aedile?" he asks me.

"In a couple of days," I answer, surprised at his sudden change in topic.

"You'll get new sandals before you go?" he asks.

I glance down at my sandals. "Why?"

He nods at them. "They're shabby."

"They've been repaired," I allow, extending my feet to look at, "but are hardly shabby."

"They're knotted and frayed and discoloured," he says, frowning. "You look worse than a beggar in them."

"*Worse* than a beggar?" I repeat.

"A beggar would be ashamed to beg in them," he maintains.

At this point Grippus appears with a question about where to store the awnings, and Orestes rises from his bench. "Get new sandals," Orestes advises me as he rises and leaves, "before you see the Aedile."

I make mixed progress with the story after his departure. The first half takes greater shape, the latter half resists my efforts. I ask Felicia to bring me soup. When she returns with it, I inquire what she thinks of my sandals. She hesitates a moment, then diplomatically asks if I have a sentimental attachment to them.

Casina passes as we discuss the matter and I solicit her opinion. She acts surprised that I have to ask. She tells me that she had thought the sandals must represent some kind of good luck keepsake. I admit to having repaired them several times. But there's nothing unusual, I assert, or wrong, about that. "Two repairs is thrift," Casina argues, "greater than three is mingy."

"Mingy?" I say. "Really?"

When I awaken the following day, I reluctantly set out to visit Festus, the one-legged leather worker who operates a small business ten streets over. The streets and alleyways between the caupona and his shop are crowded and smelly. I get stuck behind a young man carrying a lamb and am unable to slip past him. The lamb is draped around his shoulders, its legs bound, but every few moments it writhes and twists and threatens to kick free, so there is a certain concern about approaching too closely and receiving a hoof in the head.

I am grateful when I arrive at the sandalmaker's at last, and receive a drink of cool water from a wooden pail. I explain my situation to Festus, who nods gravely. "You want two sets of sandals, one for outside, one for inside?" he asks. "Correct?"

I have been satisfied with only one pair, but decide after the critique I've received over my footwear that an inside and an outside pair is probably appropriate. "Yes," I tell him.

"Stool?" he says, and I wonder for a moment if he is addressing me. He quickly clarifies the matter by throwing a scrap of leather at a boy crouched in the corner. The boy looks up. He is about ten and has a dirty face. "Bring me that stool!" Festus barks. The youngster hastens to the far corner of the room to fetch a short wooden, three-legged stool.

Festus takes it from him. "This is my brother's son, apprenticing with me," he says, and brushes dust from the seat, "He is a dimwit." He drops the stool in front of me. "Sit here."

He draws a low block of wood to sit upon and sprawls with his wooden peg stretched to one side. I have observed him from a distance, bobbing through the market at a remarkable pace, but have never had the opportunity to study the carved leg closely. It is a smooth, tapered column of polished oak. There are a number of devices etched onto it, one of which I recognize as being associated with Fortuna, and soliciting good luck. The other signs I cannot read but recognize as Etruscan.

"You see that," he says gesturing at his remaining healthy foot. "The one sandal I wear will last me my lifetime. Money spent on sandals is always a good investment. I spare nothing on the comfort of that foot. As I have only the one, I must be doubly attentive to it."

He seems comfortable talking about his condition so I ask him how he lost the other leg.

"I was carrying goods through traffic, was caught between a cart and a vending stall. The ox in the cart rebelled and backed up—oxen are nervous creatures and easily vexed by noises, never startle an ox—the cart and vending stall closed round my leg like teeth around a piece of straw, and my leg snapped. After, I had it set, but it healed wrong and impurity set in. Block. Block!" He turns to glare at his nephew. "Must I ask for everything twice, slug?"

The boy scampers to another corner of the room, brushes a halter off a heavy wooden block and carries it across the room.

Festus scowls at the perceived slowness of this procedure. "His father has not beaten him sufficiently, consequently he listens only when he cares to. I have tried to address this, but he is nimble when he wants to be, and being one-legged as I am, I cannot always catch him."

He drapes a wide strip of thick cow leather over the wooden block. "Put your foot here," he directs. I slip my right foot from my damaged sandal and place it atop the leather. "Charcoal," he says, and his nephew drops a stick of charcoal into his outstretched hand. He quickly traces the outline of my foot. "I sacrificed to the divine gods but initially hesitated to consult an augur. As a consequence, my sacrifices were rejected. The leg was severed below the knee. The impurity persisted, and more was cut away the way you might slice mould from a block of cheese. I consulted an Etruscan augur—there are Romans who make claims to augury but are a waste of money. The Etruscans invented it, and they alone know how to decode the mysteries. Finally, I was informed of what I needed to do to get my sacrifice accepted. Only then did I know I would heal." He pats my foot and I remove it from the block. He examines the pattern, then shifts the leather on the block. "Other foot," he says. I position my left foot on the block. "You offer sacrifices to the gods for the success of your plays, I imagine?"

I nod my agreement. "Certainly."

"Consult an augur," he advises me. "They can tell if your sacrifices are accepted or not. Who made your old sandals?"

"I don't remember."

"He was a fool, these are useless. The leather's rubbish," he declares, and flexes the sole between his hands. "I would not wipe myself with it. It is neither cut nor stitched properly. Look at this stitching." He tosses my sandal at his nephew who, caught unawares, receives the spinning sandal full against his forehead.

"Look and learn. The sandals I fashion will last you the rest of your life, you will be cremated along with these sandals if you want. Yes," he says, rubbing his hands against his apron, "if they are accepted, all manner of miracles are possible."

It takes me a moment to realize that he has returned once more to the matter of augury and is not speaking of the miraculous properties of his sandals.

"If they are not, nothing is possible. What the gods wish to promote will be promoted, what the gods set their countenance against cannot thrive, though everything appear to favour it." He measures two lengths of leather thong against my leg, instep to mid-calf, marks them, and sets them aside. "When I first set out on life one-legged," he continues, "I despaired at the prospects of ever operating a successful business, but I contacted the augurs and offered sacrifices and they were accepted and now, as you can see, while I am lame, my business is two-legged—running ahead of its solo-limbed master. Remove the stool, mud."

The nephew, crab-like, scuttles forward, then retreats with the stool to his station. "The young people today have not struggled as we have. Rome is a different and more prosperous place, there is greater opportunity for a life of ease and consequently young people are inclined to laziness and stupidity. You have a young person working for you?"

It is more statement than a question, and I confirm Tertius's presence among the grex.

"I have seen him—the boy that wandered the streets near here. He runs errands for you?"

"Yes, not so much for me as for my Choragus."

"Watch him. He's a devil," he states matter-of-factly. "The boy pilfered from me in the past and I was compelled to beat him." He plucks up the thongs and the sheet of marked leather. "Come back tomorrow, the sandals will be finished then."

He is as good as his word. The sandals—one pair for inside, one for out—are ready the next day, and the workmanship is very good. Strapping on my new footwear, I feel equipped to visit the Aedile.

Titus Quinctius Flamininus lives high up on the Esquiline hill, overlooking the city. The view as you ascend is glorious and clear. Looking west it's possible to observe the city in its entirety: a rolling, sprawling red and tan mosaic of rooftops and roadways; the grey-green Tiber snaking through it, coiling sinewy and lithe, north into the mountains, and south to the coast.

I approach the high gates of the Flamininus domus, and am met and escorted by a slave, first into the vestibulum, where I wait briefly, and then into the atrium.

The roof is open to the sky in this section of the estate and sunlight streams in. A fountain flows into a gathering pool in the centre of the garden. Near it a very fine cream-coloured marble statue of Ceres stands, holding a sheaf of wheat. A long wooden table has been placed—it seems to me temporarily— close to the fountain, along with two chairs.

The Curule Aedilis enters smiling. "There you are," he says. "Welcome." He gestures to his slave, who pulls a chair out for me to sit on. Titus Flamininus is still standing, however, so I remain standing.

"Please. Make yourself comfortable," Titus Flamininus insists, and sits. I fold myself into the chair across the table from him. "I am very excited about this ludi," he tells me, moving quickly to discuss the play, "very excited. I have been speaking with others at the Senate and these conversations, these discussions, confirm that a major devotion to the gods is exactly what is needed. After all, we have so much to be thankful for! After years of feeling threatened, of feeling that we have been living hemmed in, Rome is thriving once again, and it is, I believe, important to offer thanks, and bring Romans together. My nephew Varus was involved in the struggles for Cannae, it was a nightmare, but he has returned safely, and so I have a personal reason to be grateful as well. Are you thirsty?" he asks, abruptly, and then just as abruptly, answers himself. "Of course you are." He glances about and catches his slave's eye. This slave, a younger and much better-looking youth than the one who guided me to the atrium, is clearly very attentive to his master. The instant he is signalled, he fills two cups with wine and places them in our hands.

"I think you'll enjoy this vintage," the praetor says.

I take a sip. I don't believe I have ever in my life tasted anything like it—light, sweet, utterly refreshing. This is what wine is like if you can afford it.

"I saw one of your plays several years back. Found it very entertaining," he continues, "but I hadn't heard anything of you for quite a while, until this latest production you presented at the Lentulus funeral ceremonies." He takes a sip. "Which, as you know, I enjoyed. What have you been doing?"

"I have been out of Rome attending to my business interests," I tell him, a little vaguely, perhaps, but not a lie. "But now I have returned and am ready to press forward with several writing projects."

He settles back in his chair. "And what do you have in mind?" he asks.

"I saw a play, years ago," I tell him, "when I was first serving in Illyria. I've put my hands on a copy, and have been reviewing it."

"Illyria," he repeats. "They have fabulous stonework theatres there, don't they?"

"Yes they do," I agree.

"A serious drawback of our Roman heritage, I'm afraid, and something we will have to remedy one day. Building permanent theatres. The Greeks are so advanced in that regard. I've visited Syracuse, and the theatre there is a marvel of imagination and engineering. There is a particularly fine theatre in Illyria, is there not?

"At Dodona. That's right." I recall mounting the steps of the theatre, sitting in a seat and sensing its power. "It's exquisitely constructed and situated in the most beautiful environment. Right next to it is the prophetic glade of oaks, used to construct Jason's talking ship, the *Argo*."

"Imagine that," Titus Flamininus clucks and shakes his head. "Imagine that. And did the glade speak to you?"

"I'm afraid not," I confess, laughing. This interview, I think to myself, is going much better than I'd anticipated.

"So, this play you saw while in Illyria," the Aedile says, folding his hands over his stomach, "it was a comedy?

"It was," I agree. "An extremely funny one."

"And you enjoyed it?"

"Very much."

"Good," he says, sounding content. "Excellent." He looks about, and almost magically his slave appears once again, this time with dark ripe figs set amid a bowl of the reddest grapes. "And you believe you could work with it."

"With adjustments," I say. "Yes. The original doesn't completely suit the Roman temperament, but with amendments and additional music, I believe it will be a very good fit."

"Perfect. Describe it to me," he requests as he bites into a fig.

"Well," I begin, licking my lips.

"Not the whole thing," he says, waving his hand airily. "Not the details, but as if you had written about it in a letter to me."

I gather my thoughts. "To start with, there's a slave, Daos, who returns from a war, thinking his master, a soldier, Kleostratos, is dead. He's not—he's actually imprisoned, and will be freed in an exchange—but we won't find that out until later. While Kleostratos is absent, his uncle, Smikrines, tries to wrest the fortune Kleostratos made in the war from the estate, by marrying the heir, Kleostratos's sister."

"Is he a miser, like Euclio was in *The Pot of Gold?*" Titus Flamininus interrupts.

"He is," I answer, "but he will be prevented from attaining the fortune because Daos is a master of spinning stories and telling lies."

"Isn't that the way?" Titus chortles to himself, and slaps me on the upper arm, "Isn't that always the way? *I* have some fellows here who have been known to bend the truth on occasion." This is for the benefit of his slave, who has drawn closer. He grins shyly at Titus Qunctius Flamininus. "Isn't that so, Matho?" the Aedile asks and Matho nods.

"But it turns out," I continue, "that he is only lying for his master's own good. "

The Aedile throws his hands above his head. "How did I know *that* was going to happen?" Titus demands rhetorically, "I suppose you think that part is funny." Matho, once more nods his affirmation. "And then what?"

"Of course the slave, seeking to find a solution to the problems of his master, digs himself into an ever deeper hole, by—"

"—Lying more?" Titus suggests.

I raise my eyebrows in agreement, pleased that this is being received so well. "Exactly. By lying more."

Happy that he has guessed correctly, he taps the tabletop. "And then?"

This is the part I've been fretting over throughout the previous nights. There are a number of different ways the plot might diverge, but I've as yet been unable to commit to one or the other, because each outcome holds distinct benefits and risks. The moment I commit myself to one trajectory, I will in effect strike a course from which there will be no retreat. Inasmuch as he seems happy so far, I decide I might get away with a quick, confident glossing over of a few general outcomes. "By setting up one convoluted deception after another, naturally. By turns getting caught and then extricating himself again. And then, you know how it follows, punishment, revenge, renewal and, ultimately, rejoicing and feasting for everyone," I conclude glibly.

These words are received with complete silence. Titus Qunctius Flamininus stops laughing, and regards me with an expression that is both confused and a little offended. In one appalling instant I realize how greatly I have misjudged the situation. How close I am to losing my one opportunity. I feel blood rise to my face, and wonder if he is going to have me escorted out. And then, just as suddenly as he grew silent, he tosses back his head, guffaws, and slaps me hard on the thigh.

"Oh, you *are* a clever devil. Isn't he a clever devil?" he asks Matho. Matho, who is perhaps as confused as I am, doesn't answer. "You want me to be *surprised*."

I breathe a silent prayer and a sigh of relief. "Of course," I agree.

"He wants me to be *surprised*," he repeats. "Doesn't want to reveal the plot and how things turn out in advance. Why, you're as spare with information as my cook is with salt."

I smile at him and nod, as though he has caught me out in my scheme. "There's no point my writing it," I add, "if it doesn't astonish you."

"You writers," he says, wagging his finger in admonishment. "You writers have your secrets. But that," he carries on, settling back into this chair and regarding me with a level, appraising gaze, "doesn't provide me with much information upon which I can make a decision, does it? I've looked into your history, and you've certainly had your share of successes, and failures. So, on the basis of *what* am I to decide whether to include you among the writers at the Ludi of Apollo? Or not?"

I return his gaze with what I hope is my most sincere expression. "I can guarantee that this play will be a good one."

"That sounds wonderful, but," Titus sips his wine, and licks a drop that has spilled onto a finger, "how, exactly?"

He stares at me frankly, and I can tell in that instant that no amount of bluffing, hedging, or persuasion will work. He has asked me an honest question, for which I do not yet have an answer.

"You will have to trust me," I tell him finally, trying to make that statement sound confident rather than desperate.

"That," he allows, "is all very well for you to say, but it sounds like rather self-serving advice."

"I can guarantee that you won't be disappointed."

"Very good," he says and shrugs. "But again, how?"

"Because unless the play draws at least a second sitting and a second audience, you need not pay me."

He sits up and shifts in his seat. "Are you suggesting a . . . wager?" he asks, tilting his head as he considers me.

"Something like that," I reply.

"A wager. I didn't take you for a gambling man," he muses and dabs at his mouth with a napkin. "So describe the terms to me again?"

"Pretty simple," I say, taking a sip of wine to wet a mouth gone suddenly dry. "Double or nothing. Either the attending audience demands an interruption of the ceremonies and compels a second performance, or we forfeit payment."

"And you," he asks, "and your grex are prepared to assume the risk?"

I nod.

"Hmm," he grunts, tracing light circles on the tabletop with his fingertips. "When I first brought your name up with other Senators, the consensus among us was that you were honourable and honest—a dedicated poet. I felt you might be the precisely correct individual to approach. Now, I see that actually you are no better than a common player of knucklebones, throwing combinations in the dust of some alley, hoping to bring home enough money for dinner, but perhaps leaving the game with nothing beyond the tunic on your back. You are, in the final appraisal, Titus Maccius Plautus, a bit of a desperate character." He drains his drink and stares me in the eye. "I find that proposition thrilling. Have your man write up the forms and the funds you will require to begin. I'll have my man look it over, they'll haggle, then I'll sign. Well. Double or nothing—this will certainly make this ludi an interesting one."

The caupona is only moderately busy when I return to it, Pomona the sole server on the floor. I catch her eye and have her bring me a pitcher of posca.

Shortly after, Casina joins me. "Well?" she asks.

"He's accepted our submission," I inform her.

She pulls a long pin from her hair, adjusts her front locks and secures them in place. "But you don't look happy," she observes.

"I bet with him," I confess.

"Ah," she says, and raises her eyebrows. "What stakes?"

"What we'd discussed," I reply, and pour myself more to drink.

She crosses her arms and studies me a moment. "And now you feel anxious?" she asks.

"Yes. Of course," I say as I drink. "He's rich and powerful. He can hire people to sabotage the presentation. He can simply refuse to permit a second showing, regardless of the response of the audience."

"He can," Casina agrees, "but he won't."

"What's to stop him?" I ask her.

"He needs the play to succeed," she reasons, "or he loses the esteem of his peers. That's the only reason to finance it in the first place—to win support from merchants and farmers and the sorts of people he never meets. Plus he's a *gambler*—and for a gambler there's no thrill in a fixed bet."

"Even if he doesn't do anything," I say, "there's no guarantee that the play will draw a second audience."

"No. There isn't," she agrees, and pats me on the shoulder. "And that means you will have to write something wonderful."

I don't know if I find her confidence reassuring or unsettling. I stand to leave, but am reminded of what I was going to ask. "I saw Lucius Caecilius yesterday," I recall.

"Oh yes?" she replies, and then after a moment spent thinking asks, "The money lender?"

"Yes. His face was puffy and bruised. Apparently he was attacked by someone the other night."

"Is that right?" she asks as she withdraws a cloth from her sash and wipes down the tabletop, "By whom?"

"I don't know for sure," I tell her. "Rumour has it that it was a big bear of a fellow. But it was dark, and the attacker was wearing a mask."

"These street criminals are shameless," she clucks, shaking her head. "Did he steal anything?"

"No. It seems he took nothing," I answer, "which was strange. I'm only hearing this second hand, you understand, but apparently Lucius maintains that the criminal said just one thing."

"Oh," she asks, "what was it?"

"Pandora," I tell her.

Casina looks puzzled. "Curious. What does that mean?"

"According to the Greeks, she was the first woman."

She shrugs. "I'm not familiar with that story."

"She lacked patience," I say. Casina indicates a kind of distant interest, so I push that matter a little further. "Do you know anything about this?"

"Me?" she asks, surprised. "What has this to do with me? I'm too busy keeping the Cerium running to listen to gossip about what has happened or hasn't happened to people in their adventures after dark."

"Did you send someone to—" I start.

"Lucius is a money lender. I'm sure," she interrupts me, "that there are any number of people who might want to urge him to have greater patience ."

9

I put the bet behind me—what point can there be in worrying? I must simply keep my head down and trust that the play once birthed will open its mouth, wail, and thrive. In the meantime, I admit that Casina is a godsend—clever, competent, and consummately thrifty. She and Orestes begin quietly accumulating and storing the materials we will require for the next production, and Casina is almost always able to purchase the goods at a price considerably lower than our quote.

I find my usual table in the Cerium and write. As fall approaches it is evident that the caupona has become increasingly busy—a development I choose to believe can be attributed to my newly constructed latrine. In any case, the coenatio is packed this evening. Merchants cluster around two tables, laughing as they share information regarding the day's commerce. Foreign salesmen—maybe Egyptians, maybe Libyans—chat in their native tongues near the kitchen. Several hefty-looking soldiers and ex-soldiers defend three or four tables. An especially burly member of that group darts a threatening look my way. I turn my attention elsewhere. Through them all, Felicia and Prima dash, wriggling between tables, lifting dirty dishes, taking orders, fetching food, carrying drinks. Domitia busily scrubs at a message that has been scrawled above Priapus's prominent male member reading, "For a phenomenon bigger than this, come see Secundas."

"Every man thinks they're built like that," Domitia grouses as she scours the offending passage with water and vinegar, nodding at Priapus. "And then it turns out that they're built like that," she says, indicating the remaining melted stub of a candlestick on a table.

Orestes joins me for coena, but wrinkles his nose as he sits. "The place reeks like a fish market at noon."

"Nothing wrong with that," I reply as Prima sets my steaming, fragrant meal down in front of me.

"You Romans," he complains, fanning a hand in front of his face. "Cabbage, turnips and your precious, precious garum."

"How," I ask, spooning a little more of the potent fish sauce onto my bowl, "can anyone love life and not like garum?"

"Easily," Orestes replies dourly. "Very easily."

I pop a steaming spoonful of fish stew into my mouth, and am struck once more by how much dining has improved at the Cerium since Casina took over. It's astonishing. I recall that at one time the food was barely edible, but the menu has matured so much since then. For example, there's more fish in the stew than I would have found in times past—before, it would have been minnow sized! And the garum, great Neptune, the garum! Savoury and agreeably zesty, magnificently aromatic. There are many other businesses that produce the sauce, but the Cerium's is, without doubt and without exaggeration, the finest.

"The garum employed at the Cerium amounts to a cultural treasure," I lecture Orestes, and hold my bowl up to better enjoy the aroma, "If you were truly Roman you would appreciate it for the paragon it is. I know I'm not the only one who thinks this, but I would give my right arm for the recipe."

"And I would sacrifice another body part to be kept free of it," Orestes retorts, drawing his head back in distaste. "My nose, for instance. I'd certainly give my nose."

Orestes orders a simple lentil soup, and wine and water as usual, and we discuss matters relating to musical composition, and the challenges of translation, as we eat. The phrasing and metre of *The Shield* are problems, but by no means the biggest. It's irksome how essentially untranslatable humour can prove. Lines that cause great hilarity in Greek lie down like sheep with colic, to sicken and die, in Latin.

Naevius joins our table mid-conversation, and orders spiced wine from Prima. Never shy to offer an opinion, he declares that it isn't only Greek humour that resists adaptation, but the entire Greek disposition. Greeks, he argues, are deep thinkers, Romans on the other hand, doers. This, he adds, is one of the most persuasive arguments for creating a truly Roman theatre—Roman plays about Romans in Latin. He holds up as a model the work he did on *Clastidium*, his historical play. I agree but maintain that the situation is more complex than he realizes—that Roman doers, Greek thinkers, Celtic drinkers, Syrians, Persians, Ligurians, Umbrians, Samnites, are all part of the potent brew that represents something new in Rome. A new theatre should reflect that novel energy as well—and still make the audience laugh. I see that Orestes has disengaged from the conversation, and so inform him that our script will go through further adjustments before we have a proper shape for performance, but I'll try to maintain the schedule we've set.

Orestes urges me to keep writing, stay healthy, and abstain from garum. With that he claps me on the back, drains his cup, stands, and bids us both good night. Naevius nods as

my Greek friend slips past him. I reflect as he leaves that
there's always been a certain reserve between these two that I
honestly don't understand. I know Orestes respects Naevius as
a poet, and Naevius has praised Orestes's musical abilities to
me many times. Still it's undeniable, there's tension when they
sit together.

I spy Casina squeezing between tables on her way to the
culina and cannot resist complimenting her. I call her over.
"You make this yourself, don't you?" I ask, indicating my bowl.

"The fish stew?" she asks, puzzled. "Of course."

"No," I reply, shaking my head, "the garum."

"Oh! Yes, that's my own special recipe," she answers proudly.

"You should be celebrated and applauded!" I enthuse.
"The product is subtle and potent all at once, rich, complex,
aromatic—a genuine treasure!" I lean in so that my voice will
be shared with her alone. "So, tell me. What's the secret?"

"There are a few unique extras," she replies enigmatically.
"But you must be especially pickled if you think that just
because you smiled at me and offered words of praise that I'm
going to share it with you."

I pull her in close and whisper. "What difference would it
make? We both know I can't cook."

"So, why does it matter?" she whispers back.

"The recipe would be like a token of good luck for me, and
a gesture of a special trust between partners!" I deliver what
I hope is my most winning expression. "Didn't I build you a
good latrine?"

"A gesture of a special trust between partners!" she repeats
and laughs out loud. "Really! How much have you had to drink?"

"A little," I tell her. "Maybe three cups."

"More like four or five," she corrects me, but then relents. "You promise you won't reveal it to anyone else?"

"Absolutely," I swear.

"Very well," she surrenders and lowers her voice. "Take one large fish, mince it fine. Add sardine eggs and entrails, grind them until you have a thick paste. Salt it to the second joint of your thumb. Stir it. Cover it. Then leave it in the sun to cure. Let the mash ferment, beat it a couple of times a day, when it's ripe, pour the whole thing into a very fine cloth bag. Let it drip through the cloth into a container. Seal it," she concludes.

That's it?" I ask, feeling like Hercules returning home with the Nemean lion over his shoulders.

"That's it. It takes time to produce," Casina warns me. "Not everyone has the patience."

I write it down and must appear very pleased with myself, because as Casina returns to the culina, I catch Naevius regarding me pityingly.

"You don't see?" he asks.

"What?"

He clicks his tongue in disgust, and whistles through his teeth. Heads turn across the room, including Casina's. "Ask her if it's complete," he tells me. "Go on."

"Casina?" I call.

She's halts near the archway, "What?"

"Have you," I hold up the wax tablet, "held back on me?"

"Of course I have!" she calls back, "It's a *secret* recipe." And chuckling to herself, exits.

"Like a baby," Naevius mocks me, shaking his head at my naïveté. "Never trust the horse dealer to reveal the horse's age, or the cook her ingredients." He leans back against the wall, takes a gulp of his drink. "I've spoken with the Aedile today."

"Oh yes?" I say, putting away the tablet and attempting to conceal my disappointment.

"Despite assurances I received when I first returned to Rome, I'm still waiting to learn if I will be invited to submit a tragic work to the Ludi Florales."

"Have you been given reasons for the delay?" I ask.

"It's always the same question. Do I represent too great a risk? 'Too great a risk,'" he repeats as though the words themselves were incomprehensible. "Imagine. We have waged a war for our very existence, but the words of my *plays* are so hazardous they must be controlled." He shakes his head at the folly this represents. "So. I understand you have your grex scheduled in the Ludi of Apollo?"

"Yes," I reply, at this point feeling a little guilty at my good fortune.

He swirls the wine about in his cup looking for sediment. "That's been confirmed?"

"Yes."

"Good for you," he commends me and drinks. "The comedy is coming along well?"

"I think so," I admit.

He nods a moment, then takes another drink. "And you're satisfied with that?" he asks.

"What?" I reply. "That I am working on a comedy that interests me, that I have retained a wonderful cast? How could I possibly not be satisfied with that?"

"And that is all you want to do now?" Naevius asks rhetorically. "Amuse people?"

I shrug. "I believe at this point in my life I could be content to amuse people," I say. It's clear this answer doesn't satisfy. "I take it that's not enough for you anymore?"

He purses his lips. I'm not sure what that's supposed to indicate. "What do you aspire to write?" he asks.

"I would be happy enough if I wrote a successful romantic comedy," I tell him.

"And what's that supposed to mean?"

I consider the question a moment. "I suppose a successful romantic comedy should involve lovers so ardent they will accept nothing less than complete union, parents so adamantly opposed that Jupiter himself could not convince them to permit the marriage. It demands a potent mixture of sexual longing and chaste virginity. And if the female lover is both a slave and a whore who just happens to turn out in the end to be a virgin and the best friend's sister, that would probably be the best arrangement. That is a love story that Romans will cheer and remember."

"And that," Naevius responds sourly, "is precisely the kind of love story that is guaranteed to send me racing for your latrine. A love story like that represents a more powerful purgative than any herb or potion invented by man."

"Remind me," I tell him, "not to sit near you in the audience."

"Our writing shouldn't simply *entertain*," he continues, taking up his theme. "It should chastise, instruct, inspire. Words aren't just toys, they're weapons to be strategically employed."

"I have heard that before," I tell him, "and have heard laughter itself can be a weapon. Which is perhaps interesting for people who are eager to build weapons. I've built weapons, real weapons, and I'm not trying to build or deploy weapons anymore. My words serve other gods."

"Yes," he says, "now your words serve Bacchus, drunkenness, and debauchery."

"Maybe," I permit. "There are worse services."

"Really?" he demands. "What? What could be worse than prostituting your craft?"

"Well, writing—as you know—can get you imprisoned. From where I am sitting right now, that would be considerably worse. On balance I don't find there's much wrong with writing comedies."

"But writing, real writing, isn't about balance," he insists, slapping his right thigh for emphasis, "like some fat merchant weighing gold against cloth or grain or olives. Writing should be a torch, and the poet's duty is to hold up that flame and chase away darkness. Writing can do that. Maybe *only* writing can do that."

I sit back in my seat and sip my wine. "You used to enjoy writing comedy," I remind him.

"Not anymore. I am through with it," he says, and plants his cup firmly on the table. "I am through with comedy. I am finished making repulsive things seem funny, making a corrupted society seem clean. I am done oiling and massaging the bloated personalities of a self-appointed governing elite." He waits for me to bite, and when I don't, he asks, "Well?"

I shrug. "I could use an oiling and massage. Where do I sign up?"

"You're hopeless," he scoffs. He waves to someone entering the Cerium, obviously a meeting he has previously arranged, and stands. "Comedy has become a whore's art," he concludes testily and finishes his drink. He gathers himself together and stands. "A whore's art," he repeats over his shoulder in case I haven't heard him.

I watch him swagger through the crowd to another table where doubtless he'll enter into an equally passionate debate with someone else. He's thoroughly primed now, so I imagine there'll be no stopping him. I note that the swagger isn't as confident as it once was, though, and he favours his right leg as he walks. He's gotten old and cranky over the years, but I remember when he was the most admired poet in Rome. He was handsome, in a rugged, austere way. He'd fought in the first Punic war in Sicily, taken scars and won honours. He was writing comedies then, and was sharp enough to shave with. When I first began writing, with just the experience I had as a stage carpenter and a minor bit of acting to recommend me, along with the few haphazard plays I had adapted for a faltering grex, it was Naevius who mentored me, who took me under his wing, and most encouraged and promoted me. He saw to it that I received recognition and notice for my writing from people who counted—and at that time he was genuinely connected. He knew everybody. As tenuous as my future is at this time, as poised between success and disaster as I am, I wouldn't have any career without him.

I think all that as I soak up the remaining precious drops of my fish stew, then glance about the room. I note that there's a major change in the works. The first battalion of customers, having finished their meals, are abandoning the field, leaving it to the next division to occupy empty seats. Candria emerges, glittering bronze hoops dangling from her ears, her hair tied high in a brightly coloured wrap, her lithe arms exposed, and begins to sing. She glides between tables, halts briefly to attend the soldiers, then shifts her focus to the merchants. She carefully includes the lonely sailor in the corner, the Libyan merchant, and the Greek physician, welcomes them all, and at the same time she continues swaying, her castanets softly beating their own compelling rhythm.

"Stay," she sings. "The sun has set, a new jar of wine has just been opened. What better way to spend the night than here, listening to music? The lovely ladies of the Cerium would be only too happy to make your acquaintance." She introduces Pomona, Felicia, Prima, and Domitia. "Take your cue from Pan," she urges customers, "the happiest and least anxious of the Gods. He understood that it was far better to linger, a drink in hand, surrounded by beautiful women, than to slave like Vulcan working, working, working." I see passersby on the street stop to listen and moments later wedge themselves in at a bench beneath the awning. The crowd continues to swell. Candria's song finished, Pomona steps forward to announce that a new jar of wine has indeed been opened. Hands shoot up all over the room, and Felicia, Domitia, and Pomona scramble to take their orders. The evening deepens.

I stand, stumble up the steps to the latrine, enter, relieve myself and feel that guilty wave of pleasure and pride I experience whenever I see some useful object I've made employed. Outside and down the hallway on my right I hear one of the beds being vigorously exercised. When I return to the coenatio, more tables have been set up out on the streetside.

At the table nearest to me, an unruly knot of men converge, intently throwing knucklebones. "The Dog!" a squat, heavyset man to my right cries, then snatches up a small pot and rattles it. "Pay up!" he crows. His colleague tosses in two sesterii. Another sweeps up the knuckles, shakes, and throws. His pitch results in the Dog as well—he curses and adds more coins to the swelling pot.

I'm not by nature a gambler so don't understand why anyone would wager the certainty of something against the probability of nothing, and when they do, why it's expected to produce a pleasurable sensation. Though many of my comrades gambled when I was in my regiment, gaming remains as much a sacred mystery to me now as it was then.

At last one of the players throws Venus. A loud groan emerges from the losers as the winner gleefully sweeps the money from the pot into his pouch. Felicia brings me wine, smiles, drapes an arm around my shoulders, and asks if I am still working on my play. "Always," I tell her. "I am always working on it." I joke that if she's unkind I will make her one of the wicked characters in the next piece. Laughing, she claims that she would prefer that. The audience may applaud heroes, she informs me, but villains are actually the ones everyone secretly roots for. As she moves to the next customer, I feel a prickle on the back of my neck, turn and see the large soldier I'd noticed earlier, glaring at me once again.

I hear Naevius's penetrating voice and shift my attention to him. He's gesturing to a group at a table two or three over from me. Politics, of course. "He's taking his time though, isn't he?" he asks argumentatively, "Scipio? His troops are the richest, yes—and the best fed, *and why?* Because every battle represents another invitation to collect treasure! The reason his troops take so blessedly long to get anywhere is because his baggage train is so cursedly laden with swag. Are his men disciplined, though? Are they prepared to defend Rome and sacrifice their lives? And aren't those the standards a general should set?"

"But hasn't he recruited his own legions on Sicily?" one of his listeners objects. "Gathered them from nowhere, trained them at his own expense, and sent them to Africa to fight Hannibal. Doesn't that display his skills?"

"Absolutely!" Naevius exclaims. "It is precisely the same skills he demonstrated as commander in Spain, where his legions conducted themselves more like pirates and voluptuaries than legionnaires. He bribed and pampered them, but could he make time to prevent that criminal Hasdrubal from attacking our Roman soldiers? No! Hasdrubal skipped by him because Scipio's bunch were too busy screwing prostitutes in Spain. And that's exactly the problem—he's under the impression that he's running a brothel, not an army."

"Who the fuck are you?" a voice demands suddenly, cutting through the noise of the evening. It's the soldier with the ugly disposition I'd noticed earlier, and now he fairly radiates hostility.

Naevius straightens and turns his head. "I'm sorry," he replies calmly, "you're under the mistaken impression I was speaking to you. This is a private conversation."

"Never mind that," the soldier snaps. "I asked *who the fuck are you?* Are you a Consul or a Senator? Did someone elect you? You act like an expert, but do you actually know the first thing about what it is to run an army?"

"I have had the honour of defending the Roman people with my body," Naevius stiffly replies.

"Alongside Romulus and Remus, maybe, when there were only wolves and wild cats to fight. I only have to look at your grey hairs trailing behind to tell me that you're talking about wars fought before swords or spears were invented." This draws chuckles from his comrades.

"And I can see," Naevius says, "that you're an ill-mannered baboon."

This, apparently, is the invitation for the baboon to stand. As he slowly rises from the table I begin to wonder if he will ever stop. He is truly, truly massive, scarred, and impressively muscled. I remember campaigning with bruisers like this. Wonderful to march beside in battle, a disaster to drink with.

"Scipio soft?" the soldier asks rhetorically, and laughs harshly. "Did everyone hear that? Soft? He can kiss his men to bed at night, for all I care, sing them a song and comb their hair. All I know is he's poison for your Carthaginians. He will hammer them in Africa and hunt them down. Rip down their buildings and temples and leave nothing standing. If you have wasps, you must burn them out."

He steps away from his table. The cords of his neck and shoulders swell and appear to slowly haul his knotted, muscular arms up. Viewing him standing, I see that he's built like an especially powerful ox, only larger and less intelligent; and I cannot help but think that if he strikes Naevius, he is likely to punch a hole straight through to the other side.

"And you," he sneers as he approaches Naevius, "sit here, making your insolent pronouncements about him."

I reluctantly rise and attempt to adopt what I hope will be taken for a reasonable, calming tone. "Now," I coo, "everyone is going to have their own opinion—"

He pivots, and I'm startled at how nimbly he can move for a big man. He glares at me with blazing eyes. "And who the fuck are *you?*" he interrupts.

I shift my stance so my right foot is wedged beneath a stool which I can kick in his path if he takes a run at me. It won't hurt him—I'm certain he's drunk beyond feeling anything— but if I'm extremely lucky he might trip over it. "Just someone enjoying a few drinks, who wants everyone to stay calm—"

"Someone sticking his puny dick where it doesn't belong, is what I see," he snaps. "Another mouth that needs to be shut, is what I see—" And then, abruptly, he drops to his knees. "Ow—fuck," he mutters as his hand goes up to rub the back of his head.

He collapses face first to the floor and lies still. It all happens so quickly, I have trouble sorting it out. And then I see Casina behind him, her face flushed, clutching an enormous staff of polished cypress in her hands.

"I call this rod," Casina announces to the suddenly silent room, as she holds aloft the wooden pole, "presented to me by General Fabius Maximus, 'The Mediator' because it mends all arguments. And this," she gestures behind her to Vulcanus, "is my Mercury. He's Mercury, because he delivers everything where it needs to go. And this big windbag," she declares, nodding to the soldier lying on the floor, "needs to go somewhere where he can cool his temper and learn some manners. Take him to the fountain and introduce him to the calming ministrations of Fons."

The cook grabs the soldier by his armpits and with a grunt, heaves him up and dumps him into the cart he uses for hauling firewood.

"What's his name?" Casina demands.

One of the soldiers replies, "Postumus."

"Postumus will be very welcome to return," Casina announces as Vulcanus wheels him out, "another night, when he has composed himself. Is there anyone else who has issues requiring my mediation? Anyone else wishing to disrespect my establishment? Because they can take their business somewhere else right now. Anyone?" She scans the room. Although the other soldiers scowl, none stand, and I realize how clever Casina has been, first in advertising her connection to the very respected General Fabius, and then in taking care of this matter herself. Had it been anyone but her, the intervention would almost certainly have prompted a much bigger fight, but she, tiny as she is, doesn't present a challenge to anyone.

"No one," she observes after a moment. "All right. Everyone who wishes to celebrate and dine is most welcome. Felicia, Prima, send that table," she directs, gesturing to the table of soldiers, "more wine. They look parched. And send that table more wine too." She nods in the direction of the table where Naevius sits. "And everyone," she says, shooting a dark look at Naevius, "let's have no more arguments or political debate—right? Candria?"

Candria emerges to sing once more, and Casina slips back into the culina. I step out onto the street to get air. I spy a knot of soldiers lingering near the fountain, making jokes at the expense of their fallen colleague, and then gathering him up to take their carousing to another caupona. At the same time an impatient customer shoves past me to nab a seat in the Cerium. What an immensely active city Rome is, I reflect. I lift my face to the sky and view a vast emptiness dusted with luminous particles scattered by the gods. Who has not stood beneath the open night sky and felt exposed and small? The west wind puffs her cheeks and exhales, sending the combined fragrances of river, reeds, wood smoke, and grilled meats to swell the Cerium's awnings and toss my hair.

Later that night, after I have retired, the door opens a crack. Felicia steps across the sill into the close darkness of my cubiculum and crawls into bed beside me.

"Where were you?" I whisper as she snuggles close and I pull the blanket around her.

"With a client," she replies quietly.

I should have known that would be her answer; what other answer could I have expected? "That took a while," I observe after a moment. "I was expecting you earlier."

"He was in a bad mood. We argued, so I had him leave— and now," she stretches and settles her head upon my shoulder, "I'm here. It'll mean I have to find someone else later in the week, to make up for the time he wasted," she broods.

We huddle close. The straw mattress rustles comfortably beneath our bodies. Above us, doves march like centurions across the roof. "The Plebeian games are approaching," I remind her, trying to lift her spirits. "You should accompany me."

"That's a busy time for the Cerium," she replies. "You may have to find someone else."

"You won't be occupied the entire time," I reason. "Come when you can."

"What would we do?" she asks after a moment.

"We would attend the plays, of course," I tell her, "maybe view the chariot races. We could escape the crush of the crowds, slip upriver to where hot springs enter and go swimming,"

"Swimming," she scoffs, and gives me a playful nudge. "At this time of year? And how many girls have you slept with who know how to swim?"

"That doesn't matter. I could swim and you could simply admire my prowess and drape yourself on a rock in the sun looking pretty."

She makes a rude noise. "That sounds enjoyable for you, anyway."

I brush my fingers along the hollow at the base of her throat. Is there any smoother, warmer, softer, more delicate spot in all of creation?

"Beyond you ogling me, and me freezing against a rock," she continues, "what would we do?"

"I'd buy you a honeycake, in celebration of the gods," I say, and twist a lock of her hair between my fingers. "You like honeycake, don't you?"

She props her chin against my collarbone. "Honeycakes are nice."

"We could bring bread and cheese with us," I continue, improvising. "Carry fruit. Refresh ourselves in water and let the warming sun dry us—"

"—and *freeze* while waiting for the sun to dry us," she corrects me.

"We'd carry additional wine to warm us. We'd drink to Jupiter for beneficence and Dionysus for eloquence and toast one another on our good fortune. I'd amuse you—I can be amusing when I try. I'd write poetry about you." I stroke her arms. "Doesn't that sound inviting?"

"I don't know—it depends on what you wrote," she says. "What kind of poetry would it be?"

"The best kind. Poetry that praised your gifts, your wit, your beauty. Poetry that celebrated the great good luck that permitted us to find one another. And of course we'd have more wine with us—we'd have to drink a lot of wine to genuinely become warmer. The banks of the Tiber fill pretty quickly with families picnicking, but there are places you can go where the crowd thins, and the trees create a discreet shelter," I add. "There we might participate in other activities."

"You asked if I was from the country, but it's *you* that's just a country boy at heart. The simple pleasures," she scoffs, but she takes up my right hand and kisses the inside of the palm. "What other country activities do you have in mind? Would we snare birds?" she asks as she slides up my body. "Would we go fishing?"

"Perhaps," I say, as my left hand glides down her back, and draws her closer.

"What would we catch?" she whispers.

10

As I work on the play, despite my best efforts, I find the text wriggling beneath my hands, lurching in new and unexpected directions. This unsettling movement unbalances me. The unfortunate truth is that the imagination is a poorly trained horse. You never absolutely control it, and sometimes you can only barely hang on. It may refuse to trot in some directions regardless of your most urgent urgings, and it may gallop in other directions unbidden.

The noise and bustle of the Cerium provides the right ferment for my work, and I stake out the same table each day to sit and scratch my frantic notes. Toward the end of the day, just prior to the Plebeian Games, Naevius squeezes through the crowd and straddles a bench at my table. It's obvious from the way he holds his mouth that something troubles him.

"What is it?" I ask while completing a scene.

"The well has been poisoned," he announces enigmatically. "The field has been salted."

"What well?" I ask, striking as neutral a tone as possible. "What field? What are you talking about?"

"I'm no longer to be included in the Ludi of Florales," he explains. "They have cast me aside."

"How do you know that?" I ask. "And who's *they*?"

He grasps the pitcher on the table and pours from it into an empty cup he has picked up who knows where and drinks.

"I am closely connected to the gens Flamininus and have an especially long and friendly association with Titus Quinctius Flamininus following our time spent fighting in Sicily. He recently sent me private communications indicating that he has received strong pressure to strike me from the roster."

"Have you done anything to change his original inclination?" I ask. "Done something to cause alarm?"

Naevius dismisses these questions with a wave. "I've been quiet as a mouse. I might as well be invisible, I have kept such a low profile. It has to be the Metelli exerting themselves. Or maybe someone of the Scipios. Or both."

I can see that I won't be getting any further writing done while my friend is in so agitated a state, so I put the tablet aside. "I thought you had reconciled with them," I remind him.

"Obviously they have forgiven me sufficiently to set me free," he explains, "but not enough to permit me to write."

I consider the problem. There have always been powerful families striving for prominence in Rome. The poet's challenge has been to draw close enough to these figures of influence to attract their necessary support, while at the same time maintaining an appropriate distance to prevent being dragged into their conflicts. "Is there something you can do?" I ask.

"Nothing," he says, draining his cup and refilling it.

"Perhaps you should speak with them," I suggest.

"You have no understanding of the situation," he says dismissively, waggling his brimming cup at me for emphasis. "They almost had me killed. They may have set me free, but they have no desire to converse with me."

"There must be some action you can take," I insist, "someone you can approach indirectly."

"Their pride is completely out of proportion with their abilities. They're rich and powerful, and that gives them all the permission they need to do whatever they wish. They cannot bear criticism, cannot apologize, cannot forgive real or imagined insults."

"Well," I conclude, having exhausted my meagre supply of advice, "what will you do then?"

"I don't know," he says gloomily, and looks down at the graffiti that someone has scratched into his bench, a crude figure drawing of three individuals engaged in a complicated sexual act. Then suddenly his head pops up and he says, "You!"

The utterance occurs so suddenly, and seems so connected to nothing that we have been talking about that I glance down at the drawing to see if perhaps someone has scratched my name beside one of the stick figures. Thankfully, this doesn't appear to be the case. "What?" I ask.

He turns his attention to me. "You could approach them on my behalf."

"Me?" I check to see if he is joking. Unfortunately, no. "Approach who? And say what?"

"The Metelli," he says. "That I must be permitted to write."

"How can that possibly work?" I ask him. "You said yourself that I don't know them—I'll never be able to convince them of anything."

"That you don't know them is perfect," he insists. "They have no argument or issue with you."

"Listen to me," I urge, attempting to appeal to his sense of reason. "You've picked the wrong man. It's the ox asking the lamb to speak on its behalf at the sacrificial altar."

He places a hand on my shoulder. "You must do it for me."

"Why me?" I ask.

"Because the old ruling families trust you," he argues. "You are the voice of innocent and blameless comedy, comedy of mistaken identity and sexual misadventure, comedy stripped of politics, ambition, or censure. They will understand the truth of the situation coming from you."

"How is that possible?" I protest. "*I don't understand the truth of the situation. I don't even understand what the situation is.*"

"Which makes you," he assures me, "the perfect person to explain it to them."

Overhead, crows loop in lazy circles, mocking me as I walk. I had been advised that I would find Quintus Caecilius Metellus at the Circus Maximus. Apparently his passion is horses and he spends an enormous amount of his time and money preparing them for the races. I trudge the road like an ass whipped to its duty and curse like a pimp cheated of his fee. I curse Naevius, certainly, and I curse the Metelli as well, and all the self-absorbed, self-inflated patrician families and the corrupt system of appointments and patronage that governs this land, but first, principally, and most of all I curse myself. I curse myself for my weakness and inability to say no. I swear by Jupiter the greatest and most powerful, and Apollo the most just, and all the gods that ever were, that I will never, ever again find myself in a situation like this. Dust billows up underfoot. I choke on it, and curse it as well.

As I traverse the shallow bowl of the Murcia valley it is possible to detect the faint sound of horses whinnying and the drum of hooves against the packed earth of the racetrack.

The rich smell of straw and dung grows stronger. I choose the east entrance to the circus and pass under the shadowy stone archway. Crossing into the sunny expanse of the long, oval-shaped arena, I see a chariot drawn by two black horses round the bend, not truly galloping full out but running steadily nonetheless. Up in the stands I spy a cluster of men in togas, one of whom I hope, from the information I've received, will be Quintus Metellus.

Reluctantly, I climb the steps and find my anxiety makes each new step harder to mount than the last. Before I reach the top of the stairs one of the servants separates from the group and calls down to me, "What do you want?"

I halt and call up, "Your health. Is the honourable Quintus Caecilius Metellus here?"

Silence. My voice ricochets off the steps of the stadium. The servant doesn't respond, and although others must have heard me, no one answers. I feel myself break into a heavy sweat.

"I heard that Quintus Caecilius Metellus was at the Circus," I begin again, and when nobody interrupts me, or responds to the question implicit in that statement, I continue, "but perhaps my information was wrong. May I leave a message with one of you gentlemen for him?"

More silence. Then one of the toga-clad figures speaks up.

"I've seen you before," he says. "You're the playwright, aren't you?"

"Yes," I respond, still uncertain whom I am addressing.

A sudden horrible feeling strikes me that they may have mistaken me for Naevius and I awkwardly attempt to correct that impression. "That is, I am the playwright Titus Maccius Plautus," I say.

The man's brow wrinkles in confusion. "Who?"

"Plautus," another replies wearily. "One of the poets Flamininus has scheduled for the Ludi of Apollo."

"Yes? What would you want?" the first man asks. His manner is dismissive, and the tone he employs is what one would use when addressing the very slowest pet. I feel my face flush, but ignore it.

"I have come to say. That is, I have come to ask a favour, humbly. Very humbly." I had wrestled with how to phrase this request as I walked, but now that I am here, I cannot find the correct way to broach the matter.

"Yes?" he prompts. "What favour?"

"It is," I begin hesitantly, "in regards to a fellow poet, Gnaeus Naevius. He is—"

"—a pig rooting in filth," someone from the rear of the pack interrupts me.

"A wasp," another voice suggests, "too inebriated on fermented fruit to fly straight, but still able to sting."

"A rabid dog," a third proposes, "howling and biting wherever he goes. Had he not foamed and frothed he would not have been fettered."

They find this enormously funny and collapse in laughter on one another. I smile and nod, as though they had said something sensible and smart. Obviously, they're drunk. Perfect.

I feel the sweat pooling at my collarbone and trickling in slick rivulets between my shoulder blades. I recall Naevius's unhappy story of his imprisonment, and wonder what punishments an intoxicated Metellus might apply to someone impertinent enough to defend his most public critic. "That is what I have come to speak with you about. On his behalf. He is, as you know, an esteemed writer." Someone makes a scoffing sound, but I carry on as though I heard nothing. "After all, who can offer anything but praise for his celebrated poem *The Punic Wars*, which was a very patriotic work?"

One of them hoots at this. "Are you making him out to be a patriot?" he demands.

"A patriot? No. Not a patriot, exactly," I acknowledge.

"*Exactly?*" the same voice mocks.

"He has," I plow on, hoping that if I raise my voice and speak faster, they will permit me to finish a thought, "I admit, in the past developed something of a bad reputation, not entirely undeserved, that he is now devoutly attempting to put behind him. He has, perhaps, been overly candid, and his writing sometimes, like the lemon, is acerbic. But the lemon also adds savour to a meal, and without Naevius the literary canon loses its zest. The community I belong to, the community of poets and writers, is not a large one. There are so few truly talented individuals, we are not like the Greeks, blessed with artists who spring from the vineyards, like Aeschylus, or who toil in caves like Euripides. Roman writing is just in its infancy. It seems a shame not to employ the ones who have genuine talent."

My speech is greeted with stony silence. It's difficult to determine if this results from appreciation of my eloquence, or is the stunned hush of the truly bored. One of the racing enthusiasts, a man a little taller than the others, separates himself from his colleagues to address me.

"As you say, the Greeks have many writers," he says, drawing closer. "Are you familiar with Aesop?"

"A very great moralist," I answer.

A servant holds out a tray of breads, cheeses, and olive oil. He plucks a crust up as he moves closer. "He offers an instructive tale of a farmer who scared cranes away from his crops by waving an empty sling. That worked for a bit. But in time, the birds, seeing that they weren't actually hurt, ignored him. The farmer, irritated by their continued depredations, genuinely armed his sling with stones and dispatched several cranes. The others, seeing that there would be no more idle gestures, fled."

He dips the bread in oil, and draws it to his mouth. "You see," he says, "When words will no longer do, actions—" he gestures with a crust of bread, a drop of the vinegar arcing through space to spatter my knee "—actions must prevail."

I do not want to argue, nor, given the political stature and the inebriated state of those I am addressing, can I afford to even give the appearance of arguing. And, I don't think that he is the type to be swayed by argument in any case. When dealing with the powerful, I remind myself, the most important strategy is to agree and agree and agree.

"You are absolutely right," I announce. "There are many lessons to be learned from the venerable Aesop. In another fable, I believe he tells of a farmer who held a grudge against a certain troublesome fox that was eating his chickens. The farmer captured the fox, and decided to teach it, and by extension, other foxes a lesson. He plucked up a rag, soaked it in oil, tied it to the fox's tail. Then he set the rag on fire and released the fox. Instead of fleeing for the forest or his den, however, the fox raced straight into the farmer's field, where it set the entire crop aflame."

The man I assume is of the Metellus family chews his bread a long moment, then returns the crust to the supervision of a slave and wipes his hands clean of crumbs. The expression on his face changes, and not in a pleasant way.

"Do I understand you to be threatening me?" he asks quietly.

"No!" I step back in surprise. In my swift retreat, I stumble over a crack in the flooring and nearly take a tumble into another row of benches. "No, no. What could make you think that?"

"Are you warning me that you," he says, pointing, "or he, will set my properties on fire?" He presses close and I can feel his heat, every bit as much as if he had been set alight and raced to engulf me. I wonder what I can possibly say to remedy this situation. I reflect briefly on how poor my communication skills are for someone who pretends to be a communicator.

And then I hear a familiar voice speaking. "I believe," it says, "the story—murky as it is—is one that extols the virtues of forgiveness."

"Yes, exactly," I say, a great rush of relief washing over me as I turn and see Titus Quinctius Flamininus climbing the steps.

"Revenge is a dangerous emotion, it proclaims," Titus Flamininus continues. "Eschew it. Now why are you chasing my playwright about? Can a person not relieve himself without some unpleasant incident arising? As it turns out, I agree with Plautus and Aesop both. I have said it before and I will say it again, it would be far better if your gens let this rascal Naevius carry on with his craft."

"Craft," my opponent grumbles. I can see that he is not so much a debater as he is a repeater of the phrases of others.

"Be reasonable, Marcus," Titus says, finally identifying the individual confronting me: Marcus Veturius Metellus, a nephew of the high-ranking former consul Quintus Metellus. "You can't very well have him released one day and then not let him write the next. That just makes you appear petty and insecure."

"What would you suggest?" Marcus asks, turning to face Titus. "My family won't be the object of his calumny. I have told you that."

"And I say once more, let him write."

"Let him write, let him write," Marcus echoes impatiently. "What if it were you and your family he slandered?"

"I would say exactly the same things I have said, and I would act in accordance with those thoughts. Permit him licence. Offer him liberty. He will either reward your trust, or he will not. However, the law is very clear about calumny, and Naevius certainly knows by now that you are not the kind of people to permit lawbreaking of any sort to go unpunished. And yet, if your family forgives him now, it will make you appear confident, gracious, and exceedingly generous. Everyone respects confidence and grace, and there is nothing that the public loves more than generosity. And it is exactly this kind of gesture that the plebeians will recall later when votes are required. Now," he says, returning his attention to the race track, "the horses are becoming restless, they're stamping at the starting line, and our poor charioteers are looking up at us anxiously and wondering if we have abandoned them. I believe we have a wager to settle. Can we send our poet along to return to his writing, and return ourselves to matters of greater consequence?"

I recognize a cue when I hear one. I make my hurried goodbyes, turn and exit back down the stairs. As I quickly leave the stadium I hear the sound of footsteps behind me. I turn and see the slave Matho running after me.

"My master has a note for you," he tells me, and passes me a tablet. I take it from him and turn to go, but he places a restraining hand on my arm. "He asked that you read it in my presence."

"I see." I look down at the tablet and read. "I wanted to have a quiet word with you before you left," the Aedile has written. "Tell my friend, Naevius, that I will work things out with the curale, and I am sure he will be persuaded to make some arrangement, but you may want to remind him that, as they say, to lay aside Aesop for a moment and go with a more traditional Roman proverb, 'to blunder twice is not allowed in war.' Really, as you have seen, it's barely allowed once."

"And I am to take that from you," Matho says after I've finished reading.

I thank him and return the tablet. The Aedile is a cautious one.

11

The weather takes a foul turn the next day. Aquilo, the north wind, scatters leaves in his wake. Men clip briskly through the streets, clutching their robes close. I forego the early morning procession beginning the Ludi Plebei, and the sacrifice to Jupiter, Mars, and Quirinus. Instead, I make my way to the plays later in the day. As Felicia predicted, she is busy with a client, so I proceed on my own. Wrapped in a thick paenula to keep out the wind, I hike to the Circus Flaminius, where a theatre has been constructed for the ludi. It's trim and functional, although I'm proud to note that it lacks the handiwork or detail that Grippus and Pappius applied to ours. There are six plays presented in a rush over two days, three a day. I attend the first three, and run into Naevius as I return to the Cerium.

"You saw the plays?" I ask him. He nods. "And?"

"I found it hard to distinguish one dreary comedy from the other," he says, shrugging, "they were so similar in tone and style they ran together like paint on a wet surface." We pass a merchant closing his stall for the day, wrapping and packing up tiny ceramic representations of actors. "But this isn't the moment to debate the failings of the comic form. I wanted to thank you for addressing the Metelli on my behalf."

The merchant extends a pot-bellied, bearded figurine to us. "Take something funny home with you, citizens? One of the clowns," he suggests, his face lifting into the broad happy folds of his smiling ceramic statue. "Everyone loves clowns!" Neither Naevius nor I are so inclined, and the merchant drops his pitch and his smile as we pass him, tosses the figure back into his cart and draws a sheet of protective fabric over it with a snap.

"Have you heard anything?" I ask Naevius.

He shakes his head gloomily. "Nothing."

We continue walking in silence, as I try to find words of encouragement. "Beyond that, you're well?" I ask.

"The food served at my cousin's is plainer than army rations. My cubiculum is a wood box so tiny I must stand and remove myself to scratch, and so noisy at night I wrap my head in my toga to muffle the racket. Jupiter strike me if it wasn't quieter on campaign." The wind gusts and we pull our cloaks tighter. "Yet, here we are," he concludes, "and neither of us young men."

"No."

We share a few other general observations about the plays before he trudges homeward. The following day I leave early for the ludi. The weather is only mildly warmer, but there are, of course, many festive activities to observe, if one cares to. I attend a mime performance, in which I view Candria. I assume she has been loaned out by Casina for the period of the ludi. She acquits herself well, dancing the role of the sultry Barbarian Queen Omphale in *The Loves of Hercules*.

One enterprising soul has trained four tiny dogs to race around a makeshift track, leaping barriers as they compete with one another. The dogs—more comedians than athletes—participate eagerly; then, once a circuit is completed, turn like children to beg their reward from the crowd. The smallest, a scamp with drooping ears, growls if he feels the reward is not commensurate with his efforts. The audience applauds his pluck, and of course tosses additional coins onto a mat spread for this purpose by the owner.

Orestes joins me to watch the dogs, but remains unmoved by their antics and offers nothing when they finish. He says teaching performers of any kind to ingratiate themselves with the audience transforms art and sacrifice into beggary. He too has his paenula wrapped tightly about him, and his hood up. Normally he scorns cold weather, so I assume fall has truly arrived. We stroll across the field together to find seats for the plays. As we approach the benches, Orestes nudges me, "Look who's approaching," he whispers. "Stay calm." His eyes are keener than mine and I strain to identify the stranger.

"Plautus!" a voice calls. I still can't make out for sure who it is, but as he draws closer I conclude it must either be a goat someone has squeezed into clothing or it's—

"Pellio!" I return. "I enjoyed your play." This is a hideous lie, but obligatory. His play—a dreary adaptation of *Philemon* by Livius Andronicus—presented yesterday, was interminable, but I have no wish to enter into another embarrassing shouting match.

"Thank you. I missed yours when it was performed at the Lentelus funeral," he replies. "My grex was summoned to perform elsewhere—we're always being called away by fans, it's such a nuisance. What was it I heard you presented?" He appears to search his memory. "*The Pot of Gold?*"

"Yes."

"It must be a comfort to revisit those old treasures," he condescends. "I understand it went well?"

"Yes," I answer shortly. "Very well."

"Excellent. It's wonderful," he reflects, "that you are able to provide Antipho with work at his age."

"I feel blessed," I return, ignoring his slight, "to have someone with his experience and talent.

"And it's generous of you to provide those youngsters in your grex an opportunity to perform." You would believe I had snatched newborn babes from their nursing mothers, the way he describes them. "But I'm sure," he continues, "their enthusiasm does much to compensate for what they lack in genuine experience."

Not wanting to test the limits of my control, I look for an excuse to extract myself from this conversation and am opening my mouth to make my farewell when he announces, "We'll be presenting at the Ludi of Apollo as well. Will you be offering something new then, or repeating one of your previous gems?"

"New," I say.

"Perfect!" he exclaims brightly. "Though I'm sure that will prove challenging for Antipho, he'll have to start taking extra naps to make certain that he's up to the memorization."

Pricked by his insults and feeling I have contained myself long enough, I reply, "We'll make sure our play is briefer than some, so that it won't tax his memory—or the audience's patience." Pellio's smile stiffens. The play his grex offered yesterday is by far the longest of this, or several, ludi.

"I hope you are not referring to the length of our plays," he replies tersely. "Our plays are long, but we offer a value that other gerges cannot."

"I couldn't agree more," I concur. "I came away from your very valuable presentation rested and refreshed from my long sleep."

His face darkens. "Of course you slept—you're ancient! Ancient and irrelevant!"

"And *you*," I exclaim, "are an insult to acting and a blemish on the very ass of the theatre!"

He takes a threatening step closer, I take a step closer to him, and Orestes quickly moves between us.

"This conversation lacks dignity," Orestes cautions us, "and reflects poorly on both of you."

Pellio stands chewing his lower lip a moment, white spots surfacing on his flushed cheeks. "Well," he says at last between tightly gritted teeth, "this will be an opportunity to see what distinguishing character your grex offers in comparison."

"Yes," I agree, "it will be a welcome opportunity."

"Very welcome!" he snaps.

"I just said that!"

"And I will say it again! It is very welcome. I welcome it and look forward to it and anticipate it with all my heart."

Our pleasantries concluded, Pellio stiffly turns and exits in the direction of Subura. As Orestes and I make our way to the benches, Orestes attempts to reassure me. "Never mind his bluster," he says. "Pellio's grex is made up more of merchants than actors, and he is the worst offender. Noisy, artificial, and self-absorbed. Nothing he says means anything and Antipho is ten times the actor he is."

"He is," I agree, "but the audience has grown accustomed to tricks and puffery, and Pellio is thirty years younger than Antipho. His grex is experienced. He's been working with them for the last seven years, and I've been absent the last two. He's not above planting people in our audience to disrupt our performance, and will do whatever he can to outshadow our work."

Orestes shrugs, unmoved. "In the end, what matters most is what *we* do, not others."

"True," I answer. But what I think to myself and don't say is that it is also true that we will have to distinguish ourselves, just as His Most Lush and Resplendent Hairiness predicted. No person is so great a fool that they cannot be occasionally and accidentally brilliant. If I am to distinguish my work from the others on the menu, a timid vision will not serve.

This continues to run through my mind as Orestes and I find our seats and get comfortable, and I begin to envision a new direction for my writing. We have only settled in when the first play of the day commences. Just as the actors enter to outline the plot, a scowling, elderly man prowls the edge of the audience, finds his servant among the audience, climbs over benches to lay hands upon him. The actors on stage, aware of the disturbance, compensate by bellowing their lines like sailors in a storm. An irritated audience member stands, and in a loud voice commands the master and his servant to hush. The servant and master depart, still grumbling.

The actors attempt to recover, but moments later another interruption occurs, this time in the form of a tall man with a crow perched upon his shoulder. The man stalks by the audience, and carefully withdraws and juggles four, brightly coloured pieces of fabric. They float in the air, brilliant puffs of gold, green, and red. He lingers only a short time, but in that instant the damage is done. A ripple rolls through the audience. Eyes are cast in his direction to watch him go past. The deciding moment occurs when a hoarse voice summons us to "Come see Marcus, juggler and phenomenalist." The voice is particular, and when I focus on the speaker, I realize that it is the man's trained crow. Six or seven men arrive at that same realization, and immediately vacate their seats. A certain desperate stiffening can be detected in the posture of the cast, as they strive through sheer force of will to compel the audience to remain seated. The audience wavers, considers their options, and then ten or twelve others rise and race after the juggler.

Later, as we leave the Circus Flaminius, Orestes asks me, "What did you think?"

"This last play," I observe, "*The Well-Digger*, had a decent script, if somewhat thin."

"The second," Orestes disagrees, "*The Muses*, was, I thought, the more faithfully translated."

"Faithfulness?" I groan. "I don't want *faithfulness* from a comedy."

"What do you want?" he demands.

"What do I want? Merciful Gods, I want *comedy* from a comedy!"

"Faithfulness to the original intention is hardly a flaw," Orestes argues. "The plays extracted from Athenian libraries worked well when they were first performed."

"Hundreds of years ago," I reply, "in Athens. Romans are different.

"Alas," Orestes comments drily.

"Look," I tell him, "there is no point producing comedy that doesn't stir the audience. These accurate translations are wonderful for scholars and historians, but a waste of time for viewers."

"They could benefit from selective editing and better music," Orestes allows. "Nevertheless, I felt pity for the actors when that scoundrel juggler poached their audience."

"Did you?" I ask. "I didn't. We should amuse and amaze our audience. If we can't compete with distractions, then our efforts deserve to fail."

"Oh?" Orestes says, raising his eyebrows. "So if that juggler should appear at your presentation?"

"Steal his crow," I advise him. "I've always wanted a talking bird."

That night, I feel inspired. Pellio's challenge lights a fire under me. I ignore the wax tablets and set out putting words directly to papyrus. When I awaken the next morning, I continue scribbling. Orestes arrives later in the day for coena and I thrust the fresh scroll into his hands.

"There," I announce. "Take that away and read it. There are significant changes. The slave of our play is renamed Tyndarus, and his master, Philocrates. Now both are captured, and held by a wealthy Aetolian named Hegio. As before, Philocrates's winnings are carried ahead to his sister. As before, the bride-to-be pines, and is wooed by Smikrines. But in this version, Tyndarus and Philocrates swap identities—slave with master—so that Philocrates will be perceived to be the less valuable property and consequently selected to return home to negotiate a proper exchange of the more valuable captives."

"Interesting twist," Orestes muses. "Good."

"Together they fool their captor, Hegio," I add. "Philocrates is released. He promises his slave, Tyndarus—now pretending to be Philocrates—that he will return to purchase his freedom. Solo song of triumph, followed by the pair singing their farewell. The real Philocrates returns home to set things right.

"And the slave, Tyndarus?"

"Remains languishing in confinement, pretending to be someone he isn't."

"Tough for him," Orestes observes, "but courageous and dramatic."

"There's another turn, though," I continue. "Tyndarus has his true slave-identity accidentally revealed by another prisoner, so the exchange of captives is ruined. Hegio, who had intended to employ the high-ranking prisoner as a set piece in his exchange between the two warring nations to free his own captured son, becomes furious."

"An exciting turn of events—then what?"

I shake my head. "What I've given you takes us up to this point."

Orestes passes the scroll from one hand to another, as though he could determine the dramatic value of the story through its weight. "It's a little dark," he suggests cautiously.

"I thought of that, but I chewed on what that fool Pellio said the other day about distinction, and I think Roman theatre, a real Roman theatre, can afford to present a splash of garum along with its honey—this must be a comedy with a bite! And I've added a comic freedman, Ergasilus, a glutton who will assist Hegio in whatever way he can in exchange for a meal—he should generate some laughs."

"And which part do you see Antipho playing?" Orestes asks.

"He's the right age for Hegio," I tell him, "and it's a major part."

"With your permission, then, I'll have him read this aloud," he says, holding up the scroll, "I'd like to have the casting settled as quickly as possible, so we can determine which masks we'll need. Will you have enough finished by Saturnalia that I can invite the entire cast to come together? It will be early, but we'll want to get an early attack since we're doing a new play."

"Certainly."

Orestes tucks the scroll inside his wallet. I set my stylus and ink aside, and treat myself to a delicious meal of turnips cooked with pig's feet. Outside the wind bends trees, chasing most of the Cerium's customers home before the impending rain. There are only a few patrons remaining when Naevius enters and sits heavily on the bench beside me. He catches Pomona's eye and calls out rather grandly, "I will have some of your very cheapest wine."

"You seem happy," I tell him, and he does. His face is flushed, his neatly trimmed beard bristles with excitement.

"I am happy," he says. "I am extremely happy."

"Why?" I ask. "What's happened?"

"I'm officially a poet once more," he announces in a loud voice. "The Aedile has extended me an invitation to write."

The remaining customers lingering at a scattering of tables hear the news and cheer. I clap him on the shoulder, and Pomona returns with his wine.

"Then you have been included in the roster for the Ludi Florales?" I ask.

"I have not," he answers. "The invitation to submit a tragic work has been withdrawn."

"No!" I exclaim. "Then what?"

"Brother," he says, "I salute you. You and I will both be participating in the Ludi of Apollo."

"Congratulations!" I rejoice, and find I am very happy for him. I drink to his good fortune and then consider him over the cup. "But I thought you were done with comedy."

"I was," he answers.

"I thought it was a degradation?" I remind him.

"It is," he admits.

"I thought it was a whore's art?"

"Most certainly," he agrees, and takes a long pull from his cup. "It absolutely is."

"What happened?"

"Obviously," he says, refilling the cup and raising it once more to me, "I am a whore. To whores, everywhere!"

"Pomona!" I call. "More wine. This man is buying."

12

The following morning I sit at a table scratching down thoughts about Menander—he has such a wonderful knack for starting his plays with energy and surprise, he draws the audience into the story instantly—when Orestes enters. Instead of joining me, though, he remains standing. "I have to talk to you," he says.

"Go ahead," I tell him, surprised at this sudden formality.

"It's about Antipho," he continues.

"Yes," I reply, trying to finish my line of thought before I look up. "What about him?"

"He's dead."

In an instant I feel all the blood drain from my head. "Wait," I say, and push the wax tablet aside. "Wait. How is that possible?"

Orestes ponders my question a moment, then shrugs. "I met with him, as I said I would, and asked him to read from the script. He did. He read the part of Hegio and was brilliant. We went to a popina for a bite. He had just ordered. Crispus and Verinus joined us, and suddenly he stood up."

"And?" I ask. "He what . . . choked?"

Orestes shakes his head, and I can see that he is searching for the correct words to describe what happened. "No, he just . . . stood up. Swayed a moment, looked about. Then dropped to the floor."

I attempt to digest the news, but can't. It's as though I'm unable to get a firm purchase on the words themselves, they just slither past. "And he was what?" I ask. "Dead? In that instant? Just like that?"

"Yes," Orestes says.

"You saw this?" I ask. "You saw his body?"

"Yes."

"How is that possible? When has standing up killed a person?" I demand. "Nobody dies from rising out of a chair!"

"Still," Orestes replies as he rubs his brow. "Still. That's what happened."

I try to imagine what I am being told. The last time I saw Antipho, he had looked perfectly healthy, laughing and drinking as usual.

"Did he say anything?" I ask, finally.

"Nothing much," Orestes answers. "He placed his right hand over his cheek, asked if his face looked different. Rose suddenly, as I told you, and fell over."

My mind races ahead as I struggle to project myself into a future that exists without him. All I can see is the immense, gaping hole his absence has generated. "Did it?"

"What?"

"Did his face look any different?" I ask, although I don't really care. What does it matter what his face looked like?

"Not so anyone could tell," he replies. "It was quick." He sits at last, joining me. There seems nothing else to add. We remain lost in our separate thoughts a long moment. "What will we do now?" he asks me.

"I don't know."

The funeral ceremonies are held the next day. If Antipho were a richer man, his body might have been kept over for viewing, but he wasn't, so it isn't. It is to be a simple ceremony, arranged by the Actors Guild. A cremation, followed by the interment of his ashes. I walk along the Tiber late in the afternoon and smell the pine needles and wet earth underfoot. A gull wobbles low overhead, releases a little rasping cry like a sob, like it has lost something important, then glides on.

The body is simply a leather mask that the spirit slips on when we are born. This is never so evident as when a person passes away, and you observe the shell stripped of its animating inner force.

Poor old Antipho. When he first performed, I remember he made the audience laugh so hard that one indiscreet member of the audience actually sprayed the people seated in front with food. And the individuals in front who were sprayed were laughing that hard that they didn't mind. I saw Antipho—*wriggle* is the wrong word—but he was like a dog that has been praised. He shivered with pleasure at the sound of the applause, and I knew then what a blessing it is to have an actor so completely, utterly devoted to satisfying his audience. And now, there he is, a skeleton draped in a cape of mottled skin and a few wisps of limp, grey hair.

We attend the funeral procession arranged by the Actors Guild, then the cremation. His body is lifted and positioned upon a bier, anointed with aromatic oils, the kindling ignited. Inky smoke spirals up to the heavens, lifting his spirit. I contribute money to help erect a copper marker at the puticuli at the Campus Esquilinus.

After the ceremonies are concluded, we retire to his cramped home in Subura, where we drink cheap red wine and share stories about Antipho.

"He loved food. He loved drink. He loved men," Grippus says, and raises his cup. "What an actor. Goodbye."

"I will eat my next meal and think of him," his partner, Crispus says. "Nobody loved ham, sweetbreads, or cheese and wine like he did."

"I remember," Orestes says, "when he performed the part of Moschian. He didn't initially understand it. It wasn't what he was familiar with. He was used to the instant gratification of the more conventional comic roles. But he was not a man to be denied. Each day he left the rehearsal like an herbalist going out to find and retrieve a miraculous healing plant, and would return the next day with at least a couple of pieces of comic business. Bit by bit, he built that part until at last it was something real and substantial. That was *The Girl Who Had Her Head Shaved* and you all know what a success that play was. It could not have succeeded without his energy, his craft, and his dedication to Dionysus." He raises his cup. "To Antipho."

We drink and talk. Share memories. Prop each other up against our suddenly perceived vulnerability. Some drink too much—Grippus passes out. Some weep. Mostly, people adopt stoic postures, pretending that when they return home life will go on as before. We know that's false, however. We leave, when we leave, to a different life, a diminished life.

I stand and raise my cup. "A good actor is a blessing to everyone in our craft. To his fellow actors he raises the standard of each performance—he silences the noisy crowd and places them under his spell. To the playwright, he makes mediocre lines seem rich and entertaining, and he makes good lines sing and seem works of genius. That was what Antipho did. What an actor. He was my Curculio, and my Jupiter. Now he has gone to entertain the gods, whom he will, no doubt, keep very amused. Their great gain, our loss. To Antipho," I toast, and drink.

As I make to leave, Crispus follows me out into the street.

"Bless you, for your contribution to his copper marker," he says. "And for your words. You knew him."

"Thank you," I say.

"No," he continues, "no, you knew him. We poorer folk don't have money for bronze tablets or statues of carved stone. But you, you will celebrate his life in your writing."

"I don't know what I'll write about next," I tell him, "or who."

"You'll find a way. Other writers tell their stories of the rich and powerful. You celebrate the lives of people who own nothing, make nothing, and can't hire a historian to invent facts celebrating their lives. The only person who will have shared the moments of our lives will have been you." He pats me encouragingly on the arm. "You."

"I'm a comedian, not a historian," I remind him.

"You'll know what to do," he insists, nodding his head. "You'll know."

As we return home along the Tiber, Orestes remarks, "You have an admirer."

I say nothing, but keep walking. "Do you think he's right?" Orestes asks me. "Will you immortalize him?"

"Immortalize him? My job is to make people laugh. If Antipho wanted to be remembered in writing he should have kept a journal. If he had eaten and drunk less, and kept a little fitter, he might still be performing in my show. Instead, our grex is beheaded and now finds itself without a lead actor."

"So," Orestes asks. "What now?"

"What now?" I ask, and look at him. "Nothing. We're ruined."

"Surely there's someone else we can hire?" Orestes insists.

I realize he doesn't see it yet. "It's impossible. Who?"

13

I arrive late at the Cerium and, immediately upon sitting, order from Pomona. "I'll take some wine, hot," I tell her and scan the room. "Where's Felicia?"

"Out with a client," she says as she adjusts the fabric over her shoulder. "A single serving or a vase full?"

"A vase full," I answer. "Who?"

"A patron. I don't know," she shrugs and walks away.

Candria emerges and performs, accompanied by a cithara player this time, but I derive no enjoyment from it. Her singing is adept, but the musician is slow and artless, and the pairing grates. I consume my hot wine and order more. In the middle of Candria's set, a young, rather embarrassed-looking slave appears at the street entrance, delivering a request to one of the gamblers that he return home. The drunken citizen—the slave's owner, I suppose—curses him with a level of profanity I would reserve for an ox and orders him to return home at once. The slave, perhaps fearing the owner's wife more than the owner, lingers awkwardly, hoping his master will reconsider. Outraged at this disobedience, the owner leaps up, grasps his slave by an ear, thrashes him and pushes him to the street. When the slave—persistent, if nothing else—hesitates once more, the owner loses what little patience he possessed, draws a knife and threatens to sever the slave's nose. Finally convinced, the slave trudges gloomily into the darkness, perhaps to face a beating at the other end for his failure.

"Bring me more wine," I tell Prima when she passes. As she makes her way to the culina, I trace with my fingertip the steep grooves of an unremarkable rendering of a horse. It's been deeply etched into the tabletop by an individual who obviously had more patience than skill. The sounds of the caupona seem extraordinarily loud to me: the clatter of dice, the roar of soldiers betting and bragging, Candria singing over her distracted audience, the cithara player thumping ineptly upon his instrument. An old plum-faced inebriate, teetering on his elbows over his drink, shifts his bony buttocks and releases a massive, mournful-sounding fart. A lop-tailed hound slithers into the caupona like a bandit, slinks under a table and, after glancing guiltily about, snatches up the thinnest of bones. Two smaller dogs, a black and a white, lying near the counter and seemingly asleep, detect this indiscretion, leap up and give chase. The barking, snapping, growling, and racing around table legs is truly thunderous, and I feel my head will burst like an overripe pomegranate. Apparently ignored in my last request for wine, I call once again to Prima to fetch me a refill, then turn and see that she's occupied at another table where one of the gamblers is wrestling to get up her tunic.

"You wanted something?" Pomona asks, appearing beside me like a ghost.

"Yes," I answer, "wine. And Felicia."

She thumps a vase on the tabletop. "I told you, she's out."

"When will she return?" I ask.

Pomona rolls her eyes. "Am I her procurer?" she demands, and irritated, she wades back into the crowd to serve the next customer. Prima continues to politely resist the manhandling of the gambler and an associate. As their physical exertions grow ever more animated, they haggle over a fee. It's a protracted and complex discussion, complicated by the gamblers' growing excitement, and their critical inability to perform math. "So does that one fee cover two separate times?" one gambler asks her.

"No, two fees, both of you, once," Prima corrects him, pushing an indiscreet hand away.

"But the charge should come out to half-price each," the other gambler protests.

"No," Prima says patiently, "there's two of you. So two payments."

"It's like buying a cake. Lots of people can enjoy it," he nibbles at her shoulder, "but it's still only one cake. So the price," he gestures with a sawing motion, "should be split."

"No, it's like a chariot race," Prima corrects him. "If one of you starts and the other finishes, you need pay only one entry fee. But if you both wish to reach the finish line, you both have to pay." More ardent massaging and haggling ensues.

The three dogs return from their chase up the street in a state of great agitation, one of the original pursuers now in possession of the small bone and pursued by the other two. The dogs skitter across the floor, bang into benches, and release high-pitched yelps. This produces much merriment among some customers, shouts of protest from others.

When the first gambler inquires once more of Prima if it is one payment for two people once, or two payments for each person once, I feel as if time has captured me in a suffocating embrace. I can't breathe. I raise my hands and see that I am sweating.

"It's impossible," I announce loudly to no one in particular as I stand swaying, "to write or think or breathe properly, in this, this, this Circus Seximus!" I gesture dramatically at the room, fall off balance, lean against the table, too heavily apparently, because plates and cups go crashing to the floor and the table itself teeters and collapses to one side. I lurch from the wreckage, maintaining my feet, but tilt into the customers at the table next to me. Someone takes hold of my tunic, perhaps to keep me from tumbling on top of him. "Let go of me!" I object, and slap his hand away. Someone else stands and reproaches me, and suddenly Casina emerges between us. She soothes the upset patrons, draws me aside, and inquires if something is wrong.

"This place is what is wrong," I tell her, "the chaos and clamour, its unceasing uproar. Between hounds howling, over-sexed soldiers boasting of their generous genitals and carnal conquests, the annoying noise of knucklebones knocked about by knuckleheads, I can't hear myself think. I will take leave of this cacophony and go stay with a cousin."

Casina casts a glance at the darkened street. "What? Now?

"Yes."

"Where?" she asks.

"Bottom of the Quirinal," I reply, and gesture in the general direction.

"It's not safe to go wandering the streets at this time of night," she argues, "especially after you've consumed as much wine as you have. Some criminal will knock you down for sport, trample you underfoot, and then wild dogs will eat you."

"Let them try," I announce. "I have marched with my bed on my back, lived hard, and I am too tough a meat for any dog to eat."

"Titus," she says, placing a calming hand on my shoulder, "spend the night here until we can work things out tomorrow."

I shrug off her hand and remain adamant. "There's no room."

"Are you mad? There are many vacant cubiculi," she insists, pointing to the second floor. "If you don't like the one you have been staying in, choose another."

"There are none, I tell you, none that aren't already occupied by, or next to, disorderly, disreputable, diddlers engaged in non-stop scrambling, spewing, and screwing."

"Wait, wait, wait." She places a restraining hand upon my chest. "Wait."

"What?"

"Just listen and don't talk so loud. Come, step outside a moment." I see that she has already cleverly manoeuvred me to the streetside entrance. We step outside together. It's cooler, and I can feel an evening breeze waft up the roadway and brush my hair back. "If you find it too busy and noisy in the upper floor, you can spend the night next door."

This suggestion confuses me. I glance up the street. "Where? In the miller's shop?"

"Shh. It's not the miller's anymore," she says, and draws a key from a chain she has draped around her neck. "He passed away last fall. His wife has been running it this year, but it proved too much for her and she decided to return to her relatives in Antium." She lifts a lamp from one of the tables, and I follow her up the street a few steps. When she arrives at what was once the miller's place, she places the key in a keyhole, and unlocks the folding shutter. She pushes it back, and allows me in. "I purchased the lease. It hasn't become final, so I haven't announced it—and not everything has been moved out. You could spend the night there."

The lamp flickers, casting long, swaying, spectral shadows. Dust is thick in the air, and the faint, phantom smell of bread still lingers. In one corner the immense baking ovens gape like demonic mouths. In another corner enormous vessels for mixing dough tilt and rub shoulders against one another like drunken sentries. The grinding mill looms squat and spidery at the very back, with its massive basalt millstones, the long rod and a harness attached to a strap, and the bowl-like lamina to collect the milled wheat.

"What will you do with this?" I ask, turning about to look, unable to suppress my curiosity despite my temper.

"Knock down the separating wall and divide the space. Half the ground floor will go toward enlarging the Cerium, more tables for the coenatio, and the other half will become a proper separate atrium for entertaining private functions." She points. "Half of the second storey I'll set aside for more cubiculi, and the other half something a bit bigger for me," she says, nodding to the upper level. "The wife of the miller left in a hurry, so the place is a little upside down, but if you want silence, you're well away from all the howling and knucklebone throwers next door. Is it quiet enough for you to stay put?"

I've had my tantrum and now feel the full measure of the unsteadying influence of the wine. The heavy weight of my deep disappointment combines with my fatigue and piles upon me. The threatened long walk in the pitch dark to visit a relative I haven't seen in years has lost its lustre.

"All right," I mumble.

"Good," she says. "Wait here."

She leaves me holding the oil lamp and returns moments later carrying a couple of blankets. She brushes some debris from a countertop and drapes a blanket over it. "You can stretch out here. I'll leave this lamp with you."

"It will take a lot of work," I say, gesturing vaguely at the empty room.

"The sooner you begin it," she replies, "the sooner it will be done."

"Oh, you're contracting me again?" I ask.

"It could be your rent, if you choose to stay on. That is," she adds, "if you can behave reasonably and desist from turning over tables and tormenting the staff with silly questions."

I see that I've cut the knuckles of my right hand, something I must have done when I fought to catch my balance back at the caupona. I place one knuckle to my mouth to stop the bleeding. "I'd be more reasonable with everyone if I were told the truth," I tell her.

"What truth?"

"Where's Felicia?" I ask, and feel a flush of embarrassment, even as the words leave my lips.

Casina stares at me steadily across the flickering lamp, the light catching the chestnut flecks in her eyes. "She's with her soldier, Postumus," she tells me. "But you must know that already."

"When will she return?" I ask.

"She won't," she says simply. "She's moved out and taken her things with her. They left yesterday. He purchased her contract the day prior."

I am not normally predisposed to romantic posturing, but I find the news strikes me hard. "She never even bothered to say goodbye," I say.

Casina runs a hand through her hair. "Would that have made things better?"

"Did you put her up for sale without her knowing?" I ask, avoiding her question.

"Of course not—she initiated the purchase," Casina replies. "She'd been negotiating, trying to arrange it for some time." She sighs and impatiently tucks an offending lock of hair behind an ear. "Look. She's a rich soldier's concubine now. He'll set her up in a proper home, buy her nice clothes and servants, send her presents, and visit her when he returns from his campaigns. When he dies, she'll be granted her manumission. This is as good a deal as she could have wished. Any one of the girls in the Cerium would be delighted with an arrangement like this. Did you imagine she wished to continue working here forever, serving wine and sleeping with clients?"

I stand there considering the sputtering flame of the oil lamp. A frightened mouse, startled into stillness by our entrance and the lamplight, streaks for the comforting and obscuring blackness of a crack in the far wall.

"I was nothing to her, then," I say.

"Are you a child or an adult?" Casina asks. "There are many things you cannot control in life and you must have known this dalliance couldn't last. That she has a better life as his mistress should make you happy. It's the best thing that could have happened to her. Were you paying for her services?"

"No," I admit.

"Did you have any intention to purchase her?"

I shake my head. "No."

"Exactly, no. Then, stop this . . . demonstration. Be an adult. It's quieter here. You won't be disturbed." She places the second blanket in my hands. "Spend the night."

She walks out and closes the shutters behind her. I study my surroundings. The bare, abandoned walls. The upset and chaotic arrangement of the room. The lamplight shivers, endowing everything with a feeling of temporality. A temporary existence, in a constantly changing world.

Sometimes understanding drops into place of its own design. Suddenly I translate the looks and glances Felicia had exchanged with me, and others. The belligerence the soldier had shown me—this was just his response to me as a result of Felicia's attention. The thought strikes me suddenly that our entire relationship might simply have been an elaborate mime designed to make her soldier jealous and incite him to a firm offer. Our relationship had been a performance, and the soldier our audience.

I am not unaccustomed to viewing life in terms of a script, but I am most used to considering myself the principal performer in a story of my own creation. It is a bitter drink when you realize that you have only been an instrument used to advance a larger design in someone else's plot.

The longer I consider it, the more obvious it becomes. How totally blind I had been! Everyone—Casina, Orestes, Naevius, the staff of the Cerium, and all their clients must have looked at me and wondered how I could have been so dim. Casina had even tried to warn me. A hot rush of shame sweeps through me and abruptly I feel an intense need to move. I pace the length of the shop and back, and then the length of the room again. As I walk I lay out certain facts, as though I were a lawyer presenting a case. Fact—I'm fifty-some years old. Fact—I own nothing. I have no son who will attend to my funeral ceremonies, no children to maintain my grave, or propitiate the gods. I have no property. I possess a minor skill at translating Greek into Latin and bit of an aptitude for sawing and nailing boards. What kind of future can that provide? Fact. There are many ways to starve and I have perfected most of them. Failed soldier. Failed shipper. Failed carpenter. Failed performer. After being released from the architecti in the legion I stumbled into, rather than selected, the profession of writing, which is not really a profession at all, but rather a lifelong vow of poverty.

I keep walking and stagger against the leather harness dangling from the mill. Abruptly, I lift an amphora and pour grain into the feeder, slip the halter over my shoulders and strain. If I am going to be as slow-witted as a donkey, I can perform the work of a donkey as well. I take one slow step after another and gradually the immense wheel begins to turn and the stones grate against each other, grinding the kernels between the two unyielding surfaces. There. I have at last found my calling, my career, my most natural profession. I know how to turn in circles—no one better. When in my life had I done anything but? Never getting anywhere, never accomplishing anything, never having impact, just turning, turning, turning. I learned writing. Endured the switch of the tutor. For what? So I could read works written by long-dead Greeks—for what? So I could perform Latin adaptations. To what purpose? To serve the idle rich, to entertain drunks and gasbags who are barely interested in the first place, who can be distracted in an instant, and who promptly forget what they see. And why? So I can put together a tiny sum of money? For what? To piss away in failed shipping investments. To drink away in tabernae and popinae. To throw away at a girl too young for me, who knew nothing about real love, who knew nothing about faithfulness, and who never desired me in the first place.

I pour more grain into the mill and continue pulling. But then what had I ever been faithful to? To the gods of theatre and writing? Of all the gods, the least revered by the public. To the performers who brought the plays I wrote to life, and paced their own tired, tight circles in theatres in small cities and dusty forgettable towns in front of undeserving, unappreciative crowds? I suddenly see Antipho's face once again as he lay upon the bier, mottled skin drawn tight to the bone like a tragic mask shaped on stone mould. I see him again, smoking and then suddenly catching fire. The great wheel squeaks and groans as the rough wooden pole rotates in its dry socket, and the grinding stones release a low, shuddering whine. I pull harder.

I had one opportunity to lift my life out of this pit. One. One opportunity to make something of myself. And now he's dead, and how am I supposed to find anyone close to his abilities in the time I've got? Jupiter piss on him for dying. What a fool's quest and what a foolish old fool I am for believing that there could be anything but debt and failure and complete ruination in writing. There aren't sufficient ludi to perform plays in, there aren't sufficient audiences who appreciate them, there's not enough money to go around, there's a surfeit of headache and heartache. The actors can't learn their lines, and the wretched audience mutter and chatter like magpies through the shows anyway. Let all the gods strip me naked and flail me with a leather lash if I ever pick up a wax tablet to write again, let the god Dionysus plunge me deep into a vat of wine and hold me under if I ever pick up a stylus again, I am done, I am done, by all the gods who ever pulled their togas aside to piss on humans, I am done with this. If I had any other genuine talent, I would perform it, if I knew what merchandise to purchase and how to guide goods safely from harbour to harbour I would have remained in shipping, loading thin graceful boats with precious cargo destined for faraway exotic lands, and I would never again spare the slightest thought for writing, which is just designed to grind you to the finest milled dust between the twin great stones of lost hopes and crushed ambitions. I fall to my knees.

"Good morning."

I am on the stone floor, my cheek pressed flat against cut rock. A shrill scraping sound penetrates my brain. Piercing light streams through the open door. "Good morning," the voice calls again.

I shield my eyes as Casina continues pushing the shutters aside. I make a feeble attempt to rise, fail, and settle for sitting up. "What time is it?" I ask, my voice thick from drinking the night before.

"It's late," she announces. "The city is awake. Customers are arriving. Life is stirring in all corners of the city—with the exception of this one, apparently. Here is a cloth and a pan of water. Wash yourself, you will feel better for it."

I take the bowl from her, dip the cloth in water and apply it to my face. It is refreshing. I drape its wet surface over my eyes, trying to leach out the despair and desolation I had felt the night before. I wipe the back of my neck and my hands and wrists and feel cool solace. I drop the cloth back in the bowl and push it aside.

"I've brought you food," she says, and hands me a warm bun.

I take the bun from her, and as I do so, perform a quick stocktaking. I still have my tunic on, and am sitting half-covered by a crumpled blanket. I see I am coated in dust, resulting from the cloud that was thrown up as I milled wheat the night before.

"Here is some hot water with herbs," Casina places a cup in my hands. "I imagine you'll want something to drink."

I drink. Fingernail-sized buds and leaves float lazily about in it. It smells of lemon and poppies.

"What's in it?" I ask.

"Are you a doctor?" she asks, tartly. "What does it matter? Drink."

She watches silently as I swallow the mixture. "What were you up to last night?" She inquires as she stalks to the mill and taps the dangling halter. "There was quite a racket in here. I see you required freshly milled flour." The halter jangles under her touch. "Is baking another career you have decided to embark upon?"

I continue drinking and don't answer. I truly don't want to pursue it.

"Are you thinking clearer?" she asks me.

"I'm awake," I allow.

"Good. I'm speaking to you as a friend, and as a person who has a professional investment in your ludi entry. Let's talk business for a moment. Can we replace Antipho?"

I drain the substance she has prepared for me. "No."

"I would consider this answer very carefully," she advises. "The grex will be awaiting your response—"

"I don't have a *grex*," I interrupt her. "A grex is formed around an actor of Antipho's stature and I don't have that anymore. What I have now is a loose assembly of minor actors, technicians, and musicians, who came together and performed once. Once. Now that I no longer have Antipho, I don't even have that—when they comprehend the enormity of what has happened, I can expect them to scatter like dandelion seeds in a storm."

"They haven't yet," Casina objects. "They are patiently awaiting direction from you—and where exactly would they scatter to, in any case? Are there that many greges available? And there must be some actor of substance remaining somewhere."

"The ludi will take place in six months and three separate plays have already been commissioned. All the actors of any substance have been contracted."

"Think," she says. "There must be someone, somewhere who can perform this part."

My head aches, and her voice seems to penetrate some sensitive, inner chamber. "Stop saying that. Don't you understand, it is not about finding 'someone'"? We don't want 'someone.' 'Someone' won't do. Even if we could recruit some minor untrained, untalented nobody with no acting experience, reputation or following—the audience wouldn't put up with it. The audience doesn't come to see 'someone' learning their craft leading the play."

"All right," she allows, "what about extending the search beyond the city?"

"Maybe in Syracuse, but by the time we go there, and find someone and get back, there'll be no time to assemble the work."

"Then cut his part and shape the play to be performed without him," she suggests.

"Oh, Jupiter give me strength," I snap. "He was the *lead*."

"There's an actor," Orestes says. He's leaning against the entrance archway looking at us.

I raise my head. "What?" I hadn't realized he had joined us and was listening.

"I know of someone. He's living in the city. Someone with talent and a bit of a reputation."

"Who?" I ask.

"Sostratos."

I set my cup down on the floor. "He's still alive?"

14

The hallway is dimly lit by the thinnest flame of a smoking candle. The walls drip in the corners and the air is thick with the smell of sweat, sex, and urine. In an alcove to the side of the hallway, a lump stirs. I take a step nearer to examine the lump. On closer consideration I can see that it's a kind of human-looking shape, hair long and knotted, the body draped in the remaining strips and pieces of a ragged, soiled tunic. His eyes are bleary and his face framed by a greasy, matted beard.

"Who," he croaks as he slowly rises to his feet, "do you want? Do you want one each, or are you going to share?" I hear voices murmuring down the hallway, and the faint creaking of wooden bed frames.

"Are you Sostratos?" I ask.

His demeanour transforms at once from helpful to belligerent. "What are you, debt collectors?" he shouts, "Go fuck yourselves—I have nothing!"

I hold up a hand to calm him. "I'm here with a possible offer of employment," I say.

His eyes shift suspiciously from Orestes to me and back. "What kind of work?"

"I'm looking for an actor," I tell him. He doesn't respond. "You're an actor, aren't you?"

"I've performed some of the most famous," he says, hesitates as though considering his words carefully, then abruptly releases a rich, sonorous, prolonged belch. "Some of the most famous plays," he concludes mildly.

Beside me, I can feel Orestes blanching.

"What's the matter with *you*?" the lump demands of him. "You've never experienced a little indigestion? After a lavish meal I've been known to recite an entire monologue in one extended, resonant discharge."

Orestes stares impassively at him, then plucks at my tunic. "Can I confer with you a moment?" he asks, and we remove ourselves a few short steps toward the doorway.

"I apologize. This was a terrible mistake on my part," he says. "I was completely wrong to guide you here, and I advise you not to continue this discussion. First of all, clearly he's much worse off than either of us had imagined. I'd heard he had fallen on difficult times, and was struggling, but obviously he has plummeted much, much further. He stinks to the heavens, I don't know when he bathed last, and his breath could singe the hairs from your arms. When a person has descended into baseness of this kind, there's really nothing to be done. Second of all, he once was renowned, yes, but it seems he hasn't been acting for years. Who knows if he can even remember lines anymore? You thought he was dead. Looking at him now, I believe he might as well be."

"I can hear that," the man growls from the recesses at the end of the hall.

"I wasn't trying to conceal what I said," Orestes replies without turning.

"Those are terrible things to infer about someone you have just met," the man retorts.

"And I meant every word," Orestes says and glances at me. "Shall we go?"

"I have performed in some of the finest comedies," the man boasts, "and the most heartrending tragedies. I have toured places as far away as Thrace and Lydia and everywhere, near and far, have moved audiences to tears and laughter."

"Excuse me," Orestes says, turning to face him. "You are presently a kind of janitor/doorman of a lupanar, aren't you?"

The man shrugs. "Yes, *now*."

I hold up my hand to interrupt Orestes and return my attention to this man we believe to be Sostratos. "My friend tells me that you were a notable actor once, and I have heard something of your reputation—if you are, in fact, this individual. Given your present situation, you can surely understand our misgivings. But you can just as easily lay our doubts to rest. Recite something for us."

He sways a little on his feet as he considers this, then wets his lips. "Do you have anything in mind?"

"Something from a comedy," I suggest.

He runs a hand through his stringy hair. "In Greek or Latin?" he asks.

"Whichever you prefer."

He steadies himself and appears to find more solid footing. "What great sorrow," he begins, his voice suddenly clearer, "haven't I experienced in this life? How seldom my moments of genuine enjoyment? While my sadnesses have surpassed the grains of sand that fill the beach, there are only four instances of genuine enjoyment that I recall—but how rich those rare pleasures have been. I was ecstatic when Cleon was compelled by Law to—"

Whatever else has happened to him, I think, he's retained his memory.

"Dicaeopolis," Orestes says dismissively, quickly identifying the character. "That part's young for you."

The man tugs his slipping tunic back onto a shoulder. "I played him when I was younger," he explains.

"Can you do something older?" I ask.

"It was then," he says, launching into another monologue almost at once, "that the city chose to expel me, despite my age, my ill health and ailments, and it was then that my sons who should have stood by their father, chose to do nothing. My sons, who with one word might have eased my suffering, instead allowed me to become a common beggar."

"*Oedipus at Colonus*," Orestes says, raising his eyebrows. "Not exactly a comedy, is it?"

"Depends upon what you find funny," the old man replies, hacking up some horrid something-or-other from deep in his lungs and expelling it into the corner. "And you didn't ask for a comedy this time."

"You can recite," Orestes interrupts him again. "Crows can be taught to recite. Sing something for me."

And he does, just like that. Without warning, preparation, or hesitation, without even shifting his position. He simply opens his mouth and notes spill out, like swallows, one as lovely as the next. I don't recognize the song, but am transfixed. Though drinking has lent him a deep, raspy burr, he still possesses a beautifully rich and textured timbre, and a remarkable range. This is rare as eggs from a cat. All performers have penetrating voices—it's impossible to survive in the theatre unless you are able to reach the audience over the hawkers selling their goods, the crying babies, squabbling drunks, and other competing noises and annoyances of a forum—but there are very few actors who possess singing voices that can genuinely thrill. I glance at Orestes and see him weaken. He is a musician first and foremost and music is what touches his soul most deeply. When Sostratos finishes singing, we tell him to wait there and we walk back outside to consult. I note that Orestes is gnawing on the inside of his cheek, a sign that he is deep in thought.

"Well?" I ask.

He shakes his head but doesn't reply.

"It was a good audition," I prompt him. "You can't say it wasn't a good audition, and under difficult circumstances. And you've seen him in a performance."

"A long, long time ago," he says.

"And?"

"He was good back then," Orestes admits. "Very good. Probably the most complete actor I'd ever seen."

"So?" I ask. "What do you think after hearing him?"

"He was a great performer when I saw him," Orestes recalls, "but that was many—obviously a great many—drinks ago. He auditions well, yes—although he looks monstrous now, scarcely human. But a person can audition well and then present terribly. We've both known people like that."

"Still, he is the best actor we're likely to come upon in the time we have. And," I argue, "he can sing, you have to admit that. He has a gorgeous voice."

"He hasn't ruined his voice," Orestes admits, "yet. Give him a few more years. "

"Remember," I tell him, "he only needs to be good enough to perform this one part. There's no guarantee that we will keep him on after. How he manages in this role will inform whether or not we invite him back."

"Look at him," Orestes says, and jerks his head in the direction of the hallway. "Do you really want *that* performing in a play you have written?"

Sostratos has sunk back into his original position huddled beneath his cloak in the hallway, the pinky of one hand jammed into his left ear, reaming it clear. Sprawled as he is, he has the appearance of a wild animal that someone has only partially shaved and squeezed into a tunic. I struggle to imagine what he might look like after he's been cleaned up and had his hair cut, and can't quite manage it.

"Who else can we find?" I ask. "In the time we have left?"

Orestes wipes his face with a hand, and seems to find a certain resolve. Together we step back into the hallway.

"If you are hired to play this part," Orestes says, "you will drink water and vinegar to refresh yourself while we rehearse. You will work hard without complaint. You will listen to every word I say—and I mean *every* word—and if you are drunk even once during rehearsal, I will fire you. And if *you* rehire him after I've fired him," he says, turning to me, "I will quit."

Having made that promise, he turns and exits. Sostratos watches him go.

"He's Athenian, isn't he?" he asks, from his position on the floor.

"Yes," I answer.

"They're peculiar about theatre," he observes. "No sense of humour."

I nod. "That's true." I glance once more at our surroundings, and consider Orestes's misgivings, but reach the same conclusion as before. "Well," I continue, turning to him, "are you available for work? We will gather to read the script the day before Saturnalia."

"What play?" he asks

I look at him crouched upon the floor. "Does it matter?"

"No," he replies after thinking about it a moment, "I suppose not."

15

Thoughts of a broken theatre disturb my night, and sleep becomes an impossibility. I dream of a drunken Sostratos stumbling onto the stage, pissing and passing out. I see myself driven from Rome by outraged citizens. I wake to darkness and the wind raging outside. I turn on my bed, the straw mattress poking me. Finally, I stand, throw on my tunic and slip into the hall. It is midway between deep night and morning. Apart from the wind's exertions, the building is still.

I descend the steps slowly, feeling the smooth wood planking give and groan underfoot. When I reach the main floor, I detect stirring and peer into the culina. The darkness is pierced by a flickering ceramic oil lamp resting on a low table, and the dim red-black glow of burning coals upon the brazier. Vulcanus has planted himself in front of his cooking station, and is busy basting a spitted goat. The crackle of the coals and sizzle of the meat provide comforting music. His eyes flick to the doorway as I enter. He grunts his recognition and turns his attention back to his goat. "What?" he asks over his shoulder.

"Nothing," I tell him. "I can't sleep."

He nods, stirs the coals with a metal rod. Flames dance atop embers, making his beard gleam like polished copper. He's shirtless, and his great hairy belly and chest drip with sweat.

"Early to be preparing a meal," I observe.

"Silversmith's Guild coming today," he answers. "Many hungry mouths."

In the corner, on a stool, a tiny clay figure—Hestia, goddess of the hearth—squats upon an altar. Beside it, a large bronze bowl rests containing a dark, thick-looking liquid. "What's this?" I ask, nodding to the bowl.

"Cervisia. Drink of my home. I make in jug and keep private stock." He says, nodding at it. "You want?"

I peer down at it. It is a rich, earthy colour like the river Tiber when it is at full flood, and it smells of bird droppings and leaf mould. Nothing could be more unappealing. "Why not?" I reply.

He hauls a smaller bowl down from an overhead shelf and fills it from a ladle. A creamy foam surges over the lip. He thrusts it into my hand, then refills his own and raises it. I must appear doubtful, because he chuckles.

"Is good," he assures me. "Make you strong."

I raise it. Up close it looks like tidewater. I sip it, and find it tastes a bit like it too. Yeasty, thick, brackish.

"You drink that," Vulcanus encourages me, "you not fear dying."

I place the bowl to my lips again and tip it back.

"Eh?" Vulcanus grunts, asking, I think, my opinion.

"Good," I answer. "Very nice."

"More?" he asks.

I consider the wind howling outside and the discomfort of my bed and hold up the bowl to be refilled.

In the street another cart clatters by, the driver berating his mules and cracking the whip. "Is too many wagons, hey?" Vulcanus grumbles, nodding in the direction of the wagon carrying produce. "Everybodies take things to market."

"Yes, but it's not what woke me. It was the wind, then once I woke I started trying to solve problems I'm having with my play."

"And you solve?" he asks.

"Everything that was a problem," I confess, "is still a problem."

"Tomorrow," he predicts and refills my bowl.

I scan the culina. A small shuttered opening draws air from the rear alley and vents the smoke of the brazier. Two rough wood shelving units affixed to the walls extend from hip height to the ceiling. Bundles of dried mushrooms crowd the shelves, beside bowls of aromatic herbs and clusters of roots. Blackened strips of smoked, dried meats dangle from hooks next to cloves of garlic and red ribbons of salted fish. "So. Tell me," I say, as I lift the cervisia to my lips, "you must know—what ingredients go into Casina's garum?"

"Everyone asks," he replies, as though he had been expecting the question. "Is big secret, like Bacchante mystery secret, and she guard like Cerberus guard Hades. I no ask—maybe she cut out tongue."

I nod. I could have guessed he'd be sworn to confidentiality. "How long have you known her?" I ask.

"Long. I know her from other popina. I work there before she move here. She like Medea, only more smart." He saws off a piece of the roasting goat and tosses it to me. "Here. Is good to eat when drink cervisia. Take this."

The meat first scalds my fingers when I catch it, then sears my mouth when I pop it past my lips, and I have to suck in air around the edges to cool it.

"Is good?" he asks.

I can taste savoury herbs, knobs of crusted salt, a marinade of wine and olive oil.

"Very."

He nods matter-of-factly. Like all successful cooks I've known, he is utterly confident of his food-making prowess. "She know everybody, everybody," he continues. "I tell you story. Before here, at old place, stranger come one day, knocking at her door. He say he want womens—was Pomona and three different womens working for Casina then, gone now—he try to force them to come work for him. He tell Casina, sell womens to him, or he come back and take them, run her off. Big man, big talk, from Messina. Casina listen, but when he leave she tell me, sit. Watch things, tell girls to wait, wait, wait. Stay calm."

"She go off, gone all afternoon, speak with someone. Come back. Maybe next week later, city soldiers—the Tresviri—march into neighbourhood to collect taxes, why then—who knows?—that place busted up, torn down. All men working there beaten like rug, thrown into street. That fellow, Big Mouth, they beat to death, drag through alleys, drop body in Father Tiber. After that, nobody bother her. Not about girls. Not about nothing." He tilts his head at me, as though sharing a secret. "She good to friends. You don't want be her enemy."

He rotates the goat over the brazier, picks up a container of what looks to be oil and herbs and drizzles it over the carcass. He follows this with a couple of fingers full of salt he plucks up from a pile on the cutting board. As the salt scatters and clings to the sides of the goat, he whistles between his teeth, and I recognize the tune of an old marching song. My ears perk up. "You were a soldier," I say.

His face adopts a more guarded expression. "Sure," he says. "Auxiliary."

"How long?" I ask.

"Three years."

"Not long."

"Long enough," he replies, and then mutters in what I guess must be his native language. I wait for him to translate, and when he doesn't I ask what he said. He replies, "Long enough to end badly."

"You were injured?" I ask.

"Injured? Ya," he answers, and he pinches another clump of herbs and flicks them at the lamb. Some flutter past, and instead touch the coals where they flare as tiny intense bursts of blue flame. "Numistro, you know where is?" he asks me.

I think a moment. "Near Lucania?"

He nods. "At Numistro, we fight Punic. Middle of battle, Auxiliary Praefectus call retreat. Me, I'm soldier enough to follow orders. We march out. Find out later, he make deal— you know deal?" he makes a universal gesture of rubbing fingers together. I indicate my understanding.

"He make deal with Punic to withdraw troops. After, Romans capture us. Praefectus executed. Bang, bang on big cross, eh." He mimes hammering the nails in a quick crucifixion. "I try explain, only doing what told. Person above give order, you do. You don't ask question. In answer, Rome gives me three lives of animal. Penned like chicken, chained like dog, sex cut off like ram." He roars with laughter, as if he is sharing the funniest joke he has ever heard. Unsure of how to respond, I drink from my bowl.

"After that," he says, "sold as slave." He pours himself another brimming bowl of cervisia, takes a long pull, and wipes the foam from his moustache.

We stand and study the goat. Eventually I break the silence. "Bad times," I say.

"Bad times," he agrees and turns the coals. "I no want live. Nobody want buy me. I become thin like grass blade. Casina, come one day to market, put down money for me, bring me to popina, feed me. I ask what she want me to do? She tell me sit, keep eye on things. She speak gently, feed me, tell me I can work to be free. No chain, no collar, no brand, no shackles, nothing. She know I no run back home like this. I tell her I do cooking back in soldier times. Good, she say, cook. Six years now I work for her." The wind whines, and slithers through the shutters into the culina, fanning the coals a brilliant red.

"I need two goose from cellar," Vulcanus says finally, changing the subject.

I help him haul the geese up, thank him for the cervisia. He says if I ever want more, to come and see him. I find a quiet corner in the coenatio to attempt turning the story around. I enjoy my morning puls hot, brought to me by Prima, who has wakened. I stir it a long while as I consider my play. The spoon circles the bowl in resonant, repeating loops while I assemble my thoughts. There are elements of writing that in their processes most resemble the construction of a home—there are any number of ways you can develop the architecture, but only so many pieces of wood available. If you add to one room, you must be prepared to remove the timbers from another.

On investigation, I find the architecture of my play has taken on a disordered, jumbled quality, so I lay the spoon aside and begin to draft new plans. As I consider how best I might reorder things, Prima quietly enters and removes my bowl. I thank her and continue scribbling.

I work steadily and lose my sense of time. I am vaguely aware of the silversmiths arriving and banqueting, of roasted goat being served, and a stripped goat carcass being cleared away, but when I raise my head from my work I realize the daylight has come and gone. The sun has set, the silversmiths departed, and the coenatio is filling once more for the nighttime sitting—some eager customers have already finished coena. I blink and set my writing aside. I order fish soup and bread, and, feeling a little disoriented, eat it slowly when it arrives.

Naevius enters the Cerium as I savour my meal. "I haven't seen you in a while," I comment as he sits.

"I have been busy," he informs me. "My Choragus has been hounding me for a finished script. I turned it over to him yesterday. You?"

I gesture to my tablet. "Still making adjustments."

"Oh ho," he says, glancing down at the notes. "Meddling. I thought you held the opinion that the audience wants their comedy undiluted, no meddling allowed. How far along are you?"

"Almost done," I hedge.

"Almost done," he mocks. "But there you sit with your tablets and stylus. It sounds to me like you're still complicating things. Finish up, and you can join me at the symposia. In addition to crafting this play for the upcoming ludi, I've been busily negotiating my next writing project."

"Which project is that?" I ask.

"The one that will elevate me out of the prostitution of comedy. One that will permit me to perform real writing. Where's that Prima?" he says, and scans the room to catch her attention.

I take a second look at Naevius. There are dark hollows under his eyes, and his skin has an ashen hue. "You look terrible," I tell him frankly.

"My recent endeavours involved late nights and long talks," he explains. "It's thirsty work. You have to refresh yourself."

"Did you buy your colleagues drinks with money you should have used to pay me back?" I ask him.

"Of course I did," he replies unabashedly and pats me on the shoulder. "You'll thank me later. I put in a good word on your behalf, and when everything is arranged, I'll make sure there's room to wedge you in."

"It's highly unlikely that you'll catch me writing tragedy," I caution him. "Just viewing it is almost more than I can manage."

"You'll come around," he responds vaguely. "Eventually. There will be important things to write in the future. Rome won't always be like this." He flips a dismissive hand in the direction of the street. "Rome is a giant, emerging from sleep, just rising and finding its feet. Soon, Carthage will be finished—"

"I wouldn't be too quick to make that prediction," I caution. "It was only shortly ago that Punic soldiers were outside Rome's walls."

"It will be swept away," he insists, dismissing my objections, "and then we Romans will stretch out. Out into Africa and Egypt. Out west into Gaul and east into Macedonia. It's in those faraway locations that we will discover our destiny."

"And this," I ask, "was the thrust of your talk last night?"

"We talked of many things. It was interesting. You should have been there." He drinks. "That maggot Ennius was there."

"Ah," I say. I've heard rumours of Ennius, a new writer up from the south. I was wondering when he might make an appearance. "He's supposed to be a kind of prodigy. It's said he claims to be the reincarnated spirit of Homer."

"The reincarnated spirit of Homer's poetic scrotum," Naevius scoffs. "I'll give you a sacrificial bull on a butterfly's back if he's the reincarnated spirit of anything. But he is solidly connected to some important rising figures and he's been selected as the fourth for the Ludi of Apollo—did you know that?" he asks.

"I didn't know that," I admit.

"If you attended these symposia, you'd find a few things out. You won't discover anything of consequence scribbling notes and sipping your watered wine at the Cerium—except from me. Ennius," he repeats with a scornful laugh. "Let me tell you, when he dies, that arrogant pup will be escorted to Tartarus to face the real Homer and be tormented for the great crimes he committed against that esteemed poet's reputation. As for you," he tells me, tapping me hard on the chest, "it's not your failures you will be punished for, my friend, but your successes. Were you not here to play pimp to Romans for their cheap laughs, they might be compelled to look beyond to something more uncomfortable but necessary."

"And you," I ask, pointing at him with my spoon, "do you believe you will be the sole individual to escape judgment and torture when you die?"

"Not at all," he replies cheerfully. "I will, like everyone else, be conducted by Mercury to the river Styx, where I will be ferried across by Charon, judged by Minos, Aeneas, and Rhadamanthus, and then in death will once again encounter all the tiresome individuals who bored me so greatly in my former life," he tips his cup back. "And that will be my torture."

When he realizes that I can't be persuaded to join him for the evening's activities, Naevius excuses himself to meet with Lucius Flaccus and others he tells me will eventually wield enormous influence when the new, improved Rome dawns. After he departs I attempt to return to work. I arrange my tablet and stylus in front of me and order more hot wine. Pomona sets it steaming on the tabletop. I wrap a hand about it and feel its heat radiate through my palm. Two benches over, a couple of elderly men confer with one another in low tones and idly throw dice. Domitia leans against the wall chatting and laughing with Pomona. Candria somewhere, perhaps upstairs, croons a quiet song of love and yearning.

Abruptly, I feel the painful absence of Felicia. I glance about the room and wonder how many had looked at me and laughed while I had pursued her. A hot rush of shame returns, carrying equal mixtures of loneliness and loss and longing. I feel a bruised aching in some inner cavity and I realize I am simply too old for romance. It is a project best suited to the young. They recover more quickly; their damaged hearts heal more completely. It's not something that comes easily at my age. I pack up my writing materials and, leaving my wine undrunk on the table, retire to my bed.

16

The day prior to Saturnalia, we convene once again in the Campus Martius, where we had presented *The Pot of Gold*. Orestes has found benches for us to sit on, and arranged them in a semi-circle. Sostratos arrives on time for rehearsal, as he had agreed, but it is difficult to reconcile the man we hired and the man who shows up. They are so entirely different figures.

This man, this stranger, who attends rehearsal has washed, wears a clean tunic, has his hair tied back in the way of Persians. Now that he's not sprawled upon the floor of a lupanar, it's possible to see that he presents a tall, stately figure. The overall impression he offers is of a very elegant building, fallen at some point into considerable disrepair, but capable of restoration.

We sit to read the first half of the play. He reads ably, is articulate in his discussion of the text, cordial with his fellow actors—a little aloof, perhaps, but a man of even passions. After reading, Orestes has the cast slowly work through the songs. His voice is as every bit as good as I had remembered.

The only moment when things appear in jeopardy occurs later in the afternoon, just after the cast has been taught a particularly difficult melody; he turns to Tertius, who has been seated cross-legged viewing the proceedings.

"Little man," he asks. "Do you like the theatre?"

Tertius nods.

"Good. Then make yourself useful," he urges the boy, "and get me a cup of wine. Acting is thirsty work."

Tertius replies, "Orestes said you're to get nothing but vinegar and water during rehearsal."

"Of course, that's right," Sostratos corrects himself immediately, "That's what I meant. Water and vinegar it is."

So Tertius fetches a cup of water and vinegar and Sostratos takes a long drink, just as though it is what he always drinks, what he has always preferred drinking—then carries on into the afternoon rehearsals. And he's very good. Perhaps it's because it's the first day, perhaps it's because he must use the rehearsal to bend his mind away from his craving, but he is absolutely compelling. Orestes assigns the actors two songs to practice, reminds them that we will begin again immediately after Saturnalia, and dismisses them.

Once the actors have retired, and we've set things aside, I sit down with Orestes.

"What do you think?" I ask him.

Orestes lifts his hands in bewilderment, and then drops them in his lap.

"I know," I say.

"Who can predict what he'll be like in the future," he muses, "but today he's been Heracles performing his twelve labours, nothing is beneath him, nothing seems beyond him, anything is possible. It's the most amazing transformation I've ever witnessed."

"I *know*," I repeat.

"It's what he has done for the cast that is the truly remarkable thing," he muses. "They had the wind knocked out of them by the loss of Antipho, and although they stayed with us—nobody ever expressed any thought of leaving—you could sense that they didn't really believe that we could find anyone who would replace him. Today, they were reborn. And the truth is—as good as Antipho was—after today, I believe this Sostratos may be better."

"It's possible," I agree, "but we'll see."

The following day the Festival of Saturnalia begins with the ceremonial unbinding of the feet of the statue of Saturn at his pillared temple in the forum. Viewers push close as they anticipate his freeing. Excitement mounts as the unwinding commences and a loud cheer erupts from the crowd as the final pale strand of wool twine is tugged away. "Io Saturnalia!" people cry. "Io Saturnalia!"

The sacrifices are dragged forward bleating, followed by public feasting near the temple. This ritual always has a powerful impact upon me. That a god might permit himself to be bound and then freed seems a special gesture. I envision Saturn stretching his lanky immortal limbs, cramped after a year of confinement and exulting in his liberty. The public feast is a glorious event, with all attendees fed. Everyone is in high spirits, many of the people in attendance wearing the peaked felt hat the Greeks call pileus, a symbol of the levelling that occurs during the days of the festival, the mightiest and lowliest, brothers and sisters. In the crowd, one can see representations of every kind of Roman, mingling and rubbing shoulders—the poor, the rich, senators and slaves. I spy the tinsmith who repairs pots for Casina raising a cup of wine. I see Lucius, my money lender, corpulent as ever, wearing a peaked hat. "Io Saturnalia!" he calls to me across the crowd, mild as a lamb.

"Io Saturnalia!" I reply.

This begins a series of wild days when everything is the opposite of what it was, everything turned upside down and inside out. Little Tertius approaches me just beyond the temple and brazenly presents a poem—nothing really, a scandalous bit of smutty rhyming that I believe he must have discovered on a latrine wall. Of course, he recites it aloud—and then charges me for it. I pay him an as, and he runs off delighted.

"Io Saturnalia!" he calls back over his shoulder.

I stop at a sweet vendor's stall on my return to the Cerium and purchase honey and oat cakes as gifts for the serving staff. Everywhere garlands of baked goods swing from doorways. Along the streets tiny ceramic suns and stars dangle and clatter from the branches of trees. It's late when I arrive and the workers of the Cerium retire to a long table in the courtyard for our feast. I don't know where Casina purchased it, but we have a suckling pig presented on a platter, and Vulcanus has created a great work of art, the skin thin and crisp, the flesh moist and dropping off the bone. Golden cones of mashed turnips rise up from the platter like tiny steaming volcanoes; delicate, dark clumps of mushrooms gleam against the pig's flanks, and there is separate platter of dainty pig's feet cooked to perfection.

Just before we sit to eat, Vulcanus strides through the entrance draped in a short red robe, and sporting an enormous crown fashioned of interwoven twigs. He shouts for strong wine, pounds the table, and roars for the servant to come— and Casina rushes through the archway, wearing a coarse, loose-fitting slave's tunic. Vulcanus delivers a swat to her rear as she passes, and she squeals and hurries to break the seal of a new amphora and then serves us all drinks. The other girls double over with laughter when they see her in this outfit.

"At last! The real master has arrived," Candria announces gleefully, "accompanied by his faithful servant."

"Shame!" Domitia scoffs at Vulcanus. "Have you no younger servants that you must hook this elderly crone to the yoke? Grandmother," she calls solicitously, and pulls out a bench, "do you need to sit?"

"I don't know," Pomona says, choking on laughter—"the oldster looks strong as a bull to me. I'm sure she'll be able to perform the work of several servants."

Casina takes all the jibes in good humour. She heaps the plates with food, and is quick to bring cups brimming with wine. I'm pleased to see that Casina is not one who simply makes a pretense of generosity. She possesses the good sense to give with both hands when the occasion rises.

"Io Saturnalia!" the others shriek and throw semis to the tabletop to show their appreciation. Casina gleefully sweeps the coins up and brandishes them between her fingertips, claiming that at this rate she'll be rich enough to buy her freedom by the end of the evening.

"Io Saturnalia!" the butcher calls, popping his gleaming bald head in the doorway. He spies Casina serving, hoots his laughter, and presents a candle and gift of ox tails. As presiding master of the day, Vulcanus accepts the tails, solemnly. He instructs Casina to pour the butcher a cup of wine, and scowls and shakes his whip at her perceived hesitation. He brushes off a bench and invites the butcher to sit. The butcher accepts the wine and drinks our health, but has other clients to visit and other gifts to deliver.

The staff of the Cerium are, as might be expected, very popular in the neighbourhood and consequently are lavished with trinkets and gifts. They're spoiled with baked goods,

laden with fragrant garlands and the tiny clay dolls sold by
street vendors during the celebrations. They line the figurines
up along the benches, fuss over them, and name them: Salvia,
Virgilia, Juno, and Prima. I consider as they play with their
dolls how young they all suddenly look. I receive a writing
tablet—Vulcanus confides, "In case you ever want to learn
to write." I, in turn, present him with a soup ladle, "In case
you ever want to learn to cook." He claps me on the back, a
thundering crack that rattles my teeth.

"Io Saturnalia!" Festus, our one-legged sandalmaker, calls
as he pokes his head in shortly after the butcher has left. He
thumps along to our table, summons his apprentice, and orders
him to open a sack. The boy throws the sack open, Festus
reaches in and withdraws a pair of sandals for Casina and
leather hair bands for the serving staff. He lingers for a drink,
and I see that Pomona finds a pig's foot for the apprentice
as well. Moments later, Lucius, the tinsmith I'd seen at the
forum, arrives. "Io Saturnalia!" he shouts. He deposits a
small tin pot at the entrance for Casina, although of course
he pretends to present it to Vulcanus. He also shares gifts
with the girls, and he has a special one for Pomona—whom
I believe he is sweet on—a copper hairpin. Tertius is busily
making his rounds, delivering little stick figures he's woven
from twigs for the girls and a candle for the Cerium. He must
have stolen the candle, I can't imagine the scoundrel has the
money to buy one. Vulcanus accepts it gravely, and instructs
Casina to take care of him. She returns from the kitchen with
a bun and a cooked rabbit's foot. Tertius drops to a bench and
gnaws at it like a hungry dog. Orestes stops in next with his
tibia, and after he has been served his usual wine and water,
he straps the pipes on and plays some popular melodies. The

ladies sing along, and Orestes, who normally is so fierce about his music, is uncharacteristically indulgent. The female voices rise and merge in a chorus that is fresh and innocent-sounding and unexpectedly touching. Vulcanus draws up a cooking pot, beats time on it, and then chants a foreign song in his great booming voice—a selection in his native tongue that nobody understands, but is appreciated nonetheless for its novelty. Then, Orestes plays his pipes again and everyone calls for the servant to dance. Candria withdraws her tambourine and, shaking it above her head, begins the chant, "The servant, the servant!"

Casina declines, offering some feeble excuse. "The servant, the servant, the servant!" we respond, all taking up the chant, and thumping on the table. Casina stands with her hands on her hips and shakes her head at our shamelessness, but we are beyond caring and beyond shame. "The servant, the servant, the servant!" we continue braying, hammering all the harder. Then, all at once, she relents and steps out between the tables. We erupt in cheers. She performs a dance of some exotic kind, lifting her hands high in the air and spinning about in a display that is entirely barbarous, provocative, and extremely fine all once. Coins are again withdrawn from purses and sashes and flung to the table. Candria, not to be outdone, stands and begins dancing as well, a wilder dance than she normally performs for the customers, and in a moment, all the women of the Cerium have leapt up and linked arms and are leading a weaving, swaying line through the tables, wild Maenads at their spontaneous Bacchanalia.

Saturnalia rushes past, a great, frothing torrent, sweeping up everyone and everything in its foamy wake. Over the next three days the serving staff are busier than ever, the Cerium more crowded than ever. After that first day, Casina returns to her role as master general of the caupona in her campaign to extract as much revenue as she can from her customers. She orders in extra food stocks and a shipment of a special wine. Thirsty patrons storm the coenatio and drain the expensive stock before the end of the second day, and no more can be purchased anywhere. Casina responds with decisiveness. She orders in a cheaper stock, holds a special sale on hot spiced wine, at discounted prices, and this flies out of the caupona as well. The serving staff take the opportunity at nights to gamble, and Casina proves herself to be especially adept, winning time and again, and then allowing them to win most of it back so that they can start over. There is more drinking, more cooking, more eating, more gaming, more laughter, more dancing, more song, more playing of music, more singing, more raucous, rattling sexual activity in the upper floor, more activity in general, than ever.

When the festival ends, the inevitable happens. Feet move slower, smiles droop lower, and lethargy sets in. Saturnalia is the most beloved event of the year, and no one is ever happy when the great god is rebound. I feel the let-down as well, but the morning following Saturnalia I am preparing to bring my new material to rehearsal when I am surprised to see the usually calm Orestes arriving, looking agitated. I bid him good health and ask what brings him to the Cerium. He tells me he spoke too soon when he said no one in our grex was considering leaving.

I feel my shoulders give. "You're joking," I say.

"No," he replies. "Quintus has been poached."

I run my hands through my hair. "Where has he gone?" I ask. He grimaces. "Over to Pellio."

"Ah," I grunt. That's all I can manage, my disappointment is so bitter. I can only imagine the kind of offer that Pellio will have made, the kind of rosy future he will have been able to propose, while we continue to operate with borrowed masks and patched costumes.

"Yes. Exactly."

"Well," I say, drawing a hand across my face, "we anticipated Pellio might do something to interfere. Is there anyone else in our cast likely to join him?"

"No," he tells me. "I've talked to them all. They're as surprised as we are. And besides, Pellio won't be interested in approaching any of the others. Quintus was, after Antipho, our most seasoned actor. I think Pellio has heard of Sostratos's drinking proclivities and considers him more a liability than an asset. Had I not worked with him I might feel the same."

"So we must find someone to replace Quintus," I say, "but where to start?"

"I have a couple of ideas," he says mysteriously. "I've explained the situation to the grex, and told them we will adjourn for a short time and reconvene when I've secured someone new. Give me a few days." He refuses to divulge anything further, except to say that he has someone in mind and will be away holding discussions. He instructs me to watch closely over Sostratos while he's gone. "He is like one of those horses bred for racing," he counsels, "content when occupied, but dangerous to itself when left idle." He exits quickly, leaving me wondering whom he will meet, and how long it is likely to take until we have a complete cast once more.

17

Adopting Orestes's advice, I invite Sostratos up to the Cerium
to sing some of the script back to me. He agrees, and so long as
I have ample wine handy, he is efficient and willing to sit and
go through as many verses as I wish, as many times as I wish.
His voice is astonishing, and I find him a helpful workmate
and an amiable—if somewhat aloof—companion. Looking
for other tasks I can assign him, I provide him the newest
portions I've completed, material that I am just considering for
the conclusion, and ask him if he can prepare these for me to
hear in three days' time. He quickly looks the scroll over before
replying, "Why not?" Then, emptying his cup, he saunters into
the street with the scroll under his arm.

During Orestes's absence, Casina has me embark on
renovating the miller's shop. She orders timber, nails, and tools
and has the materials stacked in preparation. Grippus joins
me, and after I've shared my drawings with him and tacked
them to the wall, we begin.

We first knock out the wall separating the miller's place
from the caupona. That takes most of a morning. We stop to
eat bread and pickled fish, then commence once again, and
erect a wide archway that will connect the two buildings.
What was storage space at the top of the stairway in the
bakery, we frame for cubiculae, one a larger unit that will
become Casina's new bedchamber. Three other workers arrive

and dismantle the old roof of the former bakery to create the opening for the compluvium that will permit light in as well as rainwater for the cistern. They throw down ropes, haul up new planks, slowly piece together the new structure.

In the evenings, I maintain my writing regimen and in three days' time meet once again with Sostratos. "Have you memorized the music?" I ask as I order him his wine.

"Yes," he says, handing the material back to me. He sings, and I'm glad I requested our meeting. He possesses such a pure, penetrating voice that his singing clarifies certain lapses in the writing, and reveals potential I hadn't even been aware of. I take notes and am able to make significant improvements. I communicate some immediate revisions to him, and he swiftly grasps them and sings them back to me. He truly has a wonderfully nimble facility with music.

"Any other thoughts?" I ask absently as I write down notes to myself on a tablet.

"The representation of the Overseer is a little shallow," he replies as he refills a cup.

I'm taken aback. Of course I was speaking of the musical arrangement and wasn't requesting critique of the literary content. "Shallow?" I say, setting my tablets aside. "What do you mean shallow? In what way shallow?"

He shrugs. "Maybe uninteresting is more accurate," he corrects himself.

"That's no clearer," I reply coldly, bristling at his lack of tact.

"Well," he answers after a little thought, "the man is summoned by Hegio to seize Tyndarus, but his only contribution to the story so far appears to be devoted to posturing and threatening."

"And you feel that's a problem?" I ask.

He shrugs again. "Not for me. But he seems to go on longer than necessary, and there's almost never a reason to overwrite."

"Ah," I say, attempting to demonstrate restraint.

"And though I'm not playing the part," he allows after a slight pause, "he seems a little conventional."

"He's an overseer," I point out, somewhat tersely, "not a midwife. He's not meant to be kind and caring. His job is to compel other slaves to work and to punish those who don't."

"Yes?" he asks, as though I have not adequately explained my point.

I try again. "He is not intended to be a moral figure. He is, after all, a slave who punishes and oppresses other slaves."

"As he is compelled to do," he replies, refusing to back down the slightest. "Just as all slaves are compelled to do."

I remain silent.

"Of course," he says, wiping his mouth with the back of one hand and standing, "you are free to fashion him as you wish. Is there anything else you want me to read?"

"Take this," I answer, giving him my latest draft.

"And come back in three days?"

"Yes, yes," I say impatiently, "three days," and wave him off.

A team of masons arrives early the next morning, a couple of loud, burly Sarmatian brothers with hands calloused thick as ox hide. They knock out the ovens, yank up the grain mill, and level the central area. Laying crushed stone, they compact it, then begin to piece together a collecting basin for the impluvium within the atrium.

By week's end, what was once the bakery has been utterly transformed. The sun's rays slant down through the new opening, casting a shimmering shaft of light into the centre of the space. Casina stands next to the catch basin of the impluvium, and spins about surveying our work, like a young girl presented with a new pet.

"In the future, we'll eat here at the end of the day," she announces happily, "with the birds looking down, and butterflies resting atop tables."

"You like it?" I ask her.

"Very much," she replies, nodding. "Very, very much." She drops onto a bench I've knocked together and heaves a deep sigh of contentment.

"So. Now, you possess two miracles: an atrium and a latrine," I reflect, joining her on the bench. "Are you satisfied at last?"

"For now," she answers, still glancing about.

"For now?" I repeat.

She withdraws her feet from her sandals, stretches, folds her hands on her lap, and closes her eyes. "One day," she says, "I will purchase the next businesses over. I'll have a second culina and coenatio built, and will host exclusive private functions, where I will serve only the most expensive, exotic foods."

I chuckle to myself, amused by the entirely commercial nature of her imagination. "What kinds of exotic foods will you serve?" I inquire.

"Oh, many kinds," she replies vaguely. "All kinds. Sturgeon, venison—have you ever tasted camel?"

"No," I reply, "have you?"

"No," she says, idly testing the evenness of the stone flooring with the bottom of one bare foot, "But I have heard that cooked correctly it can be extraordinary."

I have seen camels trotted around the Circus Maximus, immense shaggy creatures, seemingly half wolf, half swan. I can't actually imagine how you would cook them, or where you would cook them, given their size. The legs alone would be the equivalent of a side of lamb.

"And I'll have a stable built," she adds as an afterthought. "Then I'll be able to accommodate coaches and guests travelling on horseback."

I scratch my back against a corner of the bench, satisfying an overwhelming itch. "A mistake," I caution her, "that you will come to regret."

"Purchasing other businesses?" she asks, opening one eye.

"No," I correct her, "Putting up horses. Nothing good can ever come from caring for those miserable, smelly, hay-eating sons of bitches."

"You!" She laughs, clapping me on the shoulder. "You have a fetish against horses and donkeys."

"Both are noisy and offend the nose," I point out reasonably. "You must feed them, water them, have someone clean up after them, throw money after someone to groom them."

"I'll charge more and hire additional servants. It will be necessary. Rome is becoming a city of international merchants and travellers, and there will be a need for these kinds of services." She rouses herself from her reverie. "But never mind—do *you* need anything?"

"Me?" I ask, and hold up a block of pine. "More wood."

"Other than that?"

"Nothing."

She stands away from the bench and brushes dust from her hands. And as she places her hands on her hips as though she were about to begin hauling timber herself, I can't help but smile. It's exactly this kind of response that makes Casina different. Other contractors will scrimp and natter that you're behind schedule, or note this or that shortcoming in the construction, as though their miserly diligence and close scrutiny will make you work harder. When Casina stops in, it's to ask 'do you need anything?'

"Oh. One other matter," she says, interrupting my thoughts.

I scratch once more; I just can't seem to satisfy that itch. "What?" I ask.

She motions for me to follow her. "Come look," she says. We mount the stairs and when we reach the top of the landing, she stops and turns to me.

"Over there," she indicates.

I anticipate what she is going to say. Haven't I heard her plans many times? "I know, you want more spacious sleeping quarters. It's already framed."

"But there's something else," she says, stepping into the still unfinished construction.

When I tell Grippus about it, I think I may have to wrestle him to make him comply. At first he flat-out refuses. "I won't do it," he says, shaking his head. "I only build useful things."

"It's what she wants," I point out.

"Did you tell her it will let noise in?" he demands. I nod. "Did you tell her birds would fly in?"

"She says birds are her sisters," I tell him, "and we will build shutters to close the world out when she wishes."

He stares darkly at the wall, and shakes his head. "It makes no sense," he blurts. "A window for the culina, yes, smoke must escape. For the coenatio, good, so many people in one place, an opening is required—but in your sleeping area? I won't do it," he repeats.

"She's paying us," I argue.

"It's bad luck!" he exclaims. "Bad luck, and everyone knows it! At night when you dream, *that's* when demons float in."

I place a calming hand on his shoulder. "They will be her demons to deal with," I tell him.

"Fine," he concludes, but shakes his head dourly. "I'll do it. But it's unhealthy. You have to be a little crazy to place a window where you sleep."

There continues to be no word from Orestes, which makes me anxious. I can only assume that he will contact me if his plans fail completely, so I attempt to maintain a calm exterior and continue working. Sostratos returns, and sings my newest verses. I make notes and further adjustments. At the end of our meeting I reach into my shoulder bag. "There," I say, thrusting a series of tablets into his hands. "Read those. It's still rough."

He sits and reads them while I watch. When he finishes, he nods to me and hands them back.

"Well?" I ask, when he says nothing. "Does the overseer agree with you more now? Does this new exchange with his master suit you?"

"The overseer expresses his own desires for freedom, even as he oppresses others, and in his blindness to his own flaws he becomes more understandably human. Both he and the master benefit from this new material," he replies. "Better." Then, nodding to me as though he were dismissing a servant who had accomplished a simple task, he exits.

"Better," I repeat as I watch him step into the street. "Next I'll be receiving text correction from the stage hands and carpenters."

Finally, a full ten days after his departure, Orestes returns, and triumphantly informs me that he has found someone to replace Quintus. When I ask whom, he confides that it's Marius Festinanter, poached from Pellio's grex! Marius has been one of Pellio's secondary musicians for years. I didn't know that he had acted before he came to Rome.

"I remember seeing him perform," Orestes confides, "and he's actually a better actor than a musician. I didn't dare share what I had in mind with you. It was so brazen an action, I was uncertain myself. I felt if I explained my plan, any argument might dissuade me."

And it is completely brazen, and rude—and brilliant. Apparently, Orestes had spent three days playing music alongside Marius at a wedding, convincing his colleague that he would better be situated with us. He argued that in Pellio's grex, Marius would never amount to anything greater than a supporting musician, but in our grex there would be opportunities both to play music and perform character. It had taken a number of follow-up conversations, and all of Orestes's considerable abilities, but at last he had been successful in persuading him.

"Of course," Orestes says, "with new talent it will mean recasting everything. I have asked our actors to meet in two days' time. You should attend as well."

I arrive two days later, as agreed. "I'm here," I announce. "What changes do you have in mind?"

"I'm having Sostratos try Tyndarus," he informs me.

I glance over to see if he is joking. "Tyndarus? I thought we'd agreed that he was best suited to play the grieved father, Hegio."

"Yes," Orestes says, nodding, "that's what I thought at first too. He's the right age, and he did a good job of Hegio, but . . . you'll see."

I do. Orestes temporarily has Fabius adopt the role of old Hegio, and Marius the role of Aristophantes, the fellow prisoner who betrays Tyndarus. He has the cast read the scenes with Sostratos in his new role and, never mind the age difference, never mind the time he's spent drunk, Sostratos seems effortlessly able to breathe life into the character of Tyndarus. It's astonishing, especially in light of the fact that he is trying this out for the first time and is working without the mask. I watch only a short while and am transported.

After he has concluded, Orestes and I retire to sit on a rough wooden bench under a tree, a little distance from the actors. Orestes opens his hands as though presenting me with a gift. "What did I tell you?"

I shake my head as I consider the performance. "He's a marvel."

"I don't dare switch him back," Orestes continues. "Your Tyndarus is such a particular construct—a slave pretending to be his master, ultimately revealed to be an individual with noble, self-sacrificing attributes—that I will need our best-equipped actor to take him on. And that's Sostratos. Hegio is a compelling character, yes, and a major character, as we both agree, but he's not in the same category as your slave. There's nowhere near the same level of complexity."

"Thanks," I say.

Orestes shoots me a glance. "It wasn't meant as a compliment. Show me an audience that wants complexity. You're writing a comedy. Your audience will want belly laughs. They'll expect jokes. That's another reason why I'm moving him over to Tyndarus." He gestures back at the stage where the cast is reading another portion of the script and Sostratos has the stage hands doubled over with mirth. "Look at him playing the audience. And it's not even a real audience."

We watch him repeating portions of the scene again, only this time adopting an attitude of fawning servility. Grippus—and even Pappius, who barely understands the script—howl. "He's good," I observe.

"Yes," Orestes agrees, nodding, "he's very good. Now," he says and pops a dried fig into his mouth, "we'll have to watch him closely to ensure that he doesn't return to excessive drinking—that is, *I* will have to watch him. You go finish this comedy."

18

The following day, Orestes continues to make adjustments to the casting. In addition to Aristophantes, he casts Marius in the part of Stalagmus—the wretch who originally kidnapped Hegio's older son. It's risky giving Marius more to do, because he hasn't performed in years, and never at all in Rome except on the tibia. "But," Orestes says, "Marius is a beloved musician, and the audience will be curious to discover what he is like as an actor. And everyone will know that he was poached, and that will entice them as well. Fronto," he adds, "I will move to the part of Ergasulus."

"Fronto?" I repeat. "In the principal comic role?"

"Yes."

"He is," I begin, searching for a diplomatic way of phrasing things, "eager, conscientious, and dedicated, I'll give him that, but—"

"But," Orestes says, finishing my thought, "just competent."

"Barely competent, is what I was thinking," I admit.

"I believe our Fronto has greater potential than has been explored. He has been permitted in his few past productions to cultivate sloppy acting habits, but this play, your play, must deliver a new Fronto. I will be the midwife and it will be a hard birthing," Orestes says, looking into the distance, "but Fronto must emerge and become the actor he is meant to be."

The new casting appears to fit overall, and the new meshing of voices seems agreeable. Everyone settles into their new roles. Later that night, after rehearsal, Orestes and I huddle in our usual corner of the Cerium and discuss the play. In the middle of our conversation I detect Orestes's attention shifting. He scowls as he watches Sostratos, seated at a table near the door, drain his cup.

"By Castor, the man has a prodigious thirst," Orestes observes.

I view Sostratos emptying the final portions of a vase. "His work day is done," I reply. "So long as he arrives sober to rehearsals, I have no complaint."

Orestes shrugs off my comment and continues to stare darkly at him. "I'll wager," he says, shaking his head, "he consumes a vase and a half, maybe two, of unmixed wine each night."

"That's a considerable amount," I permit, "but not extraordinary."

"Really?" Orestes asks. "You don't think so? I have only three cups in a night—and I have them mixed with water."

"But you are the very soul of restraint," I reason. "Not everyone shares your resolve. Many people drink more heavily than you and still live a life. Naevius must drink something approaching a vase most nights."

"Yes," Orestes snorts, "and is it wise? Have you heard the nonsense he spouts some evenings? Have his drinking habits been helpful to him?"

I don't answer, as it doesn't seem my place to answer for Naevius. I reflect once more on what a complicated mixture of beliefs Orestes simultaneously embraces, managing as he does to reconcile his devotion to Dionysus, the god of theatre, wine, and revelry, with espousing the stricter, seemingly contradictory philosophy of the stoics Chrysippus and Zeno. "It all results from the time Naevius spent on campaign in Sicily, you know," I explain. "It's the habits of islanders, all of them—Syracusians, Ionians, Cretans—to drink their wine unmixed, or mixed strong."

"Is Sostratos from Syracuse?" Orestes asks me suddenly, turning his attention back to the actor. "He carries a bit of an accent."

"Originally?" I say, and consider his question. "I understood him to be from Rhodes, but I don't know for sure, and it's hard to say what accent he carries."

At that moment, Sostratos stands and exits. His drinking habits are peripatetic, and he rarely finishes the night in the same place where he has begun. I drain my cup, bid Orestes goodnight, and as I climb the stairs to my cubiculum I consider Sostratos. I have encountered many individuals who drink to excess, it occurs everywhere, but you observe it most in Rome, where it is possible to purchase wine regularly and cheaply. It has always puzzled me that even seemingly wise men choose to squander their fortune, their reputation, and their health. Sailors, having received their payment at the end of a dangerous voyage, will piss away every sestertius, and return to the sea with no more money than the seagull, perched on the prow. Wine comes from the gods, that's true—but then, what doesn't come from the gods? I strip off my clothes and settle into my bed. Certainly not everything that comes from the gods is good. Disease comes from the gods too. And hunger. And drought. My thoughts continue in this restless vein until at last I fall asleep.

CLEM MARTINI

Sometimes the sun arrives like a soldier, sometimes like a timid suitor, peeking through a cloud before pronouncing his coming. The light of this morning is a thin, delicate thing, and the day's activities are correspondingly mild. I descend the stairs, order my puls, stir it, and eat. Shortly after I've begun, Naevius drops to the bench beside me, wearing the lines and extra years that early morning bestows on those who have lived hard the night before. He orders puls as well. We exchange nods, sit quietly, and enjoy the silence. As we eat, we each in our own way contemplate the new day.

"How are your rehearsals?" Naevius inquires as he finishes his meal.

"Fine," I answer. "Yours?"

"Terrible," he growls, wiping the corners of his mouth with one hand. "I had to walk away yesterday afternoon, or risk saying something that I might regret." Candria steps up unbidden with a warm bun for him, and you can see a slight stirring of satisfaction cross his face that she has anticipated his request. He's one who relishes receiving the extra attention that accompanies being a special customer.

"I've got the scum of the earth," he continues, as he pulls the bun apart and tucks a portion into his mouth. "Inept, incompetent, inaudible. You!" he exclaims, warming to the subject, "You were lucky. You snagged the last talented actors in the vicinity."

I respond with some vague scoffing sound, only too aware of how troubled our casting has been.

"No," he continues, "it's true! Howsoever you got yours, I've been left with the rejects, outcasts, and nitwits. I've got two, infants, I can't even remember their names—maybe they're so young they haven't been given names yet. I only know that they're still several years away from shaving or experiencing an erection or any other signal of approaching adulthood. At the same time we've hired something like the world's oldest living human."

His sense of indignation is so deeply felt, I can't help but chuckle. "Does your aged veteran possess a name?" I ask, wanting to keep the characters straight.

"Vibius," he replies, savouring the sound of it. "Vibius. I hope the old relic survives long enough for me to adapt Aeschylus's *Prometheus Bound*, because I'm sure he'll be able to offer me much rich advice about when the world was first formed. Old!" he exclaims, rapping his knuckles against the tabletop, "By Castor, he walks so completely stooped over, the other day I thought he was searching for something he'd dropped. And cheap? Every scrap of uneaten food, every bone, every morsel, no matter how meagre, he tucks away in a little fold of cloth for later use. He possesses an infinity of ancient aphorisms related to the wisdom of putting things away for later. 'What's saved now is twice precious later.' 'Something put away today is doubly savoured tomorrow.' Hercules's holy scrotum, but it's annoying." He takes a deep breath to continue his rant, but gives up. "It's all total madness," he says, exhaling. "Total, utter madness, that's the only way I can describe my rehearsals."

I listen, and see the old pirate delighting in his misery. "You're lying as usual," I tell him. "You'll perform at the ludi and I'm sure we'll all be cast in your shadow."

"I wish I were exaggerating," he grumbles, shaking his head. "Really, my only hope for salvation is my Choragus, who is the meanest man alive. Jupiter's sword, but he's tough. Now, we both know that a Choragus has got to be severe to keep the actors on task, but this one—if he'd been running our military, the Carthaginians would have fled for Africa ages ago."

"As bad as Clarus?" I ask, referencing a notoriously foul-mouthed Choragus we'd both had the displeasure of working with back in our youth.

"Worse!" he exclaims. "Think of the surliest, most hungover centurion you ever served under in the legion, then give him a toothache and piles. If anyone can whip that sorry, clueless, talentless bunch of mine into shape, it's him. He possesses a leather strap, and any time they make a mistake with the lines, go off key or move in a wrong direction— whup—that leather strap slashes their legs. He's got them racing around the set like Olympians. That oldster, Vibius, looks like he could drop dead any moment, and I think he would, but he's so cheap he won't expire until he collects his last payment. Anyway," he says, finishing his bun, "I can't say we hold the slightest hope of winning the laurel for best performance at the ludi—but if it comes to boxing, I believe my Choragus can whip any of the others in a pinch."

19

Casina and Orestes cleverly bid upon and receive the contract to construct the theatre for the Ludi of Apollo. It will not make us rich, but it means that we will have access to the structure for our rehearsals during the entire time it is being built. Grippus and I piece it together in the glade we are presently using for rehearsals. We work slowly—as once we have completed it we will have to share it with the other greges performing at the ludi.

Grippus is a virgin to the theatre; *The Pot of Gold* was the first play he had ever had any involvement with. Now it's fascinating to watch this old Samnian woodworker slowly become seduced by it. I hear him softly repeating lines of text to himself as he constructs props—sounding them out, and then saying them again. During rehearsals, he sits rapt as he studies the actors performing their parts, and when they halt for a break, he poses earnest questions about the meaning of this portion of text, or the next.

"I understand your Ergasulus well enough," he comments once, nodding at Fronto, as the cast is seated on the lip of the yet unfinished pulpitum. "He's hungry and wants to be fed. Who doesn't desire a meal? But this other curious fellow—this Tyndarus, will endure a beating and be sent to work the quarries on behalf of his master. And he does it willingly." He shakes his head skeptically. "I wouldn't have done that for my old master."

"He believes he will be rewarded for his efforts," Fronto answers, as he peels a boiled egg. "And they're friends after all, and companions since childhood."

"But he is prepared to sacrifice more than his master— torture—for the sake of that friendship. If it were me on the pulpitum advising him, I'd tell him, don't do it. You," Grippus says, turning to Sostratos, "you're performing the part—do you understand it?"

"We do things every day that don't make sense," Sostratos answers with a shrug. "How is this different? If it was just words I was employing, then it would require a longer explanation, but because it is sung you weave in hidden emotions and suppressed memories. You don't speak your character, you sing him."

Orestes, who is seated next to me on the grass a little distance away, shakes his head at this exchange. "Listen to them," he whispers ironically, "next we will transform our grex into a school of philosophy."

"So," Grippus continues, intent on arriving at clear answer, "it is music that makes the difference?"

Sostratos laughs, stands away from the pulpitum, and stretches. "You do not just sing the song. You must be the song—and the character, and the play all at once. You must penetrate the mystery of the theatre and become a world within a world. The broad sky above and the tiniest bee."

"And now," Orestes mutters, "things have descended to a new level—we have become an apiary."

"I don't know if I want bees in here," Grippus cautiously reflects. "I had to remove a hive from some scaffolding once and it was a painful business."

"That was inhospitable of you," Sostratos says, turning to the carpenter. "Recall that bees are the gods' holy messengers. The theatre possesses a special magic that occurs when words and music merge, and it is the magic of bees. Dionysus appeared as a bee once. Lips anointed with honey are endowed the gift of eloquence. Honey preserves, anoints, and sweetens. Bees hum as they move, music in motion. They are nature's most constant musicians, and their product is most like a play. The comb is the structure of the story, but without the honey—the song—it is an empty waxen husk."

"Come," Orestes interrupts at last, standing, "this is all very poetical, but it gets us nowhere and we have material to cover."

"Of course, that is true," Sostratos says, clapping his hands and nimbly ascending the stairs to the playing area. "Enough about bees! We are the sheep and you the shepherd." With that, the actors follow him back onto the pulpitum, baaing.

Orestes generally has little patience for this kind of foolery. I don't think anyone else could have gotten away with this behaviour, but Orestes is reluctant to interfere with Sostratos so long as he continues performing the way he is.

The actors work through the play up to the return of Ergasulus, following the release of the counterfeit Tyndarus. After the rehearsal concludes, Orestes detains Fronto. "Fronto," he says, "a moment."

Fronto halts and turns with an expression of happiness on his face at being detained. I believe he expects to receive praise, and I feel a hot blush of embarrassment at his innocence.

"When an army marches," Orestes begins, as he approaches Fronto, "they march to a rhythm. Isn't that so?"

"Yes," Fronto answers.

"You are precisely correct," Orestes continues. "If each soldier moves to his own rhythm chaos ensues. If an individual marches slower than his comrades or faster, he will jostle them and cause a gap to open in the formation or make them trip and fall." He checks Fronto to see if he is still following him. "Yes?"

"Yes," Fronto agrees.

"Just as soldiers have a piper who provides a rhythm to march to, you have me," Orestes says and holds up the tibia. "You must be attentive to the rhythm I play. The music informs you not only of the speed at which you should sing, but indicates how you should advance through the story itself. In the scene we just rehearsed I am piping quickly, am I not?"

"Yes."

"How should you respond, then?" Orestes asks.

"I should move," Fronto answers, "more quickly."

"See that you do." The hand holding the tibia drops to his side, indicating that the illustration is over.

Fronto, looking somewhat chastened, descends from the pulpitum and departs. Orestes watches him leave and claps dust from his tunic, "Oh, Fronto, Fronto," he murmurs to himself.

"He's not been rebirthed yet?" I ask.

"Far from it. To adopt the image of bees addressed earlier, Fronto has a sensibility that is coated in honey. He presents sweetly enough, but ideas penetrate that external sticky coating only very gradually."

"Given that Ergasulus is a little broad," I venture, broaching an observation I've been wanting to share, "Fronto is nonetheless playing him a little broadly."

When Orestes delivers me a sharp look, I realize I have made a strategic error in bringing this matter up now. "I may have him do sword swallowing," he replies testily, as he descends from the pulpitum, "or perhaps, as Sostratos threatened when we first met, have Fronto sing a song employing nothing but prolonged belches. Ergasulus is your most consequential comedic figure in this comedy."

"All I am saying is that there are subtle nuances he is missing. And he isn't the sole comic figure in the play," I argue. "Tyndarus is amusing as well."

"Is he?" Orestes asks as he places his tibia in its pouch.

"Yes," I reply, a bit louder than I intend, surprised at Orestes's confrontational tone. "The first scenes demonstrate his mental acuity, and he has many clever lines."

"Does he?" Orestes asks, picking up his cloak.

I had intended that we discuss this in a reasonable fashion, but obviously Orestes is feeling pricked at my perceived critique of his direction, and consequently can't see my comments about Fronto as anything but unnecessary meddling. If I were wise, I would simply apologize and depart, but his responses seem so designed to provoke that it gets my back up. "Yes," I answer, a little louder than before. "The passage when he attempts to prove that Aristophantes is insane is—"

"Funny?" he asks.

"Yes!" I reply, experiencing that uncomfortable sensation you feel when required to defend your writing.

Orestes places a restraining hand on my right arms. "Yes, it's funny," he agrees. "Very funny. At first. But your Tyndarus fails to secure his freedom from Hegio, so I do not believe you can expect to win many belly laughs from the audience as they see him shackled and escorted to torture in the quarries. There is no romantic line to soften this play, nor the smallest speck of sexual misadventure. Your female lead, the sister, has never materialized in your script, nor Smikrenes, the miserly uncle wishing to marry her, and I do not think they ever will. No, don't protest," he says, holding up a restraining hand, as I begin to reply. "I'm not complaining. The play is not your usual work, Titus, but it's a good work and very particular. It will require delicate handling, and consequently I ask that you give Ergasulus a big finish."

"What do you mean by a big finish?" I ask, surprised at this request and still feeling a little stung by his unexpected reproach. "A big finish in what way?"

"He's a hanger-on and a parasite. What kind of big finish does that sort require?" He asks, rhetorically. "Reward him and give the man a meal! Drop him into a barrel of food and have him eat his way out. Something!"

I consider the idea. "All right," I allow, standing, "let me think on it."

"Good. And complete the epilogue!" he calls after me.

"Yes, yes," I reply over my shoulder, "I'll finish the epilogue. You make sure Fronto learns the value of subtlety."

"I'll make sure he learns the value of fire juggling while farting folk tunes!" he calls back.

As I trudge away, digesting that conversation, I come to the galling realization that Orestes is right. There's no doubt I've neglected Ergasulus. He provides information, he incites the final movement of the play, but he never receives his due compensation. Hegio must reward him, and it will be the glutton's joy at being delivered a big meal that will herald redemption, not just for him but for Hegio and Tyndarus.

I return to the Cerium and write the scene. When I have it read, I see that it was precisely what was needed. It seems so obvious. It brings matters to a close for Ergasulus in a satisfying way and draws all the separate threads of the story together. I feel both grateful and appalled—grateful that so essential a scene is completed, appalled that I had not perceived its necessity to begin with. What else might I have missed?

The Ludi of Quinquantria occurs, honouring Minerva. I carry an offering to her temple, and thank her for her assistance. I request that she continue to direct my hand as I write. Before I leave I halt and make an additional offering and ask that she spend a little extra time guiding Fronto as well.

20

We enter that most dangerous point in the rehearsal process—a time past beginning, but a considerable distance from perfection. It's frustrating for all involved. The majority of the play has been charted and navigated in a general sense, but many of the details and specific decisions that make any production interesting haven't yet been discovered, and consequently the play tends to look undernourished, under-nurtured, and sickly.

The cast, aware of their responsibilities, plods dutifully onward. Everyone makes some slight progress, with the exception of Fronto, whose single strength still appears to be memorization. At the break, Orestes and I confer.

"The play is going relatively well," I allow.

"We are about where we might expect to be," Orestes agrees, and chews the side of his cheek as he considers the rehearsal. "Fronto hasn't yet reached the standards set by the others."

"It's curious," I muse as I trace a stick figure in the dirt, "that he manages to be lively without being . . ." I search for the correct word, ". . . good." We both meditate on the many paradoxes that Fronto represents. "The mask he's wearing doesn't help," I suggest. "What about using the Calidorus?"

It's clear from his expression that Orestes is unconvinced that this will improve anything. "I don't think that will make a difference. He's fine wearing the Gaius."

"The Gaius is only competently crafted," I assert. "It doesn't possess the same vigour or mastery as the Calidorus." That's undeniably true. While the masks fashioned by Gaius are serviceable, they are lacking in both comfort and artisanship. Orestes continues to look doubtful. "Why not try it?" I ask.

"We own the Gaius," Orestes points out. "We've only been lent the Calidorus."

I understand then that it is just Orestes's natural thrift getting in our way. "Yes, I know we've been lent the Calidorus," I agree, "but there's no point borrowing what we don't use."

"The Calidorus was lent to us knowing that if we use it overmuch we'll feel obliged to buy it."

"There is no contractual obligation," I object, "and I would feel no such obligation."

I can see Orestes stiffen. "You are not the Choragus," he tells me. "It is my responsibility to ensure we maintain our professional relationships and remain within budget."

I have a disposition that doesn't respond well to being scolded, and now I can feel my blood simmering. "It is *my* name that is attached to this work," I reply. "When the audience arrives, views the play, and finds Fronto's performance boring as fleas on fleece they will hold *me* responsible." At this point I suddenly become convinced all out of proportion to the reality of the situation that Fronto will achieve a more compelling performance from wearing a better mask, so as we are on a break I search the props cart for the old man mask crafted by Calidorus. Look as I may, that mask is nowhere to be found.

I pull aside cloaks, containers, spears, a spare tibia, drums, two old women masks, neither needed—why, I wonder, is Orestes quibbling about an expensive mask he's borrowed, when he's purchased outright two masks we won't use? There's something about not being able to find what I want, when I want it, that transports me into a kind of frenzy. Orestes makes no move to assist me in my search. When I inquire if he knows where it's been placed, his laconic response is, "No, but the fruit will not be any riper if you paint it red." This is not an answer designed to soothe me.

"The Calidorus is superior," I fume, snapping my fingers beneath his nose, "and I will see it on Fronto, if I must turn the entire set upside down."

I storm about behind the theatre like an avenging fury, and curse the lack of organization that has made me waste my time. I am interrupted when I spy a stranger engaged in conversation with Grippus.

"Who is that?" I demand, pointing in their direction.

"Him?" Orestes squints. "I imagine it's a client come to beg Grippus for a favour. Our Oscan woodsman has become very popular."

It's true, it's not the first time I have seen Grippus approached. And having worked alongside him, I've come to the realization that he is one of the two or three best in Rome when it comes to wood detailing. Still, it's impolite to solicit his services right under our noses as we work, and I'm not in the mood to endure it.

I snap the lid of the trunk closed. "I won't have our rehearsal interrupted by beggars."

I'm sufficiently devout that it feels like an interruption of our sacred art, and I am, naturally enough, jealous of every moment spent at our work. The prevailing reason for my objection is, of course, the temper I'm in. In any case, I approach the conversation, intent upon running the trespasser off.

"I was told specifically to request you," I hear the intruder say as I approach.

Grippus shakes his head and tells him, "My time has already been purchased."

"Isn't there some arrangement you can make?" the stranger persists.

"What's the problem here?" I interrupt brusquely.

"It has already been taken care of," Grippus answers me, and returns his attention to the slave. "As I told you, I've only two hands. Sorry."

"Are you certain that there isn't something you can reschedule?" the slave pleads. "My mistress is adamant. She is very concerned that the work be done right and you come so highly recommended."

"Have you packed your big ears with dung?!" I bark. "He's told you no! Nothing else needs be said. Now move off before I throw you off!"

My frustration makes me employ a sharper tone than I had intended. The grex suddenly falls silent at my unseemly show of temper.

Instantly contrite, the slave apologizes. "Please forgive me," he says, and lowers his head in submission. "I didn't mean to impose. Can you suggest someone else?" he asks Grippus. "I can't return without making an arrangement with someone of a similarly high standard."

"Try the Thracian on the street of the stone masons," Grippus suggests. "He's a craftsman who knows what he's doing."

Now that I'm nearer, and observe the slave more closely, I regret my abrupt manner. I had taken him to be older. Up close I realize he's actually youngish, but so scoured by whippings and corrections that he carries himself like a much older person. His back, as revealed above his coarse tunic, is criss-crossed with leathery scars. There are abrasions around his ankles, and around his neck a thick metal collar chafes an angry red circlet. The inscription on the collar reads: "If I am found outside of Rome I have run away. Return me and receive . . ." The writing continues on to the other side of his neck, where I assume it provides a reward and the address. Obviously the man is a runaway who has experienced a notable lack of success.

Orestes, a freedman himself, is always especially gracious to slaves. He offers him water before he goes, which the slave gratefully welcomes.

As he quenches his thirst my feelings of embarrassment grow. I take Grippus aside. "I spoke in haste," I whisper. "I'm sure, there's a way of accommodating this fellow's request, if there is extra money you wish to make."

Grippus gives a quick shake of his square head. "I could've made time," he tells me in a quiet voice, "but not for that household."

"No?"

"Just look at the man's back," Grippus whispers. "The story it tells is plain enough—slaves enter the furnace of that estate and are consumed. I want nothing to do with it, regardless of how well I'd be paid."

I watch the slave hobble off to find someone else to fulfill his mistress's command.

"Who is his owner?" Orestes inquires.

"The Domina Regulus," Grippus replies.

"Ah," I say, "I see your point."

"What?" Orestes asks, detecting something in my tone. "What's special about this family?"

While Orestes is one of the most intelligent, cultured men I know, there exist a number of odd lapses in his knowledge. For anyone else, the Regulus name would be all the information required, but Orestes, like many of his Greek compatriots, disdains what he views as the relatively brief Roman History.

"The Regulus name is tainted," I tersely explain, still nursing a grudge about the misplaced mask.

"Tainted?" he asks. "By what?"

"Marcus Regulus was one of our more celebrated generals a generation back," Fronto leaps in, eager to ingratiate himself with Orestes. "He defeated the Salenti, captured Brindisium, then later—along with Lucius Vulso—so pummelled the Carthaginians in Sicily that they sued for peace. Afterward, Marcus Regulus was left to manage the terms of surrender."

Orestes raises his eyebrows. "Hardly notoriety," he observes.

"Had things stopped there, that's how he'd be remembered today," Fronto continues, "but instead, he negotiated too hard. The Carthaginians, feeling they hadn't been beaten as badly as all that, delayed meeting. They secretly hired a new and more adept general, Xanthippus—"

"A Greek?" Orestes asks.

I could have predicted this would catch his attention. There is nothing Greeks love so much as to boast of the successes of their cousins. "Yes," I say, "a Spartan mercenary, who rallied the troops. He turned the tables, defeated our troops, and captured five hundred soldiers—among them Marcus Regulus."

"So," Orestes says, nodding, "his notoriety springs from this failure."

"The story is more complicated than that," I tell him, "and several versions splinter off the main tale from here. The first has it that Consul Regulus was sent as a hostage to Rome, having first promised to secure a peace. Instead, upon his arrival, he warned Romans that Carthage could never be trusted and urged Rome to annihilate their hated rival. Then—because he was an honourable man—he returned to Sicily, where he was tortured and executed. The alternative story is that he had, after his capture, been unable to face the shame of his inglorious failure, and killed himself. The latter," I say, "has always seemed more likely to me. The Regulus family has promoted the former legend, and Marcia, his wife, briefly achieved a kind of notoriety herself for torturing to death several Carthaginian prisoners in reprisal for the alleged mistreatment her husband received. After that, the family seemed to fall under an ill star."

"It was Gaius, her eldest, who died fighting the Gauls, wasn't it?" Grippus asks.

I nod. "And the younger, Marcus, was killed in the defeat at Cannae. That was the final blow for the mother, who died, it was said, of grief. This left only her daughter, Marcia the younger, as the surviving member of that family."

"And what is she like?" Orestes asks.

"She would be that slave's mistress," I say, "and as you can see from the stripes applied to that man's back, she possesses her own edge."

The story of the Regulus family isn't one designed to uplift and inspire, and I can see that our actors have had their spirits lowered by its telling. When I see Fronto's blank face gazing at me, I recall what upset me in the first place.

"Fronto," I ask, "do you know where the Calidorus mask is?"

Fronto says he'd tried it on, but had given it to Marius. I ask Marius, and he tells me Grippus packed it away. A tremendous whoosh of renewed temper surges through me. "By my crucified crotch," I shout, "does no one know where the mask is? Grippus! *Where* is the Calidorus?!"

Again, there's some confusion about which mask I'm requesting, and who had seen it last, but finally Grippus becomes clear about what is being discussed.

"The old man mask? I packed it away in the cart," he insists.

"Well, if you packed it away, by all that's holy, where is it?" I demand. "Show me!"

Grippus approaches the cart and brushes his hands through the top layers. "Pappius!" he calls.

They consult a moment in Oscan, and Pappius shakes his head and walks away. Grippus turns to me once more. "I don't know."

"Don't know? What kind of answer is 'I don't know'?" I demand. "This is borrowed material. We are responsible for it. Will 'I don't know' pay for it if it is lost?"

"Ah. I see your concern for returning it to the lender has returned," Orestes observes mildly as he glances off into the distance, but I am not deterred by his sarcasm.

"Did Pappius misplace it?" I ask Grippus.

"No, it's me," Grippus says. "I apologize and take full responsibility. My memory is failing."

"What do you mean?"

"This isn't the first item I've lost," he confesses. "There have been other things. I haven't said anything because I thought they'd turn up, but . . . there you go. I set things down, look around, and they're gone."

"What things?" I ask.

"Nothing big. A scarf. An apple. I left my smallest chisel— my favourite—behind when I took my meal, then couldn't find it when I returned. A carving knife." I look at Grippus, and he appears completely undone. His face is lined from years working outdoors, but when I do the calculation I realize he can't be much older than me.

"Never mind," I tell him and pat him on the shoulder. "We'll look later for these things. I'm sure they've just been misplaced."

"I hope so," he says. "I'm only fifty-eight, you know. Old, but too young to be losing my memory. I apologize that the Calidorus has gone missing."

"Rest," I advise him, "and drink the juice of cabbage."

"That helps maintain memory?" he asks.

"Cabbage juice holds many healthful properties," I explain.

Grippus looks doubtful, but says he will make some up. He expresses his sincere regret once more, thanks me for my helpful suggestions, and returns to his work.

"I believe you may place too much credit in the juice of cabbage," Orestes tells me after Grippus has left.

"It's horrible stuff," I tell him as I watch Grippus gather his tools. "I wouldn't touch it myself. I just wanted him to stop worrying."

I leave the search for the moment and return to my midday meal.

"Tertius?" I call.

"Yes."

"Bring me a bowl of the lentil stew."

He fetches me a bowl, sets it down in front of me. I break some bread, dip it in the stew, and give one piece to him. He thanks me, sits cross-legged, and begins to gnaw on it.

"You know how I am about stories?" I ask.

"Yes," he says between bites. "You like them."

"That's right." I agree, and dip some more bread into the lentils and give it to him. "Have I ever told you Aesop's tale about the frisky mouse?"

He continues eating but shakes his head.

"It's a simple story," I tell him, "but instructive. There was a frisky mouse that lived in a mouse hole. Each day he contemplated how many things he could pick up and pack off to his mouse's den. Then one day the master of the house learned that things were going missing and he lowered his enormous eye down to the deep darkness of that hole and he looked directly at the mouse, straight into his mouse's heart, and he said if I catch you stealing anything ever again, even the smallest grain, it will absolutely be the last thing you do. I will grind you into sausage meat and feed you to the stray dogs. And the little mouse, realizing he had been caught, never took anything again." I pop the last piece of bread into my mouth. "Everyone lived happily after that. Do you understand the moral of the story?

Tertius slowly swallows the bread, and nods stiffly. "Yes."

"Good," I say, dismissing him. "Go pack the props. They're in disarray. When I look tomorrow, I expect to find everything in order."

His face ashen, he hops up and races to help pack.

Orestes, who has been observing this exchange, watches him go. "I don't believe I've ever heard Aesop told that way," he comments.

I sweep a finger around the bowl to clean up the contents. "Not really Aesop," I say, as I stick the finger in my mouth. "I'm not having a lot of success with Aesop these days."

"I expect those things will turn up," Orestes says.

"They'd better," I say. "There are a thousand boys like Tertius."

Orestes picks up a cloak, folds it, and places it on the pulpitum. "To his credit, the rascal has genuinely been useful to us. And it's interesting that he chose to pilfer the mask. It might indicate a more serious interest in the theatre. Maybe there's a place for him at some point in the future as a performer."

"Maybe," I say, "but he can't stay if he can't be trusted. If the mask doesn't turn up by tomorrow, send him off."

21

Dawn slowly emerges, dripping and draped in fog, suited to this day celebrating the Feast of Lemuria, when we placate the spirits of the restless dead. Mist clings to the trees in thick, grey, obscuring ropes of trailing cloud. The world, it seems, is devoted to sombre reflection.

I enjoy my morning puls hot, brought to me by Candria, and stir it a long while as I consider my play. There are still portions of the script that remain frustratingly incomplete, and they pester me. I unfold a tablet and scribble a few idle notes.

As I reread them, Candria quietly enters and removes my bowl. I thank her and continue writing. She says something to me by way of response, but I don't catch the exact words, my mind is on my work. I hear her again moments later—not speak exactly, but release a kind of sigh—and turn to see her collapse as easily as a strip of fabric might fold. She topples so gently—one hand on a table bearing her weight even as her legs buckle beneath her—that the empty bowl she is carrying away simply rolls from her outstretched hand across the floor.

I kneel by her. My first thought recalls Antipho and his sudden failure, but when I touch her cheek, I can feel that she is still warm and breathing.

"Vulcanus!" I call, and when he doesn't respond I call again, louder.

He emerges from the culina, flushed from working close to the grill, brushing his rough hands against an overcloth he wears when he chops meat. He appears irritated and impatient at being summoned, but when he sees me on the floor beside Candria, his expression changes. "Get Casina," I tell him. "Quickly."

Casina arrives holding a damp cloth, and wets Candria's face. Candria wakes briefly, confused and disoriented; and Casina directs Vulcanus to carry her to her bed. It's only then that I spy the pool of blood on the floor.

The midwife arrives and passes a bundle of herbs to Casina to prepare. As she climbs the stairs to see Candria, I exit and hurry to meet Orestes at the dockyard, where I'm to help collect some bolts of fabric. Along the streets, everywhere, people are preparing offerings and setting out in small groups to attend to the gravesites of their deceased family members. Clouds continue to gather, following the line of the river valley, and before I have arrived at my destination a hard rain commences.

I am delayed longer on this mission than I had wanted, the storehouse being difficult to find and the merchant talkative. I locate Orestes and help him transport the bolts of fabric. Afterward, we share a meal and discuss matters related to the production. When I return to the Cerium it is late. The weather has stayed miserable, and consequently the streets, normally crawling with the most disreputable, undesirable kind of drunk and cutthroat, are deserted.

I arrive back at the caupona cold and dripping wet. It's quiet when I enter, and as I cut across the coenatio I'm surprised to see Casina seated off in a corner, a heavy wool cloak wrapped around her shoulders and an oil lamp at her side, burning low. A vase and a cup are on the table in front of her.

"Casina?" I call, and when she doesn't respond, repeat her name louder.

"Good," she says, suddenly rousing and looking up, as though noticing me for the first time, "you're here. Hold these." She hands me two bronze pots that are resting by her feet. "The others have retired. You can help me complete the ritual."

I grasp the pots by their handles and gently tap them together, then look out at the street. "It's pouring rain."

"The spirits care nothing for weather or damp. Drink," she says, pushing the vase of wine forward, "it'll warm you."

She pours a generous cupful, undiluted by water, and hands it to me. I drink from what I assume was previously her cup, while she braces herself against the tabletop, lurches to her feet, and fetches another for herself. When she returns, she sits heavily and pours herself a healthy serving. We listen to the rain strike the roof and sweep through the street in great erratic, wet gasps.

"The month of May. It either comes laughing or crying," I observe, and wipe the rain from my face. I nod at the vase. "Seems you're well ahead of me."

"Just having a quiet moment to myself," she says. "Spent most of the day dealing with Candria."

I take a seat on the bench across from Casina. "How is she?"

"Poorly," she replies, looking out at the street. "She took the wormwood late, that was the problem. To work properly it should be taken in the first month, but it's easy to misjudge." A rain-drenched dog hesitantly peeks in at the entrance. Not sensing a welcome, it sadly turns and pads off into the darkness. "I think the worst is over," Casina says. "The midwife believes the worst is over, but she'll stay on to help until we're certain."

A platter of cold food sits on nearby table, put together for Lemuria. Casina reaches over and casually plucks up a portion of lamb. She nods at me. "Eat, eat. I've already burnt an offering, I'll prepare more later if the dead are still hungry."

I select a strip of lamb as well. "At one point late in the day," she continues, "Candria experienced convulsions. It's then I was most anxious. Several years back, at the previous location, another girl I employed, Astaria, met with the same difficulties. Bled and bled, as though it would never end, and three days later she was gone. Thankfully, this time, the midwife was able to contain it." She wipes her hands on the rag she has tucked into her sash. "The Choragus for a mime company has been making inquiries after Candria. I've put him off because his offer has been low, and she's definitely a draw for customers here—but maybe she'd do better there."

I nod my agreement, then hold up the pots she handed me. "And now you are preparing for the midnight observance?"

"I own this business and am head of this home, such as it is, so will complete the Lemurian ceremonies on behalf of the household. Although I don't really have wandering spirits to appease," she says, and drinks. "You?"

"I don't think so. My father and mother passed away while I was a child, but I have no reason to believe they were unsatisfied. In any case, I made my offering to them earlier today. And my wife," I add.

"You're a widower?" Casina asks.

"Barely," I reply. "I was matched young, we were married only a year. She sickened and died before I was conscripted." A chill catches me as I speak of her. "And your parents?" I ask, to take my mind off her. "Are they still alive?"

"Both dead," she answers, "but they didn't have the kind of personalities that would bother haunting down here. If I know them, they'd stay up north where the summers are cooler and the other spirits all speak the same language."

"How far north?" I ask.

"Just east of Mediolanum."

"A considerable distance," I agree. "And your family didn't accompany you?"

"That wouldn't have been possible." Her mouth tightens in a thin, humourless grin. "My father sold me."

"Oh," I say, feeling a rush of embarrassment for having asked. I apologize, but it doesn't appear to perturb Casina, who just waves it off.

"Our household was poor," she says. "My father drank. I was a nuisance to him, and for my part I wasn't unhappy to leave."

The caupona, usually so lively, seems uncharacteristically sombre in this dim light. The mist creeps in at the corners of the room and nestles near the table legs.

I pour myself more wine. "You came directly to Rome, then?"

"Initially I was purchased to work out in the gods and beyond down south," she says, grimacing as she brings it to mind. "Some sprawling, dusty vineyard with a crush of other desperate slaves hunched over, sweating from sunup. The moment I set foot on that compound, I had one long look about and made a point of ensuring I served inside." She drinks. "But when you're young, the mistress has one idea of service and the master another, and I could either make my mistress or my master happy, but not both at the same time.

Finally, the mistress had me whipped for a whore and sold to a brothel."

I murmur some kind of expression of sympathy, but she shakes her head. "Never mind," she says. "That was my lucky day. Those big estates use and discard slaves like so much dirty dishwater. The pimp I was sold to was old, his instrument weak. It didn't take much to make him happy. I turned out to be popular with his clients and soon became his favourite and chief among his girls. As he grew older, I took over duties, including caring for him after he collapsed and took to bed. In gratitude he granted me manumission and the business before he died. I convinced him in his last years to purchase a popina where I could manage the business and where he could be more comfortable. The business thrived, I needed more room. I sold the popina and traded up. Here." She opens her hands to indicate the Cerium.

Perhaps it's the ritual, but hearing her talk about her journey here and her family, I find myself turning over my past experiences and the people I have lost, the souls I have known and know no longer. Prior to today, it has been months since I thought of the child I had been married to for less than a year, and I realize with a disquieting twinge that I can't even put a face to her any longer. For a moment I struggle to remember her name, and finally dredge it up. Abelia.

With effort I am able to bring to mind that plain, silent youngster with her blank face and long, pale neck. I barely knew her before she contracted a stomach ailment, and as with everything else she had ever done, she made her exit quietly and without complaint. I'd grieved, but the fact was that we had only begun to become acquainted. Suddenly, I feel a sharp pang that I will never have an opportunity to know her any better than that. I think back to my family and feel their shades loom close.

The weather worsens as we talk, rattling the roof tiles. "In this downpour, how will we know when it's midnight?" I ask.

Casina nods out at the dark night. "Listen for when the others begin."

We fall silent. Casina tops her cup up again. "Did he come up with you to this place, your former master?" I ask.

"No," she says, drinking, "no, he never saw it. He died at the previous location, just prior to our moving."

"And you were able to carry on in the Cerium without his guidance?"

"Guidance?" she chuckles drily. "Before he passed, in his final moments, he made me promise that I would find a man to take care of me and the business—he was that certain that all that time I had been bathing him, purchasing and preparing his medicines, feeding him, managing the accounts, cooking and seeing to it that the other girls were fed, making sure that they were turning over their money, making sure they kept enough money to save a little for themselves—that he had, in fact, been caring for me."

"Did you make the promise?" I ask.

"Of course I did," she answers and drinks. "I'd have to have been cold-hearted to not fulfill a dying man's wish."

"And then?"

"He died happily, assured that he was still in control," she says, pouring herself more wine. "And then I continued running the operation on my own, just as I had all along. And do you know what? The business performed better in the year after he died than in all the years previous."

I hold up my cup. "To business and better days."

"To prospering despite hard times," she says, and we touch cups and drink.

The wind whines, and the shutters rattle, as though all our past deeds and departed companions are trying to force their way through the slats to drink with us. The darkness beyond the lamplight crowds close and I suddenly feel an intense bitter pang of loneliness, regret, and loss.

"On this night above all, don't you long for home?" I ask after a lengthy silence.

"Home?" she repeats scornfully. "Noo." And she says it with such certainty that I'm taken aback.

"No yearning at all for your youth?" I demand.

"For what?" she asks. "For a family that no longer exists, a village I barely knew? By now the community where I was raised is as thoroughly Roman as garum, and as boring and confining as any small town can be. Here, I have a thriving business, I own property, I am surrounded by people who know, trust, and respect me. Had I stayed there, what would I have become? A farmer's wife?"

"Would that have been so bad?" I ask.

She looks me in the eye. "Have you ever slept with a farmer?"

We hear the sound of metal clanging against metal, up and down the street.

"Come," she says, "it's time."

We stand, make our way to the entrance, hesitate a moment beneath the awning, then step outside, the rain sluicing down, cold, insistent, penetrating. Casina stretches her heavy brown cloak out over her head and clutches the lamp in her left hand, safely sheltered from the downpour. I, at least, am wearing sandals, but her feet are bare as the ritual requires, and the puddled water squelches between her toes. She halts at the entrance to the caupona and removes a handful of black beans from her shoulder satchel.

"Ready?" she shouts, raising her voice to be heard over the steady thrum of the rain.

I nod.

"I send these," she proclaims, flinging a handful of beans onto the roadway, "and with these beans I redeem me and mine!" She tosses a few more. I hear some bounce and scatter where they hit stone, and others splash and sink into standing water.

I clang the pots together and recite, "Spirits of my fathers and ancestors, be gone!"

We trudge to the southwest corner of the caupona, where Casina again reaches into her bag. Again she says, "I send these, and with these beans I redeem me and mine." And because I have performed this rite with my uncle, now dead, and my father, now dead, the ceremony transports me. I abruptly see my father, and his stern face, and my family and all those who have passed away, all those I have loved, and many that I didn't love. My ailing, sharp-tongued aunt, and my resigned, long-suffering mother appear and chastise me for neglect. How could I have forgotten them, they ask. The blank face of my fourteen-year-old wife stares dumbly at me from the darkness. Hasn't she a claim on me? They all seem to demand an answer. I clang the pots to silence them. "Spirits of my fathers and ancestors, be gone!" I yell over the wind.

My comrades in the legion appear next in the darkness, the Hastati I marched alongside, dug trenches, and shared a tent with, limping. "Haven't we," they clamour, "a claim? Weren't we at one time your family?" The night is cluttered with faces, alive with voices, thick with memories. The wind keens through the street, and voices and whispers emerge from every corner, dark recess, and crevice. We repeat the ritual six more times at the corners of the caupona and around back in the alley and then directly once again at the front entrance. The ceremony concluded, we return inside, set the lamp on a tabletop. I catch a choking sound, glance over at Casina, and see that it's not the rain streaking her face, but tears. I pass a hand over her right cheek to brush them away, and am surprised to find that when she presses the warm, open palm of her hand against my cheek, I am crying as well.

We kiss hesitantly at first, then hard. We cling to one another. She slides the leather wallet from her shoulder and drops it to a tabletop. I slip my sandals off and together we climb the creaking stairway, stripping off our wet clothes, pressing close, wrapping rain-slick limbs about one another for heat, for comfort, for reassurance, to block out the darkness and memories and the insistent sound of the wind and rain as we tumble into bed.

The sleep following our lovemaking is deep and dreamless, but just prior to dawn we wake briefly, press closely, whisper softly, caress, twine hands in hair, twist limbs around one another, and find fulfillment once more before dropping back to sleep.

22

I am on a ship, the ship on the ocean. Chilly seawater spills
over the lip of the prow and sprays my forehead. We are
rehearsing a play—I don't know which one—on board, but the
turbulent waters present special challenges. The props shift
and slide with each trough we dip into and shift again with
each wave we ascend. Naevius is a one-legged sandalmaker,
fashioning leather goods that appear to have a vaguely sexual
purpose. He sits next to me and laughs uproariously at the
chaotic activities. "It is a whore's art," he cackles again and
again, slapping his one good leg, "a whore's art!"

I find this highly annoying. Consequently, I experience a
spasm of guilty satisfaction when one of those mangy black
and white spotted dogs that sailors keep on ships ambles over,
lifts a leg, and relieves himself against Naevius's wooden peg.
This, I think, will silence the smug bastard, good dog. Then
the dog calmly lifts a leg to pee on me as well. Incensed at
this crude behaviour, I seize the dog by its scruff to fling him
overboard. Abruptly, the dog wiggles free, stands on his hind
legs, and I understand instantly that he is actually Dionysus
in animal form. Simultaneous to this I realize that the actors
are approaching the end of their lines and I haven't finished the
script. I unfurl a scroll and begin inventing lines, scratching
them down, hurriedly filling the blank spaces. Casina, who
is now seated next to me, observes that the actors are nearing

the incomplete ending. I write faster. I am writing so swiftly that sparks leap from the end of the stylus and ignite the initial portion of the script. These sparks catch on the dry papyrus and set it aflame. I continue scribbling madly, choking on the smoke, but as fast as I write the other end burns. I realize there will be nothing left, I will have thrown my entire being into this venture, and will not have left a trace.

"I will never finish," I cry aloud, "never finish, and no one will even know that I began!"

The dog turns, fixes me with his flaming golden eyes, opens his mouth, and says, "That is not the script you are talking about, but life."

At once, vines spring from the oar locks, crawl up the mast, and crowd the deck. The mast itself erupts in green branches, and the branches sprout flowers. The ship's deck turns into a forest, the dog version of Dionysus transforms into a fiery cloud and ascends into the sky, the cast turn into dolphins and leap overboard, Casina turns into a seagull. I remain me—dusted in ashes, soaked by seawater, holding a singed scrap of smoking papyrus.

"It will never be finished," I say to myself. "Never."

I feel a hand on my shoulder shaking me. "Wake up."

"What is it?" I growl, still recovering from the dream. I push the hand away.

"It's about Sostratos."

I rub my eyes and yawn. "What about him?" I ask.

"He's gone," Orestes tells me.

Instantly I'm awake and see Orestes and Fronto looming large above me, their faces wrinkled in concern. "What do you mean?" I ask, trying to gather my wits.

"I mean he's gone," Orestes replies. "He didn't show up for rehearsal this morning."

I throw the blanket aside and sit up, noting in that moment that Casina has already risen and left for work. "Did you look for him?" I ask.

He nods. "I sent Fronto up to wake him when he hadn't arrived."

"And?" I demand.

"It turns out," Fronto answers, "he hadn't been there last night."

"Hercules's engorged member," I mutter, and rub a hand over my face. "Where is he?"

"Where is he?" Orestes scoffs. "What kind of question is that? You know where he is."

"Meaning," I say, "that you believe he's off drinking?"

"Of course he is," he replies. "What else would he be doing? After acting, it's the thing he does best."

I try to determine what our next step should be. "Is there a drinking establishment that he frequents?" I inquire.

"Is there a drinking establishment he hasn't frequented?" Orestes replies, determined, it seems, to answer all my questions with questions. "He could be anywhere. I warned you he would be impossible to control."

"Well, this is just chastising the wind for capsizing the ship," I say as I stand and throw on my clothes. "It may feel good at the time, but there's no use in it. We are too deep into the play to recruit someone else. We'll have to find him."

"And then what?" Orestes asks.

"Sober him up. Fetch him back to rehearsals. Prevent him from getting drunk again until he finishes the production."

I direct them to inspect the closest popinae in the nearby streets, and we agree to meet up back at the central fountain. While they are gone I clean myself and hurry over to the temple of Minerva.

"Minerva," I whisper as I place my gift on the altar, "goddess of wisdom, patron of the arts, guardian of poets and scribes and other such fools, I offer up this cake of barley and honey. Please accept my sacrifice and provide your blessing on our grex. I am asking that you have pity. Has there ever been a project so plagued with delays, interrupted, and cursed with setbacks? Isn't it sufficient that my first lead actor died? I ask you to send your watchful eye and guiding hand over my grex and help me find that irritating, drunken, unreliable, ungrateful Sostratos and chastise him for his negligence, bad judgment, and irresponsibility—but not so severely that he can't complete the play," I hasten to add, "and then help me to develop some device to keep that inebriate away from wine in the future. I humbly request this of you and vow that if this play is successful and doesn't grind me into the finest milled dust as a result of these many trials then in addition to this sacrifice I will ensure a lamb is devoted to you in the spring. I pledge this with the priests as my witness."

I bow to the priests on duty and back away from the altar. As agreed, I meet up with Orestes and Fronto at the fountain, and we continue our search. We develop a plan, moving out from the Cerium in widening circles, asking questions of the proprietors, and of the individuals who, from our estimation, look like they've been drinking there longest.

If only it were that simple. Rome at night becomes an immense sponge. Squeeze it anywhere and cheap wine runs freely. There are any number of dank, easily overlooked operations where a person may sink into the city's saturated pores if they don't wish to be found.

Orestes and I inspect dozens upon dozens of drinking establishments, and even I am surprised to discover how many unwholesome businesses exist, places where a person can quietly drink himself to death if he so chooses.

I begin to realize what a monumental task we've set ourselves. Rome has indeed stirred up an anthill, as Orestes once suggested, and the ants have raced from great distances, gathered other ant comrades, and burrowed deep into the innermost recesses of the hill, where they now gorge on the collected nectar. As we move in our expanding circles we come across leering drunks too intoxicated to speak; profane drunks whose conversation is thoroughly blasphemous; wicked gangs of threatening drunks whom we quietly step around and avoid; drunks so thoroughly steeped in wine that it is difficult to determine if they are still breathing.

In fact, if Sostratos had chosen to remain quiet, pay his sestertii, and drain his cups, we might never have found him. Instead, he involved himself in an altercation that nearly ended his life.

My understanding of the chain of events that evening, drawn from the testimony of a variety of less than reputable individuals at adjoining tables, is that after Sostratos had slipped from his chamber, he found his way by stages to Mercury's Cup, a greasy little enterprise habituated by mercenaries, sailors, and a variety of shady disreputables. There, he joined a hard-drinking company seated around a table in the corner. Everything was fine for the duration of the first few vases, but then as they pursued their libations more vigorously, events took an uncomfortable turn.

Everyone is in agreement that a situation arose between Sostratos and the individual immediately to his left—a southerner of some kind. After what had been described as a protracted, intense, hushed disagreement, a scuffle erupted. Following a short period of grappling, Sostratos abruptly seized a large vase from an adjoining tabletop and shattered it against the side of his antagonist's head. Then, demonstrating remarkable agility for one so old, and showing a surprising capacity to improvise with the implements at hand, he snatched a broken shard and in a swift, deft motion, slashed the man's throat in an arc that traced from ear to ear. The shard, not being as keenly edged as a knife, had not sliced as deeply as a knife might have, and so the man, though bloodied and frightened, survived. The fight had been broken up, and the stranger who received the cut disappeared into the night, nursing his wounds. The proprietor, understandably upset that this level of violence had taken place under his roof, took the expedient measure of having his employees thrash Sostratos senseless before roughly ejecting him into the street.

When we find him seated on the paving stones of an alley, skinny legs stretched out, both sandals apparently lost or stolen, he is nearly unrecognizable. He is by no means a young man to begin with, and he looks, in this moment, aged many years beyond old. Every feature is swollen or cut. His back is braced against a stone wall, and he presents a bleeding, beaten patchwork of discoloured, angry flesh and shredded tunic.

I hire a donkey. Together, Orestes and I haul Sostratos to his feet and strap him, groaning, to the donkey's back. His head dangles limply over the side like an ornamental tassel draped from a fancy saddle. He hiccups once, then turns his head and projects a sour-smelling stream of vomit, spattering into the gutter.

We remove him to his cubiculum, where we strip him of his soiled clothes, clean him as best we can, and put him to bed. Throughout the exercise, he says next to nothing in response to our questions. Afterward, Orestes and I scrub up, and close his door.

"Who," I ask, "can stay here and stand watch?"

"I've already arranged for that," Orestes tells me. "I have a man coming, he'll be here shortly."

"Well?" I ask as I dry my hands.

Orestes yawns and rubs his face tiredly. "I'll rehearse the others tonight," he says, "then bring Sostratos in tomorrow to carry on."

We descend the stairs on weary legs and lean against the wall out on the street. "What do you think happened?" I ask.

"What happened?" he repeats and shoots me a glance. "I think he got drunk."

"Don't be simple," I snap.

Orestes shrugs. "Wherever you have people drinking to excess, you also have brawling."

"This wasn't an ordinary drunken fight. Drunks when they fight aren't discreet. They roar, thump their chests, announce their grievances to the world. Again and again, we're told that the argument, though bitter, was private." I lick my lips, and strike a calmer tone. "So, what does that tell you?"

Orestes runs a hand through his hair. "That they knew one another?" he suggests.

"Yes, and . . . ?" I prompt.

"There was something they argued about that they didn't want others to know."

"Exactly," I conclude. "So, the question, my friend, is what didn't they want others to know?"

23

We attempt to extract this information from Sostratos the next morning, but he insists that he had been too drunk. He can't remember the events, can't recollect the individual, can't recall the drinking establishment. The night's conflicts, as far as he is concerned, have been erased.

I attend rehearsals and he does well under the circumstances. His lips are swollen, one eye nearly closed, and I'm sure his movements cause him considerable pain. Nevertheless he limps along gamely, hitting his cues and singing in a dry, raspy voice.

After rehearsal's end, I follow him and share a few encouraging words. When I return, I find Orestes and Casina engaged in quiet conversation about how best to cope with the present situation. I cautiously suggest that we try limiting his drinking.

Orestes shakes his head. "He won't be able to stop— that's been proven. He's been steeped in wine too long. It's unreasonable to expect him to simply come to a complete halt."

"I'm not saying that he should drink nothing at all, but we have to do something. Otherwise," I argue, "it's inevitable that one of these times the fit will take him and he'll leave us in the lurch."

"Orestes and I have taken care of it," Casina tells me.

"How?" I ask.

"Don't ask if you don't want to know," she replies.

I glance from one face to another, but they return my gaze blankly. I decide that she's right, I don't want to know. "Fair enough," I say, "but other than that, everything is going well?"

"Yes, yes," Orestes answers. "Stop worrying. Concern yourself with finishing the play."

I return with new material a few days later, and see continued improvement in the performances. Sostratos gradually heals, and the play takes good shape. Though he still favours one leg when he walks, his voice is as sweet as it was when we first met.

"Well, you're getting your money's worth," Orestes tells me when rehearsal ends.

"He's a gift from Dionysus for certain," I acknowledge, "a god who loves both acting and drinking."

"And that performance comes only shortly after a night on a drunk and a flogging," he observes. "Imagine what he could achieve if he managed to stay sober. When," he asks, "will we receive the conclusion of the script?"

"It's coming," I tell him. I glance once more in the direction of Sostratos. "I understand from speaking with Grippus that Sostratos is not staying where he did before."

Orestes looks at me. "That's correct," he says.

I wait for him to say more, but he remains silent. I try to restrain my curiosity but finally give in. "So tell me," I say.

"There's a servant's shed not far from here," he tells me. "Casina rented it. The slave's manacles are still there. He's chained to the floor and provided with food and a container of wine."

"Every night?" I ask.

"After we've finished rehearsals, yes, he's locked in," he answers, "and it has only been a couple of nights."

I shake my head. "And he's agreed to that?"

"We didn't put it to a vote," Orestes replies, "if that's what you're wondering."

"I see."

"And, so long as there's wine placed beside the bed each night, he's satisfied," Orestes tells me, sounding a little defensive. "It was either that or I told him I would go back to you and have him fired. In the morning, I release him and he rises like a lamb and follows. You object?"

I consider our options, then shake my head. "No."

Later that evening, though, I worry over that conversation as a dog worries a bone. If Sostratos silently resents this treatment, won't this simply provoke him to leave once more? Why would anyone with the prodigious talents that he possesses permit anyone to debase him so thoroughly? I decide to go and reason with him.

He is reclining on his bed, carving a piece of knotted olive wood when I enter. The shavings have collected in a feathery pile on the floor. The shed he is housed in is much as one would expect, primitive and small. His legs are each secured at the ankles to a length of chain that is, in turn, secured to the wall. He is able to stand, stretch out, shuffle to the door, and back to the bed.

"Well," I say, looking down at Sostratos, "this is an unhappy sight."

"I am a dog," he tells me, and rattles his chains. "You have me kennelled."

"Had you not tried to kill someone," I remind him, "this would not be necessary."

He shrugs. "I didn't say I was an unhappy dog." He reaches for the cup sitting beside the bed and takes a sip of his wine. "I am fed and watered. I have employment during the day and I am content to stay here nights and entertain."

"Who is it that you entertain?" I ask.

"Myself," he replies, and grins. "And at my age, that is all that is necessary."

"Let us be honest with one another," I suggest as I sit on an empty spot at the end of the bed. "Why did you cut this man?"

"He gave offence," is his simple and direct answer.

I think on that. "What kind of offence did he give?" I ask.

"I can barely recall anymore," he answers. "It doesn't matter."

"Clearly, it mattered that night," I argue.

"I was influenced by wine at the time," he says, offering me a thin, humourless grin, "and under its influence I take offence easily."

"Then you should drink less," I suggest, "or take offence less easily, or both."

He drains his cup and then pointedly refills it. "We are both a little long in the tooth to exchange advice about life choices," he tells me. "Whatever I am now, I have been for some considerable time and am unlikely to change."

We talk for a brief while longer but continue fruitlessly in this vein, and I receive no more information than I already have received from him. Whatever happened, he is either unable to remember or unwilling to reveal. He tells me he is comfortable enough and not to concern myself. I leave him with an apple and small piece of cake wrapped in a cloth, and retire.

Rehearsals are interrupted as the cast, excepting Sostratos, attend the wedding of Fabius and his young bride Lollia, the beginning of June being regarded by her parents as auspicious. I have heard vague rumours of preparations for this union for some time, but it is my first opportunity to meet her. She seems a pretty and pleasant match. Short, wide-shouldered, and broad-hipped, she has lively green eyes and an open, friendly face. The wedding is an uncomplicated, joyful affair: Fabius is proud and happy, Lollia smiles throughout. She wears the simple traditional white tunic and flame-coloured veil, which asserts purity and presents a kind of clean, wholesome appeal, but never truly flatters any woman. The attending priest has them chant, "Where and when you are Gaius, then and there I am Gaia." Following that, they exchange rings, and kiss. Everyone cheers. The priest bids them to sit on a sacrificial lambskin facing one another and makes an offering to Jupiter; he then has them eat a portion of the spelt bread baked by the bride. Once that has concluded, Lollia's parents begin bustling about, setting out food for the guests.

As this occurs, there is a lull in the ceremonial activities. I scan the crowd and see that there are many from the theatre in attendance. I spy Naevius standing near a doorway and wave him over. "How are things going with your rehearsal now?" I call as he approaches.

"Catastrophic," he grumbles, and shakes his head. "You cannot imagine how the gods are punishing me for my past misdeeds."

"You've committed many, so amending them may take time and prodigious effort. But an older fellow like yourself might need a drink to help cope," I suggest, and pass him the jug I'm drinking from.

"Excellent idea," he agrees, grasping it.

"So, things haven't improved since we last met?" I ask.

"Improved?" he repeats, and drinks. "Goodness, no! Our Choragus, Lucas, has the cast so thoroughly terrified that they are utterly beside themselves now."

"How do they manifest this terror?" I ask, amused at his theatrical gloom. "Do they howl like spirits, or merely chatter their teeth?"

"They sprint through the play as though chased by death," he declares, "and if they stumble over a word, turn pale as a ghost. My oldster, Vibius, accidentally reversed two lines the other day. I thought Lucas might ignite. He cursed in the most profane manner, flung his cup across the field, summoned the gods and all their compelling powers. The old fellow was completely abject, of course. I feared he might soil himself." A table is carried over to where we are standing, and Naevius and I shuffle aside to make room.

"The Choragus couldn't find it in himself to forgive him?" I ask.

"No, he remonstrated with him in the most extreme terms. Then the youngest infant in our crew screws up some terribly misguided courage and squeaks out in his thin reedy voice to 'Leave old Vibius alone.' Well, that hurled the fat into the fire. Lucus roared like a Cyclops and leapt onto the pulpitum, ready to denature him."

It's not uncommon for passions to rise in the latter stages of rehearsal, but this level of conflict—if it's true—is astonishing. "So a fight broke out in your rehearsal?" I ask.

"Well," Naevius allows as his face crumples into a lopsided grin. "More a foot race than a fight. The youngster immediately abandoned any vestige of defiance, tossed his mask behind him, and took flight. Lucas pounded after him, raging that if he had damaged the mask he would flay him alive, tan the skin, and fashion a new mask from that."

"So they tear across the field, a wolf chasing a rabbit, the infant lobbing curses over his shoulder but propelled by total, undisguised fear. 'You dog!' he shouts over his shoulder, his voice trembling. 'You dog!'"

"'I'll show you dog,' Lucas growls, snapping his leather strap. 'I'll sink my teeth in your backside, I'll grind you up and shit you out!' This only spurs the youngster to greater speed. Round and round the field they turn, my Choragus calling down fire and cracking his strap the way a charioteer snaps the reins. Finally the youngster sources a last desperate reserve of energy and leaps like a squirrel into some low-hanging branches and scales a tree. There, he perches in the uppermost canopy, snapping off cones and hurling them below. Lucas, completely exhausted, collapses at the base of the tree and releases a stream of profanity so foul my beard would ignite if I were to repeat it." Naevius shakes his head as he considers the wonder of it.

"Now," I ask, "how do things stand?"

"The artists in my grex continue to work, and it's either the greatest comedy or the greatest tragedy I've ever witnessed—I can't make up my mind which. I only know that if I could get the audience to attend my rehearsals, I would win the prize for best performance, no question."

I want to ask him if he has heard anything of the other two greges, but we are interrupted by the food being set out by the bride's family. We're both hungry, and the wedding banquet is exceptional. The bride's father—a cheese maker by profession—has laid out a superb selection of his finest cheeses, along with fresh breads and sausages, sweet figs, and dried apples.

We eat and drink our fill and then, once done, trail along after the wedding procession to the home of Fabius, showering the happy couple with nuts as they go. At one point, Fabius and his team of young men speed up the pace and take a more direct route to ensure that they arrive at his home prior to Lollia and her entourage. We continue following Lollia, some of the younger ones in the procession chanting the usual scandalous songs. Moments later, as we turn down an alley and approach the newlyweds' home, Fabius reappears. He accepts the torch from Lollia's hands and brings it into what will now be their shared dwelling—a tiny, tidy place behind his uncle's olive oil business. Inside, one can see by the flickering torchlight that the nuptial bed has been beautifully decorated with fragrant garlands of colourful flowers and rings of figs. Fabius employs the torch to light his brazier, and a lamp. That done, he extinguishes it in a bucket of water. Then, stepping back onto the street and stretching his arm behind his head, he hurls the torch twirling high into the air over the procession. Fronto eagerly leaps up, and extending his entire body, manages to snatch the torch over the competing outstretched fingers of his competitors, like a soldier seizing the sword of a vanquished enemy.

"What athleticism!" Grippus teases as he, Orestes, Fronto, Tertius, and I stumble along the road following the festivities. "He was like a young Hercules gripping the twin snakes sent by Hera."

"Or Perseus," I suggest, "seizing the severed head of the Gorgon. To Fronto, and his heroically long reach and firm grasp!"

"And to Fabius," Grippus adds, "our lucky friend who is now, even as we speak, consummating his marriage!" Grippus performs some kind of quick inner calculation. "Perhaps for the second time."

"And to Lollia," Orestes adds.

"To the bride!" we shout our agreement.

"Very much so to the bride," Fronto remarks politely after saluting her health. "She seems so nice."

"Quite nice," I agree.

"Surprisingly nice," Orestes muses, taking the vase from me. "I'm stunned that Fabius found a match with someone as pretty as she is."

"What are you saying?" Grippus objects, throwing his hands up in protest—and nearly knocking me over with one knobby elbow in the process. "Fabius isn't ugly!"

"He's not bad,"Orestes permits, "but he has that long nose."

"A long nose is an expression of virility."

"You only say that," Orestes points out, "because you possess one too."

"That's how I know," he states primly.

Grippus has had the foresight to snag a separate vase of wine, which, having finished the earlier one, we now exchange back and forth as we walk to the theatre. Tertius had brought us a message indicating that strangers may have trespassed at the theatre site and left things in disarray. Orestes has suggested that we stop by to ensure that nothing is damaged.

As the dirt track narrows, and becomes hedged about with tall reeds, our group is constricted, and Grippus, Fronto, and Tertius forge ahead like explorers. Grippus seizes this opportunity to satisfy his obsession with the craft of acting and interrogates Fronto. Fronto, like most actors, is more than willing to indulge this curiosity. Orestes and I fall back, and for a while are content to follow behind, attentive to the friendly chatter of our colleagues and the sound of Tertius's dog occasionally darting into the brush—he's adopted one of the stray pups from the Cerium, a skinny, sharp-muzzled mongrel with movable, expressive ears. It's a warm, comfortable, quiet night. We pad along, listening to the happy, hoarse pant of the dog, to the thrum of birds suddenly flushed from the bushes, to the timorous calls of owls. Orestes has plucked and stripped a long slender rod from alongside the path, and as we amble on, he casually flicks the sides of his legs to deter mosquitoes. They can be miserable at this time of year, but I find I'm not particularly bothered, a testament to either my thick skin or wine-blunted senses. Or both. "Have you noticed," I ask Orestes, "a distance in Casina?"

"A distance?" Orestes repeats and considers the question a moment, then shakes his head. "No. What do you mean, distance?"

"You haven't detected a kind of cooling?" I persist.

"No," he replies. "She remains an exemplary business partner in every way. Capable. Very willing to take matters on. Prompt. Why? Have you noticed something?" When I don't respond, he glances at me sharply. "Have you slept with her?" he asks.

This seems a discourteous question, so I don't reply. Orestes drags a hand across his face. "Was it necessary?" he inquires in a lower voice.

"Necessary? Who considers necessity in matters of this kind? She has all the many positive attributes you've just listed," I point out quite reasonably, "and in addition she's very attractive. Highly attractive. Her neck is like a poem."

CLEM MARTINI

"This has implications for everyone, you understand?" he whispers, his lips tightening. "She is an extraordinary business partner, the grex will never find another like her. A sensible person, a mature person, can feel attracted to those they work with, without sleeping with them. And if you're wise," he adds, "you resist."

"Only Stoics do that," I answer shortly.

He stares hard at me. "So now," he demands, "is there trouble between you?"

"Calm yourself. There's no trouble," I deny. "I never said there was trouble. I said she seems distant."

"Distant," he asserts, "is just another way of saying trouble."

"Not at all, it means distant. You are making a big issue out of something very small. Never mind," I tell him as the others wait for us to rejoin them. "It's nothing serious. I'll speak with her."

Grippus claps his hands as we catch up to them, "There you slowpokes are! I thought we had lost you!" he exclaims, then takes a long drink. "Eyy, that washes the grit away, doesn't it?"

"Very much so," Fronto replies agreeably after drinking as well.

"My actor friend and I have just been discussing your play. As I have told you, when first rehearsals began," Grippus says, retrieving the vase from Fronto, "I was confused when the slave Tyndarus accepted beatings on behalf of his master. I wouldn't have done that for my miserable old master, I can tell you that, I would never have done that, *never*, not if I had lived to be an ancient and forgetful old man. I would have permitted the old scoundrel to take his stripes and may the gods bless him—but, by Dionysus on a donkey, it's funny furious bit of business in the play now. The other afternoon in rehearsal when Sostratos pretended that Aristophantes had lost his mind to prevent him

from revealing the deception to Hegio, I nearly peed myself."
He checks his tunic. "In fact, I might have. This performance will
win Sostratos the laurel wreath, I feel sure of it, it cannot fail."

"Don't make premature predictions," I caution him. "And
don't boast. The gods can—and do—change things in an
instant, if that is their will."

"Happiness cannot occur where there is no wisdom,"
Orestes recites, "no wisdom can occur without submission
to the gods. Pride is always punished, and boasters learn this
lesson as they age. Sophocles."

Grippus releases a rich, fruity belch in response. "Excuse
me," he exclaims, "but piss on Sophocles. It's not boasting if it's
true. We have the best grex. We have the cleverest script—or
will have once it is completely finished. My knees weaken,
the singing is that beautiful. And our Choragus," he glances
sideways at Orestes and whistles through his teeth, "is as mean
and evil as a gorgon."

"I haven't the faintest clue what you are talking about,"
Orestes replies coolly. "I know that if you delay rehearsals
again as you did the other day, peppering the actors with inane
questions, I'll have you flogged with a bolt of papyrus."

"You see what I mean?" Grippus exclaims, shaking his
head with admiration. "How can we fail?"

We round a turn in the path, and arrive at the theatre.
Tertius has been carrying a lamp to light our way, and it's
apparent from the moment we enter the clearing that someone
has visited the rehearsal site. A bench has been overturned,
and there are roasted rabbit bones and muddy footprints on
the pulpitum. Grippus snatches the lamp from Tertius and
trots around behind the theatre to investigate.

We straighten up the disorder and try to determine if any serious damage has been done. "Hey, what's this?" Grippus suddenly shouts. "Look at what some ignorant criminal has written on my beautiful pulpitum!" He shouts for Tertius to come. "And fetch the pumice stone," he adds.

"What does it say?" I ask as we join him.

"I fucked Rufina," he reads, "against this wall." We crowd around to view the writing and consider the drawing—two stick figures engaged in an improperly aligned vertical sexual act. "By all the Gods, this fool is prolific," he fumes. "I've seen the same vulgar phrase scratched in the lane behind the Cerium and up against the docks."

"Also behind the tinsmith's," Orestes reports.

"And on the walls of the Circus Maximus," Fronto adds, "and at the Forum Boarium."

"They're insatiable! Is there any wall," Grippus demands as he traces the wording to determine how deep the drawing goes, "against which this Rufina has not been fucked?"

Tertius arrives with the pumice stone and Grippus puts him to work erasing the image.

"And is there some kind of medical condition, an arthritic hip, or bad back, that prevents the couple from lying down? Jupiter as my witness," Fronto marvels, "it's always against a wall—don't they tire of standing?"

"Here, take this," Grippus says, giving Tertius a coarser stone to employ.

Tertius and his dog end up overnighting at the theatre site to keep watch. Since he ceased his pilfering he has proven himself useful to the grex in a thousand different ways. Grippus leaves them both with sufficient food for the night, some cheeses and breads he pinched from the wedding. The boy has crafted a sling from a scrap piece of leather and he's developed a deadly eye—I've seen him knock over a dove at a hundred paces. And the dog, bony as he is, is a legionnaire at heart and will defy a foe of any size. Between the two of them, they're well equipped to withstand almost any incursion.

We bid him goodnight, and follow a path along the banks of the Tiber. The river chuckles softly through the reeds as starlight anoints us. The moon gleams, an immense saucy orb, and all our surroundings become edged with silver, the tree limbs, leaves, and glittering grass blades. As we pass the wine about, it takes on new and glorious textures: rich, coarse, and deliciously earthy.

"Well, that wasn't as bad as I had feared," Grippus announces, referring to the disorganization we encountered at the theatre.

"Yes," I agree, "it was fortunate that we found nothing seriously damaged. And wasn't it also a fantastic day for a wedding—and now a stunning evening? Look at this radiant moon!—it is a blessing on the married couple."

From behind me I hear Fronto respond, "Very much so," and there follows a brief intense argument wherein Grippus upbraids the young actor for applying this same phrase to every circumstance and Fronto answers that he hopes he will not have his conversation limited on such a festive occasion and Grippus agrees that a wedding is a special time, and permits special liberty, to which Fronto concurs wholeheartedly, shouting, "Very much so!" and they both drink. That settled, we once again toast the wedded bliss of the married couple, their fertility, and continuing happiness.

"As much as the gods have blessed the union of Fabius and Lollia," I say, raising the vase once more, "I feel the gods have blessed our grex as well." And abruptly, without warning, a great wave of sentimentality overwhelms me. "We must," I exhort my colleagues, "discover a way to maintain this group. Although that rascal Sostratos gave us all a terrible scare the other day with his drunken foolishness at the taberna—what a superb talent he has demonstrated in rehearsals!" Fronto, Orestes, and Grippus mutter their agreement. "What devotion to his craft. We must somehow tame his passions, and convince him to drink with more moderation."

"Yes," Fronto concurs, "so that he can join us when we drink to excess!"

"Exactly!" I say.

Grippus plucks the vase from my hands. "Agreed," he affirms after drinking.

"And after all," I say, looping an arm around Grippus, "it is a kind of sacred brotherhood we share in the theatre."

"True," he says, nodding. "Very true."

"A kind of unique family," I suggest.

"The best kind," Grippus amends. "No household to maintain, and an audience instead of in-laws."

"You think I am joking, but I'm not," I insist, as I see Orestes smiling indulgently at me. "Where else can I consult learned opinions like yours, Orestes? Or solicit advice on thorny matters of translation or musical composition? And who is there as able as you to construct a theatre, Grippus? And who better than we four to celebrate the theatre now, and in the future?" I demand.

"Yes, yes," Grippus murmurs softly, as though he were praying.

"Very much so," Fronto adds quietly.

"We must find a way, my friends, to remain together," I insist, returning to my central theme. "Otherwise, who will

I dine and recite lines with at night? And who, when I have grown old and infirm, will truly know me and my work and can be counted on to write something meaningful on my grave?" I conclude with a flourish.

"Never worry," Orestes assures me, patting me on the back. "If there is no one else to do it, I will compose something appropriate for your grave."

"Thank you, and what," I ask, suddenly struck to the quick by the pitiful vision of my tragic, and I'm sure, much regretted departure from this world, "will you write?"

"Something simple," Orestes muses, "but sincere." He glances skyward as if seeking inspiration from the heavens. "He owed me two sestertii," he says finally, prompting guffaws from the others. I nudge him off the trail. He loses his footing and only escapes falling on his face by clutching at a low-hanging branch of a nearby oak, where he dangles a moment, laughing to himself.

"Traitorous clown," I rebuke him as he stands and finds the path once again. "Slandering, drunken nitwit."

"Or," Fronto says, suggesting an alternate epithet, "though I begged him, he denied me a leading role."

"Or, "Grippus offers gleefully, "I fucked Rufina against this gravestone."

The three—even Orestes, who normally doesn't partake in this kind of foolishness—convulse, laughing bent over and bracing themselves each with a hand against a colleague's back.

"Laugh all you want," I protest, which, far from dissuading the inebriates, only provokes greater merriment. "The gods will reproach you for that kind of scurrilous blasphemy. They will chastise and excoriate you! In fact, unless I am mistaken, I believe I can sense them now conferring, from their lofty perch in the heavens, their faces darkening, and believe me, it does not look good for any of you."

I am mollified by a gracious toast that Grippus makes to the play, and another drink, of course; and then we break into a chorus of the opening number from *The Pot of Gold*. As we continue walking we sing every song from that play and then follow it with all the songs from *The Captives*. At last we part ways, shouting goodnight to one another as we take our separate paths, and I finally stumble into the Cerium, up the stairs, and into my bed.

24

I sleep in and neglect to attend rehearsal; consequently it is late in the afternoon when I launch into my midday meal. I am mopping up a bowl of onion and lentils with a wedge of bread when Orestes drops to a bench beside me. He helps himself to some wine and water and says, "I think we have a bigger problem."

"Bigger than what?" I ask. "Bigger than having a drunk as our lead actor? Bigger than potentially being financially ruined? Share it with me, please. It's precisely what I need to lift my spirits."

Orestes peers at me over his cup. "I see the ardour you had for our holy brotherhood has faded," he observes.

"That was last night," I reply. "Reality has blunted it somewhat today. What is it?"

"I've been doing some investigating," he tells me. "I spoke with the owner of the popina where Sostratos got into his tussle, and he pointed me in the direction of some others who had been sitting close to Sostratos. They couldn't tell me exactly what was said, but a couple of them were fairly certain that the one he tried to kill had been demanding money."

"Yes?" I ask, encouraging him to get to the point.

"And they had heard something else he said, something about someone wanting him back."

"*And?*"

"It's obvious," Orestes says, setting his cup down. "Someone, somewhere wants him back."

I wait for him to explain himself.

"Look at the way he has responded to being chained up. He has completely accepted it. There's only one possible interpretation."

"Which is?" I prompt.

Orestes lowers his voice and leans in so that only I hear him. "He's an escaped slave."

I don't reply.

"He has scars of correction," he points out. "His back is criss-crossed."

"Soldiers may receive correction as well," I remind him, thinking back to my time in the army and the men I saw punished, "and come away with the same scars."

Orestes ignores my argument. "If he has escaped his owner," he continues, "and he's discovered, it would be the end of the play, the end of our grex, and there could be enormous fines for anyone who had offered him assistance."

"Maybe," I reply, "but there are a several things to consider. If he is an escaped slave—and we have no sure evidence that he is, beyond some vague second-hand reported conversation, and old scarring, and no sign of a brand marking him as a runaway—"

"That doesn't prove he didn't run away," Orestes interrupts me, "only that he wasn't caught."

"—but if he *is* an escaped slave," I continue, "he has managed to remain free for some time. He has been performing a long while, long enough to build a considerable reputation and then drink it away. We know that."

"What else could he be running from?" he demands.

"Debts," I suggest, "destiny, a difficult wife—"

Orestes rolls his eyes, clearly unimpressed by my argument. "Don't rely on time to fix this," he warns, wagging a finger at me. "Slaves have escaped and then been identified and reclaimed by their masters even decades later."

"I know, but what it could mean is that his owner—if he has an owner—doesn't live in Rome, and perhaps lives a considerable distance away. This fellow Sostratos met in the popina may have been trying to extort money from him with the threat of revealing his identity, but it's possible that given the length of time Sostratos has been free, any theoretical owner may already be dead, or his owner may have stopped searching for him. If it proves necessary, once we determine the truth, we can find the owner and broker the purchase price through an anonymous third party."

Orestes remains unconvinced, but agrees to leave it with me for a few days more. The more I think on it, though, the more I become certain that this situation can be repaired. The penalties for an escaped slave are designed to be harsh. Yes, the owner can legally maim the slave, work him to death, torture him as a lesson to others, or kill him outright. But an owner who had gone that long without his slave would have already written the matter off as a financial loss. Any price he received now would be welcomed.

I view the rehearsals of the new material and Sostratos continues to impress. He is somehow able to dig deep and discover nuances of character in a seemingly effortless fashion. Whatever anxieties he might feel, they are put aside so completely that one wouldn't know that he had any troubles.

I choose to approach Sostratos the next day after rehearsal as he cleans himself from a bucket of water. "I want to speak to you candidly," I tell him.

"Talk away," he replies as he hangs his tunic from a branch. He plunges his hands into the bucket and, drawing water up, scrubs his torso.

I lean up against a nearby tree trunk. A small glade between us and the rehearsal site affords us a bit of privacy. "I went looking for that soldier you argued with," I tell him.

"Really?" he says, picking the bucket up and pouring water over his head. "I should have killed him."

"You almost did," I point out.

He shrugs, picks up a cloth, and wipes himself. Then, pouring olive oil into his hand, he applies a quick layer to his torso and legs. "So?" he asks. "What lies did he tell you?"

"He didn't tell me anything," I reply. "You had done your work well enough, he was sufficiently frightened that he fled and couldn't be found. So, I would guess, from the snippets of information that others have revealed of this brawl, that you were once a slave. Given that this individual served in Sicily, I would guess that you were a slave there—and he knew you."

He continues listening as he reaches into a leather pouch, removes a strigil, and begins scraping away the excess oil from his body.

"I have come to believe that you may escaped from someone's estate," I confide. He says nothing, but continues looking me in the eye. "I don't want to turn you in, that's not why I am bringing this up. I want to assist you—but for me to do so you will have to trust me."

"I see," Sostratos says as he folds up his strigil and places it back in the pouch. "You believe me to be a criminal."

I refuse to be embarrassed. "Do you have any response?"
I ask.

He wrings the damp cloth out and drapes it carefully
on a tree branch to dry. "I'm afraid it is worse than what you
believe," he answers.

I hadn't anticipated a quick, unequivocal confession.
"H-how?" I stutter, after a moment's hesitation, trying to
imagine what could possibly be worse than what I have
already described.

"I have spent nearly my entire life lying and breaking the
law," he continues, "I have slept with my mother, killed my
father, murdered innocent children with fire and with arrows.
I have committed every wicked, cruel, infamous, unworthy
deed imaginable—on stage. You see, that is the way it is. An
actor must be able to shed his skin like the snake and take on
other appearances. Do you want to know if I have murdered? I
have. Have I offended the gods? Most certainly. Whatever the
situation has called for—on stage—that is what I have done."

"I am talking about life," I object, "real life."

"As am I," he assures me. "For me, nothing could be more
real than the theatre."

"This is senseless rhetoric," I tell him. "I am offering you
help. If you were once a slave, and escaped, let me fix this
matter for you. It's time for truth."

"You don't want the truth. You want a fiction that wears a
cloak of convenience," he says, taking his tunic up from the tree
branch. "I have no such cloak to provide you."

25

A tiny black lizard, no bigger than my thumb, crouches and peers at me from its lofty vantage, high on the far wall. In many ways, I think, a lizard's life must be an enviable one. They view the world with complete serenity. They expect so little—a quiet corner of a taberna, the occasional meal of a fly. In the end it is our expectations that test us. If we desire only little, like the lizard, we are most likely to be satisfied. But then, of course, you must cultivate a taste for flies.

I'm interrupted in these lofty thoughts by Casina as she enters the caupona. She pauses briefly to adjust one of the tables, then carries on toward the culina. I rise from my seat and block her way.

"There you are," I say by way of greeting her, and she looks up at me inquiringly. I open my mouth to continue, but although I have rehearsed my lines, they escape me in the moment. "I have begun to think that you regret sleeping with me," I say at last, more bluntly than I had intended.

"No, no," she replies dropping her voice and shifting her body toward me to shield our conversation. "What makes you think that? Would we have repeated what we had already done once if I hadn't enjoyed myself?"

"And yet," I say, "the last time, my tablets and other articles were removed from your cubiculum to mine—"

"I wanted to make sure," she says, "that you could easily get them when—"

"And I observe," I carry on, afraid that if I neglect to say what needs to be said now, I will lack the resolve later, "that you maintain a certain formality in our exchanges—"

"I've been busy," she assures me, "and I've had to spend time bargaining with the—"

"It's not just that you are busy," I interrupt. "Let us at least be honest with one another."

She doesn't reply, and an awkward silence falls over us. This is not how I had envisioned things turning out. I wet my lips and start over. "You once told me that I made myself foolish when I pursued younger women. Are you now going to tell me that I shouldn't be involved with women my own age?"

She shifts her weight from one foot to another. "I am attracted to you," she answers finally, "but our relationship is complicated."

"I don't understand," I tell her.

She dries her hands on her apron. "If you board here," she begins slowly, "and sleep with me occasionally, no one can misunderstand our association."

"Yes?"

"But if you share my room, wake with me, eat with me, things become . . ." Her voice trails away.

I wait. Casina is normally a very direct person. "Things become what?" I ask when she doesn't continue.

"Unclear," she says after a moment.

I take a step closer to her. "In what way unclear?" Again, she doesn't reply, but I feel I must have an answer. "I am clear," I tell her. "I have feelings for you. And the depth of those feelings has surprised me. Is it not this way for you?"

"I have feelings for you as well," she replies, "but if we habitually rise together in the morning, the girls employed at the Cerium will eventually begin to defer to your opinion—after all, you'll be the man living with the owner, in the owner's bed. In time, Vulcanus will begin to consult you about what kinds of meats he should purchase."

"I know nothing about meats," I object. "He will learn nothing from me."

"It won't matter what you know or don't know," she responds, "he will still consult you. And he won't be the only one. Tradespeople will come to you first with their estimates, customers will approach you for advice, and one day I will find myself a stranger in my own home. And," she adds after a moment, "I am hardly your age."

"So, that's it?" I ask. "Our relationship is impossible because of these commercial complications? Despite our feelings? Despite our affinity, or passion, it comes down to the matter of—sharing your cubiculum?"

She doesn't answer me right away. I turn and walk away, angry. The first thought I have, flawed as it is, is that I will take my business elsewhere. Never mind that I am not really paying for my accommodation. Or food.

I spend the afternoon and evening drinking at the Ripe Fruits. I spend the night there as well, and only suffer for it. Bugs devour me and prevent sleep. I endure an itchy, restless night turning over my prior conversation with Casina. I am surprised, given my age at how bruised my pride is, and how totally caught off guard I am by her response. I thought we felt the same way about one another.

The next day, Orestes seeks me out and sits beside me. "I was told I would find you here," he says as he settles onto a stool.

That doesn't appear to require a reply, so I don't offer one.

"You brought this upon yourself," he comments as he waves to the owner for a drink. "I told you. Sleeping with business associates can only provoke ill feelings."

That just irritates me, so again I choose not to respond. He orders his wine and water, and when the server leaves he says to me, "She wants you to return to the Cerium."

I consider not replying once more, but instead tell him, "She is the most obstinate, contrary, hard-headed woman."

He sighs, and reaches into a pouch. "I am too old to be carrying messages, but she sent me with this for you. It's a sealed writing tablet." He slides it across the table to me. I let it rest a few moments, while Orestes busies himself with mixing his wine and water.

Once finished, he drinks and grimaces. "The wine here is terrible. I don't know how you can bear it."

"What does it say?" I ask him without touching the tablet.

"How would I know?" he demands. "Did you not hear me say it's for you?" He pushes it closer to me. "And that it's sealed?"

I break the seal, open and read it. I run a hand through my hair. Read it again. And close it. We both linger a few moments in silence, Orestes finishing his drink.

"Will you come back now?" he asks.

"Yes," I answer, and rise. I feel an enormous sense of relief that my protest hasn't gone completely ignored—I don't know how we would have salvaged our relationship if it had. Ever the sensible one, though, while I was away brooding, Casina devises a practical solution. When I return, she settles me into the cubiculum adjoining hers, and has me construct a separate, private passage from one room to the next. It is a subtle distinction, this, but sufficient for her. And in the end, it's probably for the better. She still has her glorious window to invite starlight in and bugs; and I needn't be disturbed when she rises early to her industry and new initiatives.

Mid-June arrives. The air is thick with the fragrance of blossoms; honeysuckles bloom alongside lilies and lavender. I sit, determined to finally put an epilogue in place. The finishing of plays always requires a certain delicacy. As I work, though, Pomona and Prima argue about something related to restocking the wine and I find it impossible to deliberate over top of their shrill exchange. I pack up my tablet and stylus, intending to retire to my cubiculum, but only ascend the stairs partway when I hear stirrings in a cubiculum down the hallway and realize that the silence I crave will not be found there either. I hesitate upon the steps, trying to determine where I will find a tranquil spot, and cannot think of even one place. The world is a great mischief maker and will interfere with your writing. At last I slip up alongside the latrine. I peer in and see that it is vacant. Inside, it is quiet and calm, like an ancient temple. I enter and shut the door. There I perch, the honey-coloured light slanting down, and write the very final words of my play.

When I finish, I retire to the coenatio and treat myself to a plate of raisins.

The Cerium is briefly filled with the sound of bleating as a shepherd drives his flock ahead of him on the street. One rebellious ewe wanders into the doorway and seems to consider entering. We exchange glances, she and I, but then she must hear some correction that my senses cannot detect, because she quickly pivots on her hind legs and scurries up the street. Sure enough, a shepherding dog follows not long after. He glances in, and then, confident that none of his charges have proven wayward, moves on.

There follow several glorious days of the sweetest, mildest summer weather imaginable. The temperature is consistently warm but not unpleasantly so. The flowers continue to bloom and butterflies float, jewelled brooches pinned against the bosom of heaven's breast. At night fireflies bob drunkenly, flaring glittering signals as a radiant moon elevates high in the dark sky. Food tastes better, people are more generous with one another—the weather even has a kindly influence upon Naevius. When I inquire how rehearsals are going, he cocks his head to one side and squints as he considers the question.

"I believe," he pronounces at last, "that my Choragus may actually have scared the cast into becoming adequate. I won't say they're good," he hastens to add, "that would be stretching things too far, but at this point they're almost tolerable. It's the most miraculous metamorphosis I've ever been party to. If the production actually occurs, and I'm not totally disgraced, I may turn as devout as Orestes."

Now, as we near the end of rehearsals, I am delighted to see that my play, to which I have given the title *The Captives*, continues to advance. During one rehearsal Sostratos pulls Fronto aside and assists him with the conclusion of a scene.

Fronto had been playing the moment as though he were a merchant, calculating the number of opportunities to dine he has lost. Now he plays the same scene as though it is a personal insult that he has not been invited to dinner, and his passions drive him. Sostratos plays the subsequent scene as though his life depends on it, singing like a man spirit-possessed. The high emotions infuse the music with a kind of fierce purity, and we all conclude the rehearsal feeling excited and proud.

In the same way that a disease can be caught, so can excitement. I return to the Cerium, that sensation still stirring inside me.

Casina must sense it as she sits next to me. She drapes a hand at the nape of my neck and gives it a gentle squeeze. "You seem particularly pleased with yourself," she observes.

"I am," I tell her, "and with my grex."

"Things are going well?" she asks, smiling.

"I hardly dare speak of it," I confess, "I'm afraid that, like summer snow, it will melt when touched. But, after a long passage of mixed fortune, I believe we have finally struck a lucky patch."

"Luck," she says scornfully. "How you go on about luck. What is luck?" she asks, rhetorically. "I say it is lucky when a dog has fleas because there are so many other worse illnesses it could have."

I peer at her over my spiced wine. "Have you ever even owned a dog?"

"No," she says, scooping up some of my raisins and popping them in her mouth, "they have fleas."

"I would get a dog," I venture, after some thought.

"A dog?" she says, frowning. "I have difficulty enough keeping them out of the Cerium. Why?"

"I've never had a dog," I tell her. "My uncle had a dog."

"But what would you do with one?" she asks, sounding genuinely puzzled.

"*Do?*" I ask, surprised by the question. "I'd *do* nothing. Owning a dog isn't about *doing*. Owning a dog isn't a duty; it is a title conferred. You don't 'do' anything with it. You live it. It transforms you. You become a dog owner. It makes you appear more popular—after all, from that moment on you are never alone, you have a dog. It makes you seem more kindly, you like dogs. It makes you a man of property—even if you own nothing else, you own a dog. It makes you more approachable—unless the dog is mean, in which case it makes you more feared, which," I say after considering things, "is perhaps even better."

"The baker next door had a dog," Casina recalls, frowning, "and he bit everyone."

"He provided security," I correct her.

Her frown deepens. "And he peed on everyone," she remembers.

"He held commendable notions of equality as well."

She tightens her grip on the nape of my neck, with surprisingly strong fingers.

"Ow," I wince.

26

Perhaps to goad me, perhaps because he knows of my passion for sea craft, Naevius has a copy of a play by Aristophanes dropped off for me to read. It's titled *The Merchant Ships*, and is totally ridiculous and completely unsuitable in every respect. Roman audiences wouldn't put up with it for a moment, neither the topical references nor the belaboured political satire. But his poetry is very fine, and it is a genuinely amusing play. There are a number of places where, as I read, I am caught off guard and laugh out loud.

I wonder what it must have been like in the time of Aristophanes to have had an immense chorus at your disposal, as the Greeks had, and costume them all as dancing ships—that's a spectacle you will never see in our Roman theatre. I'm musing on this, lost in my own thoughts, when I turn and am startled to find Naevius seated near me. "You're being very quiet," I observe, laying the scroll aside. "You must have slipped in like a bandit; I didn't hear you take a seat."

"Plautus," he says, "I need to speak with you."

"About what? Aristophanes?" I ask, holding up the scroll and chuckling, "because he's completely absurd—"

"No," he says, "It's something else."

"What?" I ask absently, and reach for a scraper to rub one word out and write in another in my wax tablet where I had made some notes.

I glance up at Naevius and study him more closely. His greying hairs stand askew and he seems thin and wan. Normally, he is capable of consuming a great deal of wine without showing signs, so I would guess that he must have returned from an especially serious bout of extended hard drinking.

"I think I may have made a mistake," he tells me.

"Well, given your disreputable character and unsavoury habits, that's entirely likely," I assure him. "In what way? You stayed out too late? The vintage didn't agree with you? You drank too much?"

"Yes," he answers.

"Which?" I clarify. "You drank too much?"

"All of them," he responds absently.

I am surprised by his uncharacteristic reticence. Normally he is eager to share the sordid details of his bad behaviour. "And?" I prompt.

"I recited some scurrilous poetry," he replies.

"All your poetry is scurrilous," I reply as I pack up my writing materials, but when I glance back at him, he doesn't crack a smile. He remains seated, wringing his hands, like a child confessing to pilfering from his father's purse.

"This was different," he informs me. "This crossed a line."

"How?" I ask. "What kind of line?"

"I insulted the Metelli—" he begins. I inadvertently allow my writing materials to slip from my hands, and the clatter causes old men in the corner to raise their eyes from their knucklebones. After they have returned to their game, I continue speaking.

"Tell me you didn't," I say in a lower voice.

"I didn't think anyone was listening—" he explains.

"Are you slow?" I interrupt him. "Have you no sense or memory, or abilities of restraint? There is always *someone* listening."

He nods his agreement, penitent, but continues, "And someone left the room shortly after I recited."

"Who?" I ask.

"An in-law of the Metelli," he admits, "Gaius Veturius—"

I call up his face—a sour-looking little sardine of a man. "You're joking."

"I wish I were," he replies.

I run a hand through my hair, and part of me registers that I'm doing what Naevius must have been doing ever since leaving his party. "What were you thinking?" I ask.

He shrugs. "I hadn't realized he was present."

He declares it simply, as if he were saying any common thing: 'I hadn't realized it was morning' or 'I hadn't realized it was raining.' A brief, sharp impulse of impatience runs through me and I want to shake him. "Perhaps you should have looked about," I chastise him, "before you chose to share your poems." I take a breath to calm myself. "Did you run after him to speak with him and explain?"

"He left too quickly," he replies. "I called after him but he wouldn't be stopped."

"And do you think he left in this abrupt fashion because he had heard?" I ask.

"Yes."

We simply sit a moment and digest the gravity of the situation. "What can I do?" he asks at last.

"Well," I begin, and then reflect on the Metelli and the kind of response they are likely to have.

"Well what?" he asks.

"You must go to them," I begin again, trying to assemble some kind of practical solution, "and humble yourself."

He shakes his head. "That won't work."

"You must approach their home like a supplicant," I insist, "and beg an audience. You must apologize sincerely and humble yourself—"

"That won't work!" he repeats.

"It worked before," I remind him.

"After two years confinement," he replies. "After enduring a beating, and writing long obsequious expressions of penitence couched as plays to earn their forgiveness."

"Tell them you were drunk," I counsel him. "Tell them it was the wine talking—frankly I think it must have been the wine talking, because only an idiot would open his foolish lips to recite insulting poetry in the presence of the relatives of people who had already punished him once for libel—"

"They told me," he interrupts, "that they would have me killed."

That stops me. "Who did?" I ask, "and when?"

"The Metelli, when they first released me. After they had me whipped."

"They said that?" I confirm. "That they would have you killed?"

He nods. "They quoted from the Twelve Tablets. 'If any person has sung or composed against another person a song causing slander or insult he shall be clubbed to death.' They told me that would be the next step."

I stare at him a long, long moment, trying to penetrate his wild hair and sad eyes and see into him, into his core, to truly understand him. "And *still* you recited your poetry?"

He glances down at the floor and mutters, "I wasn't thinking clearly."

"Well, no," I agree, "I don't suppose you were."

A thick silence hangs over us as we consider the possibilities. Having too few options can paralyze as much as having too many.

"Venus!" one of the elders the next table over calls. His colleagues groan as he scoops up his earnings.

"So what will I do?" Naevius asks.

"Leave the city," I tell him. "Find someplace that will hide you—"

He passes a hand over his brow as he thinks on this. "I have a relative," he says, "out near Ostia—"

"It can't be with a *relative*," I snap, and dart him a look. "Are you mad? If they come hunting for you that will be the very first place they'll look. Have someone put you up outside Rome. It should be someone that no one would consider affiliated with you."

He stares blankly at me.

"There is a place," I say at last in my quietest voice, "I stayed when I was wanting to remain hidden from my creditors. They're discreet. And not far." I scratch out directions on a wax tablet.

"How long should I stay there?"

"Wait," I tell him, "and see what response they have to your poem. I'll keep my ears open, make some quiet inquiries, and then send you a message. Perhaps the Metelli will choose to ignore this latest indiscretion." I push the tablet across the table.

"And if they don't?" he asks me.

"Have someone scout out a new location on your behalf," I advise him, "someplace far enough from Rome that the Metelli will find it difficult to pursue you, and small enough that you will detect any visiting stranger. Have funds sent ahead and escape as quickly as you can."

27

"Plautus?"

"Yes?" I answer, but I'm not truly awake. I sense a presence beside me, waiting. I open my eyes and see Tertius standing beside my bed, chewing his lower lip.

"You're to come," he says. "Orestes sent me. There's been some trouble."

We enter the vacated room, and I see the manacles that once chained Sostratos, now heaped in a pile upon the bed, still fixed at one end to the wall. Orestes leans wearily near the entranceway, his eyes closed and his arms crossed upon his chest. Fronto slumps on a stool, his head in his hands.

"Where is he?" I ask.

"How should I know?" Orestes replies.

"I thought we had someone watching the door," I remind him.

"After he was shackled," Orestes says, "the watchman didn't think it was necessary to watch every moment. He stepped away for something to eat. He says he was only gone a short time."

Frustrated, I kick the empty vase against the wall, where it shatters, sending shards bouncing in all directions. This is petulant and unhelpful, I know, but I'm not operating on reason or sound judgment.

"When did anyone last see him?" I ask once I have myself in hand.

"Last night at coena," Orestes tells me.

I look around the room for some kind of clue. "Had he said anything? Warned anybody?" I ask.

Fronto shakes his head. "No," he says.

"Was there trouble?" I ask. "Did he argue with anyone about anything?"

"No," Fronto replies, shaking his head again, "nothing."

I scan the stark, empty room, and can see nothing that would provide clues as to where he might have gone. "He didn't say anything to anyone?" I ask again. "Anything that would lead anyone to believe he was thinking of running off?"

"Not that anyone remembers," Fronto replies.

"And nobody heard any noise during the night?" I ask.

"No."

I can feel a hammering in my head. I take a breath. "Tell me what he was doing when his food was brought to him."

"We were told he ate his meal," Fronto replies, "and seemed in good spirits. He had a healthy appetite. Asked for extra portions of everything. Extra bread, extra olive oil for his bread, and a little extra wine." He glances at Orestes when he mentions the extra wine, and I can see that this is something that was supplied without asking permission. "We didn't think it would hurt."

"How much?" I ask

"Another cup or two—" Fronto explains.

"Not the wine!" I shout, "At this point I don't care how much he drank. How much oil?"

"I don't know," he answers, looking puzzled. "I didn't ask."

I bend down and feel the inside of the manacles. Oiled, of course.

"Idiot! He greased himself to slip his bonds."

I brush past Fronto as I make my way to the door.

"Where are you going?" Orestes asks.

"To find him," I reply.

"Where?"

"Where else?" I fire over my shoulder. "A caupona. A lupinar. A gutter. A large vase, perhaps. Maybe he's crawled into one and made himself at home." And as I exit the room I mutter, "And if I can't find him, maybe I'll crawl into one myself."

28

Of course, there's nothing to be done but repeat everything
we have done before. We return to Mercury's Cup, where
Sostratos was found previously. No one has seen him there.
Orestes and I divide the city into sections, and hike about like
peddlers, making queries at various popinae and cauponae.
At each establishment I enter, I pose the same questions:
"Have you seen anyone fitting this description? Older fellow,
has his hair up." They answer no. "Has there been any trouble
lately?" I ask. Most places, there has been, but none of the
participants sound like Sostratos. Once, I believe there might
have been something that involved him, but it turns out to
have been a disagreement between a sailor and an amorous
older merchant.

Eventually I find myself at the Thirsty Rooster, an
astonishingly bad drinking establishment even by the low
standards I've encountered. It's situated near the storage
containers along the river, not a great location to begin with,
but this place is especially squalid. The corners of the floor
crawl with ants, the walls are crumbling, and something like
dried blood dots the lintel. An evil-looking, toothless old
grandfather scowls and slouches in the corner, scratching
himself and drinking. His face and arms are covered with
scars and he seems like he might easily have dispatched two
or three people before his morning piss.

I ask the proprietor, a stocky, thick-bearded rogue, if he knows Sostratos. "People come and go," he grunts, "they don't share their names with me." He carries on wiping his countertop. This must be strictly for show because the rest of the establishment looks like it hasn't encountered a wet cloth, dirty or clean, since it was built.

"He's a recognizable fellow," I explain. "Older. Keeps his hair long, in a knot. Sometimes gets in with a bad crowd." The proprietor snorts when I say 'bad crowd' and shoots me an ironical glance, but otherwise doesn't respond.

"He might have caused trouble," I suggest.

"Most nights," he tells me, "there's trouble."

"So you're saying there was a fight here last night?" He shrugs. "Did any of the participants fit the description of the person I'm looking for?"

"Who can tell?" he answers. "How different is one customer from another?" The man has suddenly turned philosopher on me. I place a semi on the counter with a snap. He scoops it up.

"There was a scuffle late last night," he admits, "and one of them might have been the fellow you described. He was older. Had his hair up in a foreign manner."

"So," I continue to probe, "two men fought?"

"Two or more," he corrects me, nodding at the entrance. "It moved outside. Once that happens I don't care, or count, who's involved."

"And my fellow?" I ask.

He raises his eyebrows. "What about him?

"How did he fare?"

"No idea," he answers. "Didn't watch."

"So where might he be now?"

"It began, they fought, it finished. That's all I know."
He opens and closes his hands like one of these travelling magicians demonstrating that they are holding nothing.

"Do you know what direction he went?" I ask.

He returns to cleaning his countertop. His shoulders rise and fall once again, in an almost imperceptible shrug.

I drop a sestertius on the wet surface. He stares at me and takes the coin.

"Last time I saw him," he begins, "if he's the individual you're talking about—he was resting behind the building."

I step back into the street, then walk around the south wall to the rear of the building. The law states that it's a proprietor's responsibility to keep the street in front of his business clean, but there is no such ruling regarding back lanes. Behind this building there is a crooked dirt track that reeks of urine and old garbage and is choked with tall shrubs and undergrowth.

A willow presses close to the rear wall. Beneath a tangled spray of its branches, pushed over onto one side, lies a body. It's been a long time since this fellow was 'resting'—flies are already beginning to swarm. I consider the torn clothing, the matted hair still arranged in a topknot. What a useless, meaningless way to end a life.

I step closer, inhale, grasp the body by a shoulder and heave. As it flips over, the flies rise and surround me. I wave them off and glance down. Black eyes stare blankly back at me, and his mouth gapes. The face, disfigured by bruises, the nose pushed to one side, is still sufficiently intact that I can confidently determine it's not Sostratos.

Later that night I return to the Cerium thoroughly discouraged, and sit by myself in the corner.

Casina approaches, sets wine, water, and a cup down on the table, then joins me. "Any luck?" she inquires.

I shake my head. "He's fled into some deep, dark hole."

"No sign?" she asks.

"Nothing," I answer. "No sign. No word. It doesn't seem that he talked to anybody or gave any warning about where he was going. He just . . ." I brush crumbs from the tabletop as I try to suppress my deep feelings of disappointment. "We visited, oh, I don't know how many popinae," I continue. "Not a trace." A mottled grey and brown dove glides in, perches at the end of the table and struts, puffing out its chest and thrumming in that bossy way they have. I wave impatiently at it, but it brazenly insists on parading about. Suddenly irritated beyond reason, I seize a corner of the table and shake it until the dove departs, then slam the table down again. "Jupiter in a latrine, there is a curse, by every vengeful god, there is a curse on me. Getting this play performed is—" I run out of words and feel embarrassed by my display of temper. "I am Odysseus clinging to the slippery waterlogged timbers of his destroyed ship, desperately trying to return home, and every time I draw closer, every time I spy the shoreline, the wind, the currents, and the gods conspire to push me farther away."

Casina places a calming hand on my arm. "What can I do?" she asks.

"I don't know," I answer truthfully.

"Where have you looked?" she asks after a moment.

"Everywhere," I tell her, "I have looked everywhere. Drinking establishments, gambling dens, whorehouses, inns, large and small. The places we have never visited, and repeats . . ." I shake my head. "Maybe he's left the city."

Her glance moves to the ceiling, an expression I've seen her use whenever she is deep in thought. "And who have you asked?"

"Everyone," I reply. "Proprietors and pourers of wines, wherever wine is served."

"Proprietors?" She repeats, clucking disapprovingly. She sets her fingers to her lips and whistles. "Hey, Tertius?"

Tertius, who I notice has taken to resting nights on the floor near the culina when he's not at the theatre, sticks his head around the entranceway. "Yes?" he says.

"You know Smyrna?" she asks him.

"Tall woman, laughs like a donkey braying?" he answers. "Flirts with the delivery?"

"That's the one. Take her this message. Tell her I want her to speak to Aegyptus, have him ask on his rounds about Sostratos. He may not hear the actual name, but there might be something said about an older man getting into drunken trouble. Tell her whatever Aegyptus brings back to her about an older fellow with a topknot, we want to know. Say it's worth money to me." She looks at him. "You'll remember all that?"

He nods.

"Good," she says, and gives his head a quick pat. "Don't dawdle along the way."

Tertius nods again and runs off with the message.

"Who is Smyrna?" I ask.

"Smyrna is the busty server over at the Three Roosters. She has a passion for a certain well-muscled young slave, Aegyptus, owned by Marcus the wine merchant. Aegyptus loads and delivers wine, so he drives his wagon and a team of mules around the city from popina to popina each morning. He'll ask the slaves that unload the deliveries about Sostratos, they'll ask the other slaves. And the slaves," she concludes, "know everything."

Rehearsals carry on while we continue searching. Orestes fills in for our runaway. He gives a spirited rendition of the part but, of course, while he does that, the musical accompaniment is absent. The actors don't object—what can they do?—but there is the deadening impression that this is rapidly becoming a futile exercise.

After four days searching, and no sightings, hope begins to run thin. "We can't keep pretending," I sigh as Orestes and I sit on the grass during a break from rehearsal. "Without an actor to replace Sostratos we don't have a play."

Orestes traces a design in the dirt with his fingertip. "You'll have to inform the Aedile."

"And tell him what?" I ask

"The truth," he says simply. "That we have nothing to perform."

I pluck up a broad grass blade and carefully tear it into thin strips. "He'll want his initial funding returned," I point out, "and it's spent."

Orestes doesn't respond at once. "Have you considered performing it yourself?" he asks finally.

"Me?" I reply. "The part of Tyndarus?"

"You've acted before," he observes.

I throw my head back and laugh out loud, although it's hardly funny. "You couldn't really call what I did acting. I transported messages and props across the stage, and occasionally played the obnoxious slave." Orestes doesn't blink. "And you've heard me sing."

"Your voice carries," he observes politely.

"Casting me would certainly make our performance a comedy. The wrong kind. We'd be hooted off the stage. Scorned in every taberna throughout Rome."

"That is preferable to not having anything to show at all," he reasons. "Or returning money we no longer have. You know the lines. And as small as the parts might have been, you've performed."

We both tacitly acknowledge that this isn't really a solution, or rather, it is a solution of last resort. It is a solution that permits us to present the play, without offering any true hope of success. If I perform, it will allow us to formally fulfill our obligations, yes, but it will open us up to the most scathing lampooning by our rivals and critics. The public will see it as a feeble, faltering, ridiculous enterprise. Those who know more will view it as an act of complete desperation. Which, of course, it will be.

"There's nothing else to be done," I admit at last, and cast the shredded grass blade at my feet. "I will perform the part. I'll begin rehearsals tomorrow." And that, I tell myself, will end my career.

29

It is early yet, and cool when I wake.

I lie atop my mattress in the darkness and resist beginning my day. I briefly and bitterly contemplate the upcoming rehearsal—the deep failure it will represent, the public humiliation I will endure as a result, the doors it will close on future opportunities. I cast about once more for other alternatives, other more palatable solutions. There are none, of course. If there were any, I would not still be in bed avoiding rehearsal.

Having affirmed this gloomy reality once more, and realizing the futility of treading old ground, I sigh, rise from my bed and slip on my sandals. I descend the stairs and walk to the fountain, thirsty and still groggy with sleep. A tradesman is already at the lip of the collecting basin when I arrive, berating his servant for spilling a heavy tub of water. Had he stopped remonstrating him for a moment and simply lifted and refilled the tub himself, he would have been done and home and everyone would be happier, but his chastisement is long-winded and makes matters worse. The servant, nervous after the previous mishap, upsets the tub once more. The line waiting to get to the fountain grows.

I squint at this sorry performance and feel a vein in my temple begin to throb. I am already anxious about the upcoming day, and this fussing around the fountain seems to me especially irksome. There are some slaves who, having been freed, become worse than their masters. Afraid that they will be discovered to be inferior, they transform into the worst tyrants. This one makes a big show of berating his servant for failures that are really his own, then beats him to demonstrate how severe his moral standards have become. He raises his stick repeatedly to strike the servant, who flinches but has no choice but to stand shivering like a leashed dog, and take it.

At last I feel I can wait no longer. "Can you not," I inquire, "beat your servant somewhere other than directly in front of the fountain?"

He pivots to face me. "Who are you?" he barks, huffing and puffing, red in the face from the exertion of thrashing his servant.

"Someone," I say, "wanting water and waiting for you to conclude."

He steps closer, and I smell his sour breath. "Will you instruct me in how I am to manage my servants?" he demands.

"If you cannot find a way to manage them," I retort, "without inconveniencing others, then yes, I will."

His face, already flushed, turns a more florid hue, and his right arm, as though controlled by strings, pops up. "I will show you inconvenience!" he huffs.

Shocked, I realize that this madman is truly out of control, "If you hit me with that—" I caution him, but too late. Even as the words escape my lips, I feel his stick strike my left shoulder, not hard, but hard enough that it stings. A great burning surge of anger courses through me at this stupid ineffectual rabbit in rooster's feathers. I snatch the rod from his hand, kick his legs out from under him, and thump him in the centre of his chest. He sprawls to the ground.

"There!" I shout, catching him on the back of his head with his wand, "and there! And that one for your foul mouth! And that for your servant who has to put up with your boring, idiotic, pointless bluster! And this one is to help you to remember that if ever I catch you beating your servant for your own failings I will come by your home like a hunter and pull your insides out and use your carcass for people to wipe their feet upon so that at last you will become useful in some small way, you flabby, pitiful, blathering waste of bones and breath! Do you understand?" But I take no joy from beating him, as he cowers and cringes and shows not the slightest hint of courage or resolve.

"I asked, do you understand?" I repeat.

"Yes!" he whimpers.

"And I'll keep this," I say holding up the stick. "Now go, and let others get water."

His servant helps him stand and then gathers up his urn and tub, and together they drive their donkey away.

Festus, the sandalmaker is there, leaning on his one good leg. Ever practical, he commends me as I rub my stinging shoulder, saying, "That was well done. He was unreasonably delaying access to the fountain."

"Yes, he was," I answer, and seeing him peer around at the water, say, "Go ahead."

Festus fills his urn, and passes it to his apprentice, who lifts it and places it atop one shoulder.

"You know," he tells me, "that rascal will beat his servant the instant he gets home, for not stepping between him and your blows."

"Of course he will," I say, still massaging my shoulder, "but a fellow like that would have beaten him in any case. That kind of individual needs no excuse—and at least he'll have to find another stick."

At that moment Tertius approaches and tugs at my elbow, excitedly. "What?!" I bark, annoyed because it's my sore arm he's pulling.

"I've found where he is," he gasps.

"Who?" I ask impatiently.

"Sostratos."

At once I forget about my shoulder and the fool and his servant. "How?" I demand.

"A slave approached me," he gasps again, and doubles over to draw in a breath. He's obviously run here to deliver the news, and for a moment he can say nothing.

I grasp him by his arms. "So where is he?"

"That old estate," he says between pants.

"That old estate?" I repeat impatiently, "*Which* old estate?"

"The one," he says, and gulps air. "The one."

"I don't know what you're talking about," I tell him.

"The one you talked about with Orestes," he explains. "The estate of the Domina Regulus," he says, catching his breath.

"You're certain?" I ask, releasing his arms. "You're certain that's where he was taken?"

He nods. "He was seized and bound by four slaves."

"How did you find this out?" I ask. "Which slave exactly witnessed this?"

"The slave of Balbus the stabler called Lucan. He was grooming a horse, and received a kick in the thigh. As he walked it off, he says he saw these four set on Sostratos and bind him."

"And then they took Sostratos away?" I ask, trying to get the sequence straight in my mind.

"Yes."

"And how is this Lucan so certain that these slaves took Sostratos to the Regulus estate?"

"He recognized one of the men who bound Sostratos. A big man, an overseer." He lowers his voice. "Lucan was anxious that his master not find out that he went wandering when he was supposed to be grooming, so he said nothing until he heard there was money offered."

I perform a backward count in my head. Sostratos would have been captured five days ago. It's possible that he may still be held at the estate.

"Tertius?" I say.

"Yes?"

"Take this." I give him my money pouch. "Run to the livery and rent two donkeys. We will have to move quickly. Then run and fetch Orestes. I'll have him accompany me."

He nods, takes the bag, and sprints up the street. My mind is racing now. Casina, having heard the fuss at the fountain, is approaching.

"Tertius," I tell her, "has learned that Sostratos is being held at the Regulus estate."

"I just heard the same news from Smyrna," she informs me.

"You'll have to contact and prepare the grex. Tell them they are to pack costumes, masks, musical instruments, everything they can easily carry, and follow after Orestes and me." I step closer to her and lower my voice. "And you will find Naevius at this location." I reach into my leather satchel and scribble down some directions on a wax tablet. "Have someone you trust to forget the location after they have read this, or that they ever went there, deliver this message to Naevius. Tell him I am calling in my debt."

"Calling in your debt?" she repeats.

"He'll understand," I tell her.

She takes the tablet from me, and places it in her purse. "Very well. Anything else?"

"The Cerium will be our command central, and you our general. Every message I send will come to you first, and you must ensure the messages are delivered promptly."

"What do you intend to do?" Casina asks.

"Find out what Sostratos has done to offend the Regullae and beg that he be released."

"And if it turns out," Casina begins, searching my face, "as Orestes worried, that Sostratos is an escaped slave?"

"I will apologize on his behalf, uncover the rightful owner, and broker a deal to pay his fee." I glance at Casina for assurance. "It may require that I bargain against some of the future profits of our play, but I assume we're agreed on that? If we don't have him, there will be no future profit."

"Be careful," Casina cautions me.

"I will," I reply, and feeling the pressure of time, turn to go. Suddenly I experience a sharp nip of my sore arm.

"Ow!" I yelp, and shoot a look at Casina. She has pinched me. "What was that for?" I ask rubbing my arm.

"You," she replies, "are hot headed, but in these dealings you cannot afford to be rash. The Regulus family is proud, powerful, and easily offended; do nothing to upset them. Do you understand?"

"Yes," I reply impatiently. "Of course."

"And," she continues, placing a restraining hand against my chest, "if he is held at the Regulus estate, it may be because they have already discovered conclusive evidence and made their decision. If that's so, then there may be no chance that you will be able to bargain, and probably no fee that will be sufficient."

Her eyes catch mine, cautioning me. Preparing me for the possibility of disappointment. Having spent the past night in despair, I am in no mood for any such caution now that Sostratos has been found.

"Then I will do," I tell her, "what any inventive protagonist of a comedy would do in an impossible situation."

"Which is?" she asks.

"Throw things into confusion until some other solution comes to mind."

30

The Regulus estate is located south and east of the city, and once Orestes has joined me, we set out for it immediately. The donkeys take a brisk pace, sending up tiny puffs of dust with each step. We exit Rome by the Esquiline Arch, quickly escape the crush of insulae and tabernae, and enter a rolling landscape of farmlands and larger estates. As we approach the property, it becomes apparent how immense it is, maybe 300 jugera in total. The road cuts a line parallel to the farm, past a silvery grey cloud of mature fruit bearing olive trees. Nearer to the house, apple and plum trees blossom. As we draw nearer to the villa we hear shouts announcing our arrival.

A side road branches off as we approach the front gate, and I see an individual moving with determination in our direction. The villicus of the estate, I presume. A tall, balding individual with a sour expression greets us at the front gateway. "Your health!" I call to him.

"Yes?" he replies shortly. No 'your health' in return, or 'thank you' or 'good day.' Just his curt, dismissive, impolite 'yes.'

I dismount and continue speaking, trying to adopt a confident, friendly tone. "I understand that an individual, an actor I know, was brought here four or five nights ago. Taller fellow, older, bearded, wears his hair in a topknot. His name is Sostratos."

No response from him, so I carry on. "I'm uncertain what he may have done," I explain, "but I've come to inquire about his release. He is required for a performance, which I'm sure you can understand has a certain degree of urgency."

The senior servant gives a brusque shake of his head and says, "I'm afraid that won't be possible."

"Then you *do* have him?" I ask.

He frowns at what he perceives as my impertinence. "The affairs of this estate," he replies, "are none of your concern."

"A witness saw him taken here," I persist. "He is contracted to work for me, so I have a legitimate interest. Are you, or aren't you, holding him on this property?"

I can see that the mention of a contract raises certain issues of legality for him. He weighs his response a long moment before answering. "We may have detained a person that fits your description," he allows.

"May I ask why?" I press him.

"I'm sure I don't know precisely, it is not my place to ask that my mistress explain her every decision. My understanding is that there are certain questions that are being put to him."

"Certain questions?" I find this encouraging. If he is still being interrogated, that can only mean that there remains uncertainty. If there were certainty, he would either already have been delivered back to his owner, or be dead. "Can I ask what those certain questions are?"

The servant's frown deepens at my perceived presumptuousness. "You may not," he responds curtly.

This, to his mind, terminates our conversation, and he turns, meaning to dismiss me, but I dart in front of him. "As I have already told you, my grex has need of him," I say.

"My *mistress* has need of him," he replies haughtily, and everything in his manner implies that her need surpasses mine in every respect.

"How long can I expect him to be detained?" I inquire.

"Until the answers to these matters are discovered," is his short response.

Realizing that I am addressing an individual who possesses no social graces, I attempt to steer the conversation down another road. "There might be information," I tell him, "that we could gather and so help with the investigation."

"I will inform my mistress of your helpfulness," he replies and tries to walk around me.

I step sideways, blocking his escape once more. "I'm sure I would like to wait, but it is impossible to stage the play without him."

"It is probably best, then," he responds, unhelpfully, "if you find someone else."

"That's impossible, he is essential."

He chuckles, as though I have said something especially funny. "No slave is essential."

"Ah. That," I say, seizing my opening, "is where you make your mistake. He is not a slave."

He considers me skeptically. "He bears scars of correction on his back."

"Past corrections," I say. "He has been freed."

"Where is his manumission recorded? This has been investigated," he tells me pointedly, "and he does not appear in the manumission census."

This at least confirms for me the reason that Sostratos is being held. "There are many freed slaves," I caution him, "that do not appear on the census."

"Can you then identify the Praetor or magistrate who touched him with a vindicta, and so freed him?" he inquires.

"I believe he was freed through imposed formal conditions—"

"Can you provide witnesses?" he challenges me.

"Not immediately," I reply. "That would be impossible in most cases, but I'm sure I can find some in time."

"If you can discover that information it would be helpful," he says, and steps past me and back onto the Regulus property.

"Can you at least tell me where he is located?" I call after him.

"For the time being," he says, "in the ergastulum." The ergastulum of any large farm is an unpleasant place. Slaves are only confined there for correction, and I can only imagine what correction looks like on the Regulus estate. If Sostratos is to be in any shape to perform, we will have to find a way to have him released very shortly.

"Excuse me," I say as he grasps the upper bar of the gate, preparing to close it. "I am forbidden to leave without him."

"Forbidden?" he repeats, and looks at me as though he has unexpectedly bitten into something unpleasant. "By whom?"

"The individual you presently hold is a critical part of the upcoming ludi, and without him the failure of our performance is assured. This is not acceptable to the Aedile."

The fool makes a show of glancing behind me. "I don't see him anywhere," he says.

"He sent me ahead," I reply, as patiently as I am able.

"Do you have a written message bearing his seal?" he asks.

"No."

"Perhaps," he declares rather patronizingly, "it would be better if he came himself then."

"That's impossible. His responsibilities to the Republic and heavy workload prevent him."

"I'm afraid—"

"I must explain the seriousness of this situation directly to your mistress," I say, adopting another strategy. "Bring me to her."

He remains undeterred. "She is not available," he replies.

"When," I press, "will she be available?"

"I do not control her day, but it is unlikely that it will be soon."

"What is your name?" I ask him.

"Cassius."

"Well, Cassius, my friend and I will wait."

"I cannot tell you when she will return," he says. "You may end up waiting a considerable time." And with those words, he shuts and fastens the gate.

Orestes and I lay our goods down in the grass and wait. We pass much of the late morning reclining in the shade of a tree, Orestes sleeping, me planning.

"I'm interested to learn," Orestes asks at one point, breaking our silence, "what was in that note."

I glance at him. His eyes remain closed, his hands peacefully folded upon his chest. "What note?" I ask.

"The one Casina sent you," he replies, "when you were staying at the Ripe Fruits."

I adjust my back against the tree. "That is the question of a busybody," I tell him, but he awaits my answer, undeterred. "The note said several things. It expressed her sorrow at our disagreement," I inform him finally, "and her affection for me."

"What proof had she included?" he inquires, after a moment.

I stare at him with astonishment. "Have you no shame?"
I ask. "It is a private matter, and what makes you think there
was proof?"

"Her affection for you was already obvious to anyone
with eyes. You are obtuse in matters of this sort, though, so I
assume she must have offered you a kind of proof."

"In matters of the heart things can seem evident, and at
the same time not," I inform him brusquely. "There is no one
correct way to illuminate a passage that is dark, be it a candle,
a torch, or an oil lamp. And," I conclude, "not that it is any of
your business, but she included her recipe for garum."

Orestes chuckles to himself, in a way that I find extremely
annoying, but at that instant the grex arrives, with their props
and stage instruments. "Good," I direct Orestes. "Position
them near the road."

In a short time, Orestes has the materials they brought
arranged, masks and costumes dangling from trees like
vaporous dryads emerging from the branches.

"I see we have already attracted a few curious spectators,"
Orestes observes and points.

I turn and spy five or six children, gathered in small clumps
across the road, gazing shyly at us. I wave at them, the braver
ones wave back.

"Excellent," I say. "Send Fronto to tell them to fetch their
friends. They will have something to watch in a short while."

I consider the closed gate a moment, then call to Grippus.
I withdraw a writing tablet and quickly scratch a few notes and
hand it to him

"Hurry and bring this note back to Casina. Take the
donkey. Tell her that she needs to frame this request with
some urgency, and ensure that it happens swiftly."

He nods, climbs on the donkey and touches it with a switch. As he disappears around the bend in the road, I turn back to Orestes.

"Have you another tibia?" I ask.

"Yes," he replies, "why?"

"I'm not the musician you are," I explain, "but I can play, and together with you, we will generate a fuller, louder performance."

"Very well," he says, "I'll get it for you."

"And distribute the drums we have." I tell him, wondering if it might be worthwhile asking some of the audience to assist. "And the bells."

"What are we going to do?" Orestes asks me.

I consider the imposing stone works of the Regulus estate, the long wall and the solid gate barring the entranceway. "Lay siege to the house," I inform him.

31

The final rays of afternoon sunlight catch the dust rising from
the road and envelop the world in a fiery orange radiance. I
have Grippus place lit torches against the coming night; they
crackle and send up coils of dark smoke. We have by this time
attracted a not inconsiderable number of children and farmers,
drawn by our music. Beneath the pulsing cry of the tibia, the
tambourines and drums pound an intense rhythm driving
the songs forward. Fronto's voice carries urgency, and the
impromptu crowd that has gathered encourages him with their
rhythmic applause. As he approaches an especially passionate
moment, I detect a new sound—the squeal of the front gate
being thrown open and the voice of the villicus shouting. I
reflect that in another life, Cassius might have made a good
actor. His voice certainly has the ability to carry.

"What is this noise?!" I hear him braying, as he pushes his
way through the crowd. "What is this wretched pounding and
wailing? Who are these rustics you have brought with you?"

He stands in front of me, puffing, and mopping his brow,
demanding answers.

"They are members—" I start before being drowned out by
the singing.

"What?!" he shouts, placing a hand beside his ear.

"They are members of the play I spoke with you about,"
I answer.

"What business have they here?" he demands, scowling at the audience we have attracted. "What business have any of them here—and for that matter, what are you doing out here, still?"

"We are rehearsing," I reply matter-of-factly, "as best we can. As I told you, we don't have everything we require."

His gaze darts from one masked individual to another, and at the torches we have lit, all with a mixture of horror, disbelief, frustration—and, I note—suppressed curiosity.

"How long is this ritual likely to continue?" he asks finally.

"What do you mean?" I innocently inquire.

"How long," he bawls, "will we have to put up with your—"

"We are only trying to—"

Orestes plays the tibia louder and Fronto sings at the top of his voice, drowning me out.

"What?!" the steward shouts, his voice taking on a hoarse quality as he tries to be heard over the music.

"We are only," I cry, "trying to work around the impossible situation we find ourselves in, and we will be at it until the actor you presently hold is released!"

His eyebrows shoot up several levels. They were already raised. Soon they will be on the very crown of his brow and he will be able to view the clouds and stars and passing birds without tilting his head. "Here?" he snaps, quivering with outrage. "That is a preposterous imposition!"

"It is a practical solution," I explain patiently, "to the difficult situation we have been placed in."

"*Never mind* what situation you find yourself in!" he bellows. "Go elsewhere with your rehearsals."

"That's impossible," I inform him. As our debate grows more heated, the musical instruments gradually fall silent and the audience draws closer, curious, as crowds always are, to observe a fight.

"Of course it isn't," Cassius insists. "Return to wherever it is that you normally rehearse. Or go farther down the road, go to Hades if you wish, but—"

"Time, as I have attempted to explain to you, is of the greatest importance to us. We performers," I tell him, and gesture to my grex, "are like sailors preparing for a hard voyage, and we must catch whatever favourable breeze comes along to hasten our passage. The craft of presenting a play requires the energy and talents of each actor and technician. We cannot waste a single moment."

He opens his mouth to object once more but I plow over top of his objections, "Not a *single* moment. Our efforts are severely impeded by the absence of our comrade and so we must rehearse in the location that is in closest proximity, so that when his proper status as a freedman is at last acknowledged and he has been released we will be able to make up for those precious moments that have been lost."

"This," he says, grasping the shoulder of my tunic, "is an outrageous, deliberate insult to a noble house—"

I brush his hand away from my shoulder. "I'm so sorry," I say, "to learn that you feel this way. We are simply trying to accomplish—"

"I can *see*," he snaps, "what kind of mischief you are trying to accomplish—"

"—the work," I carry on over top of his rude interruption, "that we have been contracted to perform—"

"—and it is impertinent!" he barks. "It is insolent! It flouts authority, and believe me, you will live to regret it. I will have you, *you*, and all your sorry band of criminals and vagabonds and wandering *musicians*," and the acid touch he scores the word 'musicians' with, makes it sound infinitely worse than 'criminals,' "whipped down the road for the beggars you are—"

"You should do whatever you must. But I want you to understand," and here I raise my voice, and draw myself up. I may not be much of an actor, but I am actor enough to know how to shout down a bully and ensure that everyone hears me, "we are on public land and we are commanded to prepare for the Ludi of Apollo by the highest authority of our republic. If you, or anyone else, interferes with this mission, it will be an offence against the Aedile, against common law, against the gods whom we serve in the sacred ludi and against Rome itself. And I have sent the Aedile a personal message informing him that the Regulus estate, and you—and believe me, I have mentioned *you* specifically by name, Cassius, in my message— are impeding our progress."

His face flushes several shades of red, as he contemplates his response, and I wonder if it is possible that he will actually combust and burn to ashes and dust in front of me. Then, abruptly, he turns on his heel and retreats through the gate. I signal to the others to continue playing and join once more in beating a drum. The crowd, delighted to hear the music recommence, bursts into spontaneous applause.

Moments later, another, lesser servant appears. He gestures at me.

"The Domina will see you," he says. "Come this way."

I motion to Orestes to join me. If the questioning has been vigorous, we may need to carry Sostratos from the compound. "Keep singing until we return," I command Fronto, and together with Orestes, I slip through the front gate.

The road leading to the main house is well maintained. As we follow the servant, I examine the grounds and orchards. Although the sun has set, it's still hot and slaves continue to labour among the trees, clearing weeds and splitting wood, while others break and stack rocks. Some of the slaves are chained together, foot to foot, and are forced to coordinate their movements with a kind of shuffling, synchronized step.

Although we have only spoken of it a few times, I know Orestes served for some years on an estate of similar size. He catches my eye and gives a brief rueful shake of his head, a silent commentary on the life of servitude. We glumly march across the compound until we arrive at the house where Cassius stands attendance at the entranceway.

"The Domina Regulus will receive you in the atrium," he announces stiffly. "Follow me."

He turns and conducts us through the house. Inside, the air is cooler, cavelike, quiet. The spacious room hosts a series of statues, including one of Minerva, the Lar of the home, and one of an older man I would guess to be Marcus Attius Regulus. Death masks of the Regulus ancestors, going back many generations, adorn the walls. At the north end of the room, there is a raised dais, an elegant wooden chair placed upon it. I assume this is where the Domina Regulus greets guests.

32

Cassius leaves us, and Orestes and I stand silently waiting. I study the masks on the wall, and marvel at their lifelike detail. Judging from the images in that room, the Regulus family was a dignified tribe, but couldn't be described as very pleasant company. Each face is a study in a kind of solemnity that can only be achieved through a lifelong practice of habitually rehearsed, rigorously applied unhappiness. These thoughts are interrupted when the Domina Regulus enters and takes a seat on the dais. It's impossible to tell her age precisely, but she is elderly. Once beautiful, her face has settled in lines that express only a limited number of emotions, none of them friendly or gentle or kind. The white wool fabric of her stola is immaculate and descends in severe, ivory folds. She is an exercise in precise geometry, sitting straight-backed in her chair, stiff-necked, arms held rigidly on her lap, and even her wrinkles are straight and severe. There isn't a single curve or soft element to be found. She is as a figure carved from some ancient crystal.

"I understand that you wish to see me?" There is a slight rise in the inflection at the end of her sentence, the only indication that this is a question.

A female servant enters silently and floats about the room lighting candles that sit in tapers affixed to the walls.

"Thank you for making time to meet me," I say. "I am Titus Maccius Plautus, poet, and I have no wish to disturb you, but I believe you are holding a member of my grex. This man has been retained to perform in the upcoming ludi. He has apparently been brought here for reasons I am uncertain of, but his services are required urgently."

"Urgently?" she says, turning the word over as though it were foreign to her, and at that moment I become aware of some activity. A large, bearded servant slips in and takes his post along the wall just to the left and behind me. "I'm not sure that these matters will be resolved with any speed," she informs me in grave tones. "There are certain matters that we must yet investigate."

"May I inquire what matters they are?" I ask, returning my attention to her. "Perhaps I can help."

"Matters of corruption," she informs me.

"Corruption?" I repeat. I had not been expecting this. "What kind of corruption are you referencing?"

"All kinds. Corruption is everywhere," she observes as the candles are lit. Her gaze halts on the death mask of one of her ancestors. "Faithlessness and betrayal are everywhere," she murmurs, and I am uncertain if she is addressing the mask or me.

I attempt to develop a line of argument, but cannot because I honestly have no idea what she is talking about. "I apologize," I say, "perhaps we are not talking about the same man. I am looking for Sostratos, the actor."

"I believe we are speaking of the same person," she tells me, "but you will be able to judge for yourself, shortly." The fingers of her right hand flutter briefly, indicating an action she has taken, or perhaps the direction in which an action will be taken. "He is coming. I am having him brought here."

"In the meantime," I suggest, "perhaps there is information I can provide that would be useful."

Her eyes wander to another mask. "It is improbable," she says idly. "I have just returned from the forum, where I sought some of the answers to important questions I have."

"Did you get those answers?" I ask.

The servant lights the last candle near an altar to the house Lar, and then leaves. A long silence follows before she answers, "No."

I hear footsteps, turn and see Sostratos half marched, half dragged in. His tunic is filthy and he is sandal-less. His hands are bound; his long hair hangs in greasy strands, partially covering his face. I remember once again what his appearance was like when I first met him at the lupinar. The servant grasping his elbows, I assume the ergastularius, is an enormous slab of man, with massive thighs and knotted, muscular shoulders. He pulls Sostratos into place with a grunt, and steps back.

"This is the man you are inquiring after?" the Domina Regulus inquires.

"Yes," I answer.

"He admits to being a stranger to the city," she says, and she studies him. She draws in a breath as though about to begin a longer speech, but instead simply says, "He smells something of Carthage." She glances at her behemoth. "Don't you think?"

"Yes," the man behind me replies.

"Definitely smells of Carthage," another voice agrees. I turn and see that two other large men have quietly joined us. We are convening quite a group.

CLEM MARTINI

"Don't you find it?" the Domina Regulus asks, looking directly at me for the first time since I have come into her company.

"I can't say that I detect anything that smells particularly of Carthage," I tell her. I reflect that there is the stale odour of sweat and fear, certainly, but that could be coming from me. "Maybe it's garlic you smell."

I feel a sudden jolt of pain; my legs weaken and realize with surprise as I fall to the floor that I have been clubbed from behind.

"Do you think you can become familiar with the Domina?" the man to my right barks.

I push myself up to all fours and touch the back of my head. I can already feel a lump rising. "No," I reply as I try to gather my thoughts.

"She's not here to trade jokes with refuse like you," he hisses directly into my right ear. "I could feed you and your friends through the olive press, and leave nothing but juice and runny pulp, and no one would notice tomorrow."

"I was just saying," I explain as I try to rise, "maybe he smells of garlic, Carthage was a great trading nation, maybe that reminded her—"

He strikes me again, this time in the middle of my back, sending radiating waves of pain into the base of my neck and knocking the wind out of me.

"Don't correct the mistress. And don't stand unless you're given permission."

A heavy foot presses against my lower back and forces me to the ground. "Stay down where you belong, till you're asked to rise."

This altercation does not ruffle the Domina Regulus. She remains completely serene, as though neither words nor blows have been exchanged, or perhaps as if this were so common an exchange that it doesn't deserve any response.

"This other one is a little dark," she observes, confusing me at first, as I have no idea what 'other one' she could be referencing. Then I realize with alarm that her attention has turned to Orestes. "Is his hair curly?"

"It's straight," I assure her from my place on the floor.

"There is some wave to it," she maintains. "From where does he originate?"

"He's Greek," I reply.

"I'm Greek," Orestes volunteers quickly.

The Domina Regulus tips her head to one side, as though appraising one of the sheep at the market. "He's dark-skinned for a Greek," she notes.

"They're all darker skinned where he comes from," I explain.

"And what city does he claim as home?" she asks.

"Athens," Orestes answers.

She weighs this. "Didn't the Greeks form a league with the Carthaginians at one point?" she inquires.

"Macedonians did, Ma'am," I correct her. "They're from north of Athens, they were allies of the Carthaginians. Athenians hate them."

"What does she care about the obscure histories of those barbarians?" A voice warns from behind me.

"Domina," I say, and am apparently permitted to rise to my hands and knees to be heard, "I don't want to waste your time, about history or anything else. I am only here to fetch back this actor so that we can complete the rituals of the ludi and ensure that the gods remain happy."

"I understand your concern," she declares calmly, as though we were discussing gardening, or the weather, and I weren't on the floor with blood dripping into my ears, "and I will take care of these matters. After I have satisfied my own serious concerns."

"What serious concerns would those be?" I ask.

"This man you believe to be an actor," she informs me, "is clearly a spy."

I glance up to see if she is serious in her accusation. She placidly returns my gaze.

"He has been with our grex for some time," I cautiously disagree, "and has spent all his time in rehearsal. What can he have spied upon? What information can he have gathered and for whom?"

"That is what I am trying to determine," she replies as she rubs one thumb gently back and forth over top of the other. "My ergastularius has attempted to coax answers from him, but your servant has proven reluctant. You," she says, as she shifts her focus back to Sostratos. He doesn't respond so the overseer gives him a hard nudge with his elbow. "I have questioned the owner of the popina you frequent, so there's no point in lying. I heard that you were recognized by a Numidian soldier. Where would a Numidian soldier recognize you from?"

Sostratos lifts his head. "I don't recall," he replies, slowly and courteously, like a man responding to the repeated questions of a respected but very deaf grandmother. I can tell from the effort he makes that he is exhausted. "I was drunk at the time. Perhaps he had attended one of my performances."

Apparently, she finds this answer unsatisfying. "Why did he demand money from you, if he knew you only from viewing your performances? Why," she adds, "did he call you Traitor, if you are Greek?"

He shakes his head gently, his long hair falling over his face. "When people have drunk too much they are intemperate in their language."

She tilts her head slightly to one side and asks, "Where are you from?"

Sostratos runs his tongue over his dry, bruised lips. "The deme of Kamiros, not far from Rhodes."

"How precisely he locates his home. You see how he has rehearsed his responses," she says for my benefit, although her gaze never strays from him. "Where are you actually from?"

"Kamiros," he repeats.

"Why are you here?"

"To perform in a new play," he intones, "in the Ludi of Apollo."

"And what," she asks, "have you been sent to find out?"

"To determine if Romans possess any taste or culture."

This response is greeted with a sharp blow to the back of his knees. He is flattened to the floor, where he is kicked in the ribs.

"Where are you from?" she calmly repeats

"Kamiros," he replies.

"What is your name?"

"Sostratos."

"And what," she inquires, "did you call yourself before you adopted this false identity?

"Theseus," he replies, "Oedipus. Trygaeus."

"Ahhh, this is new," she sighs quietly, expressing her satisfaction. "I had imagined that we would eventually come upon forged identities. Who are these individuals?" she asks.

"They are characters," I interrupt, and because she appears confused by my response, I elaborate. "Characters from plays.

It is a mania with him to identify with the characters he has performed in the past."

A slight frown creases her forehead. "He is entirely too creative in his answers. See to it that he considers his responses more fully before he replies again."

The giant scoops up a length of knotted rope from a sack on the floor and slips a looped portion around Sostratos's neck. He draws it tight and as the circle contracts, Sostratos writhes and claws at it.

"Please," I plead, as I watch him struggle. "This is unworthy of you."

A gesture from the hand of his master causes the overseer to slacken the loop in the rope. Sostratos sinks to his knees as he gasps and fills his lungs.

"What are you really doing in Rome?" the Domina asks.

"Acting," he pants.

"What," she demands, "are you being paid to do?"

"Act."

"What made you come to Rome in the first place?"

"I heard that there might be employment acting."

"Who instructed you to come here?" she asks.

"The God Dionysus."

The giant grunts and drags Sostratos to his feet. With one hand, he throws the loose end of the cord through the hook fixed to a beam in the roof, and then pulls on the dangling end. Sostratos is jerked upward, and stretches to the very highest reaches of his toes. He stands, trying to maintain his balance, a bit like a person performing a kind of drunken dance. Then the overseer kicks his legs out from under him. Sostratos gives a choking gargle and his face, swollen now with blood, turns a purple colour as his legs first flail and then find the tiled floor again. The servant releases the rope and Sostratos collapses once more to his knees, gasping.

"He has been acting, that is the evident, plain truth," I tell her. "I can attest to it. Members of our cast can attest to it. Everywhere, you will find witnesses to attest to this, and you will find written records if you want, with the Actors Guild, they keep very clear—"

"*Who* sent you here?" she asks, speaking overtop of my explanation.

"—records," I continue. "Can't you see that the most efficient way to settle this would be to examine the records?"

Sostratos says nothing, and the overseer pulls hard upon the rope. Sostratos elevates once more, scrambling to keep his feet under him. His eyes bulge, and he casts a desperate glance in my direction. I lunge from my prone position but am seized by the shoulders, flung to the floor, and held there by the two servants nearest me.

"Answer her," the overseer demands once more.

The overseer pulls harder. For a moment Sostratos is completely suspended, his feet swinging, like one of those wooden and cloth puppets that are hung from trees during Saturnalia. He is bleeding from the neck, where the rope has scourged the skin away, and his tongue, a dark, leathery colour, extends beyond his lips.

"Answer her!"

From my recumbent position, my face flattened against the floor, I hear a clatter and footsteps, and sense rather than see a change in the room. I tilt my head and observe the Aedile Titus Qunctius Flamininus enter.

"My apologies for interrupting," he says, "but if you are finished playing with him, I would like to retrieve my playwright." The Aedile glances at Sostratos, who has been permitted to stand on his toes. "And why have you this other individual bound in so unusual a fashion?"

The Domina Regulus grips the arms of her chair as she considers the Aedile. "I am questioning a spy," she tells him.

"This man is no spy," the Aedile responds, scornfully. "He is an actor, which may be even more disreputable, but not nearly as dangerous."

"He is a spy, I tell you," Domina Regulus insists.

"For whom?" he asks. "To attain what?"

"That is what I am trying to determine."

"I see. Well, I will administer that investigation and make that determination. You must release him." He looks about expectantly, but the servants are like dogs trained only to their owner's whistle, and make no move to obey him.

"I cannot permit him to leave without first answering the questions I have put to him," she tells him.

"I can't imagine how he will answer your questions if he is prevented by that rope around his neck."

"It is necessary to apply additional encouragements when dealing with Carthaginians."

Titus Qunctius rolls his eyes. "This man is no more a Carthaginian than I am. Really! It is one thing to be vigilant; it is another to be obsessed. Your interest in matters related to Carthage has long ago passed from a hobby into an unhealthy fetish."

"My interest in this person is of vital importance to the Republic," she retorts, thrusting her chin out, "and I cannot release him because of your fascination for some wild oriental ritual."

"The Ludi of Apollo are a solemn and religious ceremony, that honour our victories over Carthage, and the Gods cannot and will not be profaned simply so that you may indulge yourself in your perverse pleasures as an atonement for the errors made by your father."

"My father was a great man!" she barks, her voice rising to a shrill register. "Greater than presently exists in the Republic, and his memory demands the occasional sacrifice of blood."

"Your father," the Aedile snaps, "almost single-handedly managed to lose a peace that had already been won with the costly blood of Roman soldiers—quite enough of a sacrifice, I should think. And he then failed even in negotiating terms. Now excuse me. I believe my actor is choking." He steps close to Sostratos. "Can't have a participant in our ritual unable to take his part."

He withdraws a knife from his toga and with a single sharp stroke severs the rope that is twisted around Sostratos's neck. Sostratos collapses in a heap upon the floor.

I hear a sudden light clatter of metal against metal, like the castanets employed by Candria at the caupona. I glance about and see the estate's servants have drawn weapons and turned to face the Aedile. He appears completely unruffled.

"Your concern that the captive not escape custody is commendable," he says, sheathing his weapon. "But you needn't worry, I have brought the Tresviri with me to ensure that this desperate individual, once removed, is watched." At that moment, eight soldiers of the Tresviri march in.

"Tresviri," the Aedile calls over his shoulder.

"Yes, sir," a soldier replies.

"Please prepare to take these men," he says, indicating Sostratos, Orestes, and me, "back to the forum. Put that one there," He nods at the crumpled form of Sostratos.

"—on the back of the donkey we brought."

"Yes, sir."

The Domina Regulus, so impassive up until now, for once betrays feeling as her face twists into a fierce mask of rage and frustration. "Release them!" she snaps.

I rise to my feet, dust myself off, and indulge in a push as I brush past the overseer when I exit.

Once outside, the Aedile directs the soldiers to secure Sostratos onto the back of a donkey. I apologize for bothering him and thank him for coming to our assistance. He observes that my actor looks a little worse for the wear, but says that when he received the messages he came as quickly as he could. He asks if I would feel more comfortable accompanied by the soldiers back to the caupona. Eager to escape any further questioning, I answer that we have brought donkeys as well, and along with the one he has provided for Sostratos, we should be fine.

As he bestrides his horse he notes that he has been following the events surrounding our rehearsal and if there is as much excitement in our production it should prove to be a very entertaining play. Then he kicks his mount, and he and the Tresviri depart.

33

We take Sostratos straight to the Cerium, where Casina has
him cleaned up and prepares a room in the new wing for him.
I have no faith that he won't be seized once more, and I am
equally uncertain that he will not try to flee, so I pay Tertius to
spend the night sleeping outside the door with his dog. I secure
a promise from him that he will shout for help if anything
untoward happens.

The next morning when we gather to rehearse, Sostratos
hobbles onto the stage like something crawling from the
smoking ruins of Troy. His neck is swollen three sizes larger
than normal and ringed with crusty scabs where the rope
fibres shredded his skin. His face is a rainbow of bruising, his
ears puffy and discoloured. When he walks, it is haltingly.

The rehearsals are moderately difficult by the rigorous
standards Orestes normally sets, but after a short time
Sostratos loses what little voice he has, so the cast perform
the play with Sostratos simply walking his part and Orestes
reading the lines on his behalf. The next day he is able to
recite, quietly, as though sharing a secret with the others.
His colleagues chant softly back at him, like initiates in a
religious mystery.

I glumly sit and contemplate the coming calamity. For
the life of me, I cannot see how this frail, hesitant group can
possibly be made ready to perform in time. Orestes detects my

despair and urges patience. He tells me that Sostratos is like ancient, immortal Antaeus, who could be assured to thrive so long as his feet touched the earth. So long as Sostratos has his feet on the pulpitum, Orestes predicts, he will draw sufficient strength from the theatre to perform. I can only hope that this will be the case.

That's assuming that the Domina Regulus, or some other grieved citizen, doesn't launch a public accusation, of course, or send soldiers with new charges, or that Pellio won't employ hecklers to interfere with the performance. As the day passes, these and other concerns consume me, and I gnaw my knuckles raw. I pace to relieve tension and deliver multiple offerings to Jupiter and Venus. As an afterthought, I sacrifice to Mercury as well to ensure that my messages are delivered safely.

With only a day left before the Ludi of Apollo commence, Orestes has the grex rehearse full out. They respond like hounds called to the hunt and spring eagerly into rehearsal full of energy and determination. Sostratos seizes the stage with a few powerful strides and sings, his voice soaring and powerful and filled with a wild beauty.

I press my hands together. "Thank the gods," I think to myself, "thank the blessed gods. They have heard me and our Antaeus has recovered."

It is at that precise moment that he keels over and folds like an old woolen blanket all in a heap. His mask strikes the stage and shatters. The cast halts, each actor frozen in his own attitude of shock and confusion, then everyone rushes to his side.

Orestes has everyone stand back. He gently draws Sostratos into a sitting position and offers him cool water to drink. Bit by bit he is invited to rise, and is assisted to a hastily constructed bed of cloaks and costumes prepared in the shade.

As he rests, Orestes takes me aside. It was too much all at once, he tells me, but maintains that Sostratos will be ready on the day.

Later, that evening I check on Sostratos in his room, and bring him wine. Although he appears fragile when I enter, the wine has the restorative power on him that I had anticipated. He drinks gladly, nods his gratitude, then peers over the rim of his cup at me.

"I will be fine," he assures me. "Don't worry—you will see a performance unlike anything you have ever seen tomorrow."

I look at him: old, his weary voice thin as sliced anchovy. "Just rest," I answer. "I'm sure that's what is needed most." I turn to go.

"Have you guessed?" He asks quietly as I touch the door.

I halt. "Guessed what?" I turn and see him staring intently at me. "No," I tell him, "I have not."

"I am descended from an old and noble Carthaginian family," he confesses, "and served in Sicily under our beloved Hamilcar. Under his direction I fought Roman forces until our humiliating defeat at Trapani. When we failed there, after years of terrible sacrifice, and Hamilcar was recalled to Carthage to account for the defeat like an errant servant summoned to make amends to his master, I found I'd lost my heart for it. In the dark of one night I climbed aboard a ship bound east for Cythera, and threw sword, shield, and armour overboard. I swore by all the gods that I was done with soldiering. On the first day that I set foot on that sunny island, I encountered the Nemean Guild performing *Andromeda* by Euripides. By chance, one of their actors had taken ill and perished from infection. I had studied both Latin and Greek as a child, and had cut my teeth reciting Greek plays. Now, I discovered this knowledge useful as I forged a new identity. I was reborn Sostratos, actor, and earned a happy life among the gifted performers of the Nemean Guild."

"'The grandeur of great and noble actions, the glorious, anonymity of the mask—what better calling to devote the rest of my life to?' I thought. I stayed, and studied my roles, performed and travelled with the guild and was happy." He closes his eyes as he recollects those better days.

"What happened to interrupt that?" I ask.

He licks his dry lips and I pour him more wine. "Twelve, perhaps thirteen years later," he continues after drinking, "as part of an expedition to punish Syracuse, Rome captured the island of Zakynthos, where we were contracted to perform *Bellerophon*. I was seized, bound, and sold like packaged goods into slavery. An older actor in our company perished when we were captured, and hoping to brush dust over the tracks that led to my Carthaginian past, I adopted his name, Hector of Corinth. As Hector, I was selected to become a common house slave on a Roman estate, tutor to the master's children."

I nod as I listen. This, at least, was more or less as Orestes had speculated. "And you fled?" I ask.

"Not at first. If tutoring was the worst that Fate had prepared, I considered myself lucky. I am no longer a young man, I thought. If the Gods have ordained that I teach, let them have their way. I will receive food and shelter for the rest of my days in compensation for tutoring these uneducated Romans." But less than a year later, while instructing the three unintelligent children of the household to speak passable Greek, a slave in the ergastulum loosened his chains and throttled the master. By law, because I was present on the farm at the time of the murder, I was already condemned to death unless I captured the killer. That guilty party had made his escape, so what could I do? I fled as well. I shed the identity of Hector and returned to my previous role. The resurrected Sostratos found employment in the acting profession outside of Tarentum, where my prior reputation still held currency. When it became clear that Tarentum too must fall, I, along with many other artists, migrated north to Rome to avoid the bloodshed—where you saw the kind of employment I had turned to."

"And the argument in the bar?" I demand. "You were recognized as an escaped slave?"

"No—that insolent mercenary recognized me from my earliest days fighting Romans in Sicily, and tried to profit from my awkward situation. He offered his silence in exchange for an exorbitant fee I was neither equipped nor prepared to pay."

"So, you see?" he demands, his eyes meeting mine. "You wanted the truth, the truth is I am a traitor to my native land, and a convicted runaway slave to the Romans. I cannot return to Carthage, cannot return to Sicily, cannot move any more among the guilds operating closer to Greece, where Carthaginians increasingly recruit mercenaries. Tell me, which am I? Carthaginian by birth, Greek by selection, Roman by compulsion, a slave, a noble, a criminal, a freedman? I have only one allegiance and that is to the theatre. I have served it faithfully and would have continued to serve it but for this latest war." He drains the wine in his cup. "Are you interested in receiving more truth?"

"No," I tell him. I exit, shut the door, and turn to the two servants presently guarding the entrance. "Don't let anyone in there," I instruct them.

"Tertius," I call. He mounts the stairs and I give him a handful of coins. "Take these and purchase offerings to the temple of Minerva and the temple of Jupiter Maximus."

He stuffs the coins within his tunic. "Any more?" he asks.

"And deliver something to the altar of Priapus at the end of the block." I say, and give him two additional coins before he runs off.

34

The weather for the opening of the Ludi of Apollo is
auspicious, swept clear of clouds and calm as a sleeping child.
The ludi commences in the morning with a lengthy procession
that concludes at the temple of Apollo, where an ox with
gilded horns is sacrificed to Apollo, a cow with gilded horns
is sacrificed to his mother Latona, and a bull and a ram are
offered to Apollo's sister, Diana. The meat remaining after
the offering is roasted and distributed among the eager crowd.
I eat, to accept the blessing, but am too nervous to be truly
hungry. Following this, the crowd, led by the priests, winds
down to the theatre and the plays commence. Ennius presents
first, today. We present second, tomorrow. Naevius third, the
day after, and then last, Pellio.

I tag along at the tail end of the procession to watch the
first offering—Ennius has translated Philemon's work *The
Woman Initiated into the Mysteries*. I am unfamiliar with the
play and interested to see what the young Homer will make of
it. I settle myself on a bench, and in a short period the actors
are coming to the end, and requesting applause.

Pomona is attending tables when I return to the Cerium
with Orestes. She brings us wine and sets it down at the table.
"How was it?" she asks. "The Ennius?"

"On a hot summer day," I say, "have you ever perched upon the banks of a river, thrown twigs in, and watched them flow past?"

"Yes."

"It was a little like that," I tell her, "only longer and less interesting."

"He is a rival, you are required to censure it," she says. "Orestes, how did you find it?"

"It wasn't without merit," he allows, diplomatically, "but I am not certain that comedy is his form. He will do great things for tragedy."

"I imagine so," I agree. "His comedy certainly left me feeling a little depressed."

"Well, in any case," Orestes says, raising his drink. "We are up next."

"Yes, we are."

That evening we hold a final rehearsal for a select invited audience. Clouds roll in and a brief spattering of rain falls. A meagre crowd convenes to huddle on the cold benches and watch by torchlight. Orestes directs the grex to strive for precision. This, he says, should be a performance of only two-thirds capacity. The intention, he says, is to refresh everything, and at the same time reserve energy for tomorrow. The cast performs, but it feels to me like a sad little tale as executed by people who have been heavily drugged. The actors move like solemn mourners at a funeral, slipping from one dirge to another, bidding a deceased loved one farewell. Some of the audience steal away into the obscuring darkness before the play concludes. The handful of spectators remaining at the end are charitable, but brief in their comments. Orestes shoos them off and encourages our cast to get a good night's rest.

I fall asleep dreaming that I am a bug being devoured by a particularly evil-looking lizard. It pins me, squirming beneath one clawed paw. Its mouth gapes black and vast, and its tail thrashes high above its head as it shouts down at me, "You thought you were something, but you are only a bug!"

I awaken to a beautiful day, and an astonishingly clear morning. I gaze out at the sun and feel slightly queasy. Birds wheel about a sky that is a wash of the palest blue. When I arrive at the theatre, people have already begun to convene. Hawkers bark, selling their small ceramic figurines, and amulets of luck. Food merchants offer salted, dried lentils, and roast nuts. Whores lounge near the front of the stage, and although Orestes chases them relentlessly, they are like flies—shooed away once, they immediately return—to stretch languorously and laugh. The seats fill steadily. I can't bear to sit, so I walk.

"Tertius!" I shout.

"What?"

"Take another sacrifice to the temple," I tell him, "and dedicate it to Castor."

"I'll miss the play!" he protests. "I can't get there in time."

"Then take the coins," I say, "cast them in the Tiber, and ask for the river god's blessing." I provide him with money and he races to the riverbank.

The audience is restless as they wait, and it's difficult to determine their temper. Some men laugh and drink. Seeing this, I say a little prayer of thanks—if the audience begins with laughter it's said they will end in good humour as well. But when I turn my attention elsewhere in the audience, I view with alarm the number of small children resting in their mothers' arms. I mouth a prayer to Somnus that the babies will continue to sleep, and another prayer to Ceres, goddess of fertility and motherhood, and Venus the mother of the Roman people, asking that they ensure that the children remain content and quiet, but if they don't, that the mothers will demonstrate good sense and transport them elsewhere out of hearing. A couple of ugly, scowling men settle at the rear of the audience and I worriedly reflect on what impulse has drawn them to the theatre. Throughout the audience, scattered in this seat or that, I recognize friends and acquaintances. My cousin, whom I have avoided because of my debts to him, and to whom I have just sent an initial payment, is seated near the front. Perhaps, hopeful that he will receive further payments if the play is successful, he will applaud especially loudly. Casina is there, and smiles encouragingly. Prima, Pomona, Domitia, and Candria are there, and Vulcanus crammed into a bench taking up a space and half. The butcher is there. I recognize our tinsmith. Festus the sandalmaker is there, promoting his leather goods. His silent, thin apprentice crouches in the shade of a nearby bush. I am surprised to see Felicia, seated off to one side, and wonder if she has come to be entertained or to revel in my failure.

I scan the audience and speculate on where the accusation will arise. Who will stand to condemn Sostratos and haul him away? My eyes return again to the two restless strangers, lurking at the rear of the crowd. It occurs to me that they don't appear to be displaying a festive spirit, and I can't help but wonder what their intentions are.

I feel a hand on my back, and turn to see Casina. "You've noticed those two?" she asks quietly.

"Yes," I reply, "Who are they?"

"Hecklers sent by Pellio. And those," she says, indicating four heavyset, bearded bruisers who silently squeeze into places immediately behind the two, "are individuals I have hired to ensure their good behaviour." I offer a silent inner prayer of thanks for Casina's prompt action, and then offer a further prayer that a disruptive fight won't break out between the two groups.

Suddenly horns sound, and there's no longer any time to worry. The play begins. The prologue enters, the audience, still eating, drinking, talking, grows progressively still as he addresses them directly. "The old man who lives here is Hegio," he announces and then points at Tyndarus, "but the events that have led to him being the slave of his father, is something you need to understand. Listen while I explain."

It is at this point that the focus turns to Sostratos. If someone is going to level an accusation, I think, surely it will come now. If there are people planted to halt the play and seize him, this is where they will step out of the audience. I wait for the accusation to be made, for soldiers to step forward, but the moment passes. The crowd remains seated and attentive. Then Sostratos opens his mouth.

I can only say that he gives the performance of a lifetime—my lifetime, in any case. Every portion of his own experience, his crushed hopes, his loneliness, his dislocation and desperation he distills into some kind of potent brew, which he serves line by line to the audience. His singing is so transcendent I swear that the birds themselves take instruction. His performance has not been bettered by anyone since. When at last he pleads for freedom, and is dragged away to the ergastulum and torture, the singing is so heartfelt I do not believe I have ever been so moved.

I watch my characters speak, shout, argue, sing, exit, and enter, and it is though I am in a trance. It's possible that I laugh from time to time, but I cannot testify to it. The audience doesn't shout or heckle—but they don't laugh hard either. At any other performance, at any other time, I would fret over this, but I have gone far past caring. I stop wondering if Sostratos will be arrested, or if I will be seized, or if the production will fail. I simply watch.

Then, all at once, the cast has returned to the stage and the epilogue is pronounced. "Now, if you are willing, and have enjoyed the play and haven't been bored . . . ," but before they can complete their request bidding the audience to respond, the audience is on its feet applauding and stomping and shouting out the actors' names, preventing the cast from finishing, applauding and applauding until at last the Aedile stands and sternly announces that the rituals of the ludi have been interrupted, and must be carried over once more, to tomorrow, when the play will be repeated. The audience howls its approval.

I feel the strength leave my legs. It is a sensation so complete it is as though the muscles and sinews have been severed. I totter about and must make my way to a bench to lean against for support. Titus Qunctius Flamininus and his servant push through the crowd toward me. I straighten to meet him.

"Titus Maccius Plautus," he pronounces in very loud, very public voice, "I announce, in front of witnesses, that you have won the wager we made. The audience insisted that your play be repeated tomorrow, so there will be a second sitting. I did not think that you had it in you to defeat me, but you did." Then he leans in closer to me and says in a more confidential tone, "I may even forgive you one day for planting claques to lead the crowd in applauding." He pinches my cheek, then continues. "Come and see me in a week's time, and we can discuss your next play. This one was very good, very daring, but perhaps something a little more conventionally comic, next time." He turns, and exits, his retinue following after him.

Casina, grinning a great, broad grin, runs to me, embraces and kisses me, and then hugs me again and holds me tight. Orestes reaches past and grips my shoulders and shakes me and confesses that never in his life has he been so anxious, and then he completely astonishes me by bursting into tears. Grippus and Sostratos, Fronto and Fabius clap me on the back, thrust wine into my hand, and offer me words of congratulations. Festus the sandalmaker shouts to me that it is a good work, but in the future he can do something better for the footwear of the cast if I am interested. I am still reeling from all this information and the sudden comprehension that I once again have a future as a poet, that I have been invited to write a new project, when I see a tall forbidding figure draped in a dark shepherd's robe, its hood obscuring his head, striding purposefully toward me. I am preparing for a summons from the Domina Regulus, or perhaps from someone else, and am stunned when I peer beneath the hood and see the angular, grinning face of Naevius. He embraces me and I clasp his hands.

"Thank you," I say, "for sending your letter to the Aedile when we were at the Regulus estate. I could not be confident that my note alone would move him sufficiently."

"When I received word from Casina, I prepared the most urgent message I could and had it delivered to Titus Qunctius Flamininus. I'm glad it did the job. It was the least that

spineless Titus Qunctius could do. And, he will be pleased—
your play should reflect well on him."

"It seems to have entertained the crowd," I acknowledge.

"*Seems to have entertained the crowd*," Naevius scoffs and
embraces me again. He glances about at the people milling
alongside the actors. "Look at the expressions on their faces. It
is without doubt and without exaggeration your best and most
honest work," he says. "I cannot say how much is Menander
and how much you, but however you contrived to adapt the
play, it is funny and sad and mad and thoroughly different
from anything else you have ever written." He slaps me on the
forearm. "Who would have thought you had it in you?"

"Thank you," I repeat. "But there are certain to be people
looking for you. You didn't need to attend this and place
yourself at risk."

"No, but I wanted to," he tells me, "and I'm glad I did."

"Maybe," I suggest, "you can prevail on the Aedile to
intercede on your behalf with the Metelli."

"No, that won't be possible," he says. "I received a message
back from him, same messenger I sent my note with, saying
that this was the last favour he would be able to do for
me, because the Metelli were adamant that I not escape
punishment this time. He informed me that if there was
anything he could do to assist me in quietly relocating to a
safer more distant situation, he would."

"I see." We exchange glances, and in that instant realize
that we may never see one another again. Never again share a
drink; commiserate over failures; exult in our successes; never
share thoughts on a play.

"Yes. And now, as you may appreciate," he says, glancing
about, "I can't stay—"

"But wait," I interrupt, and grasp him by the shoulder. "Surely you are going to remain to watch your own?"

"I don't think that would be wise. That above all is when I would be looked for, and truthfully, it's not very good. But then, what can you expect?" he asks as he tugs his hood further down over his face, turns and trudges away. "It's a whore's art."

Moments later he has merged with the crowd and disappears.

The next day I attend his play. He is right, it's not great art; slight, and self-consciously silly—but infinitely superior to the work of Ennius. And much shorter than the very lengthy epic Pellio presents the day following.

Prizes are awarded at the conclusion of the ludi, and Sostratos deservedly takes the wreath as an award for best performance. It is a very gracious thing he says when he takes it. He says he accepts the prize on behalf of his Jason in his quest for gold.

This reference becomes more explicit later that evening when my money pouch goes missing and in exchange I find a package left to me, simply addressed in the clear crisp writing of Sostratos: "To Plautus, our Jason." In the package, I uncover the wreath, left for my keeping. Along with it is a short piece of script scratched on a tablet. It reads simply, "My regrets for borrowing money from you—it could not be avoided. I must keep moving. I'm not sure yet where I will end up. Wherever I go, I will have no use of the prize, and it more truly belongs to you than me, anyway. I know you'll understand. Many thanks to you for recruiting me, for your loyalty to me beyond what might be naturally expected of a father, and for the gift of laughter. Working on your play has been something I will treasure forever. There are many more things I would say, but as you know, there's almost never any point in overwriting."

I don't know how far he will have to journey, but he is probably right about the need to move. Rome continues to draw more people from farther afield. It is only a matter of time before someone else recognizes him once again and perhaps then there will be no one able to intercede on his behalf. On my way home, I stop and make an offering to Dionysus, to guide his path.

The day following the performance Orestes collects the remaining funds from the Aedile, gathers our grex together, and pays out shares according to their separate agreements. Casina receives the return on her investment, and happily tucks it in the strong box she keeps in her room. I put aside a significant portion to pay down my debt to Lucius, which brings me close enough that I feel confident I will be able to retire the entire amount within a year. Fronto, Grippus, and even Tertius receive their portions.

Casina has Vulcanus prepare an immense meal of ham, figs and walnuts, lentils, and leeks. We sit in the delicate slanting light of her new atrium and drink and sop up the hot juice of the meal with fresh bread as we plan for the next play. She brings out the wine she reserves for her best patrons, and we toast one toast after another, and eat and relax like athletes after their trials, the exertions leading to the play having left us all exhausted and giddy at the same time.

"And he said you were to see him about another play?" Fronto asks again about what the Aedile had said.

"Yes," I tell him once more, "next week."

"And have you anything in mind?" Casina asks.

"Something simple this time," I tell her, "a story I saw in Syracuse, perhaps, involving twins separated at birth— but after that I would like to write one that is set outside of buildings, outside of the usual conventions, outside of the city entirely, maybe along a seascape, following a shipwreck. No doors leading off the pulpitum. Only the stark temple to Venus, the wild howling wind, and an unbroken coastline. And perhaps, in the background a chorus of fishermen singing as they draw in their laden nets." I turn to Orestes. "What do you think?"

Orestes sops up some more gravy, and recites: "Do not spoil what you have by desiring what you haven't, remember what you have now was once what you only hoped for." He reaches for more bread. "Epicurus."

"To paraphrase Grippus," I say, "piss on Epicurus. There's no point in living if you can't dream a little."

I inform Orestes and Casina of Sostratos's departure and that once more we have lost our principal actor. Neither of them is surprised. At another time, this might have crushed Orestes or me—although not Casina, who I believe has greater reserves of strength than either of us—but we will take it in stride. Orestes says that he knows of several young and upcoming actors who may serve, and we will just have to make do in the meantime.

That is, after all, the craft of the theatre—maybe the craft of every art—making do. We are all trying to right the world, in a world that continually, without fail, goes wrong. The world is a bad dog. We strive to train it each day, and each evening it settles to eat, having learned its tricks—but the next day it resolutely rolls in the mud and bites the neighbour and pisses in the corner, and though we curse it and beat it, it is the only dog, our only dog, and come dinner we scratch and pet it once more.

Tomorrow it may yet be trained.

...THE END...

Acknowledgements

The works of the ancient Greek and Roman comic playwrights have, of course, been the principal inspiration for this novel. When I consider their invention, audacity, and the sheer volume of what they produced, and the challenge that writing presented in those early days, I am amazed and humbled.

In attempting to recreate the long ago world of Plautus, I have found many texts helpful. Notable among them are Duckworth's, *The Nature of Roman Comedy*, Easterling and Hall's *Greek and Roman Actors: Aspects of an Ancient Profession*; James Rives *Religion in the Roman Empire*, Richard Beacham's *The Roman Theatre and Its Audience*, the various translations of Plautus's works by Slavitt and Bovie, Riley, P. Smith, as well as Balme's translation of Menander's works and fragments.

I am obliged to Dr. John Humphrey, Professor Emeritus of Classics & Religion at the University of Calgary, who most graciously reviewed an earlier draft of this book and gently deterred me from making the most egregious errors. Any remaining inaccuracies and oversights can all be attributed to my own failings.

I am immensely grateful to The Writers' Trust of Canada and Pierre Berton House, where I worked on a draft of this book one winter, and to the Alberta Foundation for the Arts, which provided support for its development, and The Banff Centre where I was afforded space to perform a final edit.

I am indebted to Mary Ann Wilson and Brian Cooley who hosted many delightful writing salons and offered judicious criticism and praise as I developed earlier chapters.

And to my dearest family, Cheryl, Chandra, and Miranda who read several iterations of this novel and so thoroughly engaged in the world of The Comedian, encouraged me to continue and compelled me to reconsider portions as necessary, I thank you. To quote Plautus in Miles Gloriosus, "No man is wise enough by himself."

Clem Martini is an award winning playwright, novelist, and screenwriter with over thirty plays, and twelve books of fiction and nonfiction to his credit. His texts on playwriting are employed widely at universities and colleges. He is a professor in the Division of Drama at the University of Calgary.

BRAVE & BRILLIANT SERIES

SERIES EDITOR:
Aritha van Herk, Professor, English, University of Calgary
ISSN 2371-7238 (Print) ISSN 2371-7246 (Online)

Brave & Brilliant encompasses fiction, poetry, and everything in between and beyond. Bold and lively, each with its own strong and unique voice, Brave & Brilliant books entertain and engage readers with fresh and energetic approaches to storytelling and verse, in print or through innovative digital publication.

No. 1 · **The Book of Sensations**
Sheri-D Wilson

No. 2 · **Throwing the Diamond Hitch**
Emily Ursuliak

No. 3 · **Fail Safe**
Nikki Sheppy

No. 4 · **Quarry**
Tanis Franco

No. 5 · **Visible Cities**
Kathleen Wall and Veronica Geminder

No. 6 · **The Comedian**
Clem Martini